I0715714

The FALL of a GOD

The FALL of a GOD

HOLLY RENEE

The Fall of a God

Copyright © 2021 by Holly Renee.
All rights reserved.

No part of this book may be reproduced in any form or by any electronic or mechanical means, including information storage and retrieval systems, without written permission from the author, except for the use of brief quotations in a book review.
This is a work of fiction. Names, characters, businesses, places, events, and incidents are either the products of the author's imagination or used in a fictional manner. Any resemblance to actual persons, living or deceased, or events is purely coincidental.

Cover Design: Brittany Keller Art
Editor: Ellie McLove
Proofread: Rumi Khan
www.authorhollyrenee.com

❀ Created with Vellum

FOR RAMZI

I don't need to tell you what you mean to me.

The best partner in crime I could ever hope for.

CHAPTER 1

JOSIE

This town was filled with monsters who were parading as men.

But they all revealed who they were eventually.

And the rest of us paid the price.

I thought I knew where the snakes lied. I thought I was prepared, but I was a fool. Beck Clermont was the worst of them all. He had wound his way around every part of me. He had me completely trapped before he sank in his fangs, and I was helpless.

I slipped into his plan as if I was meant to be there. He knew the part he was playing well. He was the villain, and I was the girl he fucked over without a second thought.

It had been all I could think about when I took the extra time getting dressed and doing my hair this morning. I had pulled my skirt the tiniest bit higher and lined my eyes almost unnoticeably darker, but those small things fueled me.

If he wanted to make me out to be a whore, then I would fuck up every part of his world.

I would be the whore who fucked him out of everything he ever wanted.

It had been a week since he posted the video of us on Instagram.

An Instagram account that had apparently been run by the Clermont Bay Prep baseball team for years. That was what Allie had told me. It had been passed down to the captain through the years, and it had been used to rate girls in the school based on how hot the team thought they were.

According to Allie, the good thing was that only those who followed the page saw the video. But it was still seen by someone other than Beck or myself, and that was too much.

I had given Beck more of myself than I had ever given anyone before, I had given him my virginity, and I was horrified.

I was angry. Furious. I felt insane with rage.

I never wanted to see Beck Clermont or his smug fucking face again.

But my father insisted that I go back to school. He demanded it. It didn't matter that I had begged and pleaded to be moved to Clermont Bay High. He would have none of it.

His daughter wouldn't be going to public school.

Because he apparently cared about what his daughter did or didn't do now. From what I overheard when he and Amelia were arguing, he wouldn't allow his family to be disrespected like that. He considered it a slap in the face.

I had never seen him so angry in my entire life. I had never feared him.

But he scared me when we left Beck's house. He hid none of his anger as we had climbed into his car with Beck's betrayal the only thing I could think of and my betrayal the only thing he could.

Lucas held me while I cried.

While my father yelled at me about how stupid I had been. I knew that I deserved it. I had been stupid. I had been a complete idiot.

But I didn't want to hear anything he had to say. I didn't need to be told that trusting Beck had been a mistake. That fact was clear to everyone.

They all had a front-row seat to what he had done to me. I didn't even know if you could call it betrayal because he knew what he was doing the entire time. I was just a part of his plan. Nothing else. It didn't matter that I had allowed myself to think differently.

He had never been anything more.

I just wanted my mother. She would have been disappointed in me too, I had no doubt about that, but she would have known how to fix this. She would have known how to help me.

And it wouldn't have been in the same way my father helped.

He had the video shut down within a couple of hours of it being put up, and he was on the phone with his lawyers before we had even arrived back at his house. I didn't know what he thought that would do.

The damage Beck had done could never be repaired.

That fact was evident as I walked through the halls of Clermont Bay Prep. From the way everyone looked at me and the whispers that echoed off the walls, I had no doubt that every student in this school had seen the video.

I had probably watched it a hundred times myself, and every time I just became angrier and angrier. Every time, I felt like I was sinking, and I would never find my way back to the surface.

The video had no sound, but it was clear as day what was happening. I was lying on the edge of the pool wearing nothing but a soaking wet bra. Beck's body blocked the camera from seeing most of mine, but it didn't matter.

His head was buried between my legs. Legs that were spread completely open for him. My fingers gripped his hair as I begged him for more.

You didn't need sound to know that.

It was written all over my face.

The way I wanted him was in every single move my body made.

The video was short, only twenty-three seconds, to be exact, but it was plenty long enough for everyone to see precisely what was happening between us.

What was happening right in front of me that I couldn't see.

Their view was far clearer than my own. They could see the score plastered in front of them, and all I could see was him.

I was just a pawn in his game. The lethal piece he needed for his fucked up sense of revenge.

And what he had said in his room? That Lucas had done the same to Frankie, that he had done far worse. I couldn't hear him over my anger at the time, but it was practically the only thing I had thought about since.

If Lucas had done what he said, if he had assaulted Frankie, I couldn't imagine that he would still be living the life that he was. He was totally unaffected, and I couldn't comprehend how something like that could happen with no repercussions.

When I had brought it up to my father, he had shut it down far quicker than he ever could the video. He had already been angry about what had happened, but he was furious that I even dared believe what Beck had said.

And I knew why.

This boy had just ruined my life. He had literally just fucked me, took my trust and my virginity, and I was still listening to what he said.

I was still trusting him over someone that was supposed to be my blood.

Beck was a liar. He was cruel and vile, and I shouldn't care if he looked sincere when he said that he hadn't sent the video out. I knew it was a lie even though my heart wanted to believe otherwise.

Every part of me wanted what happened to be some sort of nightmare. I didn't want to believe that Beck was capable of such cruelty, especially not after I had been falling for him. I didn't want to believe that any part of what happened could be true.

But those thoughts were foolish and being a foolish girl was what got me in this spot to begin with. I knew the moment I met Beck that he wasn't someone I could trust. Hell, he had even told me so himself.

But I didn't want to listen.

"Slut." I tried to ignore the slur that was thrown my way and pushed forward to my locker. These people didn't mean shit to me and neither did their opinion.

That was what I was going to tell myself.

These people were temporary, and I would forget them all when my dad finally handed over the keys to my mother's house.

And I refused to allow them to fuck with my head in the meantime.

I entered my combination into my lock and pulled my locker open. I wouldn't have to deal with facing Beck until second period, but I would have to deal with Cami in first. I didn't know what to expect when it came to her, but I knew that I wasn't ready.

She had been nice to me, and I had fucked her boyfriend/non-boyfriend.

I didn't feel bad, because Beck had fucking broke me. Every part of me that should have cared was now filled with blinding rage.

I couldn't bring myself to care what Cami was going to think. I couldn't care about how she had felt when she saw the video in front of her.

I didn't have room for her or her feelings.

And if she was as close to Beck as she tried to make everyone believe, I couldn't imagine that she didn't know what he had been doing to me. She had to know that he was using me. That I was all a part of his game.

She had to know what he was going to do.

And the thought only made my rage intensify.

I could feel everyone watching me as they walked by. I was nothing more than a spectacle to them, their hottest topic of gossip, and I wanted to scream at them all. I wanted to erupt and roar and ruin every one of their perfect little lives, but none of that would do me any good.

The only person I should be worried about destroying was Beck Clermont. He had shattered me, and I wanted to do the same to him. I wanted to do worse. I wanted him to feel everything he had made me feel and rip it away without warning.

I grabbed my book from my locker and straightened my spine as I made my way to class. Students steered clear of my path, and I was thankful.

The class was eerily quiet as I walked in, but I pretended not to notice. I kept my head up as I walked past desks filled with gossiping assholes, and I tried to look as bored as I felt.

I didn't think twice as I took the seat I had been sitting in since I started in this place. I didn't give a crap if it was beside Cami. I wouldn't cower.

She was already at her desk when I slid into mine, and I didn't look up at her even though I could feel her eyes on me. If she had something to say, then she could say it. They all could.

But I wasn't going to acknowledge them first.

"Are you seriously going to sit there?" Cami's snide remark came before I could even grab my notebook out of my bag.

I looked over at her, and she looked as put together as she always had. She didn't look like she was heartbroken over a boyfriend she cared about. She didn't look like a girl who had her fucking heart ripped from her chest.

"I am." I pulled out my notebook and a pencil, and I could hear whispers around me.

"Move, skank." Cami was firm in her order, and I turned my notebook to the last page of my notes. I still had to do well in school if I wanted all the things my father held in his firm grip.

I wasn't going to let them steal my future away from me.

Not when it was the only thing I had.

I got my supplies ready before I looked back over at Cami. She was so beautiful, and I knew that she knew it. She was a queen, and I was nothing to her, just like I was nothing to him.

And she had played her part well.

I was certain of it.

None of these people had ever been genuine.

"Go fuck yourself, Cami." There was a shocked gasp from behind me, but I didn't care. I could feel my blood heating and my face turning red, and all I could see was that damn video flashing over and over in my head.

She looked as shocked as the rest of them, like she had expected me to leave my backbone at home, but they had picked the wrong girl. I wasn't the girl they thought I was. I wasn't the girl to roll over simply because they thought they had won.

I wouldn't dare let any of these people treat me as if I was anything below them.

"What did you just say to me?" She looked around the room as she spoke, and I knew that she was checking to see who was watching. Cami didn't do anything if it wasn't for show.

"I'm not going to repeat myself." I faced forward and got comfortable in my chair.

"I should have known simply by your last name that you were trash."

I wasn't sure why her words bothered me so much. She was more than impressed by my last name a few weeks ago. It had meant more to her than I ever did.

I stood from my chair and watched the flicker of fear in her eyes as I moved toward her desk. Cami thought she was better than everyone else, but she wasn't. She was just like the rest of us.

Maybe even more fucked up.

I placed one hand on her desk and one on the back of her seat as I brought my face close to hers. "You have a lot of nerve calling me trash." Her eyes narrowed, but I wasn't finished with her. I lowered my voice for only her to hear. "We may have both fucked Beck, but I'm not the one fucking a married man."

Her eyes widened in shock, and I knew that she hadn't expected me to know that information. But that one move from her was enough to let me know it was true. She was uneasy that I had that information on her. Her eyes darted around the room, but there was no one here to save her.

I wouldn't tell a soul about what she was doing, but I would use it if she didn't leave me the hell alone. I wouldn't be her punching bag while she was the one who deserved everyone's hate.

"Who told you that?" Her voice was shaky, and I almost felt sorry for her.

"It looks like we both trusted the wrong boy." I pushed off her desk and returned to mine without another word.

There wasn't another word from her either.

Not a peep.

But that didn't stop the snickers and whispers that continued around me. Every time I would look to the side, their gazes would jump away from mine.

It was irritating, and I was so thankful when the bell rang at the end of the first period. I pushed out of the classroom, and I avoided looking at anyone as I went into the bathroom.

I had only been here for one period so far, and I already felt overwhelmed. I was going to have to face Beck in my next class. He was going to be there with his perfect face and his perfect body and his cruel fucking heart.

I could face girls like Cami all day, but I didn't know if I could face him.

As brave as I wanted to act, he broke me. He broke me, and I was going to have to sit there and pretend like I wasn't affected.

It hadn't mattered that he had called and text me after what happened. The first one was begging me to listen to him, to let him explain. The second had been a simple 'I'm sorry'.

His sorry was full of shit, and both he and I knew it.

And I wouldn't give him the opportunity to explain. As much as I hated him, I knew that he affected me.

I stared into the mirror and ran my fingers under the cold water. *I could face him.* I knew that I could.

I could slip on a mask just like he had and hide everything I was feeling. I just had to get through today, then tomorrow would be easier. If I could face him once, then I knew I could face him again.

I took a deep breath and turned off the water.

You can do this, Josie.

I wouldn't fear him. If that was what he wanted, he was mistaken in his plan. I didn't fear him. I hated him.

I hated him with every part of me.

Quickly drying my hands, I pushed through the door so I wouldn't be late for class and almost ran into someone coming into the bathroom. I froze when my gaze hit Frankie's.

She opened her mouth as if she wanted to say something then quickly closed it again. I had no idea what she could possibly say to me.

Even if what Beck had said about her was true. She had to know that what Beck did wasn't right.

If he thought Lucas was evil, then so was he.

But part of me knew that it wasn't the same. If what he said about Lucas was true, if he had assaulted her, then what Beck did didn't even compare.

It didn't matter if I was hurt or that I wanted to pay Beck back for every ounce of pain he had caused me. The only thing I could think of when I looked at Frankie was sadness, and it was staring straight back at me.

Whatever Frankie had been through had damaged her.

You only had to look at her eyes to see. She was good at wearing a mask too, but she wasn't nearly as good as her brother.

"Excuse me." I pushed past her, and she smiled again.

I knew she wanted to say something, and I wanted to say something to her as well. I wanted to ask her if what Beck had said about her was true, but I wouldn't dare.

Even though the lack of the truth felt like it was eating me alive inside, I wouldn't put her through that to make myself feel better.

I tightened my hands against the straps of my backpack and held my head high as I walked into second period. I knew he was in there before I ever laid eyes on him. I could feel him there.

I looked to where he normally sat, and there he was. He was staring at me like I might disappear in front of him. He looked angry and irritated, and that just pissed me off more. He had no right to feel angry about anything.

He had no right to feel anything when it came to me.

Everyone else was watching us too. They were all fucking silent bystanders as I walked toward my desk. I wondered if this was how it was going to be for the rest of the day. Would everyone be watching every single move I made?

Clermont Bay Prep was toxic, but I knew that it would be the same if I had transferred to Clermont Bay High. Allie had told me that everyone there was talking about it too. I knew she hated saying it, but she was honest with me.

Most of them had seen the video too, including her, and when I had gotten home to find my phone, I had at least fifty different messages from her.

They were all checking on me and how I was doing. The first ones were making sure that I had seen. They were warning me of what was posted and that it wasn't as bad as I thought it was.

That was her way of being nice.

It was absolutely as bad as I thought it was.

The proof was right in front of me.

I pulled my gaze away from him and took the seat behind him.

He looked shocked as I dropped my bag and climbed into my desk, but I wouldn't hide from him. Not after what he did.

If he wanted to be proud of ruining a girl's life, he would have to be proud while he faced her every day. I wouldn't give him the easy way out.

My heart raced as I pulled my books out of my bag and faced forward. He was turned in his chair to face me, but I didn't look at him. I was here for class and nothing else.

"Josie." His voice was quiet, and I knew that he was as insanely aware of everyone listening to us as I was.

I let my eyes roam over his face before my eyes met his. He looked as handsome as he always did. It was like nothing had happened to him, and I guess it hadn't.

These people didn't care that he was in that video. It did nothing but make him a god. I was just the slut that he had conquered. Those facts were black and white for them. There was no in-between.

But he would fall, and they would realize that he had never been untouchable. He was just like the rest of them.

I met his gaze, and I didn't say a word. If he wanted to talk, he would have to be the one to do it. I had nothing to say to him.

"Can we talk?"

"We are talking."

He bit down on his bottom lip, and I knew he wanted to say more. But he wouldn't do it in front of these people. They worshipped him, and he wouldn't dare disrupt that.

"Josie, I..." He looked so sincere, and I hated that my heart felt like it was in a vise. After everything he had done, those golden fucking eyes looking like they were somehow hurt was almost enough to undo me.

"Don't be shy, Josie. We've already seen." I had no idea who had said it, but it quickly brought me back to reality as the laughs rang out around us.

Beck turned his sharp eyes in the direction of whoever spoke, but I didn't care. I couldn't calm my racing heart or control the burning at the back of my eyes. I refused to cry in front of these people. I refused to let them see how much they got to me.

I flipped open my notebook and my pen shook in my hand.

"Josie," Beck said my name again, and this time he laid his hand over mine as if he cared that it shook.

As if he cared about me at all.

I jerked away from him and let every bit of the anger flow through me.

"What the fuck do you want, Clermont?"

His eyes hardened, and I knew he was getting angry. Good. I could deal with his anger. I could handle it far better than anything else he was going to throw my way.

"I want to talk about what happened." He was no longer whispering for either of our sakes.

"All right, everyone, settle down." I barely heard my teacher's words and neither did Beck. He was still facing me, and he was waiting for me to say something. But he wouldn't like what I had to say.

"I don't have shit to say to you." There were a few snickers before I saw the teacher headed our way.

"Ms. Vos, I said settle down." Her voice was firm, but I didn't care what she was saying. Not when Beck was still looking at me like that.

"Well, I have a lot to say to you." Beck clearly didn't care either.

"Not another word." Our teacher was right beside us now.

"Don't you have a girlfriend to go talk to?" I cocked my head to the side. "I thought I was just the girl who you fucked around with because you have a hard-on for my step-brother."

"Oh shit." That one came from behind me as the sudden gasps and shock rang out through the room.

"Ms. Vos, that is enough. Get your things."

I pulled my gaze away from Beck long enough to look up at her. She was pissed.

I shoved my stuff back into my bag and waited for her as she filled out a slip for the headmaster's office. My heart felt like it was going to burst from my chest, but it had nothing to do with her or the possible consequences of my outburst.

I didn't care about either.

I took the note from her hand and walked out the door

without another glance his way. The slip crumpled in my hand as I tried to rein in my anger.

I didn't know why I had expected anything different, but I didn't think he would confront me in the middle of class. But that was exactly who he was.

He thought he was untouchable and would get out of this situation completely unscathed, and I guess normally he would.

But he was wrong.

Whatever the hell these boys were used to here was unacceptable. I refused to be a doormat.

I didn't care what his reasoning was.

I didn't care how he had justified it in his mind.

I heard the door open behind me, but I didn't stop. I stormed down the hallway without a backward glance.

It wasn't until I felt a hand touch my arm that I spun around. Beck was standing there with his hand outreached toward me, and I jerked away before he could touch me again.

"We need to talk."

"We don't need to do shit." My back hit the lockers behind me, and I hated that there wasn't any more space to put between us. I would have put the world between us if I could.

"You have to know that I didn't send that video out."

I heard his words, but I didn't believe a single one of them.

I shook my head as I stared at him. I didn't know what he wanted me to say. There was no way in hell I would believe anything he said now, after everything that he had done.

"It doesn't matter."

"Like hell, it doesn't matter." He was angry, but I stopped

caring about his anger. "I didn't want for things to happen this way."

He ran his fingers through his hair, and there was an overwhelming part of me that wanted to reach out for him. I wanted to forget everything that had happened and replace his hands with mine.

But I couldn't be so stupid around him. I couldn't forget a single moment of what he did.

"Then what exactly was your plan, Beck?"

He looked up at me, and his eyes appeared desperate. "I..." He hesitated, and I knew that he didn't have any sort of excuse for what he had done. "When I first met you, this was exactly what I had planned, but things changed."

"Nothing changed," I practically growled at him. How dare he stand here and try to pretend like I was anything more than a pawn to him.

"The fuck it didn't." He moved toward me, and I didn't have enough time to react. That was what I was telling myself. I couldn't have pushed him away if I wanted to.

His body slammed against mine with no fear of hurting me. There was no gentleness as he gripped my chin in his hand and forced my face to face his. His touch was as brutal as the rest of him, and I tried to calm my racing heart as his gaze quickly searched my face.

I opened my mouth to tell him to stop, but he didn't give me the opportunity. His mouth was on mine in an instant. His kiss as brutal as everything else, and I had no choice but to allow him to kiss my mouth desperately.

The warmth of his hard body surrounded me, and it was pointless to try to block out the way he smelled or the way it made me feel like every memory of us was crashing into me.

I didn't fight against any of it. Not his smell, his feel, the overwhelming way he intoxicated me.

I let it happen, and I would deal with the consequences later.

Because after everything, he still felt too good. Even after everything he had done, I still wanted him more than I had ever wanted anyone else.

That thought made me feel sick and furious and somehow still desperate for him.

And that was completely fucked up.

He was the one who hurt me, but he was also the only one who seemed to make everything feel better. He was the only one who could make me forget.

Because I did forget, if only for a moment. I forgot about what he did and the fact that I had no one. I forgot that my mom was no longer here and my dad didn't give a shit about me.

I let my tongue roll over his one last time. I let my lips press firmly into his. This kiss felt so different than our last. The last time I kissed him, I thought that I was falling for him. This time I knew that I would never allow myself to fall for him again.

I brought my hands to his chest and pushed him away from me with as much force as I could muster. He stumbled backward and looked shocked.

He looked like he had whiplash from my sudden change of emotion, but I felt the same from him.

"Don't touch me again." I straightened my shoulders and swiped my fingers over my lips. I knew I wouldn't be able to resist him if I continued to allow him to touch me. His touch was catastrophic, and I knew that it was specifically designed to destroy me.

I refused to get lost in Beck Clermont.

I refused to allow him to use me and fuck me over as he had before.

He thought he was a god, untouchable, indestructible, but I was going to prove him wrong. He was going to fall at my hands, he would plummet from this position the others at this school had afforded him, and I was going to take back every ounce of my heart he stole from me.

CHAPTER 2

BECK

I had no idea what I was thinking.

I was fucking things up left and right.

I knew that she would be back at school eventually, and I had planned out in my head exactly what I would say to her.

I had practiced it over and over while my father had yelled at me. I almost felt as guilty about disappointing him as I did about hurting her.

His anger was raw and pure, and I knew that he was disgusted with me. He believed what I said as little as Josie did. He believed that I had posted that video.

It didn't matter that I was capable of it. That it had been my plan all along. I had planned to destroy her reputation in that exact way while infuriating her father and Lucas. I knew her father would blame Lucas for what happened. If he hadn't done what he did to Frankie, none of this would have happened.

But that was wrong.

There was no way I would have ever left her alone regardless of what happened. She was too beautiful and so different from everyone else in this town. She didn't care that I was a Clermont or how much money my family had.

It was something I loved about her.

Well, not loved, but I liked it a lot.

It didn't matter how she had reacted when I kissed her today. She had turned to putty in my hands. It had felt like nothing had happened to ruin us. That I hadn't ruined us. It felt like the rest of the world didn't matter, but I knew that feeling was fleeting and naïve.

When the only thing she saw was me, I took advantage of that fact and made her see everyone else. I made her realize that we weren't the only two people that mattered.

I made her grasp the fact that I wouldn't be the guy to protect her from the rest of the world. Whatever she had thought of me before, I demolished it.

I could see it in her eyes when she pushed me away. Every ounce of her hurt was written on her face.

Even if I had let myself forget who I was for those short few moments, she hadn't. She knew exactly who I was, and I hated that she did. I was no good for her, and I had once convinced her otherwise. Now that I desperately wanted every part of her, she knew the truth.

She knew I was nothing more than the villain in her story. I was the guy she was supposed to hate.

And I had forced her too.

This was what I had wanted, but now everything felt wrong. I had made up my mind after the night at the pool that I wasn't going to send out that video.

But I had let Lucas get into my head, and my hate for him proved to be more powerful than what I felt for her.

I looked down at my phone and read his text again.

Keep your Clermont trash away from my sister.

As if he actually cared about her. He only cared about getting back on his dad's good side, and failing to protect Josie wouldn't do that.

And he had failed to protect her. I wanted him to know that. I wanted to smear his face in the fact that his sister had wanted me, regardless of what he said. His sister had fallen for the person he hated most in this world.

I knew that couldn't have tasted as bitter as knowing what he had done to Frankie. I had trusted him, but there wasn't an ounce of trust between us now.

I still wanted him to feel it, though.

I wanted to cram it down his throat and make him choke on the fact that I had them both. Josie and Frankie. They were mine, and both were untouchable to him.

But I gave him full access to her.

The moment I sent him that video that I had already planned to destroy, I had put the power in his hands, and guys like Lucas didn't waste power.

I thought he would have done anything to protect her, but I was an idiot. Lucas didn't care about anyone but himself, and he knew the damage that video would do.

He knew that everyone would think it was me, including her.

Of course, they did. Why would anyone think her fucking stepbrother would do such a thing? Most of them had heard about our history. Even as hush-hush as our fathers had tried to keep it, secrets didn't last long in this town, and they had all expected something like this from me.

They had been waiting on my revenge, and no one questioned it.

No one faulted me for it.

No one except for her, her dad, my parents, and Frankie. God, Frankie.

She hated me for what I had done. Even if I wasn't the one to post the video, I had given him the power to do so. I had given him the power to do something that was far too close to what he had done to Frankie.

I saw the way she looked at me now. She hated me almost as much as she hated him. She knew I was capable of being fucking vile, and I broke her heart.

She would have never allowed me to do something like this if she had known my plan. It was why I didn't tell her.

I think deep down I knew that she would have never wanted me to waste another second on Lucas Vos. She was furious with me when I had beat the hell out of him after what he had done to her.

Even through everything, she still thought he was something that he never was. She didn't want me to end our friendship over what happened. She didn't want anyone to get in trouble over the stupid decisions that she had made.

Those were her words.

I had trusted that motherfucker to protect my sister at a stupid fucking party, and he took advantage of her. He took advantage of her, and she thought she was somehow to blame.

Still to this day, all she could see was her fault in what happened. It didn't matter what anyone else said. Frankie was broken by what he did, what they did, and still, she blamed herself.

"You ready?" I looked over the hood of my car and watched her make her way outside.

I knew that Frankie was gorgeous. I was her brother, but I wasn't an idiot. But I hated the way any of these fuckers in this school looked at her. I didn't want a single one of them to touch her. Especially after everything that happened.

I had failed her as a brother, and I thought about it every single day. It ate at me when her smile no longer met her eyes.

"Yeah." She nodded before climbing into the passenger seat.

It had been a long time since she rode back and forth to school with me. For a while there, she was far too cool to be seen with her older brother, but she hadn't cared lately, and I wanted to keep her as close to me as I could get her.

I wanted her close to me and far away from Lucas.

He had used her enough for a lifetime, and I didn't want her to be anywhere near him.

I knew that I couldn't protect her from everything, but I felt like I had let her down so badly that I could never let anything happen to her again.

"I saw Josie was back at school today." She was staring at me as I pulled out of the parking lot.

"Yeah. I saw her too." I didn't mention that I managed to get her sent to the headmaster's office or that I kissed her against the lockers. Frankie didn't need to know any of that.

"How did that go?" She sounded genuinely curious.

"Well, I think she hates me." I chuckled even though I didn't find anything about this situation funny.

"Good."

"Good?" I balked at her response. "I don't want her to hate me. I want her to forgive me."

"You may not want her to, but you deserve for her to. I'm glad she hasn't forgiven you."

"You're supposed to be on my side. You know that, right?"

"I am on your side." She nodded her head and typed into

her phone. "But I'm also on the side that thinks you've been a complete asshole and need to grovel if you want her to forgive you."

"Do you forgive me?" I took my eyes off the road long enough to look at her.

"I'll always forgive you, Beckham." She smiled and slipped her phone into her jacket pocket. "But I'd probably forgive you faster if you take me to the club for a hot fudge sundae."

I rolled my eyes and laughed. Frankie could be won over when it came to just about anything if you had sweets.

"We can do that."

We pulled up into the club, and I spotted Josie's car right away. I hadn't seen her since our encounter in the hallway, and that was probably what she wanted. She wanted nothing to do with me.

Even if she had a weak moment and let me kiss her, even if she had kissed me back, it didn't mean anything. Not to her.

It had meant far too much to me.

Because I was desperate to do it again.

After the way things were left in my bedroom, I was desperate to touch every inch of her and prove that I wasn't the guy she thought I was. It didn't matter that I was. I was capable of being that guy and far worse, but I still wanted to prove her otherwise.

Because she had been looking at me like I was the devil, and even though that was once all I wanted, I would do anything to take it back now.

We climbed out of my SUV, and Frankie linked her arm with mine. We didn't stop by my dad's office as we made our way to the dining room. He was probably busy, and I wasn't in the mood for another lecture.

"Let's sit outside." The dining room was mostly empty during this time of day, but I knew Josie would be in there and she wouldn't want to see me.

And I didn't want to make things awkward for her at work.

Everything was already so fucked up at school.

Between her returning, the constant gossip of the fucking sheep in that school, and Lucas running his mouth about me, everything felt fucked up.

"Okay." We pushed through the dining room and took a seat at a table that was covered in what was left of the summer sun.

We were only out there a minute before Allie came out the door and smiled at us. I searched behind her to see if Josie was with her. I didn't care if she thought I was desperate for her friend, because I was.

I felt desperate for every part of her.

"Hey, guys. What can I get you?" Allie smiled, and you would never know that I had just fucked over her friend. If Allie was cross with me, she didn't show it. Her smile was trained and friendly.

"I want a hot fudge sundae with extra fudge and a glass of milk." Frankie hadn't even looked at a menu. The two of us had been eating here since we were born, and we knew it like the back of her hands.

"I'll have the same." I nodded but still looked through the glass windows for a glimpse of her dark brown hair. "Is Josie here?"

I knew I shouldn't have asked. I should have kept my mouth shut and left Allie out of it, but I couldn't help myself.

Allie hesitated before slowly nodding. Her smile slipped then. She didn't want to tell me anything more about her friend. She had always been kind to me, but she was loyal to her friend. "Would you like me to tell her something?"

"No." I tapped my fingers against the arm of the chair and looked back toward the door. "I was just curious."

"Okay." She took a step back, and I could feel her studying me. I could feel her trying to figure out what the hell my angle was. "I'll get those sundaes started."

She disappeared through the door, and I forced myself to look away. I looked back at Frankie who was watching me and smiled.

I knew that she wasn't buying a second of it. "Where are Olly and Carson?"

"Carson needed new cleats so Olly went with him."

"Why aren't you with them?" She cocked her head to the side.

"Because I'm here with you." I placed my elbows on the table and looked over at her. She looked so much like me that it was kind of scary. The only real difference between us was that I was a spitting image of my father, but Frankie inherited lots of our mother's softness.

"Mom wants to know where we are." She tapped on her phone screen. "Apparently, you've got us both on the high alert watch now."

I chuckled, but she wasn't wrong. My mom was almost as furious as my dad about what happened, but she handled her anger in a different way.

And her way always seemed to make me feel so much guiltier.

"Did you tell her we were here?"

"Yeah." Frankie nodded. "She said she and Dad are going to meet us out here."

I puffed out a deep breath. Of course, they were. Dad knew Josie was here, and he didn't trust me around her. Not that I could blame him.

"Before they get here, who was that guy I saw hanging around your locker earlier?"

Frankie looked confused by my question, and it was adorable. "Who, Mike? He's my lab partner."

"Lab partner?" I leaned back in my chair and grinned at her. "Is that code for boyfriend?"

I was just teasing her, and she knew it. Frankie hadn't shown interest in any guy since Lucas.

"Absolutely not." She sat up in her chair just as Allie walked out carrying two glasses of milk. "I'm not interested in him like that."

Allie set our glasses down wordlessly, and we thanked her before she was gone again.

"What about anyone else? You thought about who you might want to go to the winter formal with?"

The winter formal was a big deal at Prep. Typically much bigger than prom. It was held at a different lavish location every year, and the party was far too over the top for a bunch of teenagers. This was the first year Frankie would attend now that she was a junior, and it was like a rite of passage.

"I don't think I'm going to go."

"Why not?" Most girls had been looking forward to this damn formal since freshman year.

"Because." She said it like that one word explained every-thing. "No one is going to want to go with me. Plus, it seems lame."

I hated that she thought that. Any guy would be lucky to take her. "We'll go together."

She looked at me like I had lost my mind. "I'm pathetic enough already. I will not be going to the formal with my brother."

"You are not pathetic." I practically growled out the words. Nothing pissed me off more than her thinking that. Nothing pissed me off more than knowing I had a hand in allowing her to think that.

"What's pathetic?"

Frankie and I looked up just as we heard my dad's voice. He and Mom walked out onto the patio hand in hand, and even though he was getting weaker, he still pulled out Mom's chair for her to sit down.

"Frankie was telling me that she thought she could out-hit me on the ball field, but have you seen those excuses for biceps?"

Frankie smiled, and I knew she was thankful I changed the subject. She hated talking about herself anymore, but she hated it more when our parents talked about her.

It made her feel weak and invisible, and I only knew that because I had caught her crying one night after dinner.

"Frankie's biceps are beautiful." My mom leaned over and kissed Frankie on the forehead before looking to our glasses. "Are we having dessert?"

"We are." Frankie smiled just as Allie came out with our sundaes.

"Hello, Mr. and Mrs. Clermont, what can I get for you?" Allie smiled at my parents, and this time her smile was one hundred percent genuine.

"Hi, Allie." My father smiled up at her. "Can I get my normal burger and fries?"

"Of course."

"I'll have the same and a water." My mom reached out and dipped her finger into my sundae before licking the chocolate off her finger.

"Okay. I'll have that right out."

As soon as Allie left, they were on me.

"I heard Josephine was back at school today." My mother crossed her arms and leaned against the table. It was one of the things I loved most about her. She was never like most of the other moms I knew. She wasn't a stickler for appearances and faked niceties.

She expected us to have manners, but she didn't expect us to be perfect. She never had.

"Where did you hear that?" I shifted in my seat. My mom's eyes flicked to Frankie's, only momentarily, but it was enough. "Seriously, Frankie?"

"What?" She held up her hands.

"I hope that you stayed far away from her. You know her father is on a warpath after what you did."

"I didn't do it," I said for the hundredth time. It was one of the first times my parents hadn't believed me. My father said I was jaded by rage, and he was right, but I still didn't do what they think I did.

"You didn't answer my question." She gave me her mom look that used to scare the hell out of me.

"You didn't ask one."

My dad huffed and chuckled, but my mom continued.

"Did you stay away from her today?"

"Would you believe me if I said yes?" I crossed my arms.

"Probably not." At least she was honest.

"Then no. I didn't stay away from her."

My mom rolled her eyes and knocked her hand against my dad's bicep.

"Beck, we've talked about this. Regardless of what happened, you need to keep your distance from her. Her dad is not happy."

"Her dad can kiss my ass."

Frankie laughed, but my dad didn't. He was serious. He thought the fear of her father was enough to make me stay away from Josie, but he was wrong.

I didn't care that Joseph Vos thought he could ruin me or that he thought I was trying to ruin his daughter. He was supporting the snake in his own house. His own precious stepson was the one capable of everything, and he was going to get away with posting Josie's video just as he had Frankie's.

I wanted to slam my fist into his face over and over again until he could never utter another word.

But I had been warned to stay away from Lucas too. According to my parents, the only time I was to have any sort of interaction with Lucas was during a baseball practice or game.

My dad knew that I wanted to smash his face in every time I saw him.

When I had told them that I hadn't posted the video, I saw the doubt in their eyes. It only deepened when I had blamed Lucas.

It didn't matter that I showed my dad where I sent the text. He thought I was trying to set up Lucas to take the fall.

I guess that was what Josie had thought too.

Everyone on the baseball team had access to that Instagram account. I couldn't lie and say that I didn't. I had no proof that it wasn't me. The video was on my phone, and I was obviously the one who had recorded it.

My plan had been fucking stupid. I had been a fucking idiot, but I hadn't thought out everything when I sent it to him.

I was furious with him, and I had her. That was all that mattered. That was all that I could see.

I should have known that Lucas would have never stopped. He would never just let me send him a video like that and get away with it.

I don't know why I had expected anything different from him.

I knew exactly who Lucas Vos was. He had proven that to me.

I was never going to be able to get to him through Josie. It didn't matter that their dad would be disappointed in him for not taking care of her. That would never be enough.

He didn't care about her or anyone else.

"You do realize that he could press charges if he wanted to, correct? Something like this could ruin your life."

"After what Lucas did to Frankie, I'd think he'd be a fool to even try." I hated saying that out loud in front of her, and I saw Frankie's posture change just slightly at my words.

"This isn't the place." My mom's words reached me just before Allie stepped outside with Josie on her tail.

My body went perfectly still. I hadn't expected to see her, let alone come out here carrying my parents' food while Allie carried drinks and condiments.

She didn't look at me as she made her way to the table. She smiled kindly at my dad, and I wondered how hard that was for her. She probably thought he was as cruel as I was.

She probably thought my whole family was.

"Hi there, Josie." My dad looked like he felt as awkward in this situation as I did.

"Hi, Mr. Clermont." Josie's eyes flicked across the table to me before settling on my sister. "Hey, Frankie."

"Josie, this is my wife, Ella."

Josie set her plate down in front of my mom and smiled. It was tight and uncomfortable, and I knew she wanted to be anywhere but here. I had no idea how Allie had convinced her to help her in the first place.

"It's nice to meet you, Mrs. Clermont."

"You too." My mom's smile was genuine and sad, and I knew she wanted to apologize to her for my behavior. She was ashamed of what I did, of what she thought I did, and I didn't blame her.

Josie didn't look at me again before she started to walk away. I knew that I shouldn't have, but the urge to follow her was overwhelming. The urge to scream her name and demand she listen to me was all I could think of.

She was so damn close to me, perfectly within reach, and I couldn't touch her.

I pushed out of my chair, and my mom put her hand on mine. "Beck."

I knew I should have listened to her. Not only had I just ruined Josie's life, but she was at work. I had no business talking to her here. I had no business doing anything with her.

But I couldn't stop myself.

I followed her into the dining room, and I knew she saw me. Her steps were sure and fast, and she didn't dare turn around to look at me. Allie did, though. She looked at me like she thought I had lost my damn mind, and maybe I had.

Josie pushed through the kitchen doors as if she thought that would stop me. She was insane. I wasn't scared of walking into that kitchen and making a fool of myself.

I didn't care what any of these people thought of me. It didn't matter that they could all potentially be my employees one day. Nothing mattered at that moment except for her.

"Josie, please stop."

She didn't answer me. She set down the tray far rougher than necessary and grabbed a glass from the shelf. She moved around the station as if I wasn't even there, but her movements were sharp and frustrated.

Allie was looking around at anything but me and pretending like I didn't exist.

"What do you want me to say?" I huffed out the question in frustration. "I'm sorry. Okay? But I did not post that video."

Her hand tightened around the glass she had just filled and her back went rigid. She turned to face me, and I swear I could see the fire flickering in her eyes as she stared at me.

This girl wanted nothing to do with me. Her anger was the only thing she felt when it came to me. Everything she had felt before was gone.

It didn't matter that she had kissed me back in the hallway earlier today. Nothing mattered.

I had accomplished what I had set out to do. I had ruined Josie Vos's life, and she fucking hated me for it.

"Get out." Her voice was calm, but it felt like a threat.

"I'm not leaving until you talk to me." I crossed my arms and leaned against the counter. She could be pissed all she wanted, but she had to talk to me. She had to listen.

"Beck, I think you should go." This came from Allie, but I wasn't listening to her. I was too busy staring at Josie, and her beautiful damn eyes that looked like they wanted to kill me.

When I had first met her she looked so much like her father, but I could barely see him when I looked at her now. She was nothing like him.

It didn't matter that she had his eyes or the exact shade of dark brown hair.

Everything about her was different.

"Did you even hear what I said about Lucas at my house?" I knew that other people could hear us, but I didn't care.

"Don't bring Lucas into this." She was still staring at me. "Man the fuck up and take responsibility for what you did."

"You're right." I held up my hands. "I made a fucking mistake. I would take it all back if I could. If I could just go back to what we were—"

"We were nothing." There was so much fire in her voice when she cut me off.

"We were." I felt just as angry. "We still are."

She laughed, and I knew that she was on the verge of losing it in front of all these people. These were her coworkers. She was going to have to face them every single day, and I saw the way they all looked at us. They knew what had happened.

Everyone knew.

"You are out of your fucking mind, Clermont." She grabbed a small tray and placed the glass on it.

"Then why did you kiss me today?" I knew I shouldn't have said it. I should have walked away and let her calm down, but I couldn't think rationally around her.

"You kissed me." She pointed her finger in my direction. "And I think it's perfectly clear that I have made some stupid fucking mistakes lately."

"I'm a mistake?" Rationally, I knew that I was. How in the world could she see me as anything other than a mistake?

Trusting me was a mistake.

Letting me touch her was a mistake.

Letting myself fall for the girl who was only supposed to be part of a plan was a giant fucking mistake.

"Lucas warned me not to trust you."

I felt like I couldn't breathe.

"You claim Lucas is a monster and yet, even he knew that you were toxic. What does that say about you?"

She started to walk by me, but I reached out and grabbed her arm. She was so close to me, the smell of her perfume sweet and intoxicating, and I hated what I had done to her. What I had done to us.

"Lucas doesn't know shit about me." Not anymore.

"But I do." The fire in her eyes died for a moment, and she looked so damn sad. I wanted to hold her, to comfort her, to make her see that she was worth more than what any of us gave her.

Because she was.

I wanted her, but I didn't deserve her.

And she didn't deserve what any of us would put her through.

Josie was too pure for Clermont Bay. Just like Frankie, this fucking place would change her.

"Then you know I am nothing like him."

Josie jerked her arm from my grip and her skin slipped through my fingers. I saw her fingers grip the glass before I realized what she was doing.

The cold water hit my face before I could utter a word. It dripped down my hair and into my eyes, and all I could hear were the echoes of laughter around us.

"Don't fucking touch me again." Then Josie disappeared through the doorway.

CHAPTER 3
JOSIE

The days at this school felt like torture. I avoided Beck as much as I could, but even when he wasn't around, I was reminded of him.

Of what he had done.

Every class there was someone whispering about me, every time I went to the bathroom.

The library had been my only respite.

I had been disappearing in here any chance I could.

I avoided Beck yesterday and today in class. I knew that I said I wouldn't hide from him, but I couldn't just sit there and pretend like nothing happened.

I stared out the windows I sat near and tapped my pencil against my textbook. I had no idea what I was doing. Not just with Beck. With all of it.

I had no idea what I was doing here.

My entire life felt like a giant question, and I didn't know how to answer any of it.

I felt like I was spinning, and I had no idea which way was up.

I thought I had a clue before, but I was wrong. I had been wrong about everything. Now, I didn't know where I stood. I didn't know where I wanted to stand.

I didn't want to be at school with Beck. I didn't want to be home with my dad or Lucas.

Work felt like a savior most days, but even that couldn't save me. Beck was there. He was everywhere.

I could see him from where I sat now. The baseball team was running sprints up and down the field, and I had a front-row view as he pushed himself to the limits. He was running harder and faster than the rest, and it seemed far more about pushing himself than talent.

He looked like he was as lost as I was.

But I didn't care.

It didn't matter that he had stared at me the entirety of class every day or that I had to practically run from the room to avoid talking to him. His stare did nothing to me.

His apologies fell on deaf ears.

I was no longer affected by Beck Clermont.

I couldn't afford to be.

Broken girls didn't get those luxuries, and that was the one thing I was certain about. He had broken me, and no matter what I did, no matter how busy I tried to keep my mind, all I could think about was him and how badly I missed my mom.

I missed her more than anything.

And suddenly without Beck acting as the anchor to all of my attention, I felt like I was falling apart.

Moment by moment, I could feel myself unraveling, and the only thing that made me feel sane was focusing on how much I hated him.

I looked back out toward the field just as the team was

headed to the locker room. Lucas was at the head of the group, and he looked like he had pushed himself just as hard as Beck had. He was covered in sweat, and I could see the exhaustion on his face as he passed by.

I didn't know much about team sports, but it felt odd that Beck and Lucas could even consider being on one together. A team in which none of them had each other's backs was fated to fail.

My father had told me that they were looking to win the state championship this year. This was important to Lucas. I assumed it was important to all of the guys, but it seemed like an impossible task.

I couldn't imagine them winning anything together.

After everything Beck had done to get back at Lucas, he was willing to go so far to get his revenge, and I couldn't imagine that they would be able to tolerate each other, let alone support one another.

Even the way they were walking off the field made that clear. Lucas was at the very front and Beck trailed in the back. Olly and Carson were with him, and I could see them talking to one another, but I knew that he was avoiding Lucas.

Maybe now that he had gotten his revenge, they would drop the whole thing. He had gotten what he wanted. He had done to me what he felt like he had to do, and I had paid the price for his cruelty.

I was nothing but a casualty in his game, but maybe it was enough for them to stop.

Even if Beck would never see me as anything but a Vos, I didn't care. Because he had made sure that I saw him clearly as well. He taught me a valuable lesson about who he was, and I wouldn't forget it.

Regardless of how badly I wanted to.

Beck laughed at something Olly said just before his eyes swept over the library windows. I didn't know if he could actually see inside, but I still dropped my eyes and stared down at the textbook I hadn't been able to pay one bit of attention to.

I glanced back up, and his gaze met mine. He was pushing his shirt over his head, wiping away the sweat that clung to his hair, but he was still staring into the window as if he had a perfect view of me.

The school was an old building with massive windows, but there was no way that he could see me clearly. My heart raced as I quickly closed my notebook, but he was headed in my direction, his friends forgotten behind him. There was not a chance that I was going to let him find me here staring at him like I was some lovesick fool.

I hadn't even realized they would be out there when I had picked this spot. I had come here for solitude. To get away from everything.

But it appeared that I could never get away from him.

He was impossible to hide from. Impossible to escape.

I pulled my backpack onto my shoulders just as I heard the heavy library doors open. I spun toward the sound, and my hands shook against the straps of my bag.

I didn't want to face Beck right now. I wasn't prepared.

He stood there watching me, his hair a mess, his shirt still in his hand, and I was a fool for letting my gaze leave his face and trailing down his body.

He was still covered in sweat, but it did nothing to detract from how attractive he was. His black shorts hung low on his hips, and for a moment, I let myself remember what he had looked like when there was nothing between us.

Nothing but his secrets and all his lies.

"What are you doing in here?" He was watching me so intently that I felt like every small move was under his scrutiny.

"It's a library, Beck." I held up one of the books on the table in front of me. "I'm studying."

He looked out the window as if he was imagining what I had been able to see while they were practicing, and I knew that he knew I had been watching him. Even if I would never admit it.

"You've been avoiding me." He said it as if that fact should have been surprising to him. Like he hadn't expected me to avoid the guy who had done nothing but break me.

"Have I?" I cocked my head to the side and stared at his mouth with a racing heart. "I hadn't even noticed you."

There was a flash of anger in his gaze before he stepped toward me. Instinctively, my body moved backward keeping an equal distance. My thigh hit a chair and the loud scrape of it against the floor rang out through the quiet space.

The heads of the few other students who were in there turned in our direction, and I winced at their sudden attention.

"Sorry," I whispered and turned my attention back to Beck.

He was watching me, analyzing my every move, and I could feel his gaze with a burn of familiarity.

An intimacy that I never should have allowed him.

He took another step closer, so small it was barely notice-able, but I noticed. "I think we should talk."

"I think you're out of your mind." I turned away from him before I did something stupid and listened to what he had to say. I moved through the stacks of books, racing toward the library entrance, and I could feel him following my every step.

"So that's your plan? You're just going to ignore me and pretend like you know what happened?" His voice was filled when venom, and I spun around so quickly that I smacked straight into his chest.

"How would you like me to act?" My chest heaved against his, but I refused to put any space between us. If he wanted to do this, then we would do it, and he would have to see every damn emotion right in front of him.

He would have to face it head-on.

"I saw the video, Beck. I think it was pretty fucking clear what happened."

Anger flashed in his eyes that were more green today than they were brown. "I didn't post that video."

He was so full of shit. I didn't understand his cruelty. This was his plan all along. He got exactly what he wanted, and now he was going to try to get out of it.

He was going to stand here and lie to my face.

Like he hadn't lied enough already.

"Who did then?" I held my arms out wide. "Did big bad Lucas follow us to the country club and hide to get that video? Is that what you expect me to believe?"

"No." He shook his head. "The video is from me."

I narrowed my eyes as the sound of my heart echoed in my ears.

"I pulled it from the club's security cameras. That part was all me."

"But I'm supposed to believe that you're innocent?" I took a small step back, and he caught my hand in his to keep me from leaving. His touch was rough and warm, and I knew I was a fool, but his skin against mine felt shocking.

It felt like something I would come to miss when I had no right.

I shouldn't miss anything about him.

Not his touch, not his smile, and definitely not the way his warm, smoky scent always seemed to surround every part of me when he was near.

"I'm not fucking innocent." His hand held mine even tighter. "I'm not the guy you want me to be."

I jerked my hand away from his, but he refused to let go. "I don't want anything from you."

"Yes. You do." He was so sure of himself. His words firm and unquestionable. "And I want you too."

Every part of me froze. How dare he speak to me like that? "This." I motioned my free hand between the two of us. "Will never happen again. You've lost your damn mind."

"I didn't post the video." He ran his hand through his hair, and his frustration was visible as his gaze bounced around my face.

"It doesn't matter!" I yelled, and he quickly pulled me farther into the library stacks. But I didn't care who heard us. I didn't care if we were making a scene. "You took everything from me."

"I didn't. I wasn't." He looked so lost. He was scrambling with what to say, but there was nothing he could say to make this better. There was nothing he could do that could erase what he had already done. "I made those plans before I knew you."

"And that's supposed to make what you did better?" I jerked my hand from his and pushed against his chest to move him away from me. He didn't budge an inch. "Just leave me the hell alone, Beck. You've proved your point. You've proved that you can best Lucas. That's what you wanted, right?"

He didn't say a word because what could he say? That was exactly what he had wanted.

He had sought me out to ruin Lucas.

If what he had said was true, he had sought me out to do the exact same thing to me that he was so pissed at Lucas for doing. But I had been more than willing to let him. I had been willing to give him everything without question.

"You got exactly what you wanted here."

He moved closer to me, and my back bumped into the tall bookcase. "This isn't what I wanted. Fuck." His eyes flicked over mine and to my mouth and then back. He looked so confused, so unsure of what he wanted or of what he was doing, and I felt as confused as he did. "I'm sorry."

"Your apology doesn't mean shit to me." But I knew that I was staring up at him like it did because as much as I hated it, his apology did do something to me.

It fucked with my head, and that was probably part of his plan all along.

I was nothing more than a plaything to him, and he was going to take every opportunity he could to fuck with me. It didn't matter that he had already ruined so much. Nothing mattered to him.

I could see that now.

Beck cared about his revenge and his revenge alone. I was nothing more than a casualty of war.

"What do you want from me?" I searched his face as I clenched my jaw and tried to prevent myself from spewing out everything that was running through my head. "Do you need another video?"

My heart was pounding, but it felt so different from how

my heart had raced when I was with him before. It was now anger that pulsed through me. Anger fueled everything that I thought and said.

I let my backpack slide from my back and drop to the floor, then before I could think better of it, I followed its path. I stared up at him and the way his pupils flared as I sank to my knees.

"What are you doing?" He reached for my arm to pull me back up, but I moved away from his touch.

"Isn't this what you want?" I blinked up at him and cocked my head to the side. "You weren't looking for anything but a whore, right?"

He cursed under his breath, and I let my shaking hand fall to his thigh. I had no idea what I was doing, but I wouldn't let him walk around like he had forgotten what he tried to make me out to be. If he wanted to treat me like a whore, then he needed to be reminded that was what I was.

"Get up, Josie." He gripped my hand in his and tugged me forward. My knees drug against the hard carpet, but I refused to stand. He didn't get to choose when he wanted me to be this girl and when he didn't.

"No." I reached for his shorts, and he smacked my hand away. His mouth was agape as he stared down at me, and I knew I should have felt embarrassed or worried about where we were, but I felt neither. I was too high on how uncomfortable he looked.

He was so used to being in control. He always dictated the narrative, but not anymore.

If he wanted to push me, then this is the girl he was going to get. I refused to give him any more of who I really was. I refused to allow him to have any part of me that could ever mean something real.

"You're not fucking doing this." He reached down and gripped me by the arms. "Now get up."

"Why not?" I could feel the burn of tears at the back of my eyes, and I was so damn angry with him. "Are you back with your girlfriend now that you've tricked me into thinking you weren't a dirtbag?" I ran my hand over his dick as he pulled me up, and I was shocked by how hard he was beneath my touch. "Is she back to sucking your dick now?"

"Jesus Christ, Josie." Beck looked behind him, but there was no one around us. No one that I could see, anyway. "I'm trying to fucking apologize."

I pressed my hand farther against him and took a sharp inhale as he bit down on his bottom lip. It would be so easy to fall back into him. So effortless to believe what he was saying and beg him for more.

But I couldn't do that again.

I could make excuses for myself being so fucking dumb the first time, but I wouldn't slip into him so easily again.

"Save your breath, Beck." I pressed my hand farther against him and his cock strained against his pants. I somehow felt powerful at that moment with Beck's eyes on me, his breathing rushed, his eyes dilated, and his mouth open as if begging me to close the distance between us. "I don't give a fuck about what you have to say."

I pushed away from him and grabbed my bag from the floor before he could stop me. He didn't say another word as I walked away from him.

But I could feel his gaze on me the entire time. I had Beck's attention whether I wanted it or not, and the worst part of all was that I did. His attention felt like power. The power that I needed to get over what had happened.

The power I wanted to make him pay for what he did.

But I knew that power was fleeting. Beck could turn it on me at any moment, and I would crumble under his command. He had more power over me than I cared to admit. Even after everything that had happened.

I was still hanging on to every word, every glance, and I didn't know how to stop caring. Everything had been fake for him, but it hadn't been for me.

Now, I just had to remind myself that nothing I felt was real.

I just needed to forget Beck, and not worry about him or what he was thinking or the way he made me feel. I wanted to forget everything.

I pulled out my phone and text Allie back from earlier in the day.

You're right. Let's do something tonight.

CHAPTER 4

BECK

I had no idea what I was doing. Olly and Carson had talked me into this fucking party, but I knew I didn't want to be here. There is only one place I wanted to be and that was with her.

After the way we left things today, after seeing her on her fucking knees in front of me, I didn't know what the hell I was doing. She was driving me crazy.

I knew that wasn't fair. I knew that I was the one who put us in this situation. I was the one who made her hate me, but I still hated that we were here.

I hated that I had made us into enemies when I never really hated her at all. I had hated what she represented. I hated her family, and I hated her last name.

I still hated all of those things.

But she wasn't those things.

She was so different than they were. Not an ounce of her was the same.

And it took me fucking up everything to realize that.

"You just gonna sit there and sulk all night?" Olly

plopped down on the couch beside me, and I finally raised my lukewarm beer to my mouth.

"This party fucking sucks." It wasn't like this party was any different from any of the others, but I wasn't interested in any of these people anymore. I didn't give a shit what they were drinking or how their day had been or who was screwing who. None of these people mattered to me outside of Olly and Carson. They were just noise. They were noise that used to fill up my life until I met her.

Olly nudged my shoulder before handing me his phone with a smirk on his face. He also had a beer in his hand, but I knew that he wasn't drinking it. Not really. Carson was off taking shots with who the hell only knew, and Olly was far too responsible to let all three of us get fucked up.

He had always been responsible but much more so after what had happened to Frankie.

I think he took as much responsibility as I did for what happened to her. What Lucas did hit him in a way that was irreparable, and I knew the feeling.

I think that he hated how much he had trusted Lucas before he turned his back on us. On me. Lucas had betrayed our trust in the most extreme way, and Olly would never forget that.

"What the hell is this?" I clicked on his phone and played the Instagram story that he had pulled up. It was one of the guys from Clermont High baseball team, and he was bull-shitting around with a bunch of his friends. I had no idea why Olly was showing me this because I didn't give a shit. I cared even less about them than I did about people at this party.

I went to hand him back his phone just as the next video played, but then it caught my eye. There was Josie in the background laughing with Allie by her side. I had no idea what she was laughing at or who she was with besides Allie, but I could feel my blood heat just knowing that she was there.

I was here and she was there, and I hated that they all had access to her. I hated that they all had seen her in a way that only I should have seen her. They'd seen how she looked when she writhed underneath me and begged me for more.

It was my fucking fault, every bit of it, but I still hated it. They should have never been able to see her that way. That should have been a privilege for me and me alone.

But I had given them all that privilege. I had taken it from her.

I had exposed her in front of them all, and that small part of herself that she had given to me was completely tainted.

I handed him his phone and stood.

"Where are you going?" He sounded like he had expected me to just sit there after he had shown me that, but there was no way in hell.

I turned back to look at him. "You know exactly where I'm going."

Olly quickly stood and set his beer down on the table. "You don't even know where that party's at."

He was right, but I didn't care. We knew everybody on that damn baseball team, and I would find out where she was. If she was out and about and no longer hiding in her house then I had to be around her.

I knew that was probably the last thing she wanted. That was probably why she was there instead of here. Not that I would have ever expected her to be here. The only parties I had ever seen her at before, she was completely uncomfort-able, and I had only increased that for her.

I knew she didn't want to be around these people. Most of them were as cruel and selfish as I was.

Not that many of the people at the Clermont High party were any better.

They may not have had as much money and privilege as we had, but they were still a bunch of teenagers who only thought about themselves.

The lines between Prep and High had always been pretty clear, and most of us typically stayed on our side of the line.

But not her.

I should've known the moment she got a job at the country club that she was going to be nothing like her brother, but I couldn't see anything besides how much I hated him.

"Then I'll find her." I clenched my jaw to stop myself from saying more. Olly thought me having anything to do with her was a bad idea. After everything I had done, he knew that I was toxic for her.

I knew it too.

I knew what I had done was completely fucked up. It was so similar to what Lucas did to Frankie. I was the same monster, the same kind of trash, but I couldn't stay away from her.

I knew that probably made me even worse than him because he had never bothered Frankie again after what he had done.

I had made sure of it. I made sure that he never even spoke her name again after I ran my fist through his face over and over. I could still remember it too. The crunch of his nose beneath my fist, the feel of his blood running down my knuckles when they pulled me off.

But more than anything, I remembered the look of fear in his eyes when he saw me coming for him. It was the moment that he knew that I knew what he had done. He couldn't take it back. He couldn't talk his way out of it, and I had fed on that one look every day since then.

But I couldn't just sit here knowing she was there with all of those guys who I knew probably wanted her just as badly as I did. And nothing I did to her had hindered their want in any way. Even though I knew the video was wrong, she had looked so hot in it.

I had never been so turned on in my entire life than when I was between her thighs, and I didn't need that video to remember that. That moment and the way she had pulled my hair and whispered my name was burned into my brain.

The video had only served to remind me how every little move she made, how every inch of her, was pure sin.

I had let everyone else in on that fact too.

That was the only thing I could think about as I climbed into my car with Olly and Carson on my tail.

Carson had plenty to say as we drove to the other side of town. He was talking about some chick who had given him head in the bathroom, but I wasn't paying attention. I was too busy texting every player I knew on the Clermont High baseball team. Finally, after sending five different texts, their left fielder responded with exactly where they were. The urge to ask him if Josie was still there was overpowering, but I didn't need them seeing how pussy-whipped I was.

That fact would already be evident when we rolled up to the party and I only had eyes for her.

"Are you sure this is a good idea?" Carson barely looked

up from his phone as he questioned me. "I know you have it bad for this girl but her dad and yours are going to kill you."

"I don't give a shit." My knee was bouncing, and I felt like I was going out of my mind. "I just want to see her."

"Carson's right, though. You need to be careful with her after everything."

"I didn't post that fucking video," I growled.

"And I believe you, but they don't. Why should they? You've made it perfectly clear that you had Lucas, and you were the one who recorded the video. Why would any of them believe that it wasn't you?" Olly looked over at me to gauge my reaction, but I didn't have anything to say.

I knew he was right. I knew that I should have kept my distance and give the girl some space, but I couldn't.

Space meant that she would just continue to hate me.

Space meant that I could do nothing to make her see the way I felt.

When we pulled up to the house, there were cars everywhere. Allie's old Honda was parked right on the street. If Allie was here, then she was here with her. Olly parked my car behind hers, and the three of us quickly climbed out. There was barely an ounce of alcohol running through my system, but I still felt like I was buzzing.

There is something about seeing her again, especially after the way I saw her today. With her staring up at me on her knees in front of me, I couldn't get that image out of my head. I wasn't sure I ever wanted to.

She had looked so vulnerable and so powerful at the exact same time. Everything about her being on her knees in front of me was bewildering and captivating. I knew that I should have lifted her the moment she fell to them, but I couldn't. Seeing her there in front of me, imagining what she would do if we weren't in this fucked-up place, was too much.

I shouldn't have allowed her to do it. I was attempting to apologize for something that I knew was unforgivable, but she was the most enthralling person that I had ever met.

The music blared from the house, and I could barely hear myself think as we pushed through the slightly ajar front door. There were people everywhere with drinks in their hands and smiles on their faces.

I scanned the crowd and looked for her. Every face was disposable if it wasn't hers. It didn't matter that most of them smiled at me as I walked by or a lot of the guys from the team tried to get my attention, I was only interested in finding her.

I heard her laugh before I even saw her. She was standing at a long table with Allie at her side, and Will and one of his buddies were standing at the other end of the beer pong table. I stepped back and watched her, the way she smiled at him, the way she laughed. She looked so carefree and happy, and if I wasn't selfish, I would've walked away right then.

Will was the good guy. I had always liked him, but now he was starting to grate on my nerves. There were far too many times when I had seen Josie with him, and every time she was smiling at him like he somehow mattered to her.

And she never smiled at me like that.

I knew that she had felt things for me before I fucked everything up, I would've been a complete idiot if I hadn't noticed that. But it didn't come easy. The way she was looking at Will with her dimple was present on her right cheek, I had never brought that out in her.

Most of the time, she was angry with me, and even

though she was beautiful when she was laughing, I loved seeing the fire in her eyes when she was worked up.

I hadn't seen that fire in her eyes when she was looking at anyone else. That was reserved for me and me alone, and even though Will could make her smile at the drop of a hat, I still felt like there was a part of herself that she had only shown to me. That she had given to me without even realizing it.

And that fact made me feel more selfish than I already was.

I felt barbaric and territorial, and I knew that she would hate both of those things. If I wasn't careful, I would have her running harder from me than she already was, but I didn't feel like I could be careful with her.

The cold, calculated part of me felt like it was going haywire. I could barely think when it came to her, let alone make a plan, and I sure as hell couldn't sit back and wait for things to happen the way I needed them to.

With her, I felt too irrational.

It didn't matter what Frankie or my dad or even my mom said. It didn't matter that Olly, and even Carson, thought this was a bad idea. I couldn't stay away from her.

She had been drinking. That was clearly evident by the way her hips swayed to the music and the way she seemed to not give a shit who was around her.

Because even though she normally liked to pretend she didn't care, she did. These people knew what we had done, they had seen it firsthand, and I knew that it bothered her. She already hated that they thought they knew her simply based on who her father was, she had hated me for that too, but this was different.

They had gotten to see an intimate side of her that she

hadn't given to them willingly, and I knew she blamed me for that. I was to blame.

And that was all that mattered.

But she didn't seem to care about any of that tonight.

She grabbed the ping-pong ball and dipped it in the cup of water before she lined up for her shot. She smiled at Will before she laughed, and I clenched my jaw so tightly I thought my teeth would snap.

"I'm getting pretty good at this." She teased him, and I saw the way his eyes lit up as he looked at her.

Will wasn't some dirtbag. He wouldn't take advantage of her, but he would take advantage of my fuck-up. Josie wanted nothing to do with me, and she was smiling at him. He wouldn't let that opportunity pass him by.

He would be an idiot if he did.

"You are." He leaned forward on the table, his hands resting on either side of the triangle of cups. "I might just have to recruit you for the baseball team." He winked at her, and I clenched my fingers into a fist.

My heart was racing in my chest as my eyes scanned over her. She was so damn beautiful. I was staring at her, and she hadn't seen me. She had no idea that I was there, and it felt so odd watching her be so carefree.

"What? Do you all need help smoking Beck's ass?" She lifted the ball into the air with a grin on her face, and I cocked my head as I stared at her.

Even though she was here with him, she was still thinking about me.

Will opened his mouth as if he was going to say something, but I beat him to it. "Will hasn't smoked my ass in years."

Josie's gaze swung to me and her eyes were full of shock.

Every bit of her carefree attitude dissolved in front of me within a moment's time. She hadn't planned to see me here. She hadn't wanted to.

Whatever her plans were for tonight, they didn't include me.

"What are you doing here?" Her long legs were bare, her shorts cut off at her upper thighs, and the tan she was now sporting looked so good on her. I couldn't be the only one noticing.

"It's a party." I motioned my hand around the room where barely anybody was paying attention to us as she narrowed her eyes at me.

"This isn't a Prep party." She pointed toward the door. "I think your people are on the other side of town."

"My people?" I laughed because she was torn from the same cloth as me. If those were my people, they were hers too. We were both born into it. We were both a product of our families. "I didn't realize you were such a snob, princess."

"Don't call me that," she snapped, and a few more heads turned in our direction.

That fire I had been missing was staring straight back at me. Not for Will. Not for anyone else. It was directed at me, and my cock hardened in my pants.

"Can I call the winner?" I pointed to the game they were playing. "It looks like Will is letting you win."

She cocked her hip out to the side. "He's not letting me win. But you would assume that, though, wouldn't you? You're such a dick."

Allie coughed out a laugh behind her, but I didn't move my eyes away from her face and the way her cheeks had reddened since she saw me.

"I am assuming." I nodded my head and pushed off the

wall. I saw her body tense as I moved closer to her, and the urge to gather her in my arms and attempt to take away every bit of damage I had caused her was overwhelming. "But Will has the best arm in our entire district so the only way you're beating him is if he's letting you."

She looked toward Will, and I followed her gaze. He looked guilty as hell, but he didn't say a word. We both knew I was right.

"Will, you fucking play." She pointed her finger at him, and I smiled because that lovesick smile she had been giving him was long gone.

I pulled out a chair a few feet away from her, and she tried to ignore me. Her body was as still as could be and her eyes continuously flicked my way, but she was pretending that they weren't. I let her bluff.

I leaned forward, resting my elbows on my knees and rubbed my fingers over my mouth. I could sit there and watch her pretend not to notice me all day. As long as I got to see her, as long as she was close.

I could smell a hint of her perfume from where I sat. It was mixed with the smell of cheap beer and a hint of smoke, but I could still pick up those hints of her.

The sweet smell of her drowned out the rest.

She drowned out everything.

Will and his partner took their shot, and both sank their balls with no effort at all. Josie looked over to me as Will's ball hit the cheap beer, and I simply shrugged my shoulders.

She rolled her eyes before turning back to the table, and I couldn't help the smirk that formed on my face or the way I allowed my gaze to run over her ass.

She may not have wanted anything to do with me, but that didn't mean I couldn't look at her. It felt like torture.

Being here, watching her, and not being able to touch her in all the ways I wanted.

I wanted to walk up behind her and show every one of these motherfuckers that she was mine. Even if she didn't believe it, even if I had screwed it up, it didn't change the fact that it was true.

Josie was mine, and I would do whatever it took to make her see it that way again.

But it would be torture while I waited. Complete and total agony.

And I was certain that she would enjoy every single moment of it.

She bent forward, grabbing the ball from the table, and I was positive that she knew exactly how good her ass looked in those shorts. The way she bent showed the smallest sliver of the bottom of her ass, and I was sure that was by no accident.

She knew I was watching her, and she pretended like she didn't care. But she did.

Allie took her shot first and missed the cups by a mile.

"Nice shot, Allie." Carson walked up behind me and put his hand on the back of my chair.

"Kiss my ass, Carson." She crossed her arms over her chest and moved to the side so Josie could have her turn. Allie was hot. I wasn't foolish enough not to notice that. I didn't know if Carson's aggression toward her came from pent-up sexual frustration, but the two of them needed to fuck and get it over with.

"Bring it over here," he teased her as he motioned her forward with the crook of his finger, but she simply rolled her eyes and looked away from him.

Josie was ignoring everyone. She had the ball in her

hand, and I could tell she was focused. She didn't want to lose. She wanted to prove me wrong and win because I said she couldn't.

It was endearing and a fucking turn-on.

She threw the ball, and it hit the rim of the very last cup. For a moment, I thought it might actually go in, but it slowly fell forward and hit the table with a soft bounce.

I could see her working her jaw as she took a step back, but she didn't dare look my way.

I kept my eyes on her as the game continued. Will landed his next shot as was expected but his friend didn't. The two of them only had two cups left to hit while the girls still needed four.

Allie shot again, but she didn't stand a chance. Carson also needed to give her a throwing lesson while he was fucking that animosity out of her.

Josie grabbed the next ball, but before she could throw it, I stood and quickly made my way behind her. Her body stiffened even more so than it already was, and she threw her elbow back toward me. I grabbed it before she could make contact.

Her skin felt electric under my touch. Like somehow both of us felt more alive now that we were this close. I knew that was insane. I knew that she probably felt nothing other than the urge to knock me the hell out, but my fingers zapped with pleasure just from feeling her again.

"Let me help you," I whispered at the back of her neck, and she jerked her arm away from my touch as goose bumps formed beneath her delicate skin.

"I don't need your help," she growled out her words, and if I was smart, I would have sat my ass back down and listened to her. But I hadn't done one smart thing since I met her.

"You look like you do." I pressed my chest into her back gently, and I could feel her harsh breaths as they hammered in and out of her lungs.

Whether she wanted me there or not, she was affected by me, and that knowledge felt like a fucking drug hitting my system.

It didn't matter if it was good or bad for me. It didn't matter that I wouldn't be able to stop once I got a taste, I just needed a small hit of her to tide me over.

"You always think people need something from you. Don't you?" She looked up at me over her shoulder, and her bottom lip looked red from where she had been biting into it.

"They usually do." I wasn't lying. My family and my friends, my brothers, they were the only ones who weren't always expecting something from me. But even they had their expectations.

"I don't." She was still staring up at me, and she was searching my face. I had no idea what she was looking for. Probably the truth or the secrets she thought I was still keeping from her.

"I need you." I let my hand move over her elbow, and she jerked away from my touch and my words.

She didn't respond to what I had said, and she put at least a foot of distance between us. I looked across the table, and Will was trying to hide his smile as he looked at us.

Fuck him. Fuck him and everyone else at this damn party.

She lifted her arm to throw again, and I knew she'd miss before the ball even left her hands.

"Who taught you how to throw?" I moved to the side of her, and she looked up at me with an annoyed glare.

"My mom." She attempted to line her arm up again. "My dad wasn't really in the picture, remember?"

"Lower your elbow," I instructed her and nodded when she did what I said. "Don't just fling your arm forward. Use your shoulder." I showed her what I was talking about with my own arm, and she watched. I could see a small amount of tension melt from her shoulders as she focused on what I was saying.

She practiced the movement a few times. "There you go." I took a step back and watched as she lined herself up again.

She looked over at me one last time before she threw, her lashes hitting her cheeks, and I could have sworn she wanted to say something. But she didn't. She threw the ball as I had shown her, and it landed with a small thump in the first of the four cups.

She jumped up, shocked by her own ability, and when she smiled over at me, I felt like my chest was going to explode.

She tucked her hair behind her ear and looked away from me quickly as if she had a lapse in judgment, and I took my seat back by her side.

Will and his friend ended up winning, but she played much better after my small throwing lesson.

"You playing the winner?" She turned toward me and hiked her thumb over her shoulder toward Will. She had to drink far too many cups of beer since she lost the game, and I could tell that she was feeling a little buzzed.

"No." I shook my head and leaned back in the chair. "I only wanted to play with you."

She took a step toward me and her knee bumped into

mine. I wasn't sure if it was by mistake or on purpose, but I wanted to reach out and pull her closer to me.

"I could play another game. Beat you with my new moves." She smirked down at me, and I knew she was trying to get under my skin.

"You don't think I'm better than Will?" I arched an eyebrow, but that playful smile fell from her lips.

"No." She shook her head. "From what I can tell, you are so much worse."

She was right. I was nothing like him. He would be good for her. A guy like him would be the right choice, but I didn't care.

"But here you are talking to me instead of him."

She stared down at me, and I knew that she was seconds from walking away from me. She was seconds away from telling me to go straight to hell.

"I'm sorry." I leaned forward and reached out for her hand. It was lax in mine, but I held on to her fingers. "Being an asshole is kind of a reflex."

"I can see that." She didn't pull her fingers away from mine, though. She let her soft skin settle in my rough fingers.

"Can we go somewhere and talk?" My fingers tightened around hers, and I could see the flash of uncertainty in her eyes. She wanted to, but she didn't. She wanted to be around me, but she also wanted to run so fast in the opposite direction.

"I don't think it's a good idea." She looked to her side before her gaze slid back to me.

I held up my hand that wasn't holding hers in defense. "Just to talk. I promise."

She chewed on her bottom lip, and it took everything inside of me not to tug it free from her teeth.

"You get three minutes." She held up three fingers and wiggled them in front of my face. It was three minutes I was willing to take.

She let her fingers fall for mine and walked away from me. I stood and quickly followed her, no idea where she was going, but she pushed to the back door before I had a chance to question her.

There were a few people mingling out in the backyard, but it was much quieter here than inside the house. Suddenly, I felt nervous with her.

I felt like a fucking pussy.

I had been able to do all those things with her, to her, without an ounce of fear of repercussions, but as I stared down at her with her sad eyes and her hair whipping slightly into her face, I knew that I couldn't fuck this up.

I wouldn't get another chance with her. I didn't deserve the moment she was giving me.

And even though I knew this wasn't a conversation we should be having while she was buzzing off alcohol, I was fearful she wouldn't give me the opportunity again.

She crossed her arms in front of her and looked down at her shoes. "I really don't understand what you would have to talk about."

My heart raced as she looked back up at me.

"You haven't let me explain."

She shook her head, and I knew that she didn't care about what I had to say. She didn't want to hear any other sorry excuses that left my mouth, and I couldn't blame her.

"What's your favorite memory?" I asked the first thing I could think of before she turned away and left me standing there like a fool.

"What?" She pushed her hair out of her face.

"What's your favorite memory?" I repeated myself and looked around. There was no one close enough to hear anything we were saying. I could have asked her anything and it wouldn't have mattered.

"It doesn't include you." She huffed, and I laughed.

"I wasn't expecting it to."

She rolled her eyes and walked over to the large tree that stood in the center of the yard. She kicked at the bark near the bottom before turning back to me. "My least favorite memory includes you, though."

"Ouch." I rubbed my hand over my chest. "You mean there isn't like a broken bone story or a really bad stomach bug that outranks me?"

"Nope." She leaned back against the tree and stared at me. "You're the worst."

I opened my mouth, but she quickly interrupted me. "I take that back. I won't give you that much credit. Watching my mom die was the worst."

She said it so nonchalantly, and I had no idea what I was supposed to say to that. I could deal with her hate and her sass, but I didn't know how to do this.

"I'm sorry." I tucked my hands into my pockets and her gaze followed their movement. "I bet your favorite memory is with her too."

A small, sad smile formed on her lips. "It is. It's weird, though, because it isn't some grand memory either."

"What's it about?" I needed to keep her talking. When she was talking about her mom, she wasn't hating me, and I felt like I could breathe.

"When I was about ten, she had set up this elaborate haunted house for me and my friends. Our whole house was decked out in strips of black trash bags and hanging ghosts that were probably twenty years old." She fidgeted but there was still a smile on her face. "I was so embarrassed at first, but my friends loved it. My mom had set up this entire murder mystery for us to solve, and we were scared out of our minds by the end of the night."

She looked up at me through her lashes.

"That's stupid, right? That shouldn't be my favorite memory."

"It's not stupid." I took a small step closer to her, and she tensed. "It sounds like a great memory."

"It's not even the actual memory of the night that makes me love it so much. It was just the way she cared. Ya know? I was being a brat because I was worried about what my friends would think, and she had cared enough to put so much effort into making that one night special."

She looked up at the long branches of the tree, and I followed her gaze to try and see what she was seeing.

"She was always like that, and I never appreciated her enough."

I knew I was probably going to screw this up, but I had to say something. "I don't think any of us truly appreciate what we have until it's gone."

She nodded her head. "That's so fucked up, though, right? We are all so fucked up."

"We're human." I shrugged, but she was right. We were fucked up, and I was more so than her. "Give yourself a break."

"Is that what you want me to give you?" She turned her head to the side and looked up at me. Her beautiful neck was completely exposed, her lips open and begging me to kiss them, but she wasn't mine.

I had fucked everything up, and I didn't get to do those

things anymore. I didn't get to touch her like that after what I had done.

"Do you think you deserve a break?" There was a fire in her eyes that dared me to push her. She was looking for a fight, but I wouldn't give it to her. I wouldn't demand things from her that I knew she shouldn't give me.

"No." I shook my head but didn't let my gaze fall from hers. "I just want you to understand."

She scoffed. "You want me to understand why you put a sex tape up of me?"

"Technically, it wasn't a sex tape."

She narrowed her eyes, so I decided to move on.

"And I swear I didn't post it. I know it doesn't make me innocent, but I didn't post it for everyone to see."

"No." She turned harder in my direction. "According to you, you only sent it to my stepbrother to watch. Do you know how fucked up that is? Do you know how fucked up it is that you're asking me to believe that he would do that to me?"

"You believe I did."

"Because you recorded it," she yelled, and I saw a few heads turn our way. "Even if I'm to believe that someone else posted it, you are the one who had the video of what we did. You made me fucking trust you, then you exploited my trust in every way possible."

"I know." I did know. She was right. There was no excuse for what I had done. There was no reasoning that made me any less the villain simply because I hadn't shared that video with everyone.

I was the one who had betrayed her.

I was the one who had entangled her in my fucked-up plan for revenge.

"But you're so beautiful." She reached her hand up and ran it along my jaw, and I couldn't breathe. I was so caught off guard by her words. "It's a shame you're so damn cruel."

She leaned closer to me, and her sweet smell overwhelmed me.

"You're beautiful." I pressed my hand against hers and held it to my face to keep her from escaping.

"But not beautiful enough."

"Don't say that shit." My blood felt like ice in my veins at her words. "Why would you say that?"

"Because." She pressed her body into mine, and even though I knew this was a bad idea, I couldn't help feeling intoxicated by her touch. "Cami's beautiful."

I grabbed onto her shoulders and pushed her far enough away from me so I could get a good look at her face. "Cami is beautiful, but not like you."

She shook her head slightly, and I knew that she didn't believe what I just said. I was a fucking idiot and made her compare herself to Cami. I had made her compare herself to someone who wasn't even on the same playing field as her.

"But you wouldn't have done this to her." She looked up at me, and without question, I could see nothing but hurt in her eyes.

I didn't deserve her forgiveness, but that fact didn't stop me from wanting her.

"I shouldn't have done this to you." I pushed some hair out of her face. "I'm an idiot."

She ran one of her hands up my chest, and I felt like every living part of me followed the movement. Her hand was like a magnet attracting every feeling my body could handle, and I didn't know what to do or think or say as her hand curled around the back of my neck.

"I guess we're both idiots then." She pushed up onto her tiptoes, and I knew she was going to kiss me. It was the determined look in her eyes, the way her body pushed slightly harder in the mine, and the way her lips opened slightly as her mouth moved closer to mine.

I didn't say a word as she fell into me. I could barely breathe, let alone think, but I knew that I couldn't let this happen. If I wanted any chance in her forgiving me, I couldn't let her kiss me simply because I felt like I couldn't go another moment without it.

I craved her kiss like a junkie, but it would do neither of us any good. She had been drinking, and she still hated me. And when she woke up tomorrow morning and remembered that I had let her kiss me, that I had taken advantage of the fact that she wasn't thinking clearly, she would hate me even more.

Her breath fell against my lips as her focus moved to them as well. She was so close. One of us would only have to move an inch to close the space between us, and I wanted to. More than anything, I wanted to lean forward and kiss her and not come up for air until she knew that this is exactly where she was meant to be.

I didn't want to let her go until she knew that what I said to her was sincere and that nothing else mattered besides me and her.

But I knew that wouldn't happen. Regardless of what I wished for, she wasn't going to forgive me simply because I wanted it to be so. If I wanted her forgiveness, I would have to work for it, and this wasn't how I would do it.

I leaned forward before she could do anything reckless, and I pressed my lips to her forehead. She huffed as her hand tightened around the back of my neck, and she tried to force my head down to meet hers.

"Josie, stop." I tried to push her away from me gently, but she clung to me as if she never wanted to let go.

"Kiss me." Her lips hit my jawline, and everything inside of me wanted to turn my head slightly to meet hers. No one could see us, no one was paying any attention, and I could have just devoured her mouth at that moment and made her remember why she liked me in the first place.

It would be so easy.

My body was thrumming with the feel of her against me. The idea of stopping her felt so terrible, so foreign, and every part of me was bucking against the idea.

"Josie, you've been drinking, and I want this to be more than a mistake you made."

She stumbled back from me, and I knew she was pissed. Her eyes were full of that fire that I loved, but they were mixed with so much hurt, so much pain that I had caused her. I hated that I was causing her even more right now.

"You don't want to kiss me?" She took another step back. "What, I'm only good enough if it's gonna be caught on camera? Is that how this works?" She motioned back and forth between us with her hand.

"Of course, that's not how this works. But I'm not taking advantage of you."

She laughed, and there wasn't an ounce of humor in it. She sounded like she was on the edge of snapping. "You're not going to take advantage of me? Is this the new thing you're doing? I thought that's what Beck Clermont did."

I ran my hands through my hair and tried to think about what to say to her. Her small hands were clenched in fists at her sides, and her gaze bounced over me like she was thinking of the perfect spot to strike. I would let her if that would make her feel better. She could hit me, take her anger out, whatever she needed if that meant she would forgive me after.

"Let's not do this tonight. That's not why I came here."

She stepped toward me quickly as if she was in a rush to get the answer from my lips. "Then why are you here, Beck? You just want to make sure that I'm not having a good time. You just want to ruin everything for me?"

"Of course not." I shook my head and reached out for her but then thought better of it.

"If you don't want to kiss me, that's fine. I can go right back into that party and find someone better. I can go find Will." She turned on her heels and started to walk away from me. The thought of her walking through that door and putting her gorgeous fucking lips on anyone else enraged me. My heart felt like a caged animal inside my chest, and I had no control over my body as I reached out and grabbed her hand. I pulled her back into me before she could get out of my reach. Her back hit my chest in a rush, and my breath left my lungs. Her breathing was harsh against me, and I could feel every push and pull as she tried to calm herself down.

But I had no intentions of letting her go. "I have no intentions of letting you walk into that party and kissing somebody else. I don't care if it's Will or any other guy. You are mine whether you know it or not, and I hate that I need to remind you of that fact."

I hated that I made her question the fact at all.

I wasn't here to ruin her night. I just needed to see her. But coming here was a mistake.

As much as I tried to pretend like I wasn't selfish, that I

wanted what was best for her, I couldn't let her just walk in there and find somebody who wasn't me.

"Don't say shit like that unless you want me to go in there and wreck Will's face."

Her hips moved the slightest bit, and I felt her clenching her thighs together. She may have hated me, but the thought of her driving me mad, of her driving me to violence turned her on.

"I am not yours." She turned her head and stared up at me. "You've already wrecked me. But that's what you do, isn't it? You just fucking wreck people."

She was right. It was what I did. I wrecked her, and I hurt my sister in the process. I had disappointed my parents, and it was all for nothing.

"You just use them however you want, then you throw them away when you're done."

"Is that what you think I'm doing? Just throwing you away?" My hands spasmed around her arms, and her lips parted as she stared at me.

"Isn't it?"

"No." I shook my head. "I'm not fucking finished with you."

She pressed her hand into my thigh and her fingers dug into my jeans as if she was trying to hold on for dear life. "Then prove it, Beck."

I should have done the noble thing. I should have walked away from her and let her enjoy her night regardless of who she chose to spend it with, but I couldn't.

It didn't matter that I knew it was wrong. I leaned forward and pressed my mouth to hers. She moaned at the contact, the tiniest little sound, but it was the only reassurance I needed.

I wrapped my hand in her hair, and I gripped the long strands as I held her mouth to mine. Her teeth raked against my bottom lip and I knew she was as desperate as I was for whatever the hell was happening between us.

I opened my mouth, and she deepened the kiss before I could even consider it. Her back was still to me, but it didn't stop her. She kissed me as if she had been dying for it since the moment I hurt her. She kissed me as if she thought she could erase every bit of her hate for me right there between our lips.

She turned in my arms, and I kept my hand buried in her hair as she reached for me. She tangled her fingers into my t-shirt, and she tugged me closer to her. There wasn't an inch of room between us, and I knew that she wanted it that way. She wanted this as badly as I did.

"Beck," she whispered my name, and it was like every ounce of restraint that I held on to left my body. I couldn't do the noble thing when she said my name like that. I couldn't think, let alone make a conscious decision to walk away from her.

I held her tighter against me as I devoured her mouth. Our kiss wasn't gentle, it was all teeth and tongue and a desperate chase to find something in one another.

Neither one of us cared that this was a bad idea, those fears were long gone, but I knew that they would return after we stopped. The way she hated me would return the moment her lips left mine, and I wasn't ready for that to happen.

I was desperate to keep this moment between us alive.

I was desperate to feel her and for her to feel something for me.

I never wanted it to stop. I knew that it would, I knew

that it had to, but I pushed those thoughts to the back of my mind as I hopelessly clung to this moment in front of us.

I sucked her bottom lip into my mouth, and she moaned into my mouth.

She pressed her hips into mine, and I knew that I should stop this. This felt like more than just a kiss. Neither one of us wanted to stop, neither of us cared who was around, and I knew that taking this any further would be a mistake.

But it was a mistake I was willing to make. Because no matter what I did, no matter how much I messed up, I knew that I would never regret her.

Even as fucked up as it was, I would never regret what happened between us.

"Josie," I whispered her name against her lips, but it did nothing but spur her on.

Her hands clung tighter to me, and her body begged me for more even though she didn't say it out loud. But I doubted she ever would. Josie may not have been anything like her family, but she still had their pride. I had hurt her, and she would be damned if she begged me for something ever again.

And I knew that when I pushed her away, when I stopped this, it was going to hurt her even further. It didn't matter that it was the right thing to do, that it was honorable, she would hate it and she would hate me for doing it.

It would do nothing but fuel her hatred for me.

I pushed slightly against your shoulders, and she clung to me even tighter. She knew that I was about to stop us. I was about to stop whatever mistake we were willing to make, and she hated that idea as much as I did.

Her kiss felt desperate, full of longing and pent-up aggression, and in the back of my mind, it somehow felt like goodbye. There was a part of me that thought when I stopped this she would never kiss me again.

But I still had to torture us both and put an end to what we were doing.

"Josie, we have to stop."

She finally looked up at me as she pulled her mouth from mine, and there was so much anger staring back at me that was faintly veiled with lust. She took a stumbling step, away from me, and I reached out to steady her. She jerked out of my touch so quickly you would have thought she never wanted to be there.

"Princess." I couldn't just let her walk away and think I was stopping this because I didn't want her. I wanted her more than I had ever wanted anything before.

Her gaze has slipped down to my lips before snapping back to my eyes. "Don't fucking call me that."

"Calm down." I looked around and noticed a couple of people who are now staring at us, and I tried to reach out for her again. I knew that I should have been groveling, I should have been begging for her forgiveness, but there was something about her that made me feel as angry as she was.

I knew that I was in the wrong. I knew that I was the one who completely fucked everything up, but she refused to give me a chance to explain. And her kissing me, her falling into my arms, did nothing to help how badly I wanted her.

If she wanted me to walk away, then I would do it. No part of me believed that was what she really wanted. Not with the way her body has clung to mine as if it was meant to be there or the way her lips traced mine as if she would never feel that feeling again.

We both wanted each other, but our want didn't matter.

What I had done to her was the only thing she could see

when she was looking at me like she was. I was the traitor, the villain, and even though she wanted me, she hated me more.

"Don't tell me to calm down." She tucked her hand into the front pocket of her jean shorts and backed away from me. "This will never happen again."

"It will." My words pissed her off, but they were true. Regardless of how much she hated me, this would happen again. I didn't know what to do if I was to believe otherwise.

"No, Beck. It won't." She turned to walk away from me before stopping abruptly and turning back in my direction. She pointed her finger toward my chest and her eyes were ablaze with anger. "You don't get to decide anymore. You lost any and all rights when it comes to me."

I knew she was right. I should have nodded my head, agreed with her, and kept my mouth shut. But I did none of those things. I was too far gone to be rational right now. I had wanted to talk to her ever since everything happened, and she just had her mouth on me.

I couldn't think clearly with that combination. I could barely think at all.

"I wasn't the one who kissed you, remember." I ran my hand through my hair, and I tried to think clearly about what the hell I was doing and saying. "I didn't come here tonight to kiss you."

She blinked her eyes rapidly, and I knew that I had said the wrong thing.

"Then why are you here, Beck?" Her soft tone was filled with gravel and so much hurt. "If you didn't want to kiss me, then why did you come in there and bother me when I was having a good time with Will? Is that all you wanted? To mess up my night?"

"Trust me when I tell you that I wanted to kiss you."

She rolled her eyes before the words were completely past my lips.

"Is that what you think I do? Just go around random parties looking for ways to ruin your night?" She wasn't wrong that I had been looking for her, but I hadn't intended for things to go this way. I had no idea what I thought was going to happen. I just knew that I couldn't stand another moment away from her.

"That's why you're here, isn't it? Allie told me you guys never come to a Clermont High party."

"Is that why you're here? Because you thought I wouldn't be." That thought pissed me off far more than it should. It was only logical for her to be ignoring me. I would be ignoring me too if I was her, but nothing about the way I felt about her or thought about her was logical.

She shifted on her feet before she stared at me with that same fire I knew could be heaven and hell. "What do you expect me to do, Beck? Do you honestly expect me to trust anything you say after what you did?"

Of course not. She was right again, but I hated her for it. I hated her for the way she got under my skin. For the way my plan backfired because of who she was. I hated her because my plan had still done what I had intended even though I had pussed out, and I wanted to take every moment of it back.

And it had nothing to do with the fact that I knew her father was pissed. Lucas had all the guys on the team talking about whether or not her father was going to press charges against me.

I didn't care one way or another.

Her father was nothing more than a bastard, and I dared him to try to take me down. I fucking wished he would.

If he had the nerve to try to press charges against me after what Lucas had done to Frankie, I would gladly deal with the consequences.

Consequences that Lucas didn't pay.

The only repercussion Lucas had was the day I beat his face in. There were no other consequences for him. No ramifications for what he did.

"I just. Fuck. I don't know what I want."

"Exactly." She threw her hand out to the side. "You have no fucking idea what you're doing, Beck, and I'm not some toy you can use any time you and Lucas need to have a dick-measuring contest."

"Me being here has nothing to do with Lucas."

"It had everything to do with him." Her hand trembled at her side, and I wanted to reach out and steady it with my own. But I felt as unstable as she looked. "That's the only reason we're in this mess. That's the only reason you ever talked to me on that damn beach."

I took a step toward her but stopped when she flinched. It was almost unnoticeable, but for me, it was unmistakable. "I had no idea who you were on that beach. I had no idea you were his."

"I'm not his!" she screamed, and my heart felt like a war drum in my chest. "I don't belong to anyone."

I shook my head as I stared at her. She was wrong. She was so fucking wrong. "You belong to me."

She laughed. Actually threw her head back and laughed. "I let you fuck me, Beck. I didn't ask you to marry me."

The way she said it felt so wrong. Yes. We had fucked,

but it had been more than that. I had taken her virginity for God's sake. "Don't say shit like that."

"Like what?" She stepped closer to me, and I didn't give a shit who was watching us. I didn't care what they heard or what the hell they thought was happening. "Do you want me to pretend like we didn't fuck since you didn't get it on camera?"

"Of course not." I reached out and wrapped my hand around her bicep, and every part of me wanted to slam her body against mine. I wanted to slam her against me, and never let her go.

But I knew that we would end up exactly where we were moments before. It felt like the two of us were just dancing circles around each other. We were on the same fucking loop that didn't feel like it would end.

"Everything about that night was real." I stared down at her arm with my skin against hers. "None of that was about anyone but us."

She jerked her arm away from me, and I could see her emotions storming in her eyes. "But everything before that was, right? Everything else was all a game?"

"No." I shook my head, but that wasn't the whole truth. So much of getting her, of having her as mine, started out as nothing more than a plan to fuck with Lucas. As soon as I found out who she was on that beach, it was all I could think about, but that had changed somewhere along the way.

I didn't know when. But it had.

It had changed, and I knew before I even took her to the country club that I wouldn't go through with sending out that video.

But my hatred for Lucas had proven to be far greater

than my own self-preservation. I knew how badly she would hate me after I sent that video to him, but it hadn't mattered.

I sent it anyway, and I never thought that we would end up here. I never thought he would stoop low enough to put a video of his own family on the internet to hurt me.

Obviously, I didn't know Lucas at all. I never had.

"Do me a favor." She turned her back to me, and this time I knew that she wasn't coming back. "Congratulate yourself for fucking over a Vos like you wanted to all along and leave me the hell alone."

She didn't say another word as she walked back into the house, and for once, I didn't follow her.

I let her go and tried like hell to calm my racing thoughts and my racing mind.

Getting through to her was going to be much harder than I thought, and the two of us were likely to kill each other before I did.

But I knew that I couldn't leave her alone. I wouldn't.

It didn't matter that she was still a Vos. She was so much more than that now, and I couldn't just walk away.

CHAPTER 5
JOSIE

I hated this school.

I hated being in these old walls with this stuffy uniform and these people that I didn't like.

None of them liked me either, and I was completely okay with that.

I didn't need them to like me. I just needed them to leave me the hell alone and find someone else to talk about. Because it seemed that every move Beck and I made was being watched. It didn't matter that there was no me and Beck.

I had kissed him outside of the damn party the other night, and somehow everyone found out. I had been drinking, but I didn't blame my choices on the alcohol. But it had still been a mistake.

A mistake I made in a moment of weakness when I had been drinking and he had looked so handsome and I just wanted to forget everything that had already happened between us.

My body hadn't gotten the memo that he was no longer

available to us. My mind knew that Beck Clermont was off-limits, but my body didn't care.

I kicked an old bottle of water from the bleachers and took a bite of my sandwich. The bottle rolled and clanked loudly against the metal as it fell from step to step.

I hadn't eaten lunch in the lunchroom ever since I had to hear the word slut or whore whispered under someone's breath between each of my bites. It didn't matter that Lucas had started sitting with me as if he actually gave a shit about me. None of them cared.

They didn't fear Lucas as he wanted them to. As he expected them to.

He wasn't Beck.

The bottle hit the bottom step and slowly rolled into the fence.

"That was unnecessary."

I looked up from my feet just as Cami took a seat on the bottom step. I had no idea what she was doing out here. The two of us had been avoiding each other since our run-in on my first day back, and I had no plans in talking to her now.

She may not have been the one to post the video of me, but she was just as bad as the rest of them. She was just as cruel.

"What do you want?" I was tired of tiptoeing around these people. If Cami was out here, it was because she wanted something, and I trusted her even less than I trusted Beck.

"I was just leaving the locker room, and I saw you sitting out here all alone." Regardless of what she wanted with Beck, one thing was absolutely certain. She wanted me nowhere near him.

"I really don't have the energy for you today, Cami." I

shoved my trash and the rest of my sandwich into my lunch bag and zipped up my backpack.

"I just wanted to say I'm sorry."

My gaze snapped to her because it was the absolute last thing I was expecting her to say. "What?"

She looked out to the baseball field then back at me. "I'm sorry." She shrugged her shoulders, and her blonde hair bounced with the movement.

"What exactly are you apologizing for?" I leaned forward and pressed my elbows to my knees. If I didn't head back inside within the next few minutes, I was going to be late for my next class, but there was no way I was leaving now. Not until I heard what Cami had to say.

"For what he did." She blinked up at me, and I didn't know if it was my own animosity toward her, but I could have sworn there wasn't an ounce of remorse on her face. "I knew that he was planning to use it to get back at Lucas, but..." She hesitated, and I hated how on edge I felt. I was clinging to every word that passed her lips. "I never thought that he would take it this far."

I swallowed down the emotion that was threatening to drown me. "Exactly how far did you think he was going to take it?"

"Honestly?" She turned so she was facing me more, and her uniform looked so pristine. Everything about her did. "I just thought he was going to use you to get under Lucas's skin. I didn't know he was going to post that video. I didn't realize the two of you were going to take things that far." Her eyes clouded over, and for a second, the feeling of regret washed over me.

Cami cared about Beck in whatever fucked up way the two of them allowed, and I had helped him cross a line that neither of us was meant to cross. He had planned to hurt me all along, but I also helped him hurt her.

It didn't matter what he said about their relationship or lack thereof. I should have never gone there with him. I should have seen every red flag he waved in my face and ran the other way.

But I didn't.

"He said that you two weren't really a thing," I said the only thing I could think of. It was the truth, but it sounded so weak coming from my mouth. It sounded so damn shameful and full of complete and total shit.

Both of us knew it too.

"We aren't what we used to be, but I didn't think he would do this." She shook her head, and I actually felt sorry for her. "He's just been so angry since Lucas."

I held my breath when she said his name, but she didn't go further. She searched my face for whatever she was looking for, and I knew that I was giving it to her. There was no way that I could hide my emotions at that moment. Not after everything that happened with Beck this weekend, not after I kissed him again after what he had done. Now, here I sat facing her, and I knew that I should probably be the one apologizing.

"What happened between him and Lucas?" I asked the question I had been dying to know the answer to. The true answer. Not some bullshit from either one of them.

She opened her mouth, and I stopped her. "The truth, Cami. I can't handle any more lies."

She nodded her head as she bit down on her bottom lip. "Beck and Lucas used to be close. All of us did."

"And what happened?"

She shook her head, and I felt like I was going to scream

if she didn't tell me. I had enough of all of their games. I wanted the truth. I needed it, and I didn't care if she didn't want to tell me.

I didn't care if the truth hurt her somehow.

"It was Frankie. Beck and I had left a party to head back to my house." She looked up at me, and I knew that she was watching me for a reaction. And I gave it to her. I couldn't help it. Just hearing about her and Beck together did something to my chest that I didn't want to think about.

But I couldn't stop myself from caring about him.

"Beck let Frankie stay because Lucas was there. He had trusted him. He has always been so overprotective with her, and if he hadn't trusted Lucas with his life, he would have never let her stay."

My stomach tightened with each word she spoke, and I knew that I didn't want to hear the rest of it. Even if I needed to know the truth, I knew the truth of what happened to Frankie would be much harder to deal with than my own reality.

If what Beck said was true, I didn't know how I would deal with it.

Right now, I could bury my head in the sand, but once Cami told me what really happened, I would no longer be able to hide from it.

"Frankie used to be obsessed with Lucas. Did you know that?"

I shook my head, but Beck had told me something similar when I found the video. He had said that Frankie had loved Lucas once, but the idea seemed so strange to me.

"She was. She had a crush on him since as long as I could remember. It always seemed harmless, but I think it was becoming more than a crush for her. I think that she really felt something for him, you know?"

She didn't wait for me to respond. She looked so lost in her own thoughts as if she was so vividly remembering what she told me.

"After Beck left my house that night, he went home, but Frankie wasn't there. Beck went back to the party to look for her and found her passed out drunk on the couch. She was a mess.

She was so drunk and her clothes and hair were a mess. I wasn't there, but I heard that Lucas and Beck got into it. Beck was so pissed that Lucas had let her drink that much and just lay there for anyone to bother her. But Lucas didn't care. They got into it pretty bad, and Lucas told him that he wasn't Frankie's protector."

I thought about when I had gone to a party with Lucas myself. I was his stepsister, and he had dropped me like I didn't even matter. I couldn't imagine trusting him with someone that I cared about. Not when he was out partying and drinking himself.

Regardless of who Lucas was or wasn't, he was still just a teenage boy who made stupid decisions. That didn't mean that he was a monster. Letting Frankie get drunk didn't mean that he was guilty of all the things that Beck had claimed.

And I didn't know who I wanted to believe. Part of me hoped that Cami told me Beck was a liar. I wanted her to say that Lucas hadn't done what he had claimed. I wanted her to tell me that I wasn't living with a monster in the bedroom next to mine, but a bigger part of me hoped that Beck was telling the truth.

And that was so fucked up and selfish.

But I would never forgive Beck if he had lied about this. I

didn't know that I would ever forgive him anyway, but I knew that this lie would be the nail in his coffin. Somehow understanding his need for revenge after what Lucas had done made what Beck did to me more bearable.

I didn't forgive him for it, but some small part of me could understand it.

But if he did what he did without reason, I didn't know what to think.

I would never be able to forgive him even though I knew that I wanted to. I hated Beck. I absolutely hated him for what he had done to me, but I wanted something to happen that would erase what he had done. I was clinging to that hope like it was a lifeline.

Because as badly as he hurt me, I didn't want to hate him.

I wanted to go back to that moment just before I saw the video on his phone.

I was blissfully unaware at that moment. A complete and total fool, but I was happy.

He had made me happy. Right before he ripped it all away.

"Beck was already so pissed off at him, but it wasn't until the next morning that we knew the true extent of what Lucas had done." She took a deep breath and I followed her with a steadying one of my own. "A video was sent out to the baseball team, and it was so bad. Frankie was wasted."

She looked up at me, and I couldn't decipher the look on her face.

"She could barely keep her eyes open, let alone make a decision for herself. You could clearly see it was her in the video, but it was hard to tell who the guy was at first. He was touching her. He was up her shirt when the video started, but it got worse. He went down her shorts, and she didn't stop him. She couldn't if she had wanted to. She was so out of her mind."

I closed my eyes and tried to block out the vision in my mind.

"The video never showed Lucas's face, but it was him. He had on his letterman jacket and you could hear his voice. The guy who recorded it kept saying all these derogatory things to her. They kept talking about how badly she wanted it. How she had been after his dick for so long, and Lucas kept answering. He was touching her and talking about how badly she wanted it even though she was barely awake."

I felt like I was going to be sick.

"Beck was so damn furious. No one could calm him down. The moment he saw the video, he went straight to your house. He wasn't thinking. If he had just taken a moment to think about the repercussions of his actions, he might of—" She looked truly upset now. "I don't know. I like to think that maybe he wouldn't have done what he did."

"What did Beck do?"

"Lucas hasn't told you any of this? Your father?" The way she said it made me feel like an idiot. I lived in the same home as them, but I knew far less than the people on the outside.

The people I should have been able to trust the most were complete strangers to me, and I hated that she knew it.

"No." I wouldn't lie and pretend like I knew what had happened. I didn't want to leave out one single detail because she thought I might know the truth.

"Beck beat the shit out of Lucas." She scanned my face as if she was searching for a reaction, as if she was searching to find out what I truly knew. "When Lucas opened the door, Beck didn't give him a chance to explain. He took every bit of his fury and pounded it into Lucas's face. They barely managed to pull Beck off of him. When the police arrived and took one look at what Beck had done, they arrested him on the spot."

I shook my head because nothing she said made any sense. "If Lucas did what you say and Beck retaliated, how are the two of them just walking around school like nothing ever happened? How do they not have consequences for what they did?"

"Boys like Beck and Lucas don't get in trouble, Josie." She looked back out to the field, and I had no idea what she was thinking or how she felt. Cami was almost as good as Beck when it came to hiding her emotions.

"So what? Nobody cared. They just let Lucas be a fucking monster and not have to own up to it?"

"Oh, they cared." She looked back at me. "Mr. Clermont was even angrier than Beck, but he's a businessman. He knew that he needed to protect Frankie, but he also had to protect Beck from what he did. Beck was being charged with aggravated assault, Josie."

My gaze snapped up to hers.

"Joseph... your dad, was furious. He was so sure that Lucas wasn't in that video. He was adamant, but he was also determined that Beck would pay for what he had done to him."

"So, what happened?"

"Mr. Clermont was pressing charges against Lucas. Both of them were completely ready to destroy each other's sons, and it wasn't until Mr. Clermont's lawyer stepped in and told him that he should make a deal that things changed. Unless you knew Lucas, it wasn't clear that it was him in that video, and he was worried that he wouldn't be charged."

"How do you know all of this?"

"Who do you think was there for Beck after everything happened? I was there for him, and I was there for Frankie. Frankie was so fucked up. She was miserable and confused, and she didn't want to be around anyone. Frankie was the one who convinced her dad to make a deal with yours. If it wasn't for her, I don't think he ever would have."

All I could think about was Frankie, and her gentle smile and kind eyes. I couldn't imagine anyone hurting her. Let alone someone who was meant to be my family.

The thought of Lucas hurting her, of him doing what she said, made my stomach roll, and the contents of my lunch threatened to spill over. When Beck had said it, I tried to block it out. He was angry, and I tried to chop up his words as simply that. Pure anger and revenge.

I hadn't truly allowed myself to believe them to be true.

But here was the truth staring me in the face once again.

Lucas had done what he said, and Beck had tried to retaliate against him by becoming the same kind of monster. He was so lost in his own anger that he couldn't see how fucked up that was.

But I could.

Cami had no reason to lie to me. She had nothing to gain from me finally knowing the truth.

"Beck and I have always been close, but after everything that happened, the two of us grew in a way that was differ- ent. Frankie wouldn't talk to anyone besides me, and Beck relied on me to help bring her back to who she was before your brother."

Her words made the hair on my arms stand and my back straighten. While she was telling me the truth, she was also throwing that truth straight in my face. She wanted me to know exactly what role she had played in Beck's life and the role that me and my family had played.

I shook my hand and lifted my backpack onto my back. I needed to leave. I needed to get away from her before I said something I knew I would regret. The things she had told me made me feel so angry and confused and hurt, and I didn't need to add any of the feelings I did or didn't have about Beck to the mix.

I couldn't handle it all.

"I need to get to class." I stood, but Cami wasn't finished.

"You should know that I didn't think he would go this far." She looked away from me, and it looked like she actually had enough decency to be ashamed of herself.

"How far exactly did you think he'd go?" I tightened my hands around the straps of my backpack and made my way down the bleachers until we were eye level. I wanted to see her face when she told me the truth about what Beck had done to me.

"I knew that he wanted his revenge. Beck hasn't been the same since that day. He's been so damn angry, and even though the thought of him getting close to you killed me, I knew that he needed this. I thought he was just going to make you fall for him then make you look like a fool. I didn't know—I didn't think—"

"So, you were okay with him using me, just not to the point that it also made you look bad."

She bristled, and I knew that I had hit my mark with her. Cami cared what people thought of her. I feared she cared about that more than she cared about anything else.

"I don't care how it makes me look." She stood. "I just wanted to say that I'm sorry I let him take it this far. I should have stepped in. I should have stopped him before you got so hurt."

I hated Cami. When I had first met her, I was so envious of how she looked and acted and how everyone looked at her, but now I wasn't envious of one single part of her. I didn't covet the lies she told or the secrets she kept to keep her perfect little sham of a life going.

I didn't want any part of it.

"I don't get it." I walked past her with my pulse racing like a beating drum.

"Get what?"

"This whole thing." I turned back to her and waved my hand in her direction. She still looked so beautiful, so well put together, even though she might as well have been falling apart. "Why do you think this is okay? Your relationship with Beck. The lies the two of you tell. Your affair with a married man."

Her eyes sparked with anger, or maybe even fear, but I didn't care. I wasn't going to tiptoe around her when she hadn't given a shit about me at all. She had just admitted to knowing what Beck was going to do to me. She knew, and she hadn't cared.

"That's just another one of his lies." Her gaze shifted away from me as she spoke, and I knew that she was full of shit. She just didn't want the girl who had nothing left to lose to know her dirty little secrets.

Her secrets were in danger in my hands.

We both knew that to be true.

"We both know it isn't." I shook my head and took a step back from her. I was tired of playing games with her. With all of these damn people who I shouldn't have cared anything about.

I was thankful that she told me the truth about what happened between Beck and Lucas. About Frankie.

And even though I wished it wasn't, I knew that what she said was true. Lucas was responsible for the terrors that she claimed, and deep down inside of me, I had known that to be true since Beck had told me.

And I wanted to kill him.

I had always hated my last name simply because I hated my father. It was a wound that festered and festered with every single moment that he wasn't the father I needed him to be, but now it was different.

I was really and truly ashamed to be a Vos at that moment.

I had never been more ashamed of anything in my life.

My father was an ass and a terrible dad, but even I didn't think he was capable of this. I hadn't thought he was capable of letting Lucas get away with something so terrible.

"So, what? Beck hurt you, so now you're going to use what you know against me?" She was so smug as she said it even though I knew that idea scared her, and every part of me wanted to tell her yes. I wanted to throw it in her face that Beck had betrayed her too. Even if it wasn't in the same way he had betrayed me. Even if it didn't even register on the same scale.

She had trusted him, and he had taken that trust and smashed it.

And I wanted her to taste that betrayal over and over again like I did every day. I wanted her to see it when she looked at him. I wanted her to feel it whenever she and Beck did whatever fucked-up things the two of them called a relationship.

But I wasn't like her.

I was nothing like these fucking people, and I wouldn't allow them to make me into the horrible people they were.

"I won't." I shook my head. "I'm not you. I'm not Beck. I don't give a shit who you're fucking, Cami. Just stay the hell away from me."

I turned my back to her, and I headed straight in the direction of the locker room. I knew that Lucas would more than likely be there, and I couldn't go another moment without talking to him. I had to look him in the eye and find out the truth from his lips.

I needed to hear him say it. I needed him to stop lying to me for one damn second.

Because that was all he and my dad had done since I had been here. It was no wonder his mother was nowhere to be seen. I would be ashamed to show my face too if I were her.

If I knew what my horrible son had done, and still looked people in the eye and pretended that he was something he wasn't.

He had already taken my father's last name when my father and his mother married. He wanted to erase everything he could from his former life, from whoever he was before he became a Vos, and now I truly wondered why.

I thought that he had wanted it simply because of the power it evoked.

My last name was short and simple and so damn powerful in a town like this.

And Lucas had reaped the benefits of it. It didn't matter that he wasn't a Vos by blood. He was much more my father's son than I had ever been his daughter.

A decision my father had made on his own.

A decision he would have to live with for the rest of his life.

"For what it's worth." I hesitated as she spoke from behind me. "I am sorry for what he did to you. I wish I could go back and stop him."

"But you can't." I swallowed all of the other things I wanted to say to her. I swallowed down the urge to tell her to go straight to hell and take her fake-ass apology with her.

I didn't need or want an apology from her. It would do nothing to change what happened. I wouldn't forgive her for the role she played, and if I was being honest, some part of me hated her for what happened far worse than I hated Beck.

With him, I at least had some small insignificant understanding for why he needed to get revenge. It didn't mean that I would forgive him. I knew that I wouldn't. But I could still understand it.

Even if he did go about it in the most fucked up way possible. I knew that what he did to me didn't even compare to what Lucas had done, but for someone who was so angry over those acts, he sure did come close to replicating them.

He didn't force anything on me. Every moment I had with Beck was one hundred percent willing on my part. Some of those moments I even begged him for.

But he still betrayed me. He broke my trust in the most intimate moment of my life. He took that trust that I had handed him, and he smashed it right in front of my face for the rest of the world to see.

He betrayed me and humiliated me, and I couldn't imagine how he thought any of that was right.

He had apologized since it happened. He had even said that the video being posted wasn't him, but I couldn't trust simple words from him anymore. I may have before.

I had hung on to every single word that he fed me. Even

when he admitted to hating me, and I was starving for anything he would give me.

But this was different.

I couldn't be foolish around him anymore.

I couldn't let him break me again when he had shown me exactly who he was.

I wouldn't allow myself to do that again. Even though every part of me craved to be back in his touch. When I kissed him the other night, it had felt like I was releasing a tension inside of myself that I couldn't bear for even one more minute.

His touch was oppressive and freeing at the exact same time. I felt like I was drowning while taking my first real breath since seeing that damn video.

It didn't make any sense. None of it did, but I couldn't help it.

I hated him yet I craved him.

I wanted to push him away while simultaneously searching the hallways just to catch a glimpse.

I knew how big of an idiot that made me.

"No. I can't." Cami's words were barely a whisper. "And neither can he."

CHAPTER 6

BECK

The hot water rained over me as I leaned my elbow against the shower wall. Today had been rough already.

All I could think about was Josie, but she had been avoiding me.

Not that I blamed her, but it was weighing down on me in a way that I felt like was going to make me explode.

All I could think about was her hands on me at that damn party. Her lips.

I had never wanted it to end, and I was almost certain that it would never happen again.

So instead of doing every single thing I wanted to do with her, I was dealing with Lucas's shit instead. It was the last thing I wanted to do. I had to watch his arrogance as he walked around school like he was untouchable.

I knew that fucker sent that video out. We both did. He was the only other person to have it, due to my own idiotic fucking plan, and he was more than capable.

He had ruined my sister, and he didn't give two shits about ruining his own.

It was obvious in the way he looked at me. He had a cocky smile on his face, so full of himself and pride in what he had done. He didn't care that he played a hand in helping me hurt his sister. All that mattered to him was that he had also hurt me.

Because even though I had been an idiot, it was evident that others had seen what Josie meant to me even when I didn't. Lucas knew that I was somehow going to destroy myself while trying to destroy him, and he played his hand so well.

I was the idiot who fell for his sister while trying to use her as a pawn, and he saw it for exactly what it was.

Lucas and I hated each other, but we had known each other like brothers at one point in our lives. At least, I thought we did.

If I hadn't seen that video for myself, I would have never believed it.

He was one of my best friends, and I had trusted him.

I had trusted him, and he took advantage of that fact.

Lucas had a lot of pressure on him. Joseph Vos had treated him like a damn apprentice rather than a son, and I knew that it got to him. He had a real father who had never given a shit about him, and a new one that demanded excellence in everything he did.

But he never complained. Lucas was just as privileged as I was. The only difference between us was that my father saw me for more than what I could do for him, and I was pretty sure that Mr. Vos never had.

And the way he treated Lucas changed him. It hardened him and drove him to want to be better in anything he did.

At first, I thought that drive was simple competitiveness, but it wasn't. That ambition had become cutthroat, and he was becoming exactly who Mr. Vos wanted him to be.

I should've known from the beginning that he wasn't going to care about Josie.

But there was a spark in his eyes when he first saw us together that fueled something inside of me. Even though I knew he was an asshole who cared about nobody, it was the glimpse of territorial protectiveness that made me think otherwise.

Even if Lucas didn't care for her as he should have, there wasn't a single part of him that wanted me to have her, and I thought that would be enough.

He may not have cared for my sister. He may have used her and abused her and ruined that fragile thing inside of her that made her smile become different after he was through, but I knew how much he feared Joseph Vos. I saw it in his eyes when Mr. Vos found out about the video of Frankie. Even if he defended Lucas and demanded that wasn't him in that video, he knew it was. He knew it with the certainty that I felt in my bones.

And if I were Lucas, I would have feared that flash of fury too.

I was one of the only ones left in the locker room. The baseball team had a weight training class just before lunch, and I had decided to let the heat of the shower tamp down my temper rather than heading out to the lunchroom with the rest of them.

The hard use of my muscles during our workout had taken the slightest bit of edge off, but every time I looked up and saw Lucas, it would return even stronger. It was a mad chase that I never seemed to win.

I leaned back, letting the water rain down over my face. Every time I had seen Lucas, it just reminded me of what I had done to Josie. It reminded me that I couldn't have her.

That I had once had her fully in my grasp, and I had forced her to slip through my fingers. I had forced her to hate me.

The water rolled down my body, and it did nothing to soothe the ache inside of me. Nothing seemed to. Not my hand in the quiet of my bedroom as I imagined what it had been like with her there.

Nothing took the edge off like I needed it to.

"Where's Lucas?" A female voice carried through the locker room and into the shower, and I quickly turned off the water and grabbed a towel. I was still dripping wet, but I didn't care.

I wrapped the towel around my waist and pushed the dripping strands of my hair out of my face. As soon as I rounded the corner into the locker room, I saw her. Josie was standing there talking to Benny, our right fielder, and every bit of her body was stiff.

"What are you doing in here?" My voice boomed through the almost empty locker room, and I tried to rein myself in. Seeing her in here while I still felt so out of control did nothing to help me.

It made me feel chaotic and turbulent. Every emotion swirling through me with no restraint.

Her gaze slammed into me, and I could see the same storm of emotions swirling in her eyes. She stalked toward me, and I held my ground. I planted my feet and waited for whatever she was going to do.

I would allow her whatever she needed. I would stand

and take it from her. I would take all of that swirling anger and hurt from her if I could.

"Where's Lucas?" she repeated the question that had distracted me from my shower.

"I have no idea." I held on to the small bit of towel that knotted at my stomach and shrugged. "I was in the showers."

Her gaze roamed down my body slowly and heat tinted her cheeks as her eyes stopped exactly where my hand held the only fabric that was between us. It was as if she had just noticed that I was standing almost completely bare in front of her. Whatever reason she came in here for had her distracted.

But at that moment, her eyes burned with a completely different kind of storm, and she seemed to forget everything and everyone except for me. She swallowed, deep and loudly, and I could feel every bit of my body going rigid.

She could see it too. She bit down on her bottom lip as her eyes trailed back up my body, and I could barely remember what she had asked me by the time her gaze hit mine again.

Josie may have hated me, but she wanted me.

About that, I was absolutely certain, and I wanted her just as badly. Even if I thought it was a horrible idea.

I needed to prove myself to her. I needed to earn her forgiveness before I let anything else happen between us, but I couldn't seem to remember that when she was looking at me the way she was.

I couldn't think of anything except the way her cheeks reddened and her chest heaved with heavy breaths. Each one drowning me in a trance that consisted of her and her alone.

"Why are you looking for him?" I somehow managed to

push out the words, and they seemed to snap her out of the same stupor I was in.

"Because." She shook her head and looked back toward the door. There were still a couple of guys milling about, but neither of them looked our way. I was sure they were listening to every word we said, but none of them were stupid enough to cross me. Not after they saw what happened to Lucas.

Josie balled her hands into fists, and when she looked back at me, I saw that same anger brewing there. "I need to talk to him. I need to fucking—"

She shook her head as if she had no idea what she needed.

I reached out and wrapped my hand around her elbow. She didn't stop me as I tugged her further into the locker room. We made it around the corner to where my own locker was, but I didn't drop my hand once we stopped.

"Did something happen?" I searched her face, and I was sure that it had.

"I talked to Cami." She jerked her arm out of my touch and crossed her arms.

My blood ran cold at her words. "You shouldn't be listening to anything Cami has to say."

"Why not? You do." She lifted her chin and stared up at me, but she was wrong. I didn't. I barely even talked to Cami lately.

"Cami doesn't have your best reneret at heart."

She laughed, loud and abrasive, and I knew that I had just said the wrong thing. "And you do?" She shook her head, then took a step toward me. Her body only a few inches away from mine. "I shouldn't be talking to you at all."

"But you are." My hand tightened around my towel, and I tried like hell to get a tight grip on my temper. It was no use.

I had no control over anything when I was near her. It was unnerving and frustrating, but God, she made me feel so much more than anyone ever had before. She made me feel so fucking alive that I could almost forget everything that didn't start and end with her.

Almost.

But as soon as she walked away from me, reality set back in, and reality was nothing but a cold, hard bitch.

"I didn't even know you'd be in here." She took a step back and the warning bell rang out through the school, notifying all the students that it was time to get to class. But I had no interest in getting to class. I had no interest in leaving her.

"What did Cami tell you?"

"Everything." She searched my face, but I didn't fear anything that Cami had to tell her. I had already told her the truth myself even if she hadn't wanted to hear it. What I feared from Cami were the lies I knew she spewed.

I couldn't imagine her doing anything like that to hurt me, not after the things the two of us had been through together, but my gut still tightened thinking about it.

"She told me what happened between Lucas and Frankie." I took a deep breath and tried to calm my racing heart. "She told me about the party and why you feel so guilty. She told me about what you did afterward. Is it true?"

Her voice held so much vulnerability that I knew Cami probably didn't leave out a single detail. I had no idea why the two of them had even been talking. Why Cami thought this was her place, but I was glad that Josie finally knew the truth.

I was glad that she heard it from someone who

wasn't me.

Because I could see the doubt in her eyes when I had told her the truth. I had just taken her virginity, then hurt her in a way that was inexcusable, but I had still expected her to believe what I told her.

I knew how fucking stupid that was.

"Is what true?"

"What Lucas did. While Frankie was so drunk." She shifted on her feet, and I knew that this made her uncomfortable.

"It is. I still have the video." Her father thought that he had managed to get rid of them all, but he was an idiot. I had that video saved to my computer where I knew I would one day need it again.

Joseph Vos wasn't going to ruin the only evidence that could hold his son accountable for what he had done.

Josie leaned back, just enough that I had a full view of her features. Her mouth was set in a straight line, but her eyes held so much sadness and anger that I could barely stand to look in them.

"And what you did to Lucas after? Is that true too?" She searched my face, but I didn't know what answer she was looking for. I had no idea if she wanted it to be true or if she was praying that I would tell her it was a lie.

I couldn't imagine that she wanted to protect Lucas after what she knew about him, but I had no idea where her head was at.

I had no idea what she was thinking about any of it.

"It is." There was no use in denying it. She could find out the truth even if I lied, but I didn't want to. I wasn't ashamed of what I did to Lucas. I wasn't ashamed that I had been arrested after, either.

I didn't give a damn about any of that.

The only regret I had was that I couldn't protect Frankie.

Not when it came to what Lucas did to her, and not afterward.

The ruthless actions that I did out of anger only helped the bastard. He had his face smashed in, but in doing so, I let him walk away from what he had done without a scratch.

He had walked away without any real consequences.

I would have stayed in that jail cell if it had meant that he would be right there with me. It wasn't that I wasn't scared. I was terrified when the cops put those handcuffs on my wrists and threw me into the back seat of their cruiser.

I hadn't let the truth of what I had done hit me until that moment, and even then, I hadn't realized the true consequences of my actions. I hadn't known that my father would have to choose between protecting me and protecting Frankie. If it was up to me, he should have let me rot in there with Lucas by my side.

But he didn't.

And I knew that Frankie had everything to do with it.

I had failed to protect her, but she wouldn't fail when it came to me. She had begged my dad to take the deal with Mr. Vos even when I had begged him not to.

It hadn't mattered what I said.

It didn't matter that I had made the decision to put my hands on Lucas even when I knew I would have to pay the price. He was our father, and he was trying to protect us both in the best way he could.

I had hated him for that decision. I had hated that he chose me over Frankie when she needed him the most. She needed us both.

I had failed her, and my dad had chosen to protect me.

I still remember my mother's face when I came home. She was so relieved. She was happy to have me back where she could touch me. She ran her hands over my face, my arms, every part of me, and I don't think she left Frankie or me out of her sight for at least a solid month.

And I knew that it wasn't because she didn't trust me. She was scared of what had happened to her babies.

But I had made a choice for the consequences I had. Frankie hadn't. And Frankie was what hurt my mom the most. Looking into her eyes that were so void of life. It practically killed me.

I couldn't imagine how either of our parents felt.

Josie shook her head and took a step back from me, and the look of disgust on her face fucked with my head. How could she be disgusted with me for what I had done after she knew what her stepbrother was capable of?

"That's the part that bothers you?" I jerked my locker open and let the door slam into the locker next to it with a loud crash. "After everything that you found out, you're disgusted by what I did?"

I laughed, but the sound was filled with venom even to my own ears.

"What?" she questioned, but I didn't dare turn back toward her. I could feel my anger taking hold of me, so deep-rooted that it started at my toes and crawled up my body like a living vine.

I couldn't untangle myself from that anger. That hate.

I couldn't do anything to kill it even though I had tried.

I jerked my clothes from my locker and threw them down on the bench behind me, the bench Josie was still standing by without saying a word.

"I'm not—"

I spun back toward her, and her words caught in her throat when she looked at me. I knew that she could probably see every bit of the anger I couldn't hide any longer.

If the truth was what she wanted, here it was staring her in the face. This was the real truth. The truth that neither of us could hide from. Her brother was a piece of shit, and I had been no better than him.

I had chosen the thing I hated most about him, and I had done the same to her. I had taken her feelings and used them against her. I used and used and used, and I couldn't take a second of it back.

She wasn't Frankie, and I knew that it was different.

But it was also the same.

"You should leave." I nodded my head toward the door before staring down at her. I needed to get away from her before I did something stupid.

I knew that I wasn't capable of being the guy she needed or the guy she wanted. I wasn't capable of anything good when she stood in front of me with that look on her face and this much anger in my veins.

But no part of me actually wanted her to leave. I wanted to bury my hands in her hair and slam her against this locker and never let her go. I needed her. My need was much more vast than a simple want, and I knew that she needed to leave.

If she didn't leave now, I wasn't sure I would be able to control myself. My control already felt like it was on the brink of snapping and having her here in front of me did nothing to help it.

She was the knife that could tear me apart. She could cut through my restraint with a simple touch of her hands, and I knew that her touch could be deadly.

She was the only thing that I could see at that moment. The only thing that mattered, and I hated losing sight of everything else.

She was my blind spot, and I knew that she would be the thing that wrecked me. Her and her perfect lips and her sassy mouth.

"Stop telling me what to do." She balled her hands into fists at her sides, and I knew that she also had a rush of anger going through her. Whether or not she was angry with me wasn't even important. What mattered was that as she continued to look at me the way she did, I wouldn't care if she despised me for what I had done.

I would still beg her to give me whatever she was willing to give, even through her hate I would beg her for more.

"I don't have time for this right now." I slammed my locker behind me and took a step to the side to get out of her line of sight. Nothing good was going to come from this moment, and I needed to get my clothes on and leave before she saw the bulge under my towel or the want in my eyes.

Cami has just told her everything, and all I can think about was how easily I could take her on this bench. That tiny skirt she wore would give me the easiest access to her, and I just knew that by the time I shoved it up her hips she would be dripping with as much want as me.

"So what? Only you get to decide when this is okay?" She waved her hand back and forth between us.

"I think you're the one who decided this weekend." I smirked, and I regretted the words immediately. I may have let her make the first move, but every part of me had wanted her. I had wanted her far more than she could ever want me.

She opened her mouth to say something but hesitated. I

hated the way she looked down at her feet. The way she questioned herself and what she would say in front of me.

But I had done that to her.

"What?" I asked and tightened my hand on my towel.

"Nothing." She shook her head and took an almost unnoticeable step back from me.

"No. Say it." I needed to know what she was going to say. I was dying for her to say anything that would make me feel anything other than what I was feeling at that moment.

"Why?" Her gaze snapped up to meet mine. "So you can hold whatever I say against me?"

That was fair. I knew it was, but I still hated it.

"The only thing I want to hold against you right now is me."

Her gaze trailed down my body as I spoke and stopped just as it met my cock. It jerked beneath the towel, already so fucking hard, and I could have died when her tongue snuck out of her mouth and traced the edge of her lips.

"Don't do that." My voice was rough and commanding, but she didn't care. She wasn't listening to a single thing I said.

"Do what?" She hadn't lifted her gaze.

"That." I reached out and gripped her chin with my fingers. I lifted her head until she was looking back at me, then ran my rough thumb over her soft bottom lip.

It was enough to undo me, enough to make me lose control entirely.

"I didn't do anything." Her voice was breathy and laced with seduction, and I felt the sound as if it slithered over my entire body.

"You should leave," I repeated my words from earlier, but she still wasn't listening to me. Her gaze had dropped back down my body slowly, and I could feel her assessing every inch of me.

I didn't have the restraint to walk away from her.

I didn't possess that sort of control.

I took a step toward her, leaving the smallest amount of space between us, and our breathing melded together in one harsh sound. She was as affected by me as I was her, and I hated the hesitation in her eyes as she roamed over my body.

I hated that this girl could kill me with her touch yet she feared touching me at all.

But then something snapped in her. Something broke free and that bond of indecision snapped.

She stepped forward with pure determination in her eyes as she laid her hand on my chest and pushed me back into my locker. I cursed as the cold, hard metal hit my back, but I didn't dare stop her. I barely breathed as I waited to see what she would do next.

She pushed up on her tiptoes, and her mouth still barely reached mine. She held herself a breath away, and it was pure torture sitting there waiting for her next move.

Her hand tightened against my chest, her nails digging into my skin as she pushed her own chest against her arm. Her hand was buried between us, but I never wanted it to leave my skin.

It was so hot against me, so desperate yet so small.

"I hate you." She stared up into my eyes, and I knew that she meant every single word of what she just said. Regardless of if it was true or not.

"No, you don't." I let the weight of my shoulders fall against the lockers, and let my focus be solely on her.

She was so damn beautiful.

She pushed harder against me. "Yes. I do. I hate you."

Her words should have sliced through me. They should have made me feel anything other than a raging desire to stop her words with my mouth on hers.

Every word that passed her lips only seemed to turn me on more. It didn't matter if she was angry or happy or fueled by her rage for me, every part of her was an aphrodisiac that I couldn't overcome.

"If you hated me," I looked down at her lips and watched as her bottom one trembled with the exertion of her breathing. "You would already be gone. If you hated me, you would have left this locker room the moment you didn't find what you came looking for."

She flinched, and I knew that she was seconds away from doing just that. She would walk away from me just to prove that she could, and I was an idiot for pushing her in that direction.

But it was much easier to face the fact that her body wanted me even if she didn't. Her body wanted me, and she was failing to overcome that want as badly as I was.

She pushed off my chest and turned in the direction she came from, but I had no intentions of letting her go. If she told me that she didn't want this, I would let her leave, but I needed to hear her say it. I needed her to tell me to stop because all I could see in her eyes was her need for me to never cease what I was doing.

I wrapped my arm around her bicep and her gaze shot back to me. I should have asked her if this was what she wanted. I should have made it clear that I wanted her in a way that felt uncontrollable to me, but I did no such thing.

I gave her a few moments as she stared at me, and when there wasn't a single whisper of her asking me to stop, I jerked her forward until her chest slammed into mine.

Her breath left her mouth in a rush, and I leaned down and swallowed it with my own. The first touch of our lips wasn't tentative or gentle. I didn't have the assurance to give her the opportunity to second-guess what we were doing.

I didn't want her to get stuck in her head when she tasted me on her tongue. I didn't need her to think about whether the two of us were right or wrong.

Because I knew what the answer to that would be.

I slammed my mouth against hers, and she was completely stiff beneath me. But I didn't let her go, I moved my lips, and I could feel the tension leaving her body.

She melted under my touch as she brought up her hands and clung to my shoulders. I nipped at her bottom lip before soothing the ache with my tongue, and she whimpered in a way that I thought might kill me.

"I do hate you," she whispered against my mouth as I flipped us around and pressed her into the locker. I needed control. I needed to give her something that would make her forget anything that happened before this moment.

"That's fine." I ran my tongue along the length of her jaw and down the beating pulse on her neck. "You can hate me all you want, but you still want me. You want me almost as badly as I'm dying for you."

Her hips jerked forward against mine. I wrapped my hands around the backs of her thighs, and I lifted her off of her feet. She didn't need any encouragement to wrap her legs around me. The movement opened her legs for me to fit in between them perfectly, and I wanted nothing more than to drop that damn towel and feel every inch of her against me.

I took a step back with her wrapped around me, and I dropped to the wooden bench that ran wall to wall between the sets of lockers. She held onto me tighter as she settled against me, and her hips made the tiniest movements as if she couldn't stand another second without the friction.

I pulled her jacket down her shoulders and jerked open the buttons of her white shirt. A delicate white bra encased her breasts and reminded me of the innocence I took from her.

She was still so innocent, so pure, and I was dying to taste every damn ounce of that virtue. I was dying to tarnish every bit of her with my sins.

I wanted her corrupted and dripping with the memories of what I had done to her.

Her breasts heaved as she stared at me, and I didn't waste another moment before I leaned forward and ran my tongue along the swell of her breast. Her body bowed into mine, and it didn't matter that we were in the middle of the boys' locker room.

Neither one of us cared.

I dipped my tongue beneath the thin fabric and ran it over her pebbled nipple as her hips jerked forward. The movement was enough to loosen the towel from around my waist, but I did nothing to stop it.

I let her feel how turned on I was by her. I wanted her to know what she did to me.

"Beck." My name was a whisper, and I looked up from her breasts to meet her heated gaze.

"Yes, princess?" I roughly jerked her bra down her chest, the layers of fabric on her arms pinning them to her sides, and I didn't wait for a reply from her before I dove into her flesh.

Her skin was so flush and so perfect. Her breast fit in my hand like it was made for it.

I ran my teeth along the sensitive flesh, and she jolted into me. I groaned at the contact of her warmth against me. I could already feel how wet she was beneath her panties, and I couldn't stop myself as I kneaded one of her breasts in one hand and sucked her nipple into my mouth.

Her skin was so sweet beneath my tongue, and my cock was so hard beneath her lap. I surged up against her as she mewled and watched what I was doing to her breasts.

She groaned as my cock slapped against her, and I laid her down on the bench beside me. She let her legs fall to either side of the bench as she stared up at me and I quickly straddled the bench to be perfectly lined up with her center.

I didn't waste time pulling her panties out of my way. I hooked my thumb into the edge and tugged them to the side as I took in her pussy. She was glistening with her arousal, and I moved my thumb up and down her slit at a torturously slow pace.

As soon as my thumb touched her clit, she bowed up off the bench, her tits on perfect display for me, and I knew that she was as close to falling off the edge as I was.

I constantly felt that way around her. Like I was teetering on some invisible ledge where one wrong move would have me plunging into somewhere I could never recover.

She was the gravity that held me in place and the force that threatened my fall.

I bent forward and pressed my lips on the sensitive skin of her inner thigh. She tried to clamp her legs shut, but the bench between them hindered her movement. She was spread open for me, and there was nothing she could do about it besides telling me to stop.

Her legs quivered under my hands as I forced them apart, and I ran my tongue over every inch of her. She was so sweet, the taste of her was unlike anything I had ever had before her, and I was pissed that I had been drinking so much the first time I tasted her.

It had muddled my memory of what it had been like. I knew every bit of it was good, but this felt so much better than anything I could force up in my memories.

She was so damn wet, and I lapped up at her before flattening my tongue against her clit. She jerked forward again, but I didn't let that stop me. I tasted her slow and hard, my tongue exploring every bit of her as she squirmed beneath me, and it wasn't until she wrapped her fingers in my hair and called out my name that I sucked her clit into my mouth.

I stared up at her, and I was surprised to see her watching me so intently. Her face showed every bit of her pleasure, and she watched every move of my tongue.

I flicked my tongue against her as her fingernails dug into my hair before I slipped a finger inside her. It slid in so easily due to her wetness, and I didn't hesitate to add another or to lean back and stare her in the eyes as I did.

She stared at me as I spit down onto that spot where my fingers went inside her, and I loved seeing the bit of shock in her eyes before I brought my mouth back down. I wasn't sure if she was simply shocked by the act or because she liked it so much, but I knew that her pussy was milking my fingers from the inside, and she was riding my face like she had never been so turned on in her life.

I slammed my fingers inside of her and curled them back toward me as her legs shook. She was so damn close, and even though I was dying to get inside of her, I refused to move from this position before she came all over my face.

"Beck, please." She forced her hips higher into the air,

chasing my mouth, and I put her out of her misery as I sucked on her clit with a force that I knew she couldn't stop.

She tugged on my hair to the point of pain, but I didn't stop. I didn't stop until she screamed my name again as she put so much pressure on my head that I knew I wouldn't be able to move until she allowed it.

She rode out her orgasm against my face, and I lightened the touch of my tongue and my fingers as the movements of her hips lessened.

Her fingers slipped from my hair and fell back to her sides, and when I lifted my head from between her legs, she had the smallest smile lighting up her face.

But I wasn't finished with her, far from it.

I wrapped my hands around her waist and lifted her almost lax body back into my lap. She blinked at me as I settled her against me, and I licked the seam of her lips. She instantly opened for me, and I took advantage of that fact.

I ravaged her mouth just as I did her pussy.

I didn't leave one bit of her lips untouched. I sucked them into my mouth, I caressed her tongue slowly with mine, and I knew that she could taste herself on my mouth. I wondered if it tasted as good to her as it did to me. I wondered if she could tell how much I loved it. The mix of her pussy and her mouth on my tongue.

"I need to fuck you." I pulled her bottom lip into my mouth, and she whimpered. "It's all I can think about. You're all I can think about."

She didn't reply. There was no declaration of her feelings or lack thereof, but I didn't need them. Not now. I just needed to know that she was right here with me. I needed to know that she was here, and she wanted this as badly as I did.

She ground down against me, and I was so fucking hard that I thought I might come just from that movement alone.

I lifted her hips up until the tip of my cock lined up with her, then I let her fall back onto my lap as I sank into her inch by inch. She was almost still fully dressed while I was completely bare, and there was something about seeing her like that that took every bit of composure I had left.

I buried one hand into her left thigh while my right one wrapped around her back. She began riding me without any encouragement on my part, her tiptoes barely touching the ground, and I slammed up into her every time our hips were close to meeting.

We found a rhythm that had my heart racing and my balls feeling tight. I hadn't felt like I was going to come so quickly since I was fifteen years old, but there was something about Josie that fucked with my head.

Everything about her felt like too much. She was too sweet, too pure, too fucking good for the shitstorm I brought with me.

I knew that, but I couldn't give her up.

I pressed my hand to her breastbone and let her fall back as I held her. She was still arched into me, but I had a perfect view of where the two of us met. Her tiny skirt was around her hips, and her chestnut hair was falling over her shoulders.

Her eyes were pinched closed as she faced the ceiling, and all I could think about while staring down at her was what would have happened if I hadn't fucked everything up.

"Ride me, Josie," I commanded her, and her eyes snapped open and met mine.

I let her shoulders hit the bench, and she reached up and grabbed ahold of the wooden bench above her head. She used her hands as leverage as she began to move against me. Her body rolled down the bench and ended with her hips against me.

It felt so damn good, too good.

"This doesn't mean anything." She was so breathless as she rode me, but her eyes still blazed with fire.

"It fucking does." I slammed up into her to drive my point home, and she threw her head back and moaned. "It means more than you're ready to hear."

There was a loud creaking that rang out through the locker room, and I knew that someone had just come inside. Josie froze against me, but there was no damn chance we were stopping.

Someone would have to be dying to get me out of her, and even then, it would take a lot for me to pull myself away.

"Beck," she whispered my name and tried to push away from me, but I just held her closer to me. My locker was around the corner from the door, and I knew that no one could see us unless they were headed this way, but I still stood with Josie in my arms and headed for the very back wall.

Unless someone was looking for me, they wouldn't find us here. They could hear us, her whimpers and my deep moans, but we would just have to be quiet.

"Beck. We can't," she whispered in my ear as her back hit the wall, but I didn't stop. I slammed into her and tightened my hand on her thighs.

She let her head fall back against the wall, and she bit down on her lip as she stared down at me. She was worried about who was here, but she had as little interest in stopping as I did.

If I wasn't going crazy with the feel of her around me, I

would say that the thrill of getting caught only turned her on more. Her pussy spasmed around me as I rolled my hips and her hands tightened on my shoulders.

I moved a hand between us and rolled my thumb over her clit. She cried out, and I slammed my mouth down on top of hers to swallow her cries.

"Shhhh," I whispered against her lips just before she buried her face into my neck.

She bit down on my shoulder as I picked up speed, and I knew that wouldn't last much longer.

I pounded into her over and over as my thumb moved against her clit and her breathing rushed out against my neck. Her body was so tight in my arms, and I knew that she was feeling everything as much as I was. Every part of us was overwhelming.

"Just let go," I whispered in her ear before laying a gentle kiss on her earlobe and a harsh flick of my thumb on her clit. She bit down on my shoulder as she cried out, and I followed her over the edge, my cum spilling inside of her.

It was at that moment when it hit me that I hadn't worn a condom. I had been too wrapped up in touching her, in feeling her again, that I hadn't even thought.

I saw it in her eyes the moment she realized it too.

She pushed against my shoulders, forcing me to step back and away from her. I dropped her back onto her feet and quickly grabbed a towel from a small rack.

"Josie." I reached back out for her, but she was already storming past me.

"Don't touch me." She jerked away from my hand and headed straight for my locker. She grabbed her backpack off the ground before rushing to close her jacket around her breasts.

She didn't give me another moment to say anything or try to figure out what the hell to do.

She looked over at me with a look that told me she was completely honest earlier when she said she hated me, and that feeling was even stronger now.

We had just fucked and nothing else. Whether she felt anything else between us was irrelevant.

She stormed around the corner, so eager to get away from me that she didn't care who was there.

"Lucas," she said his name as a curse passed my lips.

Her back was ramrod straight, and I rushed to my locker and threw on a pair of gym shorts.

"What the fuck are you doing in here?" Lucas's voice boomed through the empty locker room, and any amount of peace I had just gained from touching her slipped through my fingers.

My pulse thundered through me as I left my locker open and made my way to her.

"I was looking for you." Her voice shook, but there was still so much anger hiding there.

"Who are you with?"

"It doesn't matter." She didn't say my name, and I knew that she didn't want him to know it was me. Pain sliced through my chest, but I couldn't blame her.

I stopped behind her, just out of his view unless he moved to this side of the locker room. I knew she knew I was there. It was in the way her body tensed, her hands balling to small fists at her sides.

"It does fucking matter." Lucas slammed his locker, and everything inside of me went on alert. If I didn't fear her becoming even angrier with me, I would have stepped out then and let him know exactly who the fuck she was with.

"You know how pissed Dad is already. The last thing he needs is to find out you're in the boys' locker room with anyone. You already look like a whore."

Every muscle in my body bunched together, and I couldn't take another second of listening to him talk to her like that. It didn't matter that she didn't want him to know that it was me in here with her, that I had just done things to her body that neither he nor their father would approve of.

But her next words stopped me in my tracks.

"I'm not too sure that he should be worried about me at all after what I have heard about you."

My thundering pulse turned painful as if my heart might pump straight from my chest. Was she really going to confront him about Frankie with me right here?

"What the hell is that supposed to mean?"

"This isn't the right place to have this discussion." Her eyes glanced in my direction, but she didn't meet my eyes. But every part of me wanted to hear it. I wanted to know whether Lucas would lie about what he had done or if he was brazen enough to admit it.

Did he and his friends laugh about what they had done and how they had gotten away with it?

"No. Let's have it." Lucas's voice sounded closer and filled with rage. "Tell me exactly what you've heard about me, Josie."

"Fine." She lifted her chin, but I could see the slight shake of her hands. "Is it true about what you did to Frankie?"

"Which part?" Lucas laughed. "The part that your little boyfriend believes or the truth?"

"Beck isn't my boyfriend." I hated how hard her voice got as she made sure he knew I wasn't hers and she sure as hell wasn't mine. It shouldn't have bothered me like it did. I knew where the two of us stood, but I couldn't stand the thought of him thinking she wasn't mine. "What's the truth then, Lucas? Because you and Dad have told me nothing."

"The truth is." His locker slammed shut, and she jolted the tiniest bit at the sound. "Frankie Clermont has wanted me for years now. Everyone knows it."

I couldn't control myself as my fists tightened and my chest heaved. I was going to kill him. I was going to bury him for everything he did and for everything he said.

"So, what?" Josie shifted on her feet. "She had a crush on you, so you thought you could do whatever you wanted?"

"I didn't do what I wanted. We did what she wanted."

"What?"

"Frankie begged me to touch her. She begged me for what I gave her." I slammed my eyes shut and prayed that I didn't lose my shit. I wanted nothing more than to move Josie out of my way and slam his head into those lockers. My body vibrated with that need.

"From what I hear, she was drunk. I heard she couldn't even keep her eyes open when you were touching her."

"You do realize you're a Vos, right?" Lucas was over being nice. His voice was laced with venom, and I knew that I wouldn't let this conversation go on much longer. Josie had to live in the same house with him, she was forced to be his family, but I refused to allow this when I could prevent it.

"What does that have to do with anything?"

"All you do is believe what the fuck he says. You've already made up your mind about what happened before you even asked me."

"Beck isn't the one who told me." Her spine straightened,

and I felt like I couldn't breathe past the anger that radiated through me. "Just be honest for once."

"Like you were with Dad?"

I knew how much Lucas looked up to Joseph Vos, but hearing the way he called him dad in front of Josie was almost shocking. There was an air to his voice that felt a lot like he was claiming him as his own. As if Josie had no right to the name.

"Do you know what that was like for him to hear you say that you wanted what Beck did to you? That you made a decision to let Beck touch you that way after Dad strictly forbid you to even be around him?"

I was shocked by his words. Not the part where her dad forbid it, that I expected, but to hear she admitted to wanting me. She admitting that what happened between us had been as much her fault as it was mine.

And I guess it was.

At least until I took that choice away from her and recorded something that had been special to her. It had been to me too, but I had been too foolish to see it. I had been too foolish to let it be perfect exactly the way it was.

"I don't care what it was like for him." She took a step forward, and everything inside of me begged for me to reach out and stop her. I wanted to pull her back to me and never let her out of my sight. "It was the truth. Beck may have been a complete asshole for posting that video. For making me think we were ever anything more than what we were, but he didn't force me."

"So, what?" Lucas's low growl vibrated off the lockers. "You think he's better than me? He posted a video that made you look like nothing but a whore and you think he's better than me?"

Josie opened her mouth to answer, but I couldn't take another second of it. I couldn't listen to him talking to her like she didn't even matter. Like her feelings were inconsequential.

I stepped around the corner and not even the shock of his face could make me smile. I was ready to murder him. Every part of me burning with my need to make him pay not only for what he did to Frankie but Josie too.

"What the fuck are you doing in here?" His gaze snapped from me back to Josie, and his eyes darkened so quickly that I knew he truly hadn't thought that she'd been in here with anyone before.

He had believed her when she said she was just looking for him.

He would die to know what I had just been doing to her, that I could still taste her on my tongue.

"I'm getting dressed." I shrugged my shoulders like it was no big deal, but I couldn't help noticing the way Josie winced at my words.

She may have been as desperate for me as I was for her, but she was still ashamed of what we had just done. She was ashamed and possibly even angry with herself, and I knew that I deserved that.

I deserved it, but it still hurt. It was irrational, but nothing felt rational when I was around her.

Nothing I did or said made any damn sense.

"Why are you here?"

He nodded toward his stepsister before turning his stern eyes back to me. "Can we have some privacy?"

"No." I stepped closer to her until I could feel the heat of her body against mine, and his eyes narrowed at the movement. He didn't want me anywhere near her, and my feelings toward him were the same.

"Get the fuck away from her." His chest puffed out and there was a dare in his eyes. If he wanted to do this here and now, then we could. I didn't fear him or the consequences I would face because of him.

The only thing that mattered to me was making sure that Frankie wasn't hurt by those ramifications and now Josie. I couldn't stand the thought of something happening to either of them because of a hotheaded decision that I made. I had already been there once, and I knew what that had cost my family. What it had cost Frankie.

"After what you did." Lucas ran his fingers through his hair. "You're really going to sit here and act like you give a shit about her. We both know you were just using her to get back at me."

He was right. Of course, he was, but it was different now. Everything was different from the way things had begun, but that didn't stop the hurt from filling Josie's eyes or the way she took a step out of my reach.

"I'm not staying here for this." Josie's hands tightened around her backpack straps until her knuckles turned white. "You two can have a whose dick is bigger than whose contest without me here."

She didn't look back at me as she strode toward the door, and neither Lucas nor I tried to stop her. I wasn't foolish enough to try to have any sort of conversation with her while he was here.

After what had just happened between us, I wanted to know where her head was. The sex between us was amazing. There was no question about that, but I had felt more.

Everything about us felt like more, and I knew that she felt some of that too.

Even if she hated me, she still felt something, and I let the small bloom of hope take over at the idea that maybe she didn't hate me as much as she thought she did. If she did, she would never let me touch her like she just had. She would never let me devour her and fuck her and need her like I did.

Lucas looked over at me as the door slammed behind her, and I knew that he was ready to kill me. He hated me every bit as much as I hated him.

He was the villain in my story and I in his.

It didn't matter which one of us was right and which one was wrong. I would never see him as anything other than what he was to me, and he would do the same.

It felt so foreign to remember him as anything other than this, but we had been friends once. We had been so close that I had trusted him.

Fuck, I had really trusted him.

"Don't go around her again." He backed away from me, and I let him have the parting shot. I didn't need to prove anything to Lucas. Josie was mine whether he wanted her to be or not. She was mine, and the only person that could stop that was her.

And I would fight to prove to her that I was worth it. Even though I had fucked up beyond repair, I was willing to do whatever it took to convince her otherwise.

I was still the villain in her story too, but I would either fall or rise at her hand alone. She had the power to destroy me if she wanted. She held all the power, and I was completely at her mercy.

CHAPTER 7

JOSIE

I needed to get out of here.

It had been over an hour since I walked out of that locker room, and I had been watching every tick of the clock until that final bell rang.

I wanted to get away from this place. Away from Lucas and Beck and the memory of what I had just done with him. I could still feel him between my legs. I could feel the low ache there and in my lower stomach, and even though I had loved it when it was happening, I regretted every minute of it now.

I regretted that I had let him get to me when I should have been shoving him away.

I felt insane. I knew that Beck wasn't good for me, I knew exactly what he had done, and I still couldn't just walk away.

What Cami told me didn't change anything. Not really.

Not for me and Beck.

I knew his reasoning behind what he did, but that didn't erase his actions. He still made his choice to fuck with my life, even if he did so out of his anger for Frankie.

Out of his care for her.

I wouldn't lie and say a part of me hadn't softened toward him when I heard the truth from Cami's lips. Even if it had still hurt me.

I pushed past the heavy front doors and out toward the parking lot. There were a ton of students milling about, and I wanted to avoid them all. I had no interest in talking to any of these people.

I had to work tonight, and I just needed to get there and talk to Allie and have her talk me off my ledge.

She was the only one I had to talk to, the only one I truly trusted, and I knew that she wouldn't judge me for what I had done. She never judged me.

I made my way to the far corner of the parking lot where my car was parked, and I finally felt like I could breathe as the sounds of everyone around me faded with the distance I put between us.

I felt like I had been suffocating under their constant stares and judgment.

I had almost made it to my car, my dad's car, when I saw Frankie standing next to Beck's SUV. She was messing with her phone, and I tried to quickly walk by without her noticing me.

I had barely ever spoken to the girl, not really, and I honestly didn't know what I would say now. Now that I knew the truth.

I felt guilty that I hadn't known before, that I hadn't known and she had to face me like I wasn't Lucas's stepsister.

She looked up just as I passed his SUV, and her gaze hitting mine caused my steps to falter. I couldn't just look her in the eyes and walk away like I knew nothing. I couldn't just let this girl think I was somehow as cruel as my stepbrother.

"Hi." She blinked up at me, and I shifted on my feet in front of her. We were only a few feet from each other, but it felt like we were miles apart. She was Beck's sister and I was Lucas's stepsister.

She had never done anything wrong to me nor I to her, but somehow, I still felt like I was her enemy. We were on opposite sides, the line drawn in the sand by the men who surrounded us, and I hated that I felt like I couldn't cross it.

"Hey." I felt so foolish standing in front of her not knowing what to say, but part of me realized that she probably felt the same way. Her brother hadn't done to me what my stepbrother had done to her, but in a way he had. They had both taken advantage of our trust, and in doing so, hurt us irrevocably.

Neither one of us spoke for a couple of seconds, then we both try to talk at once. Our rushed words were mumbled over each other's. We both laughed before I mustered up the courage to say what I needed to say.

"I'm sorry for what Lucas did to you." She looked shocked by my words, and I could see the shame fill her eyes as soon as they passed my lips. She was still wholly affected by what he had done to her. It didn't matter that it had happened in the past or that Lucas thought she had wanted what he did to her. Every part of me knew that she hadn't simply by looking at her face.

And my stomach felt like it was in a constant flip as I saw it. That truth staring back at me.

Lucas had taken from her, and it was something I wasn't sure she would ever get back. Some piece of her armor, her dignity, her heart. And I knew that even though it had felt like it just a moment ago, what had happened to us was nothing alike.

I was pissed at Beck for what he had done, but Lucas had truly hurt this girl. He had taken from Frankie, and I had wondered what she had been like before he had. Had her smile been different? Her laugh?

Had she always looked like there was a shadow clouding her eyes?

"And I'm sorry for what Beck did to you."

"Don't." I held up my hand and tried to shut down her apology. I couldn't stand to hear it.

Frankie owed me nothing.

Not an apology. Not her sympathy.

It made my chest ache just hearing it pass her lips.

"You don't owe me any kind of apology." There is a sadness in her eyes that told me she knew what I meant. What Beck had done to me was wrong, but it wasn't the same thing.

It wasn't even comparable.

I could apologize to her for the rest of my life for what Lucas had done, and it wouldn't be enough.

Nothing would ever be enough to erase what he had done.

"You don't owe me an apology either. Neither of us can help the fact that our brothers were jackasses to two girls that loved them." Her words struck me in my chest, and it was on the tip of my tongue to tell her that however she had felt about Lucas was vastly different than how I felt about Beck. She may have loved Lucas, but I couldn't say the same. I had thought I was falling for Beck, I may have even used that damn L-word before, but now it felt so stupid.

How could I love someone who could hurt me so easily?

It didn't make any sense.

I knew that I felt something for him, I knew that I had been a fool, but saying out loud that I had thought I had loved her brother made me feel so idiotic. I wasn't like her. Beck hadn't been my friend before. I hadn't known him for years.

From the moment I met Beck, I knew he didn't like me. He didn't like me, but I still fell for him. He had shown that he hated me, but I still gave him parts of me that I had never given to anyone else.

I shifted on my feet, and by the way Frankie watched me, I knew that she knew I was uncomfortable with what she said. She had been so brave, to admit that she had once loved someone who had hurt her the way Lucas had, I couldn't imagine having that much strength.

I couldn't imagine the amount of strength it took for her to get up in the morning and come to school and face him all day. For her to pretend as though nothing happened. That thought alone had my blood boiling inside of my veins.

Lucas had hurt her in unspeakable ways, and he suffered no consequences.

Simply because he was my father's stepson. My father had gotten him out of things that he should've paid for. It didn't matter that his own freedom was what afforded Beck his. It should've never been on the table. My father should've made Lucas pay for what he did. If he protected him from the legal system, he should have punished him at home, but I knew that Lucas hadn't had those consequences.

He had disappointed my father, and that was the extent of it. But in a way, I knew that that part alone had to fuck with Lucas's head.

He was so desperate to impress him, so desperate to be

just like him, and instead, he embarrassed him in front of all the people he ruled. Because, even though I knew what had happened and how they had decided to keep everything hush-hush, a place like Clermont Bay couldn't keep secrets that tightly. Everybody whispered, everybody talked, and eventually everybody's secrets would come out.

It hit me then that that was why my father wanted me to stay so far away from Beck. It wasn't because of what he had done to Lucas. He could probably give two shits less about that. But Lucas had hurt his image, and he knew that Beck and his family were the only ones who had the power to keep that secret for them.

They were the ones who held the key to this particular set of sins.

He never actually cared about me, or what he thought the Clermonts were capable of. That was all a part of his act. The caring, loving father who wanted people to see him for everything he wasn't.

And I knew it was irrational, but part of me thought he was just as guilty as Lucas. I knew that was wrong, I knew that every bit of that was the deep-seated bitterness I had toward him, but I couldn't stop myself from feeling it.

There wasn't a thing I could do to change the way I felt.

"I know that what Beck did was wrong." Frankie leaned against his car and tucked a piece of hair behind her ear. She looked nervous about what she would say to me next. Like she didn't know how I would react. "But he does care about you."

I shook my head against her words. She saw Beck how she wanted to see him. She was his younger sister who loved him, and in her eyes, he could do no wrong.

He had been the one to protect her, to defend what had

been taken from her, and I knew that she probably saw Beck as some sort of hero. I guess in her story, he was.

But he wasn't in mine.

The way she felt about him wasn't wrong, but she was wrong about this.

Beck may have wanted me, I was absolutely certain about that fact, but wanting someone and caring for someone are two different things.

They were incomparable.

Even if a small kernel of hope formed in my chest, I knew that I had to shut it down. I was already too naïve when it came to him, and I couldn't afford for his little sister to make me believe anything other than what was right in front of me.

Beck had already shown me who he was, and it was time that I believed him.

"He doesn't." I shook my head again. There is so much sympathy in her eyes that I had to look away. I didn't need or want her sympathy even though I had given it to her.

Especially not from her.

"I know you don't want to hear it, but he does. He's just so fucked up in his own head right now."

Being fucked up in his head was nothing but an excuse. I understood why he did what he did. Why he felt the need.

Logically, I could make sense of his reasoning, but it didn't mean that I would forgive it. He was fucked up in his head, but he still made a conscious decision to do what he did to me. He made a conscious decision to make me fall for him so that he could slap everything that I had done and said and hoped for right back in my face.

And even though I wanted to believe what she said, I wanted to believe it and cling to it and let everything else fall away, I knew that it would do nothing but end up getting me hurt.

Beck only led to one path, and I knew where that ended. Thinking anything else was insanity.

"I don't..." I hesitated. "I don't know that I'll ever forgive him."

She stared at me for a few moments, and I knew that she understood what I was saying. But there was so much sympathy in her eyes, and I wasn't sure whether it was meant for me or for her brother.

Because regardless of what he did to me, he was still her big brother, and I knew that she was going to have his back. But another part of me knew that she wouldn't have said what she just said if she didn't feel it was true. Frankie seemed so far from fake, and I knew she hated the position that Beck and put me in.

She loved him, but she still hated what he had done.

She opened her mouth to say something else just as someone walked in front of Beck's car. My spine straightened as I heard the footsteps move closer to us, and I wanted to run away as fast as I could.

I didn't want to see him.

I didn't need him catching me here with his sister, especially after everything we had just done. I didn't need to give him any ammunition or time to mess with my head.

I just needed to get as far away from him as I could and to stay there.

But it wasn't Beck who rounded the hood of his expensive SUV, it was Olly, and when he looked up and saw me, I saw that same sympathy staring back at me that Frankie had shown. Regardless of how hard Olly acted when he was with his boys, I could see how much he hated what Beck had done from that one look alone.

"Hey." He gently knocked his shoulder into Frankie, and I watched a blush fill her cheek. "Hey, Josie." He nodded his head toward me, and I tighten my hands on my backpack straps.

"Hi." I took a step back, ready to retreat from him. He may not have been Beck, but I had no interest in being around any of them. It didn't matter if he felt bad for what had happened.

Olly and Carson were his best friends, and I knew that they had known what he was going to do. They had known, they had watched, and I felt so foolish standing in front of him.

All I could think about was that night the three of them had come to the country club. How badly Beck had treated me. Olly and Carson had watched him do so, then he watched me fall for him anyway.

He had to think that I was a complete and total idiot. That I was nothing more than a desperate girl who couldn't walk away from Beck even when he had been pushing me.

I pointed in the general direction of my car. "I have to get to work. I was just about to head out."

Frankie stepped forward as if she was going to stop me, but Olly caught her hand in his. The touch was almost too intimate for a girl and her brother's best friend, but I was sure that all three of them had to be more protective of her after what happened with Lucas. I couldn't imagine that any of them would stand by and watch her get hurt again.

"I'm glad we got a chance to talk." She looked down at her fingers, then back to me.

"Me too." I nodded.

And I was being honest. Regardless of what Beck and Lucas had done, the two of us were nothing more than collateral damage. And I didn't want her to hate me. If I were her, I would have hated me knowing what my stepbrother had done to her, but I didn't realize until that moment how badly I didn't want that from her.

I wasn't Lucas, I wasn't my father, and I wanted to be so far detached from them that no one would think twice about bunching me under their name.

My mother was nothing like him, like these people, and even though she had tried to make me think positively about my father until the day she died, his actions spoke so much louder than anything she would have to say about him.

And it mattered that Frankie didn't think I was like them; it mattered that she knew that I was disgusted by what he had done to her.

It didn't matter that she had wanted me to have a good relationship with my father. All that mattered was that he had never cared one way or another.

Lucas was my stepbrother, but I would hate him for the rest of my life knowing what he had done. He had irrevocably hurt the girl that stood in front of me, and I would never forgive him for the pain in her eyes. I would never forgive him for the things that haunted her.

And I hope she knew that.

"I'll see you around?" She sounds so hopeful, and I couldn't stand the thought of telling her no. I didn't want to see the disappointment in her eyes.

"Yeah." I nodded and backed away toward my car. I couldn't stop my gaze from trailing over to Olly who still held her hand. I knew that he would tell Beck that the two of us were talking.

But I didn't care what he told Beck. Beck wasn't my concern, and I wasn't his.

I was nothing to him.

"Just make sure your brother isn't with you."

She grinned, and I couldn't stop myself from smiling back at her.

CHAPTER 8
BECK

Everything inside me screamed for me to go find her as the last bell of the day rang. I hated the way we left things.

It was a constant circle of how I felt. I felt like I was dying to be around her, but every time I was, we left in a worse place than we started.

I had no intentions of letting things go where they went when she walked into that locker room. I hadn't even known she would be there, but once she was, I could let her go. I couldn't stop myself from touching her, from consuming every moment with her I could get.

Because I knew that sooner or later those moments were going to run out.

They should have run out already. If Josie was smart, she would never let a guy like me touch her again, but I didn't want that. I didn't want her to wise up when it came to me.

Because I would be doomed.

If she didn't want me, I wouldn't stand a chance.

But I knew she did. The proof was in the way she reacted to my touch, the way she begged me even though I knew part of her wanted to push me away.

It was the only thing I had. The way she physically wanted me, and I knew that it made me an even bigger asshole, but I was willing to use it. If it meant that I got more time with her, that I could possibly convince her to forgive me for what I had done, I would exploit that want until she no longer had it.

My dick was hard just thinking about it.

But that wasn't what I wanted from her. Of course, I wanted her. I wanted her in every way she would possibly let me have her.

But I wanted more. I wanted her to see that I was capable of more. Of more than being this guy who fucked everything up.

Because that was what I did.

I fucked up everything.

I had fucked up things when it came to Frankie, and I had fucked them up with Josie.

I had been so wrapped up in my rage for Lucas both times that I hadn't thought of what the consequences would be. I had known, but I hadn't cared.

Nothing had mattered to me either time as much as making Lucas pay, and I knew how fucked up that was.

I kept telling myself that I needed to quit thinking about her. I needed to stop obsessing and give her space. I would do nothing but continue to push her away otherwise.

"Where are we going?" Carson asked from the back seat as I drummed my fingers against my steering wheel.

"My house. Then to the water." They both knew what

that meant. It had been so long since any of us had been out on the water, especially together, and I needed that today. I needed it to clear my head and dampen my want.

Frankie was quieter than normal in the back seat, and every few moments I couldn't help but look back at her through the rearview mirror. She stared out the window the whole time, and I was dying to know what was in her head.

I wanted to know what she thought about day to day, moment to moment. I wondered if the memories of Lucas haunted her as they did me. And there was no comparison. What she had gone through was heinous, and the guilt of not being there for her ate me alive.

It kept me up at night as I dreamed about what it had to be like for her. Did she think that I was going to come to save her? Did she hate me the moment she realized I wasn't? Did she hate me like I hated myself?

Knowing that she had feelings for Lucas, whether she called it a crush or something more. I didn't know how far her feelings went, but she had liked Lucas and he took advantage of that fact.

We pulled up to the house, and she climbed out of the back seat without a word. It wasn't abnormal, but something just felt off today. It felt like she wanted to get as far away from me as she could, and I hated just the thought of that.

Carson and Olly followed me into the house where all three of us quickly changed into a pair of my boardshorts. This used to be one of our things to do. We had survived on surfing and baseball. They had been our only loves before we realized that girls had tits.

And I knew they had to be jonesing for the water as hard as I was. None of us spoke as we grabbed the surfboards from the garage and made our way out to the beach. The sun was strong overhead, and the waves crashed against the shore, teasing me with their beauty.

They were exquisite yet deadly, so unpredictable and so perfectly disguised. It wasn't until that moment when you picked a wave that you could feel the truth beneath you.

That was the part that I loved and needed so much. My heart raced at the unpredictability, my soul craved it.

Carson was the first one in the water. He paddled out toward the waiting sea, and I knew that he loved this as much as I did. Carson had always needed this rush, the fear of not knowing what was going to happen, it settled him in a way that I wasn't sure even I felt.

All three of us reached a point in the ocean, a couple of dozen yards from the shore, and we sat up on our boards and stared out at the ocean.

"Frankie seemed off today." This came from Carson, and I knew they had felt that same shift in her that I felt.

"She was talking to Josie when I got to the car," Olly said nonchalantly, and my head spun in his direction so quickly I almost fell from my board.

"What? What the fuck were they talking about?"

"I don't know." He shook his head. "Frankie was telling her that she was glad they talked, though. She got spooked the moment I walked up."

"That's it? That's all they said." I wanted to know everything. Every word that was exchanged between them. Did Josie approach her? Did Josie ask her about what she had found out about her stepbrother?

"Well, Josie made a comment that she'd be seeing Frankie as long as her brother wasn't around." Olly laughed, and I couldn't help smiling just thinking about Josie's sass.

I could imagine her saying just that.

"Of course she did." I chuckled and couldn't stop thinking of her.

"So what's the deal with her anyway?" Carson had his fingers wrapped around the edge of his board, and even though he was trying to act nonchalant, I knew both of them well enough to know they were dying to know my answer.

They had known my plan for her, known what I was capable of when it came to Lucas, but neither of them knew what to think now. They had no idea where my head was at, and neither did I. It felt so fucked up that I didn't even know how to explain it. I had accomplished exactly what I wanted with Josie, and I regretted every second of it.

I regretted it, and I never thought I would.

"There is no deal." It wasn't exactly a lie. I had no idea what was going on with us. She was adamant that she wanted nothing to do with me, but everything about her screamed otherwise.

"When the hell are you gonna stop lying?" Olly didn't look toward me as he spoke. He just stared out toward the water as if he was lost in his own head. "You know we can sniff out that bullshit faster than it takes for you to say it."

"What do you want me to say? That I was an idiot who pushed Josie away, who fucking forced her away, and now I wanted her back?" I ran my wet fingers through my hair.

"Well, that would be a start." Olly finally looked over at me, and there is a small smirk on his face. "Admitting you have a problem is the first step."

I rolled my eyes at him, but he was right. I had no idea why I was trying to keep this from them. We never kept anything from each other. Hell, I knew things about Carson that another person should never know. But each of us had our own secrets too. I knew that.

"Do you really think she's going to forgive you?" Carson asked, and I knew it was a fair question. She had no reason to forgive me.

If she was smart, she wouldn't.

"If I was her I wouldn't, but I hope she does."

Olly drummed his fingers against his board, and he looked like he was hesitating with what he was saying next. "Are you sure that it was Lucas who posted the video?"

"Who the fuck else would it be?"

He lifted his hands in defense. "I'm just asking. I just can't understand why he would want to do this to her. Like, what did he get out of it?"

It was the same question I've been asking myself every day. The question ran over and over through my mind.

What did Lucas have to gain from hurting Josie?

The only logical answer I could come up with is that he took her away from me. I had given him the keys to do so, and he took full advantage of it. I should've known that he would use it against me from the beginning, but I have been so stuck on hurting him, on making him pay in any way possible, that I completely underestimated his ability not to give a shit.

He just simply didn't care. There was no other explanation for it.

But part of me rebelled against that thought. Even through everything Lucas had done, even through all the hate I carried for him, he had once been my friend, and I never could have imagined him doing anything like this.

"Besides making her want nothing to do with me, I don't know."

He seemed to think about what I had just said, and I knew that it didn't sit well with him either.

Olly and Carson had been friends with Lucas, too, before everything happened, and they were forced to choose between their two friends. Neither of them hesitated when they found out what he had done, but I knew that it still took a toll on them.

"I guess." Olly shook his head. "It still just doesn't make any sense. After everything he got away with, you would think he'd keep his fucking head down and his nose clean."

"You would think, but I didn't keep my nose clean either."

"That's different." Carson chimed in. "You didn't sexually assault anyone."

Olly and I both winced as he said the words. We all knew what happened to Frankie. It stared us in the face every single day, but I still hated hearing those words out loud.

They were a blaring reminder of how badly I had failed her.

"No. I just made her fall for me then exploited her."

"It's not the same," Olly echoed Carson's thoughts. "You were in the fucking wrong, but it's still not the same."

"Frankie hates what I did."

"Of course, she does." Olly's words were muffled by the rise and fall of a harsh wave beneath us. "I don't know how you thought your plan could end in any other way."

He was right. He had told me the same damn thing before I had even gone through with it, but I hadn't listened.

"But she'll forgive you. She always has." Olly was right. Frankie did always forgive me, regardless of what fucked-up thing I did.

"We should take Frankie to do something. Cheer her up,"

Carson said just as he laid down on his stomach on his board.

"Like what?" Frankie hadn't wanted to do much of anything lately.

"I don't know. Shopping or something."

"She would hate that. It would just force her to be around more people when she doesn't have to be." Olly shook his head.

"Then what do you suggest?"

"We could take her up to the cabin like we used to. She used to love that when we were younger."

"Yeah." I nodded. "She did." We had spent so many nights at my parents' cabin during our summers growing up that it had become a second home. Frankie would never let me go with the boys without her tagging along, but I really didn't mind.

Not until I found girls and invited them to our trips instead of her.

Guilt lashed at me.

There were so many things that I had pushed her away from. That I had thought I was too damn cool to have my younger sister with me. I wish that party that night had been one of those things.

"Let's plan something."

"Okay, but first we need some water therapy." Carson looked behind him at the large wave that was headed our way and he started paddling as soon as he caught the swell.

He was right. I needed to get lost in the ocean beneath me, and not think about everything that was going on. I needed just a few minutes where I didn't have to think about how fucked up everything was.

It was just me, my boys, and the ocean, and the task of

riding the waves. Nothing else mattered at that moment. Nothing could reach me.

That was what I told myself as I paddled forward and tried to catch the next swell, but the thoughts of Josie wouldn't stop. Not even the ocean could chase them away.

CHAPTER 9
JOSIE

"I don't really care what you want, Josie. Your wants have gotten you into enough trouble already." My father's voice was stern, and I knew that I didn't have any room to argue.

But I didn't want to do this.

I didn't care if his damn party was for charity or not.

"I don't want to go." I stomped my foot like a bratty-ass toddler, and I knew that I was being ridiculous.

"It doesn't matter." My father slammed his hand down on the counter between us, and I flinched at the contact. "You are a part of this family, and as such, you are expected to attend these things. Amelia will buy you a dress, and we will arrive at the gala as a family."

As a family.

He was out of his damn mind.

We weren't a family, not really, but that wasn't what mattered to him. It was all about his image, and I had already done enough to tarnish that. He made sure I remembered that fact too.

"After what happened with Beckham, I can't afford any more bad attention where you're involved. Everyone will want to know why you aren't there. You're coming."

"I did nothing wrong." I could feel my pulse racing. I had heard my dad talking about what happened between me and Beck, about the video, a million times, but he never spoke to me about it.

It was as if my opinion on the subject didn't matter.

It had never mattered to him.

"Did you see that damn video, Josie?" His eyes that matched mine were filled with so much anger and fury.

Of course, I had seen the video. I had seen it far too many times to count, and I hated, I fucking hated, that he had seen it as well.

I didn't even know how much he had seen, but even one second was too much.

"Yes. I saw it." I squared my shoulders and waited for whatever he would say next.

"Then you know what everyone who saw that video saw. You know what they think of you."

I felt like he had slapped me. My heart raced so fast that I felt like I would never be able to slow it down. "What exactly do they think of me?"

I wanted to hear him say the words. I wanted to know exactly what he was thinking, exactly how he felt about me.

"You look like a whore," he roared, and I couldn't stop the way my vision became foggy with unshed tears.

I had promised myself a long time ago that I was done wasting my tears on a father who didn't give a shit. I had made myself that promise on the third birthday in a row that he had missed. I was eleven at the time.

But I couldn't stop them from forming now. It didn't

matter what I told myself or how badly I wanted to be unaffected by him, the truth was that his opinion mattered far more than I should have ever allowed it to.

He mattered regardless of how badly I tried to prove otherwise.

"I..." I stuttered over my words because I had no idea what to say to him. I wasn't a whore. I wasn't even close, but I knew that was what he saw when he saw that video. He had seen exactly what Beck had wanted everyone to see.

"So, why do you want your whore daughter at the event then?" I took a small step back from him. "If that's what everyone thinks, then I want to stay as far away from them as I can."

I knew the kind of people who would be at any kind of event that my father was attending, and I didn't want to be around any of them. I didn't care what they thought of me.

They were all as vile as he was, and I had no interest in flaunting myself in front of them and pretending like I was a perfect girl with a perfect life.

I was no such thing.

"You are going to go because I refuse to allow the Clermonts to tarnish our name the way they have. I refuse to cower because some teenage boy got it in his head that he could play God."

"And what about Lucas?"

My father's gaze snapped to mine.

"What about him?"

"You're fine with what he did? You just choose to pretend like Beck didn't have a reason to do what he did to me?"

My father's rage filled the room, and I knew that if I said another word, I would feel his wrath like I had never felt it before.

But I didn't care.

He had to know that I knew what Lucas had done, and more importantly, that I knew what he had done to help Lucas get away with it.

"You have no damn clue what you're talking about." His voice was eerily calm. "I don't know what Beck Clermont has been telling you, but he doesn't know shit."

"Beck's not the one who told me." I shook my head. How he could just sit there and continue to lie for Lucas made me feel sick to my stomach. I couldn't understand how even a man like my father could be okay with what Lucas did. "It was Cami."

My father was completely still as he assessed me. I could feel him calculating exactly what he would say to me next.

"What happened with Lucas was unfortunate, but I'm not going to damn the boy simply because he made a drunken mistake."

A mistake?

A fucking mistake?

"He didn't make a mistake. He assaulted her."

"That's her word against his." His gaze was so damn cold, and I knew that I didn't know anything about my father. Not really.

He was as much a stranger to me as he was to everyone else.

"So you just take his word? Even though you saw the video? Even though he released a video just like Beck had?"

"And what would you have rather I done, Josephine? Let him go to jail for a mistake? Prosecute him for letting his friends share that video of them?"

"Yes!" I was practically screaming. "He should have been held responsible for what he did."

"And what about Beck?" His knuckles were turning white from his grip on the counter. "Do you want me to press charges against him for what he did?"

My heart lurched into my throat. "No." I shook my head. Of course, that wasn't what I wanted with Beck. "But Beck didn't assault me. What I did with him was my choice."

"And it's a choice you're going to have to live with. It's something that will haunt you for years to come."

"Because I'm a teenager who let a guy touch me?"

"Because you let a Clermont touch you. You let him touch you when I told you to stay away from him and look what happened."

Deep down, I knew he was right. I knew that he had warned me to stay away from Beck, and even if his reasoning was shit, he was right. I should have stayed as far away from Beck as I could.

But every part of me screamed to defend him against my father. Even though he had given me absolutely no reason to.

He deserved everything my father thought of him, but I couldn't make myself truly believe that.

Even if I knew I should have.

"Why should it matter? Why should I listen to what you have to say?" I knew the moment I said the words they would only infuriate him further, but I didn't care. I had no reason to care about his reputation and how these damn people saw him or me. I saw him exactly for who he was, and it was about time that everyone else did too.

"Because you are my daughter. And as such, I expect you to act a certain way. Regardless of if you don't want to listen to what anyone else has to say. Their opinions are important to me." His words were low and slow and precise, and I knew that he wasn't telling me simply what he expected out of me but what he demanded.

"You can continue to act however you want to, Josephine, but there will be consequences for your actions."

"Like what?" My blood ran cold in my veins. Lucas hadn't had consequences for what he had done, but he would punish me?

"Like your mother's shitty old house and that measly bit of money she left you."

"You can't do that." I didn't care about the money, even if it was the only thing I had once I left this place, but I did care about her house.

I wouldn't let him take it from me. I couldn't.

"I can do whatever I want. You are a minor, and I have full legal control over your assets until you turn eighteen." He actually had the nerve to look sympathetic about what he said next. "Your mother didn't have anything in place like she should have before she passed. I can take everything if I want it."

He would do it too. I had no doubt, and he knew how much that house meant to me. I had fought tooth and nail not to leave it when he was granted custody of me.

And I knew it was just a damn house, but it was the last piece of my mother that was still tangible. It had still smelled like her when I left.

We had spent our entire lives in that house.

"So, what? I have to do what you say or you're going to continue to hang this over my head?"

"No." He shook his head and straightened from the counter. He picked at an invisible piece of lint from his jacket, and I knew that he was all business now. "This will be the last time we speak of it."

I wanted to rage against him, to tell him that he had no right to do the things he said, but that wouldn't get me anywhere. Because the truth was that my dad would find a way to take everything from me if that was what he wanted.

He had power and money, and I had neither of those things without him.

"You can either act like you belong to this family, or you cannot. That choice is completely up to you." What he said and what he meant were two different things. To act like I was a part of his family was to obey his every command. And I didn't know if I could do that, but I couldn't lose my mother's house.

He had used this against me before, but I hadn't believed he was truly capable. But with the way he stared at me now, I knew that he was. He was capable of anything.

The stupid charity gala that he wanted me to attend was this weekend, and I knew that I should just shut my mouth and attend like he wanted me to. It was just an event, just my father proving who he was to these people, and I could handle one night. Even if I had to dress up and let him parade me around like I was his fucking princess daughter, I could handle it for one night if it meant getting him off my back.

"Fine. I'll go to the gala and wear whatever Amelia deems appropriate for me." I couldn't stop the sass in my voice. "Can I go to Allie's now? I haven't got to see her in days."

And I needed her.

I needed to get so far away from all of these people and just be with my girl.

With both of us being back in school and our new work schedules being only part-time, I felt like I never got to see her. I talked to her every single day, but it wasn't enough. I needed to see my friend and have her help me straighten out what the hell was going through my head.

She was the only one who could.

"Fine, but I expect you to be back home tonight. Amelia will want to talk to you about your dress."

"Fine." I grabbed the keys off the counter and turned away from him before he could change his mind. "I'll be back later."

I didn't wait for him to respond as I headed out the door and climbed into my car. I tried not to think about my father or Lucas or Beck as I rolled down my window and blared music through my speakers.

I let memories of my mom cloud my thoughts as I drove down the street of pretentious houses and headed to the opposite side of town. I let myself remember her hair that was lighter than mine and the way her smile was lined with laugh lines.

Her memory wasn't fading. I could imagine every part of her as if she was still right in front of me.

I could still smell her soft perfume and feel the softness of her skin.

Those memories crashed into me, and even though I hated thinking about them, I hated thinking about the fact that she was gone, I forced myself to go through the steps of remembering everything about her that I could.

Because I knew that one day those memories would slowly start to fade, and I would regret it. Even if it hurt right now, I knew I would regret it.

By the time I pulled up to Allie's house, I felt lighter yet heavier at the exact same time. It was something that I couldn't explain, the way thinking about my mom made me feel.

Allie ran out as soon as I pulled up and waved me inside. I had never been inside her house before. It had always been a simple pick-up or drop-off, and I found myself anxious to meet her parents.

She wrapped me in her arms as soon as I stepped out of the car. "It took you long enough."

"I know. My dad was riding my ass."

She made a face that told me she understood. She had let me vent about my dad more times than I could count. "About what now?"

"Some dang gala he's forcing me to go to."

"The Clermont Bay Helping Hands Gala?" She looked back at me as she led me toward her house.

"Yeah. Wait. Are you going?" Hope bloomed in my chest.

"I'll be serving." She laughed. "I work the event every year."

"Ugh. I wish you could just go with me."

"Me too." She grinned. "The event is so glamorous. You'll have fun."

"With my dad, stepmom, and Lucas?" I made a face, and she laughed again before pushing through the front door.

"Well, at least you'll get to eat all the good food."

"That's true." We walked into her house, and I was instantly bombarded with the smell of home. A real home.

"Mom!" Allie called for her mother, and a pang of jealousy or something that felt a lot like it hit my chest.

"In here."

I followed Allie through the small living room and into the kitchen. Her mom was stirring something on the stove and moving to the sound of music that played from the radio on the counter. Allie was a spitting image of her. From her blonde hair and her eyes to the smile that lit up her entire face.

She looked over and saw me with Allie and immediately dropped her spoon into the pot. "Oh, hi." She turned toward me and wiped her hands down her jeans. "I'm Molly."

"I'm Josie. It's nice to meet you." I took her hand in mine that she stretched toward me, and it was just as warm as I had expected.

"It's nice to meet you too, Josie. Allie has told me a lot about you." She smiled, and I prayed that Allie hadn't told her everything.

"I hope it was all good." I laughed, and I could have sworn her eyes twinkled.

"It is." She grinned. "But she leaves out all the juicy details. All she told me was that you're dating that hunk Beck Clermont."

"Mom!" Allie looks like she's about to kill her mother, but I couldn't help but laugh.

"We are definitely not dating." We were so far from dating that I wouldn't even know what to call us.

"Well, whatever you all call it these days. Allie never brings any boys home so I have to get my dating gossip from somewhere."

"I'm afraid my own dating gossip is rather boring." I set my keys down on the kitchen table and took a seat beside Allie as her mom moved to the fridge.

"Now I may be old, but I'm not that old. I know boys like Beck Clermont are nothing close to boring."

Allie put her head in her hands, but her mom was right. Beck was many things, but boring wasn't one of them.

"Well, you're right. He's not boring. But he's not really good either."

She pulled out a pitcher from the refrigerator, then closed the door with her hip. "They never are, sweetheart. But that's what makes them fun. I had a thing for bad boys when I was your age too."

"Mom, that's so embarrassing." Allie truly looked mortified that her mother was saying all of this in front of me, but I already loved her. "I don't want to hear about you being with anybody other than Dad."

I couldn't stop laughing at Allie's reaction, but I had a feeling her mom was like this most of the time. Because even though Allie was embarrassed, she still couldn't stop smiling at her mom.

"Who said anything about it not being your dad? Your dad was very bad when we were young." She wiggled her eyebrows.

"Oh my God." Allie covered her ears, and I looked up at a picture of her family on the wall. It was of Allie, her dad, and her mom, and I had never seen a more perfect-looking family. It wasn't because of what they were wearing or how they were styled, they just looked so dang happy.

Her father was handsome and had dark brunet hair that was completely in contrast with her and her mother, but I couldn't imagine him being a bad boy in high school. I can't imagine him being anything like Beck.

"I'm sorry about my mom. I didn't realize we were going to get all of this or we would've gone somewhere else."

Allie's mom laughed, and I knew that she was enjoying embarrassing her daughter. "And where would you have gone, Allie? Is there some boy I should know about?"

Allie rolled her eyes, and I knew this was probably a constant subject. "I'm almost convinced that she wants me to date more than she wants me to graduate high school."

"Well, all she does is work. She's too good. She needs to break a few rules every now and then."

Allie looked over her shoulder at her mother like she was crazy. "I'll remember that when you get a call at midnight saying I'm in jail."

"I didn't say you had a go out and murder someone. But maybe just quit pining for Carson Hale and meet somebody new."

What?

Allie's gaze snapped to mine, and I was shocked to hear what her mom said. I knew that there had been something going on between her and Carson, but I would have never guessed that she was the one who was pining after him.

They always seemed like they couldn't stand to be around each other.

"I am not pining after Carson." Allie's words were firm, but even I heard the lie in them. Whatever the deal was with her and Carson, she had feelings for him whether she wanted to admit it or not.

"Okay, dear." Allie's mom set two drinks down in front of us and winked at me.

"Hello." A masculine voice boomed through the small house.

"Oh. Thank God." Allie leaned back in her chair just as her father walked into the kitchen.

He looked nothing like my father did when he got home from work. His jeans were worn and covered in dust, and his shirt had splatters of paint and dust covering it.

"There are my two favorite girls." He didn't hesitate or even notice me as he wrapped his arms around Allie's mom and pulled her into him. She didn't fight him either. Her body sank into his as he held her, and I had to look away as he kissed her like he had missed her every dang second that he had been gone.

"Keep it PG. We have company." Allie grumbled with a smile on her face, and I wondered if she knew how lucky she was to have this. To have these parents.

"My house. My rules." Her dad's words were muffled against her mom's cheek, but then he let her go with a kiss to the forehead before he turned toward us. "And who is this?"

"Dad, Josie. Josie, my dad."

I nodded in his direction. "It's nice to meet you."

"You too. Are you the one who has a group science project with Allie?" He assessed me, but her mom interrupted him.

"No. She's the one who goes to Prep and has a thing for bad boys."

I could feel the blush creep up my cheeks as he laughed and Allie groaned.

"We're going to my room." Allie grabbed my hand, and I quickly stood from the table to follow her.

"Don't be influencing my baby into liking bad boys too." Her dad called after us, and the lightness in his voice told me that he was joking.

"No. Please, do. Teach her your ways." Her mom's voice carried down the hall, but Allie closed the door before I could hear another word.

"I'm so sorry." Allie leaned against the door as I took a seat on her half-made bed.

Her room was small but filled to the brim with a life's worth of things, and I loved every inch of it.

"It's okay. Your parents are funny."

"Please don't let them hear you say that. They already call

themselves the cool parents." She held up her fingers and made exaggerated air quotes.

Allie climbed on the bed beside me and the two of us stared up at the ceiling that had a couple of dozen plastic glow-in-the-dark stars stuck to it.

"What happened? You look off."

"You first." I turned my head and looked over at her. "Pining after Carson?"

"Ugh, my mom." She growled. "I am not pining after him."

"But?"

"But I used to have a thing for him. A long time ago. My mom thinks I'm not over it."

"Are you over it?" I asked hesitantly. Allie didn't owe me any kind of explanation, but I wanted to be here for her. I wanted her to want to talk to me about these things.

"Honestly, I don't know." She shook her head, and I knew that she didn't want to talk about this. "What about you?"

"I had sex with Beck."

Her gaze snapped to mine, and if I didn't feel so much concern rolling off her, I would have laughed. "Again, or are we talking about the first time?"

"Again." I slammed my hands down over my face and tried to make sense of what I was going to say. "I wasn't planning on it. It just happened."

"Umm... I'm no expert, but I don't think sex just happens. You don't slip and fall on someone's dick."

I couldn't help the laugh that stormed out of me. The bed shook beneath us as Allie laughed with me.

"It wasn't exactly an accident, more of a seduction."

She leaned up on her elbow and looked down at me. "You seduced him?"

"Other way around." I swirled my finger in the air. "I'm not even sure if he meant to. It's just who he is."

"He is so hot." She dropped back down to the bed. "Well, was it worth it?"

Yes. No. I had no clue in hell. "The sex was worth it, but I don't know about the aftermath."

I didn't wait for Allie to respond. "Cami told me what really happened between Lucas and Frankie."

Allie turned on her side and tucked her hand under her head. "What did she say?"

"Basically that Lucas assaulted Frankie. Apparently, Frankie used to have a thing for him, and he did things to her while she was drunk at a party and his friends recorded it."

"That's so fucked up. I knew that he, Beck, Carson, and Olly all used to be close, but I didn't know about that."

"Like, part of me didn't want to believe it. You know? I just wanted to bury my head in the sand and pretend like it really didn't happen. But I ran into Frankie after school, and I knew that it did. As soon as I looked at her, I knew it in my gut."

"I'm sorry, Josie." Allie's voice was soft and made my chest ache.

"What are you sorry for?"

"That you had to find this out about your stepbrother. That Beck used you to get back at him. That you're caught in the middle."

I knew that she was right, but not one part of me deserved that sympathy. "The most fucked up thing is that I understand why Beck did what he did. I'm not saying it's right. He really fucking hurt me, but I feel like I understand where his head is at."

"That doesn't make it right."

"No." I shook my head and concentrated on the stars above me. "But it doesn't make me hate him either. I honestly just feel so confused."

Allie laid beside me silently for a few minutes before she finally spoke again. "I think you really like Beck and that's why everything feels confusing. You don't want him to not have a reason to have done what he did because then you'd be forced to not forgive him."

I thought about what she said, and I knew that she was right. Even though I continued to tell myself over and over that I hated him, I really wanted to forgive him for what I did. "He doesn't deserve my forgiveness, though." It sounded more like a question than a statement.

"That's up to you and no one else. Do you believe what he said about not being the one to share the video?"

"I don't know." I turned on my side and faced her. "Like, part of me does, but I don't know if that's the part that wants it to be true. But regardless, he still took that video and sent it to Lucas. Even if the video was never shared, that is bad enough."

"It is." She nodded.

"But I still like him."

"I know." There was zero judgment in her voice.

"Do you think I'm an idiot?"

"No." She shook her head. "I think you just fell for a guy in a shitty situation."

"And you?" I nodded toward her and prayed that she felt like she could be as honest with me as I was with her.

"I fell for a guy who didn't want to fall back." She shrugged, and my heart broke from the sadness in her eyes.

I scooted closer to her and wrapped my arm around her

side. There was no hesitation as she put her own arm around me. Neither of us spoke for a long time as we just laid there and held each other, and I hadn't realized how badly I needed this. Just to be held by someone who loved me, by someone I loved.

It made me miss my mom even more, and I buried my head into her shoulder to stop myself from going too far into my head.

It wasn't until a couple of hours later when her mom woke the two of us up for dinner that we finally let go of each other. I hadn't meant to fall asleep and neither had Allie, but I felt so much better when I climbed out of her bed.

Because no matter what I would have to face, I knew that I had her.

CHAPTER 10

BECK

I had exactly zero interest in going to this damn gala. I knew it was for a good cause, but the entire thing felt so pretentious and stupid.

If they simply took the money that was put into this damn thing, they could give a lot more to the charity.

But what did I know?

I was dressed in my tux, and my mom messed with the bowtie at least fifteen times before we left the house. I was ready to get this damn thing off.

Frankie was on my arm, and I could feel how nervous she was as we walked into the event. She was dressed in a light pink dress that flowed to the floor, and she looked beautiful.

It was the same damn people that we were used to seeing, but I knew that she felt different now. The fear of their judgment of her was paralyzing, but most of these people had no idea what had happened.

Joseph Vos wasn't good for much, but he was good at

keeping secrets and making sure those around him kept his secrets too.

But I knew that she felt like she wore her truths like a banner, that everyone could see her secrets without her ever saying a word. I knew because she had told me that once. She had let it slip out as she cried and begged my parents not to make her go back to school. That was shortly after everything had happened, and it had broken something inside of me.

"Are we going to dance together?" Her hand tightened around my arm.

I looked down at my beautiful little sister and smiled. "If you think you can keep up with me, then sure."

She rolled her eyes, but I didn't miss the small smile that formed on her lips. "I know that you think a lot of yourself, Beck, but has anyone ever told you that you have two left feet?"

"You're insane. I am perfect." I ran my fingers over my jaw, causing her to snort.

"Of course, you are." She patted my arm like she was talking to a toddler. "Mom needs to quit feeding your ego."

"It's not just Mom." I wiggled my eyebrows at her, and she looked like she might slap me.

We followed our parents through the throng of people, most of them clamoring for my father's attention, until we made it to our table clearly marked with the Clermont name.

The large space was filled with opulent round tables covered in long white linens and expensive china, and there was a small dance floor right at the front of the room, right in front of our table.

Both Carson's and Olly's families were seated with us,

and I wasn't surprised. My dad had taught me a long time ago that you should only let a select few people in, and Lucas had instilled that lesson in all of us.

Olly stood as we walked up and quickly pulled a chair out for Frankie before slapping his hand against my shoulder. "Well, don't you look handsome."

"Fuck off." I rolled my eyes and scoured the room.

"She's not here."

"Who's not?" There were dozens and dozens of people already milling about the room, but I didn't care about any of them.

"I guess it depends on which one you're looking for, but I haven't seen Josie or Cami yet."

"Low blow," I growled. He knew where I stood with Cami. He knew exactly what was and wasn't happening between us.

"I know. I just wanted to get your feathers riled." He laughed, and I rolled my eyes.

"Where's Carson?" His mom and dad were already seated at the table, but he was nowhere in sight.

"He's already off chasing some girl he spotted." Olly rolled his eyes and took a seat next to Frankie.

I pulled out the chair on the opposite side of her and unbuttoned my jacket before taking a seat. There was so much chatter around me, but I barely heard a word any of them were saying.

I was too busy running my gaze over every last table to see if Josie was here. I knew that she probably wouldn't be. Not unless her dad forced her to be, but I hoped that she was.

I hadn't talked to her since the damn locker room, not that we did much talking, and I couldn't stop bouncing my leg as I thought about going a whole other day without talking to her. Without seeing her.

"When are you going back to work?" Olly leaned forward and asked from across Frankie.

"Monday. Dad's giving me my working privileges back finally." Because that was basically the only thing he took from me after the video surfaced.

He said that I wasn't mature enough to work for his company, and I sure as hell wasn't mature enough to take over when I needed to. Those words stung like hell, but I knew he was right.

"He's no longer grounded." Frankie chimed in with a small smile. "And thank God, he's getting grumpy."

"I am not getting grumpy." I was, but it had nothing to do with my dad or his punishments.

"I think he's lovesick," Olly teased, and Frankie's smile became even bigger.

"Are you two done?"

"No," they answered at the same time.

I looked away from them, and I didn't care that they were going to see me scouring the entire place looking for her. They could call it whatever they wanted. I didn't care.

The moment I finally found her, every bit of their teasing fell away. I had no idea what either one of them were saying, and I didn't care. Nothing mattered except for her and how beautiful she looked.

I quickly stood from my seat and almost knocked my chair over in the process.

"Beckham, are you all right?" my mother asked, but I was too lost on her to answer.

I moved around the table and buttoned my jacket as I

tried to straighten it out. Josie hadn't seen me, but God, I could see her. She was the only thing I could see.

She was wearing a cherry-red dress that fit tightly against her chest before flaring at her waist in several layers of ruffles. It was held up by the thinnest of straps that disappeared beneath her softly curled brown hair.

The dress would almost seem girly if it wasn't for the color and the way Josie's body filled it out. Her lips were painted the same color red, and I felt like I couldn't breathe as I watched them move.

She was standing next to her father and stepmom, and I knew that Lucas had to be close by.

I had no idea where I was going as my feet led me closer and closer to her, but I knew that I couldn't just sit there and stare at her from across the room. Everyone else could do that. But Josie was mine.

Whether she wanted to be or not, whether she ever wanted to admit it, she was mine, and I refused to just sit back and let the most beautiful girl in the room walk in without being told how gorgeous she was.

It didn't matter that I could feel her dad's gaze on me as I approached or that I was sure my own parents were watching my every move. I just needed to talk to her. To hear her voice for a moment.

I stopped in front of her, and Josie's surprised gaze met mine. She wasn't expecting me to approach her, especially not in front of her dad, and I couldn't blame her. I hadn't expected that this was what I would be doing either.

I just knew that I had to.

"You look beautiful tonight, Josie."

Josie's gaze bounced to her father before it met mine

again, and I knew that she was careful with what she said next. I could feel her tension in the same way I had felt Frankie's, and I didn't know if it was simply caused by me or because her father was watching us with an unrelenting stare.

"Thank you." Her voice was curt and dismissive, and I wanted to pull her into my arms and kiss the living shit out of her.

"Mr. Vos." I nodded my head, and his scowl only deepened. I knew the man hated me, and if I was smart, I would have walked away as quickly as I had approached.

But I was never smart when it came to his daughter.

I didn't think I would start being so now.

Not when she looked like that.

"Beckham, it looks like your father is looking for you." His voice was as dismissive as Josie's, and I wondered if that was where she had learned it from.

I looked over my shoulder to my dad, and Mr. Vos was right. He was staring daggers into my back. He was probably worried that I was causing an even bigger shitstorm than I already had.

But the truth was that I didn't care what Mr. Vos or my dad thought when it came to me and Josie. I only needed to convince her, and everyone else would melt away.

Their opinions and disproval wouldn't matter at all if she really wanted to be with me.

"Josie, would you like to dance?" I could have sworn her eyes sparkled as I ignored her father and spoke directly to her. I wanted her to know how little I cared about him or his opinion of me. I wanted her to know that I only cared about her and making up for all the shit things I had done.

And I knew that what I did to her in the locker room

didn't help with any of that. What I did in the locker room was the exact opposite of what I was trying to accomplish.

"Not right now." She tucked in closer to her father, and I swear everything in my body ran cold. I knew that she didn't like her father, and I couldn't believe that everything I had done had made her feel like she needed his protection over me.

It made me feel sick.

"Okay. Later then." I smiled at her and tried to keep the anger out of my voice. I didn't acknowledge her father again as I let my gaze run down the length of her dress, then turned away from her.

I had to get away before I said something I would regret, before I made her hate me even more with something stupid I knew I was likely to say.

I didn't go back to my table either. I went to the back of the ballroom and grabbed a glass of champagne from a wandering waiter. Everyone here knew that I was far too young to be drinking, but not a single one of them stopped me.

That would be up to my parents and them alone, and I made sure to stay out of their line of sight as I swallowed down the entire glass in a few gulps. I spotted Carson leaning against the back wall with a slim brunette on his side. I didn't recognize the girl, but that didn't mean anything.

I walked up to him and smiled at the girl. She was pretty and smiling up at Carson like he was the best thing she had ever seen, and I knew that he already had her on his line.

"You coming back to the table?" I interrupted him, and he looked up at me with a bored expression that told me to get lost.

"Do you need me?"

"I do." I put my hand on his shoulder and gave the girl a gentle smile. "I can't keep your girlfriend company much longer. She's starting to worry where you are."

The girl huffed before stomping her foot and storming away from him. He ran his hand down his face and groaned as I laughed.

"You are such a dick. You know that?"

"I do." I leaned my back against the wall next to his and stared out over the ballroom. "But you don't need any more notches on your belt. That girl looked like she would be in love with you before you even got off."

"So, what? You were saving me?"

"Exactly."

Carson pulled a small flask from his pocket and took a sip before passing it to me.

"I saw you over there with the Voses. What was that about?"

"You saw that through your flirting game?" I took a long sip from the flask, and the dark liquor burned my throat.

"I'm a multitasker, Beck. You should practice that talent."

I handed him his flask back, and he tucked it back down into his pocket. "I was over there asking Josie for a dance."

"Shit." He laughed, and I turned my head to look at him.

"What's so funny about that?"

"She turned you down."

I couldn't help smiling because he was right. She had. "Technically, she said not right now."

"She was just being nice. I bet you a hundred dollars she doesn't dance with you at all."

"You're so full of yourself. Of course, she's going to dance with me."

He shook his head like he didn't believe it for a second. "I'll even sweeten it for you. A hundred dollars says she doesn't dance with you. Two hundred says I can convince her to dance with me."

There was no way in hell she was dancing with Carson, and not just because I didn't want her to. I knew that she wouldn't fall for his charms like every other skirt he chased. "Fine." I held out my hand, and he took it in his.

"All right. Let's head back to the table to eat, then I have to go on the hunt."

I rolled my eyes because he was absolutely absurd, but I still followed him back toward the table where we had to pass his almost conquest before I had interrupted. She was staring daggers at him, and I couldn't help laughing as he tried to look anywhere but at her.

By the time we got back to the table, some chairperson for the charity started talking into the mic. He was droning on and on about what the money that was being raised tonight would be used for and how this was the biggest and most beneficial event of the year.

He named both my father and Joseph Vos as top contributors to the charity, and everyone clapped as the two of them lifted their heads in acknowledgment.

I spotted Josie sitting next to her father. She was paying close attention to the presenter, but all I could look at was her. I had never seen her look so... I didn't even know the word for it. Beautiful felt far too simple and overused.

She looked like she was right where she belonged. In that dress with her head held high and her gaze empty of worries.

If I cared about her at all, I would just walk away and let her live in peace. It would be the gentlemanly thing to do. It was what my father had told me over and over was the only option between me and Josie, but as my phone buzzed in my pocket and I checked the text that had just come through, I knew that wasn't possible.

Stop staring at me. I'm not going to dance with you.

My gaze flicked up to hers, but she still wasn't looking at me. She looked like she had no concerns in the world, especially no concerns with texting me.

I can't. You look so freaking gorgeous tonight.

She bowed her head and looked down at her lap, and I knew that she was reading my text. She raised her head, staring straight at me, and I had not a damn clue what she was thinking.

It took several minutes before she text back, and I could feel myself getting more and more anxious as the seconds ticked by.

Too bad it's not for you.

I smiled because I knew she didn't mean it. She just wanted to get a rise out of me, and it was working.

Then who is it for? Is there somebody else you were hoping to catch the attention of tonight?

She looked down at her phone again, but this time she didn't look back my way. She was typing on her phone without a single look up.

I don't know. I'm weighing my options. Olly is looking rather handsome tonight.

My gaze snapped over to my friend, then back to her. She wouldn't dare.

Sure. If you want to see me fight my friend tonight.

There was a small upturn of her lips, but that was all she gave me.

That could be kind of hot.

As soon as she sent the message, Lucas pulled out the chair next to her and took a seat. I couldn't stop staring at her or how damn close he sat next to her. It was almost enough to make me forget how playful she was being in her text messages, that thrill of her flirting leaving me at the sight of him.

But she wasn't paying one bit of attention to him or he to her. She had her elbow resting on the table, and her chin resting on her fist as she looked over at me.

She was waiting for my reply.

Is that what you want? The two of us?

The mere thought made my blood boil. I wouldn't share her with anyone. Regardless of if that was what she wanted.

I couldn't do it.

I could feel insane jealousy taking over me just thinking about it.

Does it matter what I want?

Of course, it does.

My answer was immediate and honest. I knew that she thought I was some kind of monster, but I wasn't. What she wanted was all that mattered to me at this point. I just hoped like hell that it was me.

I want you to take off that tux jacket.

I looked up at her, but her attention was back on the speaker just as food started being served at the tables. I paid no attention to the food that was laid in front of me. I simply pulled my arms from the jacket and let it fall against the back of my chair.

That better?

She looked back over at me and let her gaze run all over me. I could feel my cock stirring in my pants, and I prayed that she didn't ask me to get up next because everyone here would know how turned on I was getting.

Yes.

But you should roll up your sleeves. You have incredible forearms.

I did what she said. I unhooked my cufflinks and slowly rolled the sleeves of my white shirt until they laid just beneath my elbows.

Okay. Is it my turn now?

That depends. What do you want?

I thought about her question, and there were a million different things I wanted from her. The presenter finished his speech and everyone clapped just as soft music began to play.

Everyone around us started diving into the exquisite food that was set before us, but not us. Neither one of us touched our food as I sent her my next message.

Dance with me.

It took her several minutes before her next text came through. So long that I felt like my heart was resting at the back of my throat.

I can't.

Her words felt like a blow.

She couldn't or she didn't want to? Either way, I knew that I deserved that decision. I had been cruel to her, and now I just expected her to dance with me in front of everyone.

After everything I had done.

My dad will be pissed.

Her next text came through, and somehow it both soothed something inside me while pissing me off even further.

She wasn't saying no because she didn't want to, but because that asshole was sitting right there. And I was sure that he had tried to fill her head with everything he could about me.

He had hated me ever since the moment everything happened with Lucas, and I hated him. But I didn't care if he didn't want me with his daughter.

It wasn't up to him.

I'll find a way.

I sent that last text before I finally lifted my fork and dug into the food. So many people in this town were scared of Joseph Vos, but I wasn't one of them. There was nothing he had that I wanted with the exception of her, and I knew that he didn't truly have her.

She wasn't some fool like Lucas who worshipped the man due to his money and power.

And I knew that she wanted me regardless of what she knew was best for her. Some small part of her wanted me, and that was all I needed to know.

Because I could prove to her that I was worth it.

Even if I had shown her otherwise before. I wanted to be with Josie Vos regardless of who her family was, and I would do whatever it took to get her back.

CHAPTER 11
JOSIE

I couldn't stop my leg from shaking beneath the table.

I just wanted to get up and leave this damn table and go somewhere.

Anywhere, really.

I wanted to go straight over to Beck and take him up on his offer to spin me around the dance floor, but I knew my father would be furious.

That wasn't specifically in his rules for today, but staying away from Beck was in his everyday rules.

Rules that I freaking hated but needed to listen to.

Because whether I liked it or not, my father was the key to my future, and I knew that I would have nothing if I didn't listen to him. It didn't matter that he was my dad. He was a businessman through and through, and he would hold up to what he said.

He would rip my mother's house and the small amount of money she left me away without a second thought. It wouldn't hurt him at all, but it would kill me.

"Would you like to dance?" My father held his hand out

to Amelia who gladly accepted it with a genuine smile on her face. She had been far too excited about this event, and when I shot down the light yellow dress she had first picked out for me, I had actually felt a little guilty by the way her face fell.

I knew that it was unfair to be cruel to her just because I was starting to hate the two people that she loved most. Amelia had done nothing to me, but I still hated the way she looked at my father like he hung the moon. Like he hadn't abandoned his first wife and kid before he chose her.

But I had still softened myself as I told her the kind of dress I liked. She had beamed at me like it was our first true bonding experience, and I may have even enjoyed it a bit once I tried to let go of how I felt about her with my dad. She brought out the red dress, and I knew that it was the one.

I loved it immediately, and she had agreed once I tried it on. I tried to not think about Lucas or my dad or my mom as I let her zip up the back of my dress and push my hair over my shoulder.

Amelia had almost nothing in common with my mother, but I knew that fact didn't make her evil.

The two of them moved from the table and onto the dance floor, and I couldn't stop my gaze from immediately going to Beck. He was laughing with his sister and his friends, and every part of me wanted to go over there and be a part of it.

I wanted to see this Beck. So carefree and fun.

Not the Beck who felt like he was constantly for show.

"Stop staring over there. You look desperate." Lucas snapped from beside me, and I quickly pulled my attention away from Beck to look at him.

I didn't say a word as I stared. I didn't have anything to

say to Lucas after everything I found out. Neither of us had uttered a word to each other since the locker room.

"You do remember what he did to you, right? Do you need a reminder?" He pulled his phone out of his pocket. "I'm sure one of my boys still has the video if you need to watch it again."

"You're such a prick." I said it under my breath, but I had no idea why I was showing him any courtesy in front of these people when he had absolutely no respect for me.

"I am." He nodded before looking toward the table where the Clermonts sat. "But so is he."

He leaned forward and I leaned back out of instinct. I wasn't scared of Lucas, but something inside me screamed for me to get away from him. I didn't fear him, but I didn't trust him either.

"Beck told me that you were the only person he sent that video to."

Lucas laughed low and humorless, and I felt a few eyes turn our way from the people who shared a table with us. I didn't know who any of them were. "Of course, he did. That's exactly what I would say if I was trying to fuck you again."

I scooted my chair back from the table and stood. There was no way in hell I was going to sit here and listen to another word from his lips. It didn't matter that what he said was probably the truth.

I searched the room for Allie. I had seen her walking around with a tray of food in her hands earlier, but she had been far too busy to stop and talk to me. But now, she was the only person I wanted.

When I didn't spot her anywhere in the ballroom, I pushed through the heavy double doors and out onto the small garden that was attached.

I took a deep breath and tried to wash away everything Lucas had just said. There were small lights strung overhead that lit up the small concrete garden from the darkness that surrounded it. There were flowers everywhere, along with a few benches, and a tall ashtray meant for smokers.

I went to the far edge of the garden and looked out over the rail. We were in the middle of the city so there were no grand views here. It was all buildings and concrete and more parking lots than I could count.

But it still felt better than being in there at that damn table.

There were a couple of people milling around. One man was chain-smoking his cigarette like he had been waiting for hours to finally get a hit, and I watched him blow out his smoke over and over as I tried to clear my head.

He didn't pay one bit of attention to me, but I couldn't stop watching him until my phone buzzed in my hand.

Where did you go?

It was from Beck, and I knew that I should have never text him to begin with. But I was so shocked when he had walked up to me in front of my dad and told me that I had looked beautiful.

Beck may not have truly known the extent of my father's dislike for him, but he knew that he didn't like him, and he simply didn't care. It shouldn't have made my heart race or my stomach flip.

Beck wasn't good for me, but my body didn't realize that. It didn't matter how much I repeated that over and over in my head. Nothing else was listening.

I ran away for a bit.

I pressed Send then tucked my phone away. I would be

lying if I hadn't thought about how Beck would react when I picked out this dress. I shouldn't have even cared, but I did.

Can I find you?

I stared down at his question, and I knew what he meant. He was giving me the opportunity to tell him that I didn't want to be found. That I wanted to be alone, and I was so shocked by it, that I could barely respond.

Beck didn't ask permission for anything.

Since the moment I met him, it was clear that he was the kind of guy who went after what he wanted and didn't let anything stop him. The fact that he was giving me this choice meant that he was giving me more than he usually allowed, and there was only one answer that I could send back.

Even if I knew I would probably regret it.

Yes.

He didn't say another word as I sat outside and counted down the minutes. The smoker snubbed out his cigarette and walked back inside, and the couple who were drinking as they spoke left the short rocks glasses on one of the benches as they walked back into the ballroom hand in hand.

The music that was playing inside was filtering out into the garden even if it was much gentler out here. I let my head fall back on my shoulders, and I stared up at the stars as I listened.

I wondered if there were dozens of couples crowding the dance floor at that very moment. If my father was wondering where I was or if he was too busy talking to his business associates like that mattered most in the world.

The music blared through the space, and I knew that someone had just walked through the door. I knew it was

Beck before I even raised my head. When I finally did look his way, he was standing with his back against the wall, and he was watching me with unhindered focus.

I let my hands fall to my sides as I stared back at him, and he was so damn beautiful.

He always was, but tonight in that tux, he looked every bit the man that his father was trying to make him into. He didn't look like he belonged in high school or anywhere near a girl like me.

He looked handsome and ruthless and so damn dangerous.

I tightened my thighs as his gaze ran over me. He looked so hungry, absolutely ravenous, and I knew that I was the thing he desired.

Beck was bad at so many things, but he had never made me question how much he wanted me. Even after his stupid games of revenge, I knew that his body wanted me regardless of what was going on in his head and in his heart.

He walked toward me slowly, and I could have sworn that he could hear my heartbeat with every step.

He stopped right in front of me and simply held out his hand.

"No one can see us out here." He nodded toward his hand, and I didn't hesitate as I took it.

He pulled me into his body and quickly twirled me around. I smiled and held onto his shoulders.

"Aren't you supposed to be schmoozing people in there?" I nodded toward the door, but he didn't look away from me.

"My dad can handle that. I have my hands full."

"Oh yeah?" I raised an eyebrow at him, and the smile he gave me in return was so lethal that I felt it all the way to my core.

"Yeah. I have some major making up to do." My heart ached at his words. I wished like crazy that he didn't need to make up for anything. I wished that he had never done anything to hurt me in the first place.

He knew it too. He lifted my chin with his fingers and brought my eyes back to meet his.

"Did I tell you that you look beautiful tonight?"

"You did." I nodded and let him move me over the concrete pavers.

"Did I tell you that I was sorry for the locker room?"

My chest felt like it was on fire just at the memory. "Why are you sorry about that?" I would die if he said that he regretted it. To know that he regretted anything with me would hurt me far worse than anything he had ever done before.

Not even that video could hurt me as bad as knowing that he hated what had happened between us.

"Because I didn't want that to happen until you wanted it to. I feel like I keep fucking this up."

I searched his face for his lies, but I couldn't find any. I knew that I would be a complete and total fool just to believe the words he said to me, but I wanted to. I wanted to be a fool with him for at least one more night.

"There really isn't a *this*, though. There is you; then there is me."

He shook his head, and his hands tightened around my back. "There is definitely a *this* whether you like it or not."

"So, what? Even if I don't want this to happen you're going to force it on me?" I knew it was the wrong choice of words as soon as I said them. His body tensed against mine, and I could have sworn his eyes instantly darkened.

"I would never force you to do anything."

"That's not what I meant." I shook my head and held him closer to me as I could feel him pulling away. "I know you wouldn't."

Because regardless of what he did do, I knew that he wasn't capable of that. He wasn't capable of being anything like Lucas. Not really.

"Are you telling me that you don't want this? That you want me to leave you alone?" His gaze searched mine, and I knew that he was as desperate for an answer as I was. But I had no clue what to tell him.

Of course, I wanted him, but he had hurt me. I couldn't just forgive what he did like it didn't matter at all.

"I'm out here with you right now, aren't I?"

"You are." He nodded, and I watched as his Adam's apple moved beneath the smooth skin of his neck.

"Then that will have to be good enough for now."

He nodded, and I knew that he wanted to say more. He wanted to demand more from me, but he wouldn't.

"I am sorry, you know. For the way everything happened. For what I did to you."

I let his words wash over me, and I tried to take them at face value. Whether he was sorry or not, he did what he did with clear intentions.

He looked away from me for a moment before bringing his gaze back to me. "When I first met you, I didn't care whether or not you hated me. I couldn't see anything past getting revenge."

My body stiffened even though I knew his words were true, but he kept his hold on me and continued to move me around the garden.

"I didn't realize how fucked up my plan was until far too late."

"Until when?" I was so desperate for his answer. I needed to know exactly when he came to regret his plan. I needed to know if he only regretted it after everything was said and done.

"Until I started falling for you."

I shook my head to block out his words. They were just a bunch of pretty letters slung together that didn't mean anything.

"You aren't falling for me." My words were so firm and sure. I wasn't sure of anything when it came to Beck, but I was certain about that.

I pushed away from him, but he didn't let me go. He wouldn't give me a single inch of room.

"You have no clue."

His words pissed me off. He thought that I didn't have a clue, but I knew far better than he did. I was the one who had to sit back and watch what he had done to me. I was the one who had to deal with all the consequences of being used by him for everyone to see.

I pushed on his chest again and forced his hold to loosen.

I couldn't just stand here and dance with him and act like some idiot who didn't see what was staring her right in the face.

"I have no clue?" I laughed, and his hand was still clinging to my side despite how hard I was trying to get away. "You don't get to say things like that to me after what you did."

His hand finally fell from my side, and I tried to control my anger along with my breathing.

"So, when do I get to say things like that to you, because I'm confused?" I could see the same anger swarming in his eyes. "Because you didn't mind me touching you or talking to you in the locker room."

I stared at him, and I wished that I had never even come out to the stupid garden. Because I knew that the moment I walked out here I was doing so to see him.

There was no use in lying to myself.

And I knew that it was a mistake.

It was a damn mistake, and I had let him make me look like a fool over and over again.

"Don't worry. It won't happen again." I pushed past him, but he snatched my hand in his before I could escape.

"We both know that isn't true."

"You don't know shit." I jerked my hand away from him, but he held tight.

"I know that you still want me regardless of what you think you should or shouldn't do. Regardless of what they tell you to do." He nodded toward the ballroom.

"What they tell me to do is to stop being a fucking idiot." I pointed to the room. "They all saw what you did to me. They all had a front-row view of you between my legs."

"I've told you that I was sorry."

"And what?" My hand was shaking in his, and I felt like every part of me was about to snap. "That's supposed to mean something? I'm simply supposed to forgive you because you claim to be sorry for something you did on purpose? You meant to do what you did to me. You knew exactly what you were doing, and you don't get to say you're sorry with a smile on your face and expect me to give a shit."

He finally let my hand fall from him, and I stumbled back away from him.

He ran his fingers through his hair, and I knew that he

didn't know what to say to me. "What do you want me to say, Josie?"

"Maybe the truth for once. Maybe just admit that you are happy with what happened. That you're ecstatic my father is so pissed off that he has threatened me with the only things I have left."

"He threatened you?" Rage took over his face, and if I wasn't careful, it was enough to make me feel like he cared. But I blocked that out before it could take over.

"Don't act like you care, Beck. You don't get to care."

"So, what? I make one fucking mistake and that's it."

"You didn't make a mistake," I yelled at him, and I knew that we were probably drawing attention from those in the event. I prayed that the music was loud enough that none of them could hear us. "You made a choice, and you need to man the fuck up and deal with it."

I didn't wait for him to say anything else. I couldn't listen to him and not let his pretty words mess with my head. Because I knew that was what he would do. He would continue to fuck with my head until I could no longer see that he was the villain and I was his prey.

So, I walked away and reminded myself that I wasn't this girl. I wouldn't just let him have whatever part of me he wanted whenever he wanted it. I couldn't. But I couldn't help the overwhelming feeling of regret that took over me with every step I took away from him.

CHAPTER 12

BECK

Josie pushed through the door back into the ballroom, back into the sea of people who didn't want us together, and I followed her without thinking.

I didn't care what her dad thought of me or how her stupid-ass stepbrother felt. But I did care that they had threatened her. I had no idea what she meant by that, by her dad taking away everything she had left.

Was he talking about cutting her off financially?

I couldn't imagine that Josie really cared about being bankrolled by her father, but I knew that she had nobody else to rely on.

I didn't even know what her plans were for after she graduated. Did she plan on staying here or running as far from her family as she could get? I was driving myself crazy over the girl, and I barely knew her.

But I somehow felt like I knew everything.

She didn't look back once as she stormed through the ballroom. She was pissed. Everything had been fine until I told her that I was falling for her. Her reaction was immediate and shocking, and I didn't know what to think.

I knew that I had a lot more making up to do before I could ever expect her to think differently of me. I had painted the picture of myself perfectly in her mind, and only I could make her see differently.

But I didn't know if she ever would.

After what I had done, I couldn't imagine how she could ever see past it, but I thought for a moment that she was. She had been so different from one moment to the next. When I walked out to the garden and she looked at me like she wanted me more than she had ever wanted anything, I had hoped for a different ending.

And I didn't mean sexually.

I just wanted her to trust me, to want me, to give me a fucking chance.

But I couldn't get angry with her for not wanting to be around me or trust me. Hell, if I was her, I wouldn't want to be around me either.

But I couldn't think like that.

Because I didn't know what I would do if she refused to talk to me or be around me. I felt desperate to be around her.

I was following her step for step. I had no idea where she was going, and I didn't care that she probably didn't want me following her. Her father could be angry if that's what he wanted, but I couldn't just let her walk away and leave things the way we just left them.

A hand shot out and landed on my chest, and her words stopped me in my tracks. "You look desperate." Cami blinked up at me, and I hadn't even realized she was here.

I looked away from her and back to where Josie just was, but she was still moving forward, still trying to escape me. I pulled Cami's hand from my chest and dropped it to her side.

"Everyone is watching you chase that girl." I looked around us, and she was right. There were people pretending not to stare at me, but I didn't care. I didn't care what any of them thought.

"I don't give a shit."

"You should." She stepped closer to me, and I wanted to push her away. I wanted to push her so damn far away from me and chase after Josie without a single thought of what these people thought of me. "Don't forget who you are, Beck, and who she is. You made your choice when you did what you did to her."

I stared down at Cami, and I could feel my anger pulsing through me. It didn't matter that what she said was true. I didn't want to hear a word of what she had to say to me.

"I didn't post that video."

I could see the disbelief in her eyes. She believed me as much as Josie did, but I had no reason to lie to Cami. She knew my secrets. She knew that I had nothing to hide from her.

"It doesn't matter." She shook her head. "You are in that video, exposing her to the world, and everyone knows that you hate Lucas. There is no way for you to get out of it. You are guilty whether you want to be or not."

I knew she was right, but I didn't want to believe what she said.

"Just leave her alone, Beck. You got what you wanted from her."

"Cami, stay the fuck out of this." I shook off the instant hurt that filled her eyes.

"You don't get to decide who gets to be in it or not. You

gave up that right when you let all these people see how much you hate her and her family."

"I don't hate her."

"You hate who she is. You hate her father and you fucking loathe Lucas. How do you think that's going to work out for you, Beck?" She moved further in front of me and blocked my view completely. "Do you think Joseph Vos is just going to welcome you into dating his daughter after everything that has happened?"

"I don't give a fuck what he thinks."

"Well, you better, because you may not, but that's her father. No matter what, she will pick her family over you. You're nothing more than a boy who needs to fuck her out of your system."

"And what, you're just some girl who wants to fuck everything? Regardless if they belong to somebody else?" It was a low blow, and I knew it would hurt her before I even saw the look flash across her face. I shouldn't have said it.

"Cami, I'm..."

"Beckham." Her dad's voice boomed between us as he slapped my back and brought his arms over my shoulders. He was smiling down between Cami and me, and I tried my hardest to school my emotions.

"Hello, sir."

"How's baseball going?"

"It's good. We have our first game coming up." And my head wasn't in it at all. If I wasn't careful, Coach was going to bench my ass, and I would be watching Lucas lead my team from the damn sidelines.

"That's good to hear." He tightened his hand on my shoulder. Her father always treated me like I was some son he had always wanted. "We're excited to see you all take the championship this year."

"Yes, sir." Cami hadn't said a word. She was staring down at my chest, and I knew that she was probably still replaying the words I had said to her over and over in her head. Words that I didn't mean to say.

"I haven't seen you out on the dance floor tonight. Why don't you take my girl out for a dance?"

"Of course." I nodded and reached out for Cami's hand. She hesitatingly placed hers in mine, and when she looked up, her smile hid anything and everything she was really feeling.

The two of us walked silently to the dance floor hand in hand, and I couldn't help searching the room for Josie as we did. Neither of us said a word as I wrapped my arms around her back and she wrapped hers around my neck. We just began to move like we had so many other times at these events over the years.

"I'm sorry. I shouldn't have said that." I looked down at this girl that was tucked against my body, and even though we weren't what we once were, I still didn't want to hurt her.

"No. It's fine. You didn't say anything I wasn't already thinking." She looked away from me, and I hated myself for it.

"I just don't understand why you're even with that guy."

"And I don't understand why you're chasing a girl who you only planned on using. So, I guess we're even."

"I guess we are." I looked away from her before I could say anything else that I would regret.

I searched the crowded ballroom until my gaze finally met Josie. She was looking at me, but she wasn't. She was staring at my hands, where they held Cami, and my hands instantly loosened around her.

Cami looked over her shoulder to where I was looking, and I knew that she saw her too. Her body tensed, and I hated that I wanted to push her away from me. But every part of me did. I wanted to reassure Josie that she was the only thing that mattered.

But I knew that wasn't the truth. No matter what I wanted or whatever Josie did or didn't want, it wasn't just about us. This room alone was filled with people who had a say in the way both of us lived our lives.

And Cami was right. I was just some guy to her.

And she should have been nothing but some girl to me, but she wasn't. No matter how hard I tried to convince myself otherwise. She was more than I ever wanted her to be.

I let my hands fall from Cami, and I took a step to move away from her before she stopped me.

"Don't forget what her brother did to Frankie. Don't lose sight of what you started."

I jerked my arm out of her touch, but when I headed in Josie's direction again, she was gone.

And Cami's words kept running through my head over and over as I tried to find her. I didn't need a reminder of what Lucas had done or what I had caused. Both of those things constantly lived at the front of my mind, and I didn't think that I would forget either of them anytime soon.

CHAPTER 13

JOSIE

Today had been busier than usual.

My feet were killing me, but I was thankful for the distraction. Because anytime I let myself think for too long, all I could see was Beck with Cami in his arms.

He had her in his arms the moment he left me. The moment I pushed him away.

"Have you decided on what you would like?" I pushed my hair out of my face and looked down at the two men who had already drunk two glasses of whiskey each.

I barely heard them as they ordered, and I tried to ignore the way the one on my right kept smiling at me the entire time.

He was still smiling at me as I walked away, but I didn't care.

I didn't smile back or give a crap if he thought I was being rude.

"You okay?" Allie saddled up next to me as I put in their order, and I tried to relax my shoulders.

"Yeah. I'm just tired."

"Let's do something tonight. You need to relax."

"I have school tomorrow and so do you."

Allie held her hand up to her ear as if she was holding a phone. "Bring. Bring. Yes. This is Mrs. Vos. Sweet ole Josie came down with a cold last night, and she won't be at school today."

I laughed and tucked my pen back into my apron. "You'd do that for me?"

"Bitch, I would do much more than that."

I knew she was being honest, and after last night, I knew she was right. I did need to relax. We both did.

"Okay. Yeah. Let's do it."

"Sweet." She held up her hand, and I high-fived her. "Only an hour more of this bullshit then it's girls' night."

The next hour passed by quickly, and I was eager to leave by the time Allie and I clocked out and headed toward the door. We were almost there when I spotted a head of dark brown hair in the hallway, and I quickly pulled Allie in that direction without a second thought.

"Hey." I held Allie's hand in mine, and I tried not to second-guess what I was doing.

"Oh, hi." Frankie put her hand over her chest as if we had scared her.

"What are you doing here so late?" It was only eight-thirty, but I didn't know what teen spent their Sunday evening in an old country club unless they had to.

"I had to drop off a few things for my dad." She held up her keys. "I was just leaving."

There was an awkward silence between us, but Allie quickly filled it. She held her hand out toward Frankie. "I'm Allie. I know we've met but not officially."

"It's nice to officially meet you, Allie. I'm Frankie." They both smiled at each other, and I couldn't help asking what I did next.

"We're having a girls' night and playing hooky tomorrow." I blurted, and Allie's hand tightened in mine. "Do you want to join us?"

Frankie looked hesitantly between the two of us. "What are you going to do?"

"Eat some greasy food, maybe park by the beach for a while, play truth or dare. Who knows!" Allie's answer was far too excited, but it brought a quick smile to Frankie's face.

"I'm in. Can you all pick me up at my house so I can change?"

"Of course," Allie answered before I could. "We need to change too."

"We'll meet you there in an hour?" I asked, and Frankie nodded.

We parted ways, and I tried not to obsess over the fact that I had invited Beck's sister to hang out with us while Allie and I changed clothes at her house. I didn't even bother going home. I sent a quick text to my dad letting him know I was going to stay the night with Allie and go to school from there.

He didn't bother responding, and I didn't really care.

Allie didn't even attempt to lie to her parents. She simply told them that we were in desperate need of a girls' night and would be skipping school tomorrow.

Her dad gave us each twenty bucks as we walked out the door, and her mom hollered for her to find a boyfriend while we were out.

"Your parents really are the coolest." We had just pulled up to Frankie's house, and I couldn't stop my foot from bouncing as we waited for her.

"I know. They are a little too into PDA, but otherwise, I can't complain."

I laughed because she wasn't wrong. When we walked into her house tonight, the two of them had been making out on the couch like a couple of teenagers.

"There she is." Allie pointed to the side door near the garage where Frankie was hurrying out of the house with a small bag over her shoulder.

I breathed a sigh of relief when she walked toward us alone, but it was only a moment later when light shot out from behind her and Beck stormed toward the car.

I stared straight ahead and tried to avoid looking at him entirely.

Frankie smiled at us before opening the back door and throwing her bag into the back seat.

"Beck, I'll be fine. Go." She sounded so frustrated as she climbed in the back seat, but Beck wasn't having any of it. He was still storming our way, and he looked pissed.

"Can I have a word with you?" He was looking straight at me, but I still looked behind me to Frankie and Allie as if he was talking to one of them.

"Me?" I pointed to my chest.

"Yes. You." He leaned into my window and rested his arms on the window seal. "Frankie's not going with you all unless I talk to you first."

Frankie groaned, and I knew he was embarrassing her. "You are not my dad, Beck."

"It doesn't matter, Frank." He didn't look at her as he spoke. He was still staring down at me.

I unbuckled my seat belt, and he took a step back once I opened the door. I followed him a few steps away from the car and crossed my arms over my chest as I looked at him. "What?"

He ran his fingers through his hair, and for a moment, I was actually really concerned about what he was going to say. "I know you're mad at me, but please don't hurt her."

"What?" He was out of his mind.

"Frankie."

"I know who you are talking about. What I don't understand is why the hell you would think that I would hurt her."

He searched my face for a moment, and I knew then that it was because he had chosen to hurt me. "I'm not you, Beck. I would never do that to her."

"I know you wouldn't." He shook his head, but he didn't mean what he had just said. "But Frankie is important to me, and she's already been hurt so much. If you're mad at me, take it out on me. Not her."

"I'm not mad at you."

"Aren't you?" He stepped closer to me, and the smell of his cologne wrapped around me. "You acted mad at the charity event."

I bit down on my bottom lip because I didn't know what he wanted me to say. Of course, I was mad at him, but I was madder at myself. I was mad because I couldn't fucking remember that I wasn't supposed to like him. That he wasn't good for me in any way.

"I came to my senses at the event. What did you want me to do? Spend the night dancing in a garden with the guy who fucked me then showed the whole world?"

He flinched at my words, just slightly, but it was plenty enough for me to notice. "That is not what happened."

"According to you." I poked my finger into his chest and moved closer to him. "But from this side of the fence, that's exactly what happened. It doesn't matter how well you can spin the story otherwise. The only truth that matters right now is mine, and in my truth, you are toxic, Beck."

I shouldn't have watched his eyes as I said the words. I shouldn't have allowed the slight hurt that filled them to affect me the way it did, but I couldn't help it.

Everything about him affected me. It was part of the reason he was so bad for me.

I should have been able to walk away from him without a second thought, but even now, so much of me wanted to wrap my arms around him and pretend like nothing bad had happened between us.

"You're right." He backed away from me, and I wanted to reach out and stop him. I wanted to tell him that I didn't have a clue what I was talking about. I wanted to do anything other than what we were doing. "Please be careful with whatever the hell the three of you are getting into tonight. Frankie hasn't been out with friends in a long time."

Not since Lucas. I knew what he was saying without him ever actually saying it.

"I won't let anything happen to her." I looked back toward the car, and Frankie and Allie were both staring out the windows at us while talking.

"Okay." Beck nodded, then walked past me without another word, and I hated it. I didn't know what I wanted or expected. I had just told him that he was toxic, yet I still wanted him to push me, I wanted him to demand more from me than I was easily willing to give.

And that was so fucked up.

"You all have fun." Beck was standing by Frankie's window as I climbed back in the car. "Call me if you need me. If you all get arrested, call me, not Dad."

"We are not going to get arrested." Allie laughed, but Beck didn't look like he believed her.

"With you three, who knows what could happen."

"Fine," Frankie replied to him, but she didn't look pleased at all by his overprotectiveness. "I will text you later."

Her answer seemed to suffice Beck, and he nodded before leaning into my window slightly. "Allie, drive carefully, please."

She saluted him with her hand. "Aye, aye, Captain."

He rolled his eyes but put his hand down on mine where it rested on the window seal. He didn't say a word to me as he gently squeezed it, then backed away from the car. Allie started the engine and began pulling away.

"Oh my God. I'm so embarrassed." Frankie buried her face in her hands, but I was still looking back at Beck. He was running his hands through his hair in that way he did any time he got frustrated, and I knew that he was honestly worried about Frankie going out with us tonight.

"Do not be embarrassed. We know your brother, remember?" I knew him better than I was willing to talk about tonight.

"This is true." She laughed. "You all know how he can be."

"Exactly." Allie turned out of the driveway and onto the street. "Plus, he probably should be a little bit worried because it's girls' night!"

Allie's laughter was contagious, and I couldn't help feeling excited to be out with two girls that I genuinely liked. I barely even knew Frankie, but I already like her more than most of the people I had met.

"Where are we heading first?" I pulled my knees up to my chest and rested my feet on her dash.

"Milkshakes and cheese fries, then we'll see where the night takes us."

"Deal." Frankie's smile was so big and genuine, and it didn't stop the entire ride to the diner Allie highly recommended.

It felt awkward while the three of us looked over the menu, and even more awkward after we ordered and the waiter took our menus away. It was already pitch-black outside, and there were very few people eating in the diner.

"So, Frankie, what's it like to be Beck's sister?"

"Allie!" I whisper-yelled at her and kicked her under the table.

"What?" She looked between me and Frankie. "I know you're thinking it."

"It's all right." Frankie chuckled. "He's an awesome brother. He's a bit overbearing as you all can tell, but he has the right intentions."

"Does he work out a lot?"

"Oh my God, Allie." I buried my face in my hands just as the waiter set our milkshakes on the table.

"He can't look like that naturally. He has to work out a lot."

"He does." Frankie laughed. "If he didn't, he'd be huge. He eats like a pig."

"Josie, what's it like for you to be Lucas's sister? Or stepsister, I mean." She tucked her hair behind her ear, and I knew that it took a lot for her to ask that question.

"It's weird." I was honest with her. "When I first moved in, I felt like he was the only person that I could talk to, but now..." I shook my head because I couldn't bring myself to say that I no longer trusted him after I knew what he did to her.

She seemed to understand that too. "Do you not get along with your dad?"

"No." I laughed. "Not at all. I don't really know him that well, to be honest."

"What about your mom?" She took a sip of her milkshake, and I stared ahead. It was a simple question, an innocent one, but it still hurt like hell.

"She passed away this past year. Cancer."

"Oh my God." Her face was filled with shock. "I'm so sorry. I didn't know or I never would have asked that."

"I know." I gave her a small, reassuring smile. "It's okay. It's good to talk about her."

The three of us were silent for a moment, and Allie gently squeezed my hand on the bench beside her.

"I was really close with her, actually. I was basically her mini-me."

"So, that's why you moved here?"

"Yeah." I nodded. "My dad didn't have much to do with me until she passed away, but he refused to let me live alone until I was eighteen. The judge sided with him."

"I'm so sorry."

I waved off Frankie's concern. "It is what it is. What about your parents? You get along with them?"

"Yeah." She nodded, and I could tell she was uncomfortable. People typically were if they had to talk about their parents after just finding out that I lost one of mine. "My dad is amazing, but a major workaholic as you two know."

We did know. I saw Mr. Clermont's car at the country club more than anyone else's.

"My mom's my best friend. That's kind of sad, isn't it?" She shifted in her seat.

"Absolutely not." I smiled at her. "My mom was my best friend too."

"They've both been super overprotective since everything happened with Lucas." Her gaze flicked back and forth between me and Allie, and I felt so damn bad for her. "I think that they think they're helping, but sometimes I just want to be left alone. You know?"

"My parents just want me to find a boyfriend." Allie rolled her eyes playfully.

"Really?" Frankie laughed.

"Yes. My mom thinks I'm going to become some sort of a troll or something."

"Didn't you and Carson used to have a thing?" Frankie asked just as the waiter set a huge plate of cheese fries between the three of us.

"We were friends." Allie was quick to correct her.

"Did he know that?" Frankie laughed, and I couldn't help laughing with her. I knew that Allie didn't want to talk about whatever happened between the two of them, but the face she made when Frankie asked was too funny to keep a straight face.

"He definitely knew that. He was the one who made sure I knew that."

"Ouch." So Allie was the one who had a thing for him?

"Yeah." She nodded toward me. "I was his friend who didn't realize she was firmly planted in the friend zone."

"I don't believe that." Frankie picked up a fry and shoved it in her mouth. "He definitely had a thing for you, or still does. He gets super grumpy any time anyone talks about you."

"Trust me, he doesn't." Allie looked so uncomfortable,

but she kept talking. "Plus, from what I hear, he's been fucking anything that wears a skirt."

Frankie winced. "That's what I've heard too."

Allie looked down at the fries then away from both of us.

"What about Beck? What's the real deal with him and Cami?" I had no intentions of asking her anything about her brother tonight, but I needed to change the subject off Carson, and he was the only other thing I could think of.

"Well." Frankie took a long drink from her milkshake before she spoke again. "They've been friends or dating for a long time, but it's like they're never really dating. It's just like they are always there for each other."

I don't know why, but that hurt far more than it should.

"But not in that way," Frankie quickly clarified. "I haven't seen him be interested in Cami in years."

"But he still sleeps with her." I was talking more to myself than her.

"I don't know, honestly. But that's what everyone says."

"He says it too. He told me that before the two of us ever did anything together. He told me that they were just a convenience thing. That..." I almost told her that he was helping Cami cover the fucked-up decisions she was making, but I stopped myself. That wasn't mine to tell. "It doesn't matter."

"Do you still like him? Like really like him?" She looked at me with such sincerity that I couldn't lie to her.

"Of course, I do."

"But you don't trust him." It wasn't a question, but I answered her anyway.

"Not at all."

"But she wants to." Allie wiggled her eyebrows at the two of us before shoving more food in her mouth.

"You don't know that." I shook my head.

"Yes. I do."

"I don't think it will matter at all, but I believe him. What he says about not posting the video. I trust him."

"So you think Lucas did it?" The thought had crossed my mind again and again, and I felt horrible that a huge part of me hoped that it was true. Somehow I felt like I could deal with the fact that Lucas posted the video easier than if Beck did.

And it was just my foolish feeling for Beck that made me think like that.

"He's done it before." She shrugged her shoulders.

"I just don't understand what he would get out of it. You know? Like, what would be Lucas's motive?"

"He got you away from Beck. Didn't he?" Allie looked between us. "He's been warning you to stay away from him since the moment you arrived."

"This is true." Frankie nodded.

"Okay. Enough about boys." I tried to clear Beck from my head. "Where are we off to next?"

"Let's go swimming!" Frankie was far too excited about that idea.

"At night? In the ocean?" There was no way in hell I was getting into that black water at night.

"Are you scared of the ocean?" Allie actually sounded shocked.

"Am I smart? Yes." I looked between the two of them like they were crazy. "You can't see what is under the water at night."

"We could go to my house and use the pool," Frankie offered with a shrug of her shoulders.

"I'd much rather take my chances with the sharks."

She and Allie both laughed, but I wasn't kidding.

"What if I message a few friends from my school? A lot of them go to the public pool to swim at night sometimes."

"How do they get into the public pool at night?" I looked over at my best friend.

She shrugged, but there was a smile on her face.

"Oh my God. They break in?"

"Break in is a strong term. A couple of the guys work there and have keys."

"I'm down." Frankie was practically bouncing in her seat.

"We promised your brother we wouldn't get arrested," I reminded her.

"We're not going to get arrested." Allie dug her phone out of her pocket before typing out a message. "These guys do it all the time. Trust me."

I loved her, but I had a feeling I should probably not trust her on this one.

Her phone buzzed on the table after only a few seconds, and her grin lit up her face. "Told you." She shook her phone in her hand. "They are there now."

Neither of them wanted to hear my arguments on why this wasn't the best idea. They were too busy paying our server and pushing me back out to the car so we could head that way.

"You know these guys well?" I asked as Allie parked her car next to theirs in the dark parking lot.

"Yes. Will is here. You know him. Plus, there will be other girls."

Will was here? I didn't know why that suddenly made me feel nervous or like I was doing something that I shouldn't be, but the only thing I could think about when she said his name was Beck. He would hate it if he knew we were here with him and these other guys.

But I couldn't sit around caring about what Beck would hate.

He had made the decision not to have that right anymore.

The three of us locked arms as we made our way up to the pool. There were a few lights on, but the large overhead lights were pitch-black. If you hadn't known that someone was going to be here, it would be hard to notice from the street.

We could hear laughter as we moved through the entrance and the smell of chlorine assaulted us. Allie was right. There were five guys around the pool, one of them being Will, and three girls.

They all looked up at us as we walked in, and I felt completely out of place.

"Hey, Allie." One of the girls waved, and I didn't dare drop Allie's arm as she led us over to a couple of pool chairs.

"Hey, guys." She pointed to me and Frankie. "These are my girls, Josie and Frankie."

If any of them knew either of us, they didn't let on. I had expected to walk in here and get a million dirty looks or snide comments over the video, but no one said a word about it.

Allie dropped her shorts and tossed them on the chair beside her. She was wearing panties and kept her shirt on, but there was no way I was getting down to my skivvies in front of these perfect strangers.

Frankie wasn't either. I knew it from the way her hand tightened around mine.

The two of us followed Allie toward the water, and when

she climbed in, I sat down on the edge of the pool and dipped my toes into the cool water. Frankie joined me, and we sat side by side as she slowly dragged her feet back and forth.

"Hey, stranger." Will swam up to where we sat, and he had such a genuine smile on his face that I couldn't help returning it.

"Hey, Will. How are you?"

He looked so handsome and so carefree, just like the first time I saw him. "I'm doing well."

His grin was warm and inviting, and I tried not to think about how much easier things would be right now if I had just been into Will. Will didn't look like he would be capable of breaking my heart. He didn't look like he was capable of any of the things Beck had done to me.

"This is awfully lackluster in comparison to the ocean." He ran his fingers over the pool water. "But we've got to do what we got to do."

"Don't you have school tomorrow?" All of them were out here swimming when normally I would already be tucked in bed.

He cocked his head to the side and studied me. "Don't you?"

"Touché." I laughed. "This is Frankie. Frankie, this is Will."

Frankie nodded gently and her cheeks turned the lightest shade of pink. "We've met before."

"Yeah." Will agreed. "You're Beck's sister, right?"

"Right." Her voice was tight, and I knew that she had to hate to be referred to as that. As if she didn't matter except for being something to Beck.

"So, are you all going to be late or are you skipping

tomorrow?" His chest was above the water, and I knew that Frankie was probably thinking the same thing that I was. Will was attractive. Hugely so.

"We're not sure yet." I tucked my hands under my thighs.

"Well, we have some beer over here if you all want some."

"I'll take one." I was shocked as hell by Frankie's response.

"Yeah?" Will smiled and started moving away from us. "Let me grab you one."

I had the overwhelming urge to text Beck. I knew that wasn't fair. Frankie wasn't doing anything wrong, and the poor girl was allowed to go out and live her life, but I felt overprotective of her. I didn't know if it was from seeing Beck's reaction before we left or because of what I knew my stepbrother had done to her.

"When's the last time you drank?"

"It's been a long time." Frankie shifted beside me, and I felt like I already knew the answer. "I haven't drunk since that night with Lucas."

"Are you sure it's a good idea?" I didn't want her to feel like she needed to drink or do any of this stupid shit to fit in with us. I already really liked Frankie, and none of this shit mattered to me.

"Yeah." She nodded her head before looking down at the water. She stared down at the clear pool for a few moments before she spoke again. "Drink one with me." She grabbed ahold of my hand before looking back up at me. "I just want to feel normal for one night. I never get to go out without Beck and my parents or somebody watching over me, and I just want to be normal."

I couldn't pretend that I knew what she was going through.

I had no freaking clue, but every word she said was like a stab through my chest. Because regardless of how she felt about Lucas or what she blamed my family for, I knew that every bit of her pain was due to him. And even though he would not take responsibility for what he had done, I felt this overwhelming urge that I needed to. I wanted to make it better even though I knew I didn't hold the power to do so.

I held up my finger. "One drink."

She grinned, knowing she had won this battle and clapped her hands together. "That's all I'm asking for, just one drink."

We stood, walking to where Will was pulling a beer out of the cooler, and I quickly grabbed one for myself. I watched Frankie's every move as she brought the beer to her lips. She hated it as much as I did, but that wasn't the point.

Frankie hadn't felt this much freedom in a long time, and I watched the smile slip over her lips as the first taste of alcohol slid down her throat.

But I couldn't help thinking that Beck would think this was a terrible idea. If he was here, I bet he would demand that she didn't drink, that he may even jerk the bottle from her hand, and even though a part of me knew that he would probably be right, I wouldn't stop her.

Not tonight.

I would sip my beer by her side, and I would make sure that she was having a good time.

We all got along with Allie's friends easily, and before I knew it, one beer turned into two. Then somehow I let Frankie talk me into the third. But that smile stayed on her face the entire night, and I didn't want to let her down. She was having so much fun, and I knew it had been so long since she'd had true fun with friends who weren't her

family or constantly thinking about what had happened
to her.

It was just us and fun, and pretty soon, everyone else at
the pool disappeared into the background.

It was nearly midnight by the time the three of us
lounged across each other on the damp pool deck. Allie and
Frankie had been swimming. Frankie had left all her clothes
on, but they didn't hinder her at all. I had only kept my legs
in the entire time because I wasn't comfortable enough with
these people to strip down in the pool with them.

They had most likely seen the video of me and Beck,
even though not one of them said a word about it, and I
couldn't stop myself from looking at each of them and
wondering exactly what they had been thinking about me.

"Are we gonna sleep under the stars tonight?" Allie was
staring up at the dark sky, and luckily she hadn't drunk a
single drop.

"My parents are cool and all, but they probably'll frown
on me bringing you all home drunk."

"I'm not drunk." Frankie giggled, and even though the
sound made me smile, I knew she was at least a bit tipsy
because so was I.

It was on the tip of my tongue to offer to sneak them into
my own house. It wouldn't take much sneaking either. My
dad nor Amelia would notice us coming in at this late hour,
but there is no way in hell I was going to take Frankie back to
my house. Not with Lucas there, but probably not ever.

I would never put her in that position if I could help it.

"We can go back to my house." Frankie raised up on her
elbows. "My parents won't say anything. I don't get in trouble
for anything these days."

That sounded like a terrible idea.

"Or we could just sleep in the car," I suggested, making both Frankie and Allie laugh.

"Beck won't notice us coming in. He has baseball work-outs in the morning, and he's probably been asleep for two hours by now."

"Aww, Beck's a good boy, huh?" Allie giggled, and I loved hearing the sound of my two friends being so happy and carefree.

"I don't know." Frankie looked over toward me. "Is he, Josie?"

I slapped her arm, causing her to laugh harder. "I cannot believe you just asked me that, Frankie."

"I'd wager that he's not good at all." Allie wiggled her eyebrows at us. "For Josie to be this twisted about him, he's got to be pretty bad."

Frankie dropped back down onto her back. "Oh my God. That's so disgusting."

"You're the one who brought it up." I rolled over on my stomach and rested my chin on my hands. "Do you want to hear all the nitty-gritty details about your brother?"

"I think I'm going to be sick." Frankie playfully gagged, and I couldn't help laughing.

"At least you're not denying that you are in fact twisted."

"I don't even know what that's supposed to mean." I rolled my eyes.

"It means that you like him. You can't stop thinking about him. You want to have his babies."

I looked at Frankie like she was insane. "You two were meant for each other." I pointed between them. "Yes. I like Beck regardless of him being a complete and total ass to me. Is that what you wanted to hear?"

"Yes." Allie's answer was quick.

"But it still doesn't mean anything." I shook my head.

"It doesn't have to." Allie looked over at me. "Whatever happens between you and Beck is up to you. No one else."

"Not true." I groaned and laid my forehead down against my arms. "My dad has made it very clear that I am to be nowhere near Beck Clermont."

"What's he going to do if you are?" Allie teased, but she had no idea the power that my father held.

"He's threatened to take the money my mother left me and her house."

"What?" I couldn't decipher one voice over the other. They both shot up and were looking at me with shocked expressions on their faces.

"Yeah. He made it very clear."

"What are you going to do?" This was from Frankie.

"I don't really have a choice." I pushed up off the ground and got to my feet. "I'm going to have to stay away from your brother whether I want to or not."

"And do you want to?" Her voice was much calmer, and I knew that she was worried about how I was feeling.

"I honestly don't know, but let's not worry about this tonight." I dropped a hand down for both of them. "Let's go sneak into one of our houses."

CHAPTER 14
BECK

I t was after one o'clock in the morning, and I had to resist the urge for the hundredth time tonight not to grab my phone and call Frankie.

I knew that she was probably just at Allie's house or doing something fun, and even though I knew Josie was pissed at me, I knew she would never do anything to hurt her.

But I still wished that one of them would have let me know they were okay. Because it had been a long time since Frankie had decided to go out, especially on a school night with two girls she barely knew.

My mom and dad were happy that she'd gone out. Neither of them giving a shit that she was going to skip school, and I did share their same enthusiasm, but I was still worried about her.

My mom had told me to stop acting like a worried mother hen and to let her have a little fun. And I knew by the look in her eyes that she was just as concerned as I was, but she was even more concerned by the way Frankie had changed.

"Shit." There was a loud whisper in the hallway, followed by sounds of uncontrollable laughter.

"Which one's your room?" I couldn't tell who was talking, and I could barely hear any response from the uncontrollable laughter.

My parents' room was downstairs and basically on the opposite side of the house, but they had to hear them come in when they were this damn loud.

I jumped out of bed and quickly made my way to my door. All three girls were holding onto each other, and they were leaning against the wall next to Frankie's bedroom. Frankie looked like a drowned rat, but she was laughing so hard that she could barely stand up.

"Shh." Josie held her finger up to Frankie's lips, but she was laughing herself.

"What are you all doing?"

All three of them jerked around in my direction as if they hadn't even heard the door open before Frankie started laughing all over again.

"I'm trying to get these two loudmouths into Frankie's room." Allie was grinning, but she was the only one who seemed to have her shit together. "Don't mind us." She waved me off. "Go right back to bed."

"Why don't you let me help you?" I walked past all three of them and opened Frankie's door. Her room had looked the same for as long as I could remember, and there were piles of clothes thrown everywhere from where she was trying to decide what to wear earlier tonight.

The three of them walked into the room behind me, and

Josie didn't dare look in my direction. She and Frankie were still holding hands, and I didn't know how I felt about that. I didn't know why I couldn't take my eyes off of where their hands were clasped together.

"Do you know where her pajamas are?" Allie asked as she pushed her hair out of her face and looked up at me. "Her clothes are still damp."

I walked to Frankie's dresser and threw three old t-shirts and three pairs of shorts onto the bed. "What the hell did you all get into?"

"A little of this and a little of that," Allie said nonchalantly.

"Girl code, Beck." Frankie plopped down on her bed before looking over at me. "We're not telling you anything."

Josie snorted out a laugh, and Frankie quickly followed suit. They had clearly been drinking, and I couldn't bring myself to be mad about it. Frankie was so damn happy.

"Fine. Girl code." I pointed to the three of them, but Josie was still looking anywhere but at me. "I'm going back to bed. Do you think you three can get into bed without waking up the entire house?"

"We've got this." Allie saluted me. "We're sorry we woke you up, but actually I'm not." She shook her head and smirked at me. "You hurt my best friend."

Josie laughed again, but this time her gaze finally met mine.

"And I'm sorry that I hurt your best friend." I didn't let my eyes move an inch away from hers. I was standing in the middle of my little sister's room in nothing but my underwear, but I just wanted to tell her how sorry I was again and again.

I wanted to say it until she finally heard it. Until she believed me.

"That's not good enough, pretty boy." Allie snapped her fingers, and I jerked my gaze away from Josie. "Now bye-bye."

Damn. Allie had always been on my side, but not anymore. I held up my hands in surrender and walked toward the door. "Okay. You all have fun. The bathroom is through there." I pointed to the door at the far edge of Frankie's room.

None of them acknowledged me again as I stepped out of her room and slowly shut the door behind me.

I could hear them laughing again as I walked back into my room, and the sound was barely muffled when I closed my door. I leaned my back against the hardwood and took a deep breath.

Josie was in my house. She was so damn close but still so far away.

I wanted to march back in there and drag her back here with me, but I knew I wouldn't. If I wanted Josie to forgive me, then I couldn't be a barbaric idiot who demanded things from her that I didn't deserve.

Even though every part of me screamed for me to do so.

I pushed off the door and walked across my dark room to climb into bed. I couldn't stop thinking about her and wondering what they were doing across the hall, but before I knew it, my eyes were feeling heavy again, and sleep found me even though I tried to deny it.

I didn't know how much time had passed when I felt a weight press down on my mattress and warm skin sliding against mine. I blinked my eyes open, lack of sleep taking its toll on me, but all I saw was a mess of brown hair against my chest.

"Josie?" I shifted, but her arm was wrapped around my stomach and she tightened her hold. "Is everything okay?"

I reached down and pushed some hair out of her face so I could get a clear view of her. She blinked up at me, sleep filling her own gaze, before nuzzling into my chest.

"Can we just not make a big deal out of this?" Her breath puffed in and out against my chest, and I wrapped my arm around her back.

"Okay." I tried to control my racing heart because I knew she could hear it beneath where she laid. I tentatively raised my other hand and ran it down her hair. "Did you all have fun tonight?"

"Mmhmm," she hummed against my skin as she nodded her head softly.

We were silent for a few minutes, and I thought she might be asleep. "Frankie was so happy tonight."

"Before or after the drinking?" I chuckled.

"Both." She tightened her arm on me. "I think she just needed a night away from everything."

"Away from me." Frankie would never say that, but I knew that I had been overbearing since everything had happened with Lucas. She hadn't been the same since then, and I hadn't treated her the same since that moment passed.

I couldn't.

Even though I had tried.

I just couldn't let go of the guilt that felt like it was eating me alive.

"No." Josie shook her head. "I think just away from everything. I think she just feels lost."

I knew Josie was right, but hearing those words out loud made me feel helpless.

"I know. I just don't know what to do to help her."

Josie leaned up and rested her chin on my chest. She looked up at me, and even though she had been drinking earlier, they looked so perfectly clear now. "I don't think you need to do anything besides be there for her and maybe stop babying her. She needs to know that she can take care of herself."

"I can do that." I nodded and stared down at her. I couldn't stop my gaze from falling to her lips, and it took everything inside of me not to lean forward the slightest bit and take her mouth with mine. "We should get some sleep."

She nodded gently but didn't move another inch. "We should."

She pushed up on an elbow, her body pressing closer to mine, and her mouth moving minutely forward.

"Josie." I searched her eyes, but they were roaming over my mouth, along my jaw, down my chest.

"Yeah?" She sounded so breathless, and it did nothing but make me want her even more.

"We can't do this."

"Why not?" She still wasn't looking at me.

"Because." I ran my hand through my hair and tried to remember the reason I thought this was a bad idea.

"Yeah?" she asked again and ran her soft hand over my chest.

"Because I hurt you and you haven't forgiven me." Neither one of us needed me to say that out loud. We both knew the truth.

But I needed her to hear it. I needed her to know that I couldn't keep doing this when she hated me. I wanted her to forgive me for what I had done, it was the only way that I would ever get more from her, and I didn't want to take these small moments she was willing to give me because I was desperate for something.

I knew it would just make her hate me more and more.

"I don't need to forgive you for this." She pushed further against me and raised her lips to mine. I grabbed ahold of her shoulders and held her in place.

"We're not doing this. You've been drinking and you'll hate me in the morning."

"I'll hate you in the morning anyway." Her voice was soft, and I knew that she wasn't trying to be cruel. She was just being honest.

I lifted my hand, pushing a stray hair out of her face, and let my touch linger against her cheek. There were so many things I wanted to say to her but none of them would be appropriate. None of them she would believe.

"You're so beautiful."

She looked up at me, and I knew that she wanted to say something. "I don't need all of that, Beck. I just want you to touch me."

"I'm not going to touch you tonight, Josie."

She huffed and lifted on her hands as if she was going to leave, but I quickly wrapped my arm around her and held her in place. "Stay, please." Her body was so stiff underneath my touch. "Just let me hold you tonight."

She shook her head slightly before opening her mouth to say something before closing it again.

"Please, Josie." My hands shook slightly, and I was preparing for her to pull away from me again.

But she didn't. She stared up at me for a moment before she laid her head back down on my chest.

I ran my hand over her hair again and again, and even

though I thought she might stop me, she didn't. She let her tight body go loose against mine, and her arm slid back around my body.

And I held her while she let me. I didn't let go of her for one second as my eyes drifted back to sleep.

CHAPTER 15
JOSIE

I was so freaking hot.

That was all I could think about as my eyes blinked open and memories from the night before came flooding back.

I looked down at the half-naked body that I was completely wrapped around and groaned. When I had decided to come to Beck's room last night, not only had Frankie and Allie given me shit over it, but I also did it with only one thought in mind.

A thought that Beck had shot down quicker than I could ask.

I had been tipsy and sloppy, and he had turned me down.

One of his arms was wrapped around me, his hand resting on my hip, and I was thrown across him like I belonged there. I leaned back, slowly trying to peel myself from his body without waking him up, and I peeked over at his alarm clock.

It was just after ten in the morning.

It was after ten in the morning, and Beck was still in bed with me.

His hand that still rested on my hip tightened, and he quickly pulled me back down against him. "Good morning." His voice was muffled as he nuzzled his face against my neck.

"Beck." I put my hands in between us and attempted to push him away far enough to put a little space between us.

"Hmm?" He wasn't having it. He pushed his body against mine, and I could feel the length of his hardening cock against my legs.

"It's after ten. You missed your workout and school."

"I'm aware." He leaned up slightly so he could see my face. "I called and let my coach know this morning that I wasn't feeling well. Luckily, you were barely snoring in the background."

"I do not snore."

"Whatever you say." He pushed some hair out of my face before he let his weight fall back to the bed and against me.

I could barely breathe or think with him being so damn close, and the last time I was in this room, he had damn near broken my heart. I hadn't let myself think about that last night when I had snuck across the hall.

But it was all crashing into me now. What we had done in this bed. My dad's face when he barged in that door.

If he knew where I was now, he would be furious. He would... well, I wasn't sure what he would do, but I wasn't stupid enough to try to challenge my father on his threats.

I knew that he would do exactly what he said if he wanted to. There was nothing that I could do to stop him. Except to give him what he wanted.

To stay away from the boy whose body was currently so damn warm against mine.

"I should go check on Allie and Frankie." I needed to get out of this room. I needed to get away from him before I did something stupid.

"I checked on them about an hour ago. They were both sleeping like the dead."

"You checked on them?" I looked over at him, his face was so close to mine that I wouldn't even have to lift my head to close the space between us.

"Of course, I did." He tucked one of his arms beneath his head and looked at me. "I took them both some water. I knew Frankie had obviously been drinking last night, but I wasn't sure about Allie. I'm hoping not if she drove you all home."

"She didn't." I shook my head. "She was the mama bear last night."

"Good." He searched my eyes for a moment before he nodded to his nightstand behind me. "I brought you some water too and some Tylenol."

"Thank you." I rolled over onto my back before turning away from him. I quickly grabbed the two pills from the stand and the water and swallowed them. I downed the entire glass of water, my mouth feeling impossibly dry, before I fell back onto my back.

Beck was still watching me, his gaze undecipherable, and I didn't want to spend too much time trying to figure out what he was thinking. I would drive myself mad trying to figure out what was going on inside of his head.

"I'm sorry I made you miss school and baseball this morning."

"You didn't make me miss anything, but there was no way

in hell I was climbing out of this bed while you were still in it."

There was no cockiness in his tone. None of that self-assured Beck who knew that I was putty in his hands.

And I wasn't sure if that made me happy or not.

Because as much as he pissed me off, he also really turned me on.

But right now he was just being honest, and that made me feel so much more uncomfortable than it should have.

"I shouldn't be in it." I took a deep breath and looked up at his ceiling.

"Well, I'm glad that you are." He reached out his hand and let his fingers slid over mine. "I was going crazy thinking about you in the next room."

I laid there and let his fingers run over mine. I should have stopped him. I should have gotten up out of his bed the moment my eyes had opened, but I did neither of those things. I just let the touch of his fingers jack up the speed of my heart, and I tried to remind myself of why I didn't want him.

I needed to remind myself of why he was a bad idea.

"I'm going to go shower." His hand slid from mine, and I watched the muscles of his torso bunch and shift as he pushed onto his feet. "Don't leave." He ran his fingers through his hair, and for the first time since I met Beck, he looked so vulnerable.

"Maybe we can all spend the day on the beach today." He nodded out his window. "Frankie will love that."

My answer came much too quickly. "Okay."

"Yeah?"

Say no. "Yeah." I nodded and climbed from his bed that

smelled just like him. "I'm going to go wake up the girls." I walked past him, but he stopped me with his arm around my middle before I could leave his room.

His breath rushed out against my neck, and I wondered if he could feel the butterflies that were taking flight in my stomach. I felt like every part of me was being pulled so tightly in a hundred different directions. One wrong move and something inside me would snap.

"I'm so glad you came in here last night. Even if you're not."

"I didn't say that I wasn't," I whispered back to him even though I should have told him that I wasn't. It didn't matter that my heart was racing or I felt like I could barely breathe when he was touching me. I had no business being back in this room.

"No." He pressed a gentle kiss to the back of my neck. "But I know you. You regretted the decision the moment your eyes opened."

He was right. I had or at least I had tried to convince myself that I did.

When I didn't answer him, he let a harsh breath out against my skin before pushing himself away. "Go get the girls, and I'll meet you all downstairs."

He walked away from me before I could answer and tried to pretend like every part of me wasn't begging me to go after him.

"I cannot believe you went in there last night." Allie shoved half a granola bar in her face.

"Well, I'm known not to make the best decisions around Beck." I quickly tied my hair up in a ponytail.

They were awake when I had walked back into Frankie's

room, and both of them were looking at me with expectant eyes as soon as I walked in. I hadn't spilled any of the details, though. I avoided both of their questions and told them to get ready for the beach.

Now here we were, all three of us dressed in one of Frankie's bikinis, waiting while Beck packed a cooler.

"So, what bad decisions did you make exactly?" Allie shoved my shoulder, and Frankie laughed as she brought her coffee to her lips.

"Nothing juicy." I looked to where Beck stood next to the fridge to make sure he couldn't hear us. "He turned me down."

"He did what?" Allie practically shrieked, and I smacked her arm just as Beck turned in our direction.

"This is why I don't tell you things." I shook my head as Allie gave Beck a little wave.

"I have way more respect for him now." Allie leaned back in her chair.

"Because he wouldn't give me any?" I looked at her like she was crazy. "Sorry, Frankie." I knew this was probably the last thing she wanted to hear about.

"No worries." She grinned, and I knew that she was getting as much enjoyment from my awkwardness as Allie was.

"Because he turned you down when you had been drinking and weren't thinking clearly." Allie nodded to where he was now carrying the cooler out the back door. "I had expected him to take full advantage of you coming to his bed last night."

"I was thinking plenty clearly, unfortunately."

"Oh. I know you were." She stood and grabbed the towel

Frankie had loaned her. "But he didn't know that, and I appreciate that he didn't give in to your ho ways."

Coffee shot out of Frankie's mouth and landed on the table. "I cannot believe you just said that." She coughed out every word.

"Are you all ready?" Beck had his hands on his hips, and he was looking back and forth between the three of us.

"Yep." I jumped up from the table before Allie could open her big mouth and repeat what she had just said. "Let's do this."

I walked toward the door and pushed against his chest to get him to walk away.

"What are you all talking about?" He raised an eyebrow at me even though he walked backward as I pushed him in that direction.

"Nothing. I'm just ready for the beach."

"More like she's ready for your..."

"Nope!" I yelled above Allie's voice, but Beck was already grinning from ear to ear.

"Is she talking about my dick?" He cocked his head to the side, and if I didn't hate him so much, that damn smile on his face would be enough to make me go weak in the knees.

"Absolutely not." I grabbed my towel and one of the bags he had packed and threw them over my arm.

"Uh-huh." His grin only deepened, but he picked up the cooler and led the way to the beach just as Allie and Frankie stepped out of the door.

"I'm going to kill you." I knocked my elbow into Allie's side, but it didn't faze her.

Nothing fazed that girl.

Allie and Frankie plopped down onto the towels as soon as we hit the sand, and I rolled my eyes at them.

"Are you not even going to get into the ocean?"

"Soon." Allie waved me off as she slid her sunglasses over her eyes. "I need a little relaxation first."

Frankie chuckled and laid down beside her. "Same."

Beck was watching all three of us but didn't say a word. Instead, he reached his hand out in my direction and I allowed him to take my hand in his as he led me to water.

My chest felt so hesitant with my hand in his, but my steps were sure. I followed him, never looking back, and I let the cool ocean waves lap against my shins.

"How much trouble are you going to get in for missing practice today?" We stopped in the water as it hit our shoulders, and I let my hand fall from his.

"Ah. Coach will be pissed, but he'll be fine. I'm one of his star players, you know."

"You don't think you're a little cocky there? Who says you're the star player? Maybe they just make you think that."

He rolled his eyes and swam toward me as I backed away. "You just want to piss me off. Don't you?"

"Maybe." I chuckled, and I could have sworn that something felt lighter in my chest than it had in a long time. "I just don't think you get challenged nearly enough."

"I get challenged plenty."

"No. You don't." I pushed some of his hair out of his forehead and stared at the way the sun glistened off his skin. He was so handsome. "That's why you have this pretty boy complex."

He snatched my wrist in his and slowly pulled me toward him with a grin on his face. I tracked the movement like a hawk as he pressed his lips to the sensitive skin of my wrist. "Did you really just say that I had a pretty boy complex?"

He looked up at me as his tongue poked out and lapped at the ocean water against my skin.

I nodded as I watched him. "It's not your fault, really. You can't help it with a face like that."

He rolled his eyes and tugged me harder toward him, but I quickly swam away with a deep laugh rolling through my chest. It only took him a moment to catch me, and I was flying into his arms then through the air before I even knew what was happening.

He threw me.

He actually threw me.

I came out of the water sputtering and narrowed my eyes at him. "I cannot believe you threw me." I swam backward to get away from him.

"Believe it." He shrugged his shoulders, and every part of me wanted to fall right back into his arms and kiss that smirk off his face. "I'll throw you again if you don't give me a minute and let me apologize."

I looked up at him, and he was completely serious. Every part of playful Beck was gone. "We don't have to do this." I shook my head. I didn't think I was ready to do this.

"Yes. We do." He moved closer to me, and his hand brushed mine under the water. "I want to be with you, Josie, and I can't do that unless I apologize for being a complete and total ass."

"You kind of already have."

"It wasn't enough." He searched my face, and I knew he was trying to gauge my reaction. "I should be apologizing every day for what I did, and even then, it won't be enough. I hurt you, I did so on purpose, and I wish I could take it back."

"Beck..."

"I should have never taken the video to start with, but I was so angry. And I couldn't see past that anger. If I had never taken the video, if I hadn't sent it to Lucas to fucking taunt him with the fact that you were mine, this would have never happened."

He gripped my chin in his hand and forced me to look up at him. "That's all on me, Josie. I should have never done any of it, and I can't blame Lucas for my fuck-up. I sent him the video, and that's my fault. It's my fault that anyone was able to see it."

"You hurt me." I said the only thing I could think of. "I don't know if I can just forgive you."

He nodded his head. "I know." He stared down at me, and I knew that what he was saying was true. "I know that it will take work for you to forgive me and trust me again, but I'm willing to do that. If you're willing to try, I'll do whatever it takes."

"You don't deserve another chance." But God, I wanted to give him one. I knew that probably made me weak, and I shouldn't want anything to do with him, but I did. I wanted him more than I was willing to admit.

"I know that too." He played with my fingertips under the water. "But I really hope you give me one. I thought I couldn't see past who you are. That was all I could see when I first found out you were Lucas's stepsister, but I don't care about that anymore. I was so angry by what he did to Frankie."

Beck shook his head and looked off into the distance.

"I'm sorry for what he did."

His gaze slammed back into me, and I could feel the weight of the world under his stare. "Don't apologize for him."

"I'm not apologizing for him." I shook my head because I

wasn't. I knew that I couldn't answer for what Lucas had done. No apology from me could ever change it, but I still needed to say it. I still needed him to know that I hated what Lucas had done to Frankie. I hated that he ever had the power to do what he did to her. "But I am sorry for what he did. I hate him for it."

"I do too." Beck lifted one of his hands and ran it through his hair. He barely seemed to notice the water that dripped down his face as he seemed to be lost in his head. "I can't get past that hate either. No matter how hard I try. I can't get past the fact that I trusted him and he did that to her."

"I know."

"No." He shook his head before looking back at me. "It's something I really need you to understand. I want to be with you, but I will always hate Lucas and your father. There will never be a time when I will get along with them. It's not something I'm capable of."

"I don't need you to like them to be with me." I could feel myself moving closer to him as he talked, like something inside me was so drawn to him. "You can hate them for the rest of your life, but you can't hold what they've done against me. You can never use it against me again."

"I won't." He looked so sincere, but I needed to make myself clear.

"I'm not kidding, Beck. I know that Lucas hurt you and you have every right to hate him and to want revenge, but I can never be a part of that. If you want me to give you a chance, you have to let go of the idea that I belong to them at all."

"Are you saying you are going to give me a chance?" He laced his fingers with mine and pulled me impossibly closer to him.

"Can you look past the fact that my last name is Vos?" I hated that I even had to ask that question, but it was my biggest fear. Regardless of how he thought he felt about me right now, I needed to know that he could separate me from the hate he had for my family. I needed to know that I wouldn't be paying for the sins of my father for the rest of my life.

"That's a stupid question. Of course, I can."

"It's not stupid." I shook my head and grounded myself in my resolve. "You couldn't before. You hurt me because you couldn't see past that."

"You're right. But I see past it now. I'm sorry I couldn't see past it then. I'm sorry that I was such an asshole."

"I suspect you'll still be an asshole, though."

He smiled, the first glimpse of relief on his beautiful face. "I would say you're probably right. I think it's a bit of a personality trait at this point."

"Absolutely." I laughed and pulled away from him. "I don't know if I'd even like you anymore if you weren't an asshole."

"Ha ha." He swam toward me, but I was still moving away. "I'm a nice guy."

"You most certainly are not."

He caught up to me quickly and pulled me back to him until my chest pressed against his. "I am." He nuzzled his nose against my neck, and I couldn't stop myself from opening up for him.

"You're not."

"But you're still going to give me another chance regardless?" He pressed a featherlight kiss against my skin.

"I am." I nodded and ran my fingers through his hair.

"You won't regret it." He pulled back to look at me, and I

knew he truly believed that. I may not have trusted Beck fully or even fully forgiven him, but I knew that what he said now wasn't a lie. He would do whatever it took to make me not regret my decision to be with him, and I really hoped that I wouldn't.

Because I didn't know if I would survive being broken by him again.

CHAPTER 16
JOSIE

I followed Beck step for step into the cafeteria. Not that he gave me any choice. My hand was securely held in his as he pulled me along.

Everyone turned in our direction as we walked in, and I knew what they were all thinking.

There was no hiding what had happened between us.

It was just me and him and the rest of this damn school that was in on our business, and even though I had made the decision to forgive him for what he did, that thought still ate me alive.

As soon as Cami's gaze landed on us, I tried to pull my hand from Beck's, but he didn't budge. He held my hand firmly in his and pulled me forward as if he didn't even feel my hesitancy.

We walked up to the table he normally sat at, a table I never would have even walked near, and he sat down and pulled me down beside him as if it was the most normal thing ever.

I pulled my lunch from my bag as everyone watched us,

and I tried to keep my trembling fingers to myself. I knew the moment I gave into Beck that he wouldn't be able to not make this more than it was.

He was incapable of being subtle. The boy was all or nothing, and right now, I hated that fact about him.

"What's up?" Olly pulled out the chair across from me and didn't act one bit affected by me being there.

"Hi," I replied hesitantly, and quickly unscrewed the lid on my water bottle.

"Coach talk to you?"

"Yeah," Beck replied as he took a bite of his sandwich. His hand slid under the table and squeezed my knee. I knew that no one else could see it, but my legs still tightened together and my back straightened. "He gave me shit about missing. Apparently, I'm going to have an extra grueling practice today."

"He can't be mad at you for being sick."

"Was he sick, though?" Olly cocked his head to the side. "The reports I'm getting are that he skipped with a certain someone because neither of you were at school."

"And where exactly do you get your reports?"

"Frankie," Beck said, and his hand tightened on my knee. "Those two are like a couple of gossiping old women."

Olly shrugged his shoulders and didn't deny it for a moment. I kind of loved that about him.

Frankie walked up before anyone could say another word and pulled out the chair beside Olly. Her eyes practically twinkled as she looked between me and her brother, and I kicked under the table to get her to stop with the lovey eyes.

"Ow," Olly hissed before looking under the table.

"Oh, shit. Sorry." I laughed.

"I think that was meant for me," Frankie whispered to Olly as she laughed. "So, how has your day been?"

I had been texting with her and Allie all morning so she knew exactly how my day had been, but the small smile on her face told me she was enjoying watching me be uncomfortable next to her brother.

"It's been good. You?" Beck leaned back in his chair and pulled his hand from my knee, only to move it behind my shoulders. The smell of his cologne was smoky and sinful, and it shouldn't have been allowed on high school boys in the middle of school. It did nothing but make me want to taste every inch of his skin.

I didn't know how they expected anyone to concentrate when they had boys who smelled that damn good walking around.

I leaned back against his arm just slightly as he tugged my chair closer to him, and I looked up at his handsome face. He had shaved this morning, his sharp jaw perfectly smooth, and I wanted to lean forward and press a kiss to his skin.

"It's been good. Pretty uneventful." I wasn't listening to Frankie. I was too busy staring at Beck. "Until now."

"Oh hey, Cami." I pulled my gaze away from Beck as soon as I processed Olly's words.

Cami was standing at the end of the table, and her gaze was directly on Beck. She didn't care that Olly had just spoken to her. She clearly had no time for niceties. She was looking at Beck like he owed her something, and every part of me wanted to pull away from him while simultaneously make sure that she knew he was mine.

It was the most confusing and maddening thing ever.

"Beck." Her voice was so firm as she said his name. So damn demanding. "Can we talk?"

I dropped my gaze from her because I didn't want to see that triumphant smile on her face when Beck pulled his arm away from me and went to her.

"Not right now." He lifted the fork in his hand. "I'm eating lunch with Josie."

She leaned forward with her hands on the table, and I knew that she was trying to avoid everyone hearing her. "Then do you think you can do it without making a fool out of me. Get your arm off of her."

I stiffened at her words. There was no way in hell he thought we were going to become anything more than what we were when he was still doing his bullshit game with her.

I started to scoot my chair back to get as far away from the two of them as I could, but he held firmly against my chair and refused to let me move away from him.

"Beck," I whispered his name because I simply wanted to be done with this, but he wasn't listening.

"I'm not making a fool out of you, Cami. I told you that I am done with this shit." He motioned his fork back and forth between them, and even though he wasn't being loud, I knew that everyone around us was listening to their conversation.

Cami's face was tinged with pink, and I knew that she was embarrassed by his words. She stood to her full height, and she looked around her before quickly looking back at him.

"I thought you were done with your little game." She motioned toward me. "You proved that she was the whore you said she was. What else do you need?"

I felt like she had slapped me in the face. Right here where everyone could see.

"Don't fucking say that again, Cami." Beck's hand felt like it was going to break the back of my chair.

"Why not? It's the truth." She looked around the table and finally her gaze hit mine. "You used her to get back at her brother. You did the same shit to her that Lucas did to Frankie, and now the two of you are sitting here like none of it ever happened."

I could feel Beck's fury rising to an uncontrollable level as so many people looked in Frankie's direction, and I couldn't keep my mouth shut for another moment.

"Beck is nothing like Lucas. Don't you dare compare them."

"Isn't he, though?" She cocked her head to the side and studied me. "You can't tell me that you don't see how fucking sick it is that he wanted to hurt your brother more than he ever cared about you. Yet, here you sit at his side like the little tramp that you are."

"You know that I didn't post that damn video," Beck practically growled.

"No." She pushed her finger into her chest. "I had to do it for you because you were too big of a pussy. You didn't even have the guts to carry out your plan after everything."

"What?" I couldn't believe what I had just heard her say.

"That's enough, Cami." This came from Frankie, but Cami didn't even look her way.

"You just sat back and let Lucas do what he did to your sister, and you were just going to let him get away with it because you were too pussy-whipped by his sister."

I turned in my chair to face her fully. "That doesn't make sense. How did you have the video?"

I was so damn confused. So confused and so frustrated, and I just wanted to walk away from all of it. I wanted to leave every one of them behind even though I knew I couldn't.

"Aww, Josie." She looked at me with so much sympathy, and I wanted to slap it from her face. "Beck isn't the only man in your life who prefers me over you. I was with your stepbrother when he got the video."

She was with Lucas? Did he give her the video?

I didn't know which was worse. The fact that I had thought he was the one to post it this entire time or the fact that he had handed it over to her.

Every possible scenario raced through my head as I stared at her.

"What the hell are you talking about?" I shook my head because I couldn't wrap my head around it. I hadn't ever seen her with Lucas. I didn't believe what she was saying for a second, but in the back of my mind, I knew that he was capable of it. I knew that what she said could be true.

"Cami, you didn't post that video," Beck said exactly what I was thinking. He looked so angry as he stared up at her, so betrayed.

"I did." There wasn't an ounce of regret on her face. "You couldn't do the one thing you needed to do so I took care of it for you. Because I care about you."

Despite Beck's grip on my chair, I forced it back and stood to my feet. Cami was taller than me but I didn't care. I was so fucking over her. "You have the nerve to call me a whore? What do you think your other lover calls you? He already has a wife so you have to be nothing but a whore to him as well."

Cami went so damn still that I knew she had lost every bit of gall she had just stormed to this table with.

"You're lucky my father doesn't put your ass in jail for sharing that video of me. If I were you, I wouldn't say my fucking name again."

Cami looked back and forth between me and Beck, but Beck could do nothing to help her here. I would shut that shit down if he even tried.

"Fuck you, Josie." She was as angry as I was, but I didn't care. "You don't know shit about me."

"Don't I?" I leaned forward, not worrying about Beck sitting between us. "I think I know far more about you than you realize."

Her gaze snapped down to Beck, and I knew that she was waiting on him to defend her. That was what she had been used to. She and Beck against everyone else, but he wasn't going to defend her now. Not with what she had just said. That fact was perfectly visible on his face.

When he didn't answer, Cami motioned in his direction. "You know that he'll be back, right?" She let her gaze slide back to me. "He always comes back to me. Even when you think it's just you and him, I'm always in the back of his mind."

Beck opened his mouth to say something, but I didn't let him. I let Cami watch every single move I made as I leaned further into him and slid my hand along his jaw. He quickly turned in my direction, his face so damn handsome, and I didn't let my gaze fall from hers until my mouth met his.

Then I kissed him.

I kissed him in a way that let Cami and every other person in this damn school who was watching us know that Beck was mine.

He was mine. That was the only thought that kept running through my mind as my tongue slid over his.

He was mine and that was all that mattered at that moment.

It seemed to be the only thing that mattered to him too. He buried one hand in my hair while the other pressed firmly against my jaw. His kiss felt as desperate for me as mine was for him. It felt so damn frantic to prove to everyone and ourselves that this was all that mattered.

When I pulled away and let my lips fall from his, he was staring up at me with so much lust. He pulled me back to him and pressed a gentle kiss to my lips before letting me go.

I looked up at Cami, who looked so damn disgusted, and I made a show of running my thumb over my bottom lip gently. "You don't have to worry, Cami. I think he'll forget about you soon enough."

She didn't say another word. She looked down at Beck as if she expected something from him, and she wasn't the only one who was shocked by what he said next.

"Cami, go the fuck on with your bullshit. I'm with Josie. I want Josie."

I fell back into my seat just before Beck tugged it impossibly closer to his. I knew that people were still watching us but I didn't care. My heart was racing and my hands were trembling, and I had no idea what was going through Beck's head.

"Josie is my girlfriend, and nothing you say or do is going to change that. I don't know what this bullshit is about Lucas, but I don't believe you. You're just trying to hurt Josie because you think that's the way you can get me back."

I looked up at him, ignoring everyone around us, and

there was so much hunger staring back down at me that I had to press my thighs together to stop the ache.

Beck didn't say a word as he leaned forward and kissed me again. This one was much gentler than earlier, so much slower and deeper and breathtaking.

Cami looked genuinely hurt before she walked away, and a part of me felt sorry for her.

But I couldn't think about her.

I could only think of him.

All I knew was that I didn't want him to let me go. I just wanted him, and I didn't want to take the time to think about anything else.

Everything about him felt too damn good. Too perfect, and I didn't want to ruin that by thinking too much about what would happen.

About what my father had threatened me with.

Because I knew the moment Lucas found out about us, he would run straight to my father.

But I suddenly didn't care.

When Beck was kissing me like this, like nothing in the world mattered to him, nothing seemed to matter to me either. Even though I knew it would once he was finished. Nothing would disappear simply through his touch, but I liked to pretend that it would.

I just wanted to pretend for a few short moments that there was nothing that could tear us apart. Not even us.

But that was foolish.

I knew that, but I couldn't bring myself to care.

When Beck finally pulled away from me, he looked just as dazed as I felt. He leaned forward, his lips a whisper away from my ear, and his words ran through me as if they were a touch. "Have I told you lately how much I like you?"

I shook my head and tried to lean closer to him.

"Well, I do." He pressed his lips just below my ear, and my eyes closed at the contact. "A whole fucking lot."

"You two are going to have to get a room." I registered Carson's voice, but I didn't move away from Beck.

"Mmhmm." Beck's answer vibrated against my skin.

"I think they're cute." This was from Frankie, and I blinked my eyes open to look at her just as Beck pulled back slightly.

"Oh. They're cute all right." Carson pulled out the seat next to Frankie and sat down. "So damn cute the entire school will need a cold shower after that little show."

I snorted out a laugh, and Beck grinned at me. I should have been embarrassed, but I wasn't.

I couldn't bring myself to feel an ounce of shame.

"So, are you two officially a thing now?" Olly motioned between the two of us.

"I don't know," I answered at the same time as Beck's, "Yes."

I glanced over at him before looking back down at my food and picking up my sandwich.

"Well, if you were, I was going to invite Josie to the cabin this weekend, but if you're not..." He shrugged.

"Are you trying to bribe me in to officially dating your friend?"

"No." He shook his head. "Absolutely not."

I didn't even know what cabin they were talking about, and I wasn't sure if I even wanted to go. "I have to say, I would expect something like this from Carson but not from you."

"That's fair." Carson nodded.

"It doesn't matter whether you invite her or not." Frankie

looked at Olly before looking at me. "Josie's my friend, and she's my plus-one."

"Then how are you all going to sneak Allie in?" Beck asked as he smirked beside me.

"Carson, you could bring her?" I smiled sweetly at him, and I knew that I was opening a can of worms I probably didn't want to open.

"That's going to be a hell no for me." He barely looked up from his food.

"Then she'll be my plus-two." Frankie crossed her arms and looked between the three of them. "And I dare any of you to tell me no."

I grinned because I freaking adored Frankie. She winked at me, and I knew that they wouldn't dare. Even though I had no freaking clue what the hell the cabin was or why we were going, I knew that they wouldn't deny Frankie.

All three were wrapped around her little finger.

"Well, I'm not sharing my bed with any of you." Carson jabbed Frankie with his elbow. "So, you can pile them all in your bed."

"Deal." She stood from the table and nodded toward me. "Come on, Josie. We have plans to make."

I stood from my seat, but Beck quickly pulled me back down against his lap. "Lips," he demanded, and even though I should have balked, my stomach flipped, and I pressed my mouth against his.

This kiss was much tamer than the others, but it still hit me just the same.

"Go make your plans." He patted my thigh. "But you are not sleeping with my sister this weekend."

I stood from his lap and scooped my backpack off the floor. "We'll see." I grinned just as I walked away.

CHAPTER 17

BECK

I was going to kill Cami.

I didn't care that we had been friends, or more than that, for as long as I could remember. I had trusted her. I had lied for her and helped her hide her fucked-up relationship and for what?

I didn't know what the hell was going through her mind.

Cami had always been selfish, but this was something else. She had gone further with this than I had ever seen her go with anything else before.

I heard what she had said to Josie, but I didn't believe a second of it. Lucas didn't have anything to give to Cami. He didn't provide her with any kind of step up, and I knew that was how she worked.

You were only as valuable as what you could give her.

Which made Lucas nothing. Not to her.

And I didn't believe what she said about posting the video. It just didn't make sense.

"What the fuck were you thinking?" I stormed into her

room and closed the door behind me. Her parents weren't home from work yet, but they wouldn't care that I was here either way.

"About what exactly?" Cami was lying on the bed with a pile of homework laid out in front of her. "I've been thinking about a lot lately so you'll have to be more specific."

"Don't fuck around with me, Cami. I'm not in the mood for your shit today."

Her gaze snapped up to meet mine, and I knew that my tone pissed her off. "Well, that's too damn bad. You clearly haven't been in the mood for me in as long as I can remember."

"Is that what this is?" I unbuttoned the top button of my shirt because I felt like I was smothering in the damn thing. "Are you pissed off because I'm actually interested in somebody else?"

"Oh please." She rolled her eyes and sat up in the bed. "If there was anything for me to be worried about, you'd know it. I can deal with you having some sort of fucked-up kink over how much you hate her brother."

I shook my head because Cami was so fucked up, and I was going to lash out at her. I knew I would, and I didn't want to.

That had never been who we were, but the urge to walk away and never talk to her again was overwhelming.

"Can we not do this?" I waved my hand back and forth between us and pulled out the old wooden chair at her desk before taking a seat. "I'm confused on how you're upset that I have feelings for someone else when you're fucking one of our teachers."

"I'm not..." She paused and shook her head, and I leaned forward with my elbows on my knees.

"You're not what?"

"I'm not fucking him."

That was news to me. "Since when? Did something happen?"

I could practically see the walls slamming down over her eyes. She was going to shut down.

"No. Nothing happened. I never..." She shook her head again, and whatever she was going to say was right on the tip of her tongue. But she clamped her mouth shut before she could say anything more.

"So, what? You two stopped fooling around, so now you're fucking Lucas? That's a little low even for you, don't you think?" I knew my words would hurt her, but I was so damn angry. I didn't even know what the hell I believed, but I was still angry over what she told Josie. Over what she made her believe. Over her making Josie question herself even more.

Cami waved her hand in my direction. "Says the guy who's been fucking Lucas's sister, for what? Revenge? And you couldn't even pull it off. You try to act like you're so fucking hard, but you got pussy-whipped by the goody two-shoes."

"I know you didn't post the video." I shook off her words.

"I did." She stood from her bed and made her way toward me. "Lucas showed me the video when you sent it to him, and I knew that meant that you couldn't go through with it. I knew your plan to ruin his family would do nothing but ruin you."

I stared up at her, only a foot or so away from me, and searched her face. "Why were you with Lucas? After everything he did to Frankie?"

Pure regret took over her face, but she quickly hid it. "Is

this really what you came here for?" She leaned forward, placing her hands on the arms of the chair. Her mouth was so damn close to mine, and once upon a time, it wouldn't have taken anything for me to lean forward and close the space between us.

But I couldn't.

Not anymore.

Not after Josie.

"Yes." I nodded and didn't take my eyes off of her. "I want to know what the hell is going through your head."

"I'm not your little watchdog, Beck. If you get to be with whoever the fuck you want, then so do I."

"I think you've made that abundantly clear."

"Are you jealous?" There was a smirk on her face as she leaned forward and whispered in my ear. "Does it drive you crazy thinking about him touching me?"

It did, but not for the reason she thought. It drove me mad thinking about him touching anything that belonged to me, and even though Cami wasn't my girl, not anymore, she had been my friend for a long time.

"Cami." I pushed on her shoulders, and she didn't fight as I pushed her away from me.

"Yeah?" She dropped to her knees in front of me before I could utter another word and gripped my knees in her hands. "What do you want from me, Beck?"

"Not this." I leaned forward and pushed her hands from my thighs. "I want to know why you're trying to take the blame for Lucas."

"I'm not taking the blame." She pushed forward and blocked me in with her body. "I'm telling you the truth. I posted that video because all you've talked about since Frankie is getting revenge on Lucas. Then when it's right there in front of you, you puss out." She shook her head like she was disgusted with me. "No fucking way. You'll thank me once you get over her."

"I'm not going to get over her." My words were firm. "And my plan was fucked up. It did nothing but hurt Josie. Lucas doesn't give a shit about her."

"No, but he gives a shit about Joseph Vos. And you successfully pissed him off." She cocked her head to the side and studied me. "Did your little girlfriend tell you that he's threatened her?"

My body went rigid. "What?"

She nodded her head slowly. "Oh, daddy dearest has threatened to take away everything she has if she doesn't stay the hell away from you." She dug her fingernails into my thigh. "Apparently something you did worked."

I couldn't lie and say that it didn't fuel me to know that he was pissed, but I couldn't be happy about it at the expense of Josie. It was what I had wanted, but I didn't think of the risks. I didn't think that I would fall for the daughter of a monster.

Why wouldn't Josie tell me about her dad? Why wouldn't she stay away if she was risking things to be with me?

"Her dad is a piece of shit." I spit out the words, and something I couldn't place clouded Cami's expression.

"You cast a lot of stones for a boy who's made his own mistakes."

I looked at Cami like I hadn't ever really seen her before. I pushed her off of me and stood.

"What? I was good enough to suck your dick a few weeks ago, but not now? You scared Josie will find out?" She smirked, and I had no idea who this girl was.

"What the fuck is wrong with you, Cami?" I ran my fingers through my hair and grabbed my bag.

"You're acting like a bitch, Beck. That's my problem. We've had a plan for as long as I can remember, and you are fucking everything up."

"What exactly am I screwing up for you?" I slung my bag over my shoulder and looked at her. "You've had this plan stuck in your fucked-up head for as long as I can remember, and in the beginning, it made sense, but now?" I held out my arms and shook my head. "Your dad isn't going to stop being an asshole because you're with me, Cami. It may have made him happy for a while, but it isn't going to magically make him better."

"I'm well aware, Beck." She tugged at the bottom of her shirt and lifted it to expose her stomach.

I stared at the fading bruises that marked her beautiful skin and tried to breathe. "He's hitting you again?"

She jerked her shirt down so hard that I was worried it would rip. "Don't act like you suddenly care, Beck." She climbed off her knees and stood to her full height with that look on her face. That look that I had seen so many times before. The one that tried to pretend that everything in her life was perfect, but I knew better.

"You told me that he stopped." If I had known, if I had seen, fuck. I didn't know what I would have done. Cami's father was almost as powerful as my own, but that didn't give him the right to hit his daughter. Or his wife.

That didn't give him the power to be a monster that was left completely unchecked.

"Well, he didn't." She shrugged her shoulders like it wasn't a big deal, but that was bullshit. I could see it on her face. I knew that every time he touched her or yelled at her or treated her like she wasn't worth anything it cracked something inside of her.

"Come stay the night at my house tonight." My voice was soft, but her gaze was hard.

"Don't be ridiculous." She began moving around her room and straightening things that were already in perfect order. "I can handle my father, and you can go right back to your little girlfriend. You're right, though. You were a good buffer for a while, but it would appear that your allure has worn off."

She stared up and every bit of that hard girl who could cut anyone with a simple look or harsh word was looking back at me.

"If you don't mind, get the fuck out of my room."

"Cami." I reached out for her, but she backed out of my reach.

"Don't, Beck. Don't even try to pretend like I suddenly matter because you can't take the sight of it. I'll deal with it just like I always do."

I didn't know what to do. I didn't know how to make things better for Cami. She was always the one who had a plan when it came to her father, and for a long time, her father seemed placated that she was with me.

But it seems that had run out.

And I couldn't run out on her too.

"Then I'll stay here tonight." I dropped my bag back to the floor and ignored the way she looked at me as I took a seat in her desk chair. "He won't do a thing while I'm here."

"You don't have to do that." She shook her head, but I could see the relief in her eyes.

And I hated that the first thing that popped into my head was Josie. I knew that she would hate that I was here. She would hate it if she knew that I was laying in Cami's bed and protecting her. She would never understand.

Even if I tried to make her. She wouldn't see past what she wanted to see with Cami, and I couldn't blame her.

Cami had created that.

Cami had made people hate her because it was her way of staying on top. It was her way of making others fear her so they never got too close.

And Josie would never understand.

But I couldn't leave Cami because I knew Josie would hate it. I couldn't leave her in the hands of her cruel fucking father, with nothing to protect her. It was the reason that I always fell back into this damn cycle with her. No matter what she did or what she said, I couldn't not protect her.

I couldn't just walk away from the girl, even if I loved someone else.

But Josie didn't need to know about me being here. Nothing was going to happen between Cami and me, so I wasn't doing anything wrong.

But it still felt wrong. The urge to run from her room and straight to Josie was overwhelming. But I couldn't.

No matter how badly I wanted to. I couldn't.

"Let's just watch a movie, Cam." I nodded toward her massive TV. "We haven't hung out in forever."

A small smile lit up her face, and I felt so much damn guilt that that was all it took.

"We haven't." She grabbed the remote before hopping in her bed and pulling her blanket over her legs.

I should have left.

But she looked up at me and she looked so content and

happy, and I couldn't do any more harm to this girl who pretended to have it all. Her parents would cause enough harm to her for a lifetime.

So, I leaned back in the chair and tried my hardest to swallow the guilt that I felt was suffocating me.

CHAPTER 18
JOSIE

Work was slower than usual.

Allie wasn't here tonight, and I had no one to talk to besides the few tables that still lingered in my section.

And chatting it up with old men who were on their fifth scotch for the night was not at the top of my to-do list.

Instead, I was leaning against the bar and checking my phone for the hundredth time. Beck had barely text me since we got out of school, and even though that wasn't exactly abnormal, things felt different now.

And he text me all day today during school.

But I was being crazy. I tucked my phone back into my apron and resisted the urge to text him. He was probably with his friends. He may have even been getting things ready for our cabin trip tomorrow.

Apparently, it was just going to be him, Carson, Olly, and Frankie, but he seemed more than excited over the idea of me and Allie joining them. I was excited about the idea of it too.

I wanted nothing more than to spend the weekend away

with Beck where there was no one around to have any expectations or demands of us. There would be no one there to judge me for falling for the guy who had irrevocably hurt me.

But even knowing that, I couldn't help thinking that maybe Beck really did mean what he said. Maybe he really was sorry for everything that happened.

I was more than shocked by what Cami had said, but part of me didn't believe her. It wasn't that I didn't think she was capable of doing exactly what she said she did, but I just didn't understand her motive.

Did she truly want Beck for herself when she was sleeping with another? Or multiple others, according to her.

I just didn't get it.

Cami felt threatened, but I didn't know where she saw the threat. I didn't understand how a girl like her who had everything she could ever want could ever be threatened by anything.

But she was.

There was no other explanation for it.

She wanted me out of Beck's life, and she was almost successful. If I was smart, she would have been.

But I couldn't seem to stay away from him. Even through her efforts and my father's threats, there was something about Beck that made it impossible to walk away from him.

I pulled my phone out again. No new messages. Shoving my phone into my pocket, I took a deep breath before heading back to my tables to see if they needed another round. I was so ready to go home and climb into my bed. I wanted to sleep off everything Cami had said today.

I wanted to sleep off the idea that she had been with Lucas when he had gotten the video from Beck.

I couldn't wrap my head around it.

But by the time my shift ended, it was all I could think about. Lucas.

Why did Lucas do anything that he had done? I hated him, yet I wanted to understand him. I wanted to know what the hell ran through his head to make him the way he was.

I slept in a room across the hall from him, and he hated me enough that he would let the girl he's fucking to post that video of me.

I climbed up the stairs one by one as the questions kept rolling through my head. Beck still hadn't text me and that just made my mind race harder. I wanted to trust Beck. I wanted to understand everything that was going on around me, but I didn't.

I didn't know what came over me or why I decided it was a good idea, but I didn't stop my feet until they were planted directly in front of Lucas's door. I hesitated as I raised my hand to knock, but I didn't do it for long.

I could hear him moving around behind the closed door, and it only took him a minute before he answered the door in nothing but a pair of gym shorts.

"Yeah?" He looked as confused by the fact that I was standing outside his door as I felt.

"Are you fucking Cami?" I didn't know why that was the first question that popped out of my mouth, but somehow it felt like the most important one. It felt like the one question that I truly needed the answer to.

"Hello to you too, sister." Lucas moved away from the door and picked up his gaming remote before plopping down on his bed. He left his door completely open so I took it as an invitation and walked inside before closing it behind me.

"You didn't answer my question." I leaned against the door to relieve my tired feet.

"If you had asked me a serious question, I might have." He was staring at the TV and didn't spare me a glance.

"It was a serious question. She told me that she was the one who posted that video and that she got it from your phone." He finally looked at me. "She told me that the two of you were fucking."

"She's insane." He shook his head. "You'll believe anything anyone says to make your precious Beck look innocent. Won't you?"

My chest bloomed with doubt. I had no reason to believe Lucas. No reason at all, but those simple words from him made me doubt all the words Beck had said before.

"So, you're not fucking her?" I asked my question again as my heart raced.

He paused his game and looked me over from head to toe. "No, Josie. I'm not fucking her."

There was a long stretch of silence between us, and I wasn't sure what to say.

"You know. I'm not some fucked up monster like you think I am." His eyes were clouded with pain or anger, I couldn't tell which. "You believe everything anyone says about me, but they don't know shit."

"Did you give Cami the video?" I asked him exactly what I needed to know. I knew that Lucas and I could never go back after what I knew, but there was some part of me that couldn't stand the thought of him being the one to post it.

"I did." He nodded, and he actually had the nerve to look guilty.

"Why?"

"I don't know, Josie. I was pissed off that he had sent me the damn video in the first place and Cami was here to pick something up from Dad, something for her father, and when she asked me to send it to her, I thought she was going to use it against Beck. I didn't realize she was going to post it online."

"Would it have made a difference if you did?" I asked as I clenched my fists at my sides.

"Honestly, I don't know."

I felt my own anger rising at his honesty. "What about what happened with Frankie?"

I crossed my arms over my chest and stared at him. I wanted to hear the truth from his lips. I wanted him to look me in the face and be honest about what he did.

"I didn't rape the girl." His knuckles were white around the remote. "I know what I did was fucking stupid, but I was drunk too. I should have never touched Frankie, but she was the one who was flirting with me. She was the one who wanted it."

My stomach was in my throat as I listened to him. "I heard that she couldn't even hold her eyes open in the video."

He looked away from me before looking back my way. His face was red and his chest heaved, and I knew I should have walked away then and went to my room. I didn't need Lucas's answer. I trusted Frankie far more than anyone I would ever trust in this house, and I knew what he had done to her. It didn't matter if he had been drinking or not.

It didn't matter if he thought that was what she wanted.

Those were nothing but excuses.

They were disgusting excuses that got rich boys out of their consequences.

"It doesn't matter what you say." I shook my head. "I'll never forgive you for what you did to her."

He let out a loud laugh that held no humor. "Do you really think I give a shit about your forgiveness?"

I knew that he didn't. I didn't even know why I had said it, but I needed him to know. For Frankie's sake, I needed him to know that I believed what she said and that I hated what he had done to her.

"What exactly do you think is going to happen?" He cocked his head and watched me, and I fucking hated it. "Do you think that you're going to go back to the guy who shared a video of you looking like a slut and you're just going to live happily ever after? He may not have posted it online, but he sent it to me. That's bad enough. You are out of your mind if you think Dad is going to let that happen."

"Dad," I exaggerated the word, "doesn't really have a say in what I do or don't do."

"Doesn't he?" He leaned back in his bed and rested on his elbows. "Look, Josie, I don't want to be enemies with you. We're family now, for God's sake. But Beck and I will never get along, and Dad will never approve of him."

I didn't know why he thought I would care about either of those things, but I didn't. "I don't..."

He interrupted me before I could finish my thought. "Dad has hated their family before all of this happened. Mr. Clermont thinks he runs this town, but he doesn't. Dad has more power than he'll ever have."

I pushed away from the door and turned the handle.

"I won't be home this weekend." I looked back at Lucas

before I stepped out of his room. "I'm going on a trip with Allie and her family."

He knew I was lying. It was all over his face. We stared at each other, and we both knew that he knew.

"Be careful, Josie." He picked his gaming remote back up and resumed his game. "You're playing a game that you don't want to play."

I hated every single one of his words. "Don't pretend like you care about me, Lucas."

He saluted me even though he was already staring at his TV. "I won't, but don't say I didn't warn you."

CHAPTER 19
BECK

Josie was pissed at me.

There was no hiding it even if she said that everything was fine.

She had barely spoken to me the entire drive up the coast to the cabin. The cabin was a place my father owned further down the coast, and it took us a couple of hours' drive to get there. We had initially decided to go to help cheer Frankie up, but I was more than happy to have her and Allie with us.

My parents thought it was only me, Frankie, Olly, and Carson going. They had even offered to join us, but I had convinced them that Frankie needed this. That Frankie needed to get away from everyone.

It was a shitty thing to do, but pulling the Frankie card had worked. My mom had backed off the moment the words passed my lips.

And I did think Frankie needed this, but I also knew that I wanted this with Josie. Just a weekend away where there was no one there who could interfere with us. Who could fuck it up?

None of her family. None of mine.

No Cami. No Lucas.

I just needed a few damn moments with her where there was nothing but me and her. And now she was pissed off at me.

By the time we pulled up to the cabin that was nestled between the trees, I felt like I was going to go crazy. I put the car in park and climbed out. The girls were already climbing out of the back seat, and I didn't hesitate as I hooked my finger in the belt loop at Josie's back and pulled her toward me.

Her back slammed into my chest, and I hummed against her neck as her hair whipped gently around my face.

"You smell so good."

She moved against me just slightly, but it was enough to make me feel impossibly hard. God, I wanted her.

I always wanted her.

And I'd be lying if I said I didn't want her so badly because I knew that she wanted me too. That there was nothing between us besides the way we felt about one another. No stupid fucking agendas or hate to fuel us.

Even if she had barely spoken to me.

She turned her head, her lips so damn close to mine. "I need to get my bags."

"I can get them." I ran my nose along her neck, and the sound of her sharp inhale was like fuel to my flame.

"You seem a bit preoccupied. I can get my own bags." She reached back and patted my cheek before pulling away from me with a small smile on her face.

There was no way in hell I was letting her get away that

easy. I grabbed her hand in mine before she could get away and tugged her back to me.

"I need to catch up with the girls." She nodded in their direction where they were grabbing their bags from the back of my SUV. Olly and Carson were already inside, no doubt setting up the plethora of alcohol that they brought, but I didn't care about any of that.

"Go on." I motioned to my sister and Allie. "But don't get any ideas because you are in my bed tonight."

She tugged her hand away from mine and took a few steps backward before she shrugged her shoulders. "We'll see."

"No." I shook my head and smiled at her. "This is non-negotiable, Josie. You are with me."

"I'm not your plus-one, remember?" She turned on her heel while still talking to me. "I already told Frankie that I was sharing a room with her."

They were both out of their damn minds because that wasn't happening.

She was going to end up in my bed tonight, and no matter how hard she wanted to play this, I knew that was what she wanted too.

It was written all over her face.

But I would let her play this her way for now. I would get to the bottom of whatever reason she was angry with me, even if I had to force it out of her.

I grabbed the bag from her hand and pulled it over my shoulder. She rolled her eyes but didn't fight me. She grabbed her smaller bag and purse, and walked up the steps that led to the front door of the house.

The moment we walked in, I knew something was off. Frankie looked pissed, and Allie was nowhere to be seen. I was so damn confused until I spotted Carson on the couch with a leggy brunette who had on barely any clothes.

"You finally made it!" Carson smiled at me and lifted his beer in the air. "Let the weekend festivities begin."

Frankie rolled her eyes and grabbed Josie's hand. "Let's go find Allie." She didn't hide an ounce of her irritation. It was written all over her face, and even though I knew it probably bothered Carson, he didn't even look her way.

"Way to go, asshole." I smacked him in the back of the head just as the girls disappeared down the hallway.

"What did I do?" He rubbed a hand over the spot I had just smacked and stared at me.

I looked down at the girl who was now kissing his neck and completely oblivious to the conversation we were having. "Don't act like an idiot. You know."

"They'll get over it." He shrugged his shoulders like it was no big deal, and I had the urge to slap him again. Instead, I set Josie's bags down at the back of the couch and walked into the large kitchen where Olly was making a sandwich.

I hiked my thumb over my shoulder as I pulled out a stool across from him at the island. "Who thought that was a good idea?"

"Don't look at me." He shook his head as he spread mayonnaise across his bread. "I had no idea about her until she showed up with a bag."

"Who the fuck is she?"

He looked up at me like I was insane, and I already knew the answer. She was just some girl. Some girl that Carson used who was more than happy to use him back. "Her name is Carrie. That's all I know."

"He's such an idiot." All three of us knew this would piss Frankie off. I knew she had her own reasons due to her new loyalty to Allie and whatever the hell was going on between her and Carson, but this was also supposed to be just us. He knew it too.

And even if he was a bit of a manwhore, he normally never would have brought a girl here. I had a feeling he didn't make the decision to do so until he found out that Allie was coming.

When the girls didn't come out of the room after a few minutes, I grabbed Josie's bag and carried it down the hall to my room. All of the bedrooms here were basically all the same, but Frankie and I had claimed our own personal bedrooms when we were young.

The room still looked exactly the same as it always had, and I dropped both Josie's and my bag in the middle of the bed before I went on a search for her.

All three girls were in Frankie's room, only a couple doors down from mine, and they all sat at the head of the bed with their heads huddled together, talking.

"You're not going to spend the entire weekend holed up in this room. Are you?" I laid across the foot of the bed and leaned up on my elbow to watch them.

"Who's that girl?" Frankie nodded toward the main living area where we both knew Carson was still probably all over that chick.

"Her name is Carrie."

All three of them wrinkled their noses, and I couldn't help but laugh. "I didn't take you three for the mean girl type. You all don't even know her."

"I didn't say anything about her." Frankie crossed her arms. "It just would have been nice to give us a heads-up." Her eyes glanced toward Allie, and I actually felt bad for the girl. I had no idea what the hell was happening or had happened between her and Carson, but I knew that he wasn't the kind of guy a girl like her should fall for.

Not that I could talk, but Carson had no interest in being with any one girl. It wasn't his style.

"If I had known, I would have told you, but I didn't. He sprung this on me too."

"It's fine." Allie stood from the bed and shook her head gently. "What's the plan for today?"

"Well, first." I grabbed ahold of Josie's ankle and tugged her toward me as she squealed. "I need to have a little chat with this one. Then I say let's head to the beach."

"Deal." Frankie hopped off the bed and started rummaging through her bag.

"I didn't agree to this deal." Josie tried to pull away from me, but I quickly stood and tugged her along with me.

"You can walk with me or I'll sling you over my shoulder and carry your ass." I stared down at her beautiful flushed face, and if my sister and Allie weren't currently staring at us, I would have leaned forward and kissed the hell out of her.

"You wouldn't dare." She sat up and attempted to push me away, but I gripped my hands around her waist and lifted her. "Beck, no." She laughed, and I swear it was the most relieving sound in the world.

She may have been mad at me for whatever reason, but she still liked me whether she would admit it or not.

She wrapped her legs around my waist before I could manage to lift her higher, and I pushed past Frankie and Allie and out of the room.

"Get ready. We'll see you all in just a bit."

I left them before either of them could reply and kicked the door to my room closed behind me as soon as we entered. Josie rolled her eyes as I sat down on the bed with her still attached to me. She attempted to push away, a very weak attempt, but I held onto her.

I didn't dare let her out of my grip.

I pressed my lips to her jaw, and her body softened against me.

"Are you going to tell me why you're mad at me?" God, she smelled so good. Did she always smell this good?

"I'm not mad at you." She stretched her neck just slightly, but I smiled against her skin at the access she gave me.

"Irritated? Frustrated? Upset? Whatever you want to call it. You are something with me."

She rolled her eyes again, and this time, I did lean forward and catch her mouth with mine. Her lips were so damn soft, and I couldn't stop myself as I wrapped my hand in her hair, holding her closer to me.

"I'm just confused." Her words were muffled against my lips, but she didn't stop kissing me.

I leaned back, putting some space between us, and looked at her. "What are you confused about?"

"You."

"Can you be a little more specific?"

"Why didn't you text me at all last night?" She looked down, but I lifted my hand and raised her chin until she was looking at me again. I couldn't tell her that I had been with Cami. Nothing had happened between us. Not a damn thing.

But her father was more than ecstatic when he saw my car there. He put on a grand show of how perfect his little family was. There wasn't a trace of the dad I knew he was when I wasn't around.

And even though I felt guilty for not telling Josie, I didn't regret staying with her. I didn't regret giving her some reprieve from her horrible fucking father.

"I need to be honest with you." I took a deep breath. I knew that what I was about to say was probably going to piss her off, but I needed to be honest. If we were going to trust each other, I couldn't lie to her about this.

"Okay?" She was watching me skeptically.

"I was with Cami last night." As soon as I said the words, I regretted the way they sounded. "Nothing happened," I rushed to clarify. "I was with her and her family."

She stood there for a moment, and I knew that she was trying to think through what she was about to say. If I were her, I would be pissed at me. I knew that she had every right, but I wanted her to understand. "Why?"

"I know that you don't like Cami, and you have every reason not to. But Cami and I have been friends for a long time, and..." I hesitated because it wasn't my place to tell all of Cami's secrets. "Her home life isn't good. She acts like she has everything together, but she doesn't."

"And you're the one she falls on when things are bad?" There was no judgment in her voice, and it killed me how understanding she was.

"I have been for a really long time."

She bit down on her bottom lip as she stared at me, and part of me thought that maybe she was going to tell me to go to hell, but she didn't. Instead, she took a deep breath and said the last thing I expected her to say. "Don't keep things like this from me. I don't like Cami, and I probably never will. But I don't expect you to hate her simply because I do. But you can't keep things like this from me."

"You're right." I pulled her closer to me. "I was just scared about how you were going to react."

"I can understand that, but even if you think I'm going to be pissed, you have to tell me."

"Okay." I pushed some hair out of her face and stared at this girl that I didn't deserve.

"And I have to be honest, it makes my chest hurt that you were with her last night."

My own chest ached at her words, and I lifted her chin for her to look at me. "Nothing happened. I would never do that to you."

She nodded, but I wasn't sure if she believed me. I hadn't given her any reason to believe me.

"Okay." She leaned forward and pressed her mouth to mine in a gentle kiss. She started to pull away from me, but I ran my tongue over her exposed collarbone.

She was too good for me. Everything about her was.

"Where are you going?"

"I told you that I'm rooming with the girls." She chuckled softly as I nibbled against her skin.

"I think I can convince you otherwise." My words were lost against her skin as she arched into my mouth, and I was dying to touch her. I wanted to feel and taste every damn inch of her skin. I wanted to burn it into my memory so I would never forget what it was like at this moment with her.

"Convince me then." The words had barely fallen from her lips before I swiped my tongue beneath the seam of her tank top.

"God, I've missed the taste of you." Her skin pebbled beneath my tongue, and I traced the small ridges like a puzzle.

I pushed her off me and dropped to my knees beside the bed. I looked up at her as I pressed a kiss to the inside of her knee. She leaned up on her elbows and watched me as I tugged her shorts down her legs.

Her thighs were trembling as I ran my tongue up them,

and her moan was deep and throaty as I kissed over her panties.

"What do you want, Josie?" She was staring down at me, watching my every move, and it made me so unbelievably hard. Everything about her did. "Do you want my mouth or do you want me inside of you?"

"Both." She was already panting as she spread her legs just slightly wider than before, but it was enough to push me over the edge. It was enough to make me forget that I had something to prove to her, that I had ever even considered taking things slow.

That thought felt so irrational now when I was in front of her, so wholly impossible.

I pulled her panties to the side and ran my tongue through the center of her. She was already so damn wet, and I knew that she felt as desperate for me as I did for her.

I didn't give her any warning as I dove into her flesh. I tasted every inch of her pussy, I didn't leave an inch of her untouched by my tongue, and she met every movement of mine with one of her own. I lifted her thighs over my shoulders, and she tightened her ankles behind them as she rode my face.

There wasn't an ounce of modesty between the two of us, neither one of us caring if the other knew how badly we wanted it. It was just me and her and this frantic need that I couldn't control.

"Oh God, Beck." She laced her fingers into my hair and tugged my head impossibly closer to her as I sucked her clit into my mouth. "I need you."

"You have me, baby. You have all of me." Every last ounce of me. It was hers. To do whatever the hell she wanted.

She cried out, just before covering her mouth with her

hand, and I thrust a finger inside her. She moved and moved, her hips grinding against my mouth, and I didn't let up on her until her legs shook uncontrollably by my ears.

I let her ride out every ounce of her orgasm before I climbed up her body and tugged her panties down her legs. I gripped the back of my t-shirt, pulling it over my head, and my hands shook as I raced to undo my belt.

I wrapped my arms around her waist and pulled her up to meet me. "Tell me you're mine." My voice was hoarse and full of lust, but I needed to hear her say it. After everything that had happened between us, I needed to hear her say that she wanted this as badly as I did.

"I'm yours, Beck." She pushed against my chest until I moved on the bed and laid on my back. She climbed over me, straddling my lap, and I groaned as the slickness between her thighs hit my cock.

"Fuck." I reached into my jeans and quickly tugged out a condom. I could barely concentrate enough to rip it open with my teeth, and it took every bit of power I possessed to slide that latex barrier between us when I could already feel how fucking perfect she felt against me.

She didn't wait a moment before she sank down on me, and I sat forward and held her body against mine as she began to move. "God, Josie. I..." It was on the tip of my tongue to tell her I loved her. I had never said those words to any girl before, no one outside of my family, and I felt insane for thinking them now.

Josie and I barely even knew each other, and yet, here I was thinking that I loved the girl. Desperate to tell her as she rode me like she was fucking made for me.

If I hadn't considered myself pussy-whipped before, I

definitely was now. I was so far gone when it came to her that I had no damn clue what I was doing.

All I knew was that I needed her, and nothing and no one was going to stand in my way. In our way.

Not now. Not anymore.

Not after everything.

"Kiss me." She gripped my face in her hand and directed my mouth to hers, and I did as she said. I kissed her with everything I felt, and I didn't care that she knew how badly I needed her. I didn't care that it was perfectly visible how desperate I was for her touch.

I broke my mouth from hers and flipped her around in front of me. She settled back down against my lap. Her back pressed against my chest, and I ran my tongue along her neck as she sank back down on my cock.

She lifted and fell against me, her body working me like a fucking sin, and I tugged her tank top down her body to expose her breasts. She didn't stop. She just leaned her head back on my shoulder as she rode me, and I gripped her hand in my hand as I watched.

I thrust up into her, my body meeting hers with every drive, and I couldn't think straight. I couldn't remember where her body ended and mine began. I couldn't think about anything past the fact that she was here with me right now at this moment, and I never wanted to let her go.

I bit down on the soft spot where her neck met her shoulders just as I thrummed my fingers over her clit, and she moaned so loudly that I knew everyone in the house could hear her.

But I didn't care.

"Beck." Her voice was desperate as she rode me harder,

her body chasing the same pleasure mine was, and I moved my fingers faster against her.

"What do you need, baby?" I kissed her neck again. It felt impossible not to touch her, to taste every inch of her skin I could reach.

"You." Her answer was rushed and demanding. "I just need you."

I wrapped one arm around her stomach as I snaked my other against her chest and gripped her chin in my hand. I turned her face in my direction and pulled her bottom lip between my teeth.

She moaned just as I slammed up inside of her, and I swallowed her cries with my mouth. I lifted her back away from my body before slamming her back down against me, and her body was so damn tight.

She kissed me as she cried out, her lips ravenous as I took over, and it wasn't long before her fingers dug into my arm as if she was begging me to hold on and let her go at the exact same time.

But I didn't let her go. I refused to.

I just worked her body harder against mine until I felt that snap inside of her and she cried out against my mouth. I milked her orgasm from her body as I continued to chase mine, and it wasn't until we were both laying back in the bed in a panting mess that I loosened my grip on her.

We were here where no one else could touch us, where the rest of the world didn't matter, and I still couldn't let her go. I couldn't drop my touch from her for more than a moment because I feared that something would happen and this girl who I was so damn undeserving of would disappear.

And for this moment in time, she was mine.

CHAPTER 20
JOSIE

I couldn't lie and say I wasn't having fun. Even if Carson's little friend had put a damper on our plans. At least, she felt like a damper because Allie couldn't quit watching the two of them together.

And I swear, he was rubbing the fact that he had that girl here in her face. If he wasn't, then he was really into her because I hadn't seen him leave her side for even a moment since we arrived.

Even now, as we walked down the boardwalk toward the crowd of people, he had her hand in his and was acting like they were some sort of long-lost lovers. I had seen Frankie roll her eyes more times than I could count as Allie tried to not look in their direction at all.

"You want ice cream?" Beck tugged me closer to him, and I pulled my attention away from Carson.

"Is that a serious question?"

"Rollercoasters first, then ice cream." Frankie slung her arm over my shoulders as she bounced on her toes, and it felt so good to see her so happy. According to Beck, he hadn't seen her smile this much in a long time.

And I knew that it made him happy to her this way. He couldn't hide it even if he tried. If he wasn't touching me and trying to sneak me away from everyone, he was watching her with just as big of a smile on his face.

"Frankie has a weak stomach." Olly grabbed Frankie's hand and tugged her toward the rickety old rollercoaster that looked like it wasn't safe for anyone to ride on. "We all have nightmares from a few summers ago when she lost her funnel cake on us."

"Hardy har." Frankie rolled her eyes but smiled. "I was already feeling sick, thank you. I have the stomach of a Viking."

"Okay, little warrior." Olly grinned at her and pushed her hair out of her face, and I looked up at Beck. He didn't seem to notice how Olly looked at his sister, but I did. It was impossible to miss. "Whatever you say."

Olly may have been overprotective of Frankie like a big brother, but he wasn't looking at her like a brother should. He was looking at her like someone who cared far more than a brother.

And I was pretty sure that Beck was clueless to it.

"I'm pretty sure that rollercoaster is going to come crashing down any second now." I nodded toward the screaming kids who were being flung around on the hunk of metal.

"Agreed." Allie looked as hesitant about the machinery as I did. "It looks like a deathtrap."

"Oh. Come on." Carson walked in front of us, and I was surprised to see he left his girl standing on her own near Olly. "Don't tell me Allie is scared."

"I'm not scared." She narrowed her eyes at him just as Beck tightened his fingers around mine.

"Then prove it." Carson held his hand out to Allie with a spark in his eyes, and I knew that she was going to tell him to go to hell. I could see it in the way she stared at his hand with disgust, but then she stepped forward, knocking his hand out of the way.

"Let's go."

Carson didn't even look back at his girl as he followed Allie toward the ride with a chuckle.

"Those two seriously need to fuck." Olly tugged Frankie toward the ride behind them, and we followed.

"I've been telling Josie that for weeks. The tension between the two of them is enough to give me a chubbie."

I laughed at Beck's words before Carrie scoffed. "You all do know that I'm standing right here, right?"

"Oh shit. My bad, Carrie. Maybe they'll let you join." Beck was so serious as he said it. "But I don't know if I'd want to. I think they have some hate-fucking to do."

I smacked my hand into Beck's chest, and he caught it with a grin. "Well, they do."

We followed Allie and Carson into the line, and neither of them spoke as they climbed into the rollercoaster together. Beck and I climbed in behind them, followed by Olly and Frankie, and I wasn't surprised when I noticed Carrie still standing by the gate. She looked pissed as she typed furiously on her phone, but I didn't care.

"This ride is completely safe. We've been riding it since we were little," Beck reassured me as he tightened the metal bar over our laps.

"I don't think that means it's safe. That just makes it old."

He chuckled and leaned forward and ran his nose over my neck. "You're cute."

"You're just trying to distract me from this deathtrap you've put me on." I opened my neck for him and let him trail his lips over the sensitive skin. He smelled so good. Felt so good. He felt so irresistible now that I wasn't trying to force him away.

Ever since I met him, we had been fighting this push and pull with one another, and I wasn't sure how to feel now that all I wanted to do was pull him in. He was right there in front of me, and all I wanted was to take, take, take.

"Is it working?" His small laugh ricocheted against my skin, and I felt the movement all the way to my core.

"Maybe." I turned my face toward his just as the rollercoaster started forward, but he didn't stop. He lifted his hand and cupped my jaw before running his thumb over my bottom lip. He didn't wait for my permission before he closed the space between us and captured my mouth with his.

I knew we were just two kids buying our time together. I knew that once we returned home, things would most likely be different for the both of us, but I couldn't let that cloud my head. I couldn't focus on what was to come when there he was, right in front of me.

He grinned at me as the rollercoaster started picking up speed, and I laced my fingers in his as my body jerked to the left from the fast turn we just took.

I couldn't stop smiling as we sped over the track and my hair whipped into my face. I clutched Beck's hand in mine as he laughed, and I couldn't stop staring at him. The rest of the world was speeding past us, and all I could care about was him.

When the ride finally slowed, my heart was racing and my stomach was still doing somersaults. But my hand was still in Beck's, and I couldn't calm down even if I wanted to.

He pulled me all over the boardwalk, showing me things from his past that he had loved, and I loved watching this side of him. Here, with just me and his friends, he was the carefree Beck that didn't give a shit what anyone else thought of him.

It was just me and him and these people that he loved. He wasn't the rich Clermont boy that so many people depended on, and I wasn't the girl he was supposed to hate.

"I swear to God, if one of you don't get me a caramel apple soon, I'm going to faint." Frankie was walking in front of us and the sun was setting over the ocean.

"She is so dramatic." Beck wrapped his arms around my shoulders and ran his nose over my neck. I hadn't gotten quite used to him touching me so much, but it was nice. Nicer than it should have been.

"I am not being dramatic." Frankie spun around and stared at her brother. "I haven't had one in, like, two years, and I've been thinking about it the entire trip."

"Fine," Beck grumbled before placing a kiss on my shoulder and letting me go. "Let's go feed you before you become a monster."

Frankie smiled before locking her arm with her brother's. "We'll grab Josie one too."

"Of course." Beck winked at me just as I took a seat on an old bench next to Allie. She had barely spoken since we had gotten off the rollercoaster, and I was dying to talk to her to see what was going on in her head. But we weren't alone, and there was no way in hell I would let Carson or Olly overhear us.

"So, Josie." Carson took the seat on the other side of me, and I looked up at him just as Carrie saddled up to his side like a puppy. "What are your intentions with my friend?"

Allie scoffed at his question as I narrowed my eyes. "What do you mean? I think my intentions are pretty clear."

"Are they?" He cocked his head to the side and stared at me. "He was a pretty big dick to you, but you've forgiven him. I can't decide if it's because you actually forgive him or if you're planning on fucking him over somehow."

"You're such an idiot, Carson." Allie rolled her eyes.

"No. He's actually got a good point." Olly leaned back against the rail that separated the boardwalk from the sandy beach.

"So, what?" I looked between the two of them. "You two don't think I should forgive him?"

"We didn't say that. We just don't want him to get hurt."

"But you had no problem with him hurting me?" In fact, they were almost just as guilty. They knew exactly what he was doing, and neither one of them stopped him. Neither one of them gave a shit about what he was doing.

"We didn't really know you." Carson shrugged like it explained everything. "And honestly, neither of us have much love for your family either."

Logically, I knew that. They loved Frankie almost as much as Beck did. That was easy to see when they were around her. But that didn't mean that I had to be okay with what they did, even though I had truly already forgiven them for it.

"Lucas used to be our best friend too, you know?" Olly rubbed his hand down the front of his shirt as he looked over to where Frankie and Beck stood in line for apples. "He didn't just fuck over Beck and Frankie. He ruined our entire group. We used to be inseparable."

"I know that." I nodded. I had heard it all already, but I really hadn't thought about it like that. I hadn't thought about how Lucas's actions had affected all of them. "But I'm not Lucas."

"We know that." Carson nodded. "We just want to make sure that you're with Beck for the right reasons. He acts tough, but he's had a few rough years."

"Don't worry." I put my hand over my heart. "I'm with Beck for nothing more than his pretty face and his ginormous dick."

I thought Carson might actually fall off the bench as he laughed and grabbed his stomach.

"All right, Vos. I think I might like you." He stood, grabbing Carrie's hand, before patting me on the top of my head.

"I wasn't really concerned about it, to be honest." I looked back and forth between him and Olly who couldn't stop smiling.

"That just makes me like you more."

"Are they harassing you?" Beck held out the most delicious apple I had ever seen in my direction as he stared at his friend.

"Nope." I reached forward and grabbed the apple before quickly sinking my teeth into it. "Carson was just asking for advice on how to please a girl with such a tiny penis. Apparently, he's been getting a lot of complaints."

Beck laughed just as Carson winked at me. "Carrie hasn't been complaining."

Allie groaned next to me, and I couldn't just let him walk away with that parting shot. Not when he had just questioned where I stood with Beck and definitely not after the way he had been treating my best friend.

"Carrie doesn't seem like she complains about much." I pointed toward her with the apple that was good enough to make me moan. "She seems pretty content to just follow you around."

I knew I shouldn't have said it. I was being petty and cruel, and I didn't even know this girl. But Carson made me stabby when it came to Allie.

"Says the girl who had a sex tape on Instagram but is still out here with Cami's man."

The apple was halfway back to my mouth when her words registered. All I could do was stare at her, this girl I didn't even know.

"Fuck you, Carrie." That came from Allie at my side, and I knew that she was as angry as I was.

"He's not Cami's man." It was the only thing I could think of as her words repeated over and over in my head. I didn't care that she thought I was an idiot for being here with Beck after what he had done. I didn't care what anyone thought, but I did care that Cami still had some sort of fucking claim on him.

At least in everyone else's eyes.

"That's not what she said." She shook her phone in my direction. "She said that she was with him last night."

She thought she had something over me. Some secret information that would make me crumble, but she didn't.

"I'm well aware of where Beck was last night," I said it as calmly as I could manage. "I trust Beck, and he already told me that he was with Cami."

"Drop that shit, Carrie." Carson's words were firm, and she actually had the audacity to look embarrassed.

"I was just saying."

"Well, don't." I stood and walked away from her. "If someone needs something from you, I'm sure Carson will snap his fingers."

I could hear Olly snickering behind me, but I didn't care. I was too busy focusing on not letting what she said get to me. Because it was. No matter how hard I tried to push it aside.

It mattered that people thought Beck was still hers. It mattered that I couldn't seem to compete with Cami even when Beck was here with me.

Beck caught up to me quickly as I walked away, and he wrapped his fingers around mine without a second thought. "Don't let her get to you."

"I'm not." I shook my head even though it was a lie.

"You are, but don't. I'm yours." He squeezed my hand, and that one simple move, that one little phrase, calmed something inside me instantly.

"All mine?" I looked over at him and the way the setting sun seemed to glow against his skin. He was so damn gorgeous that it was unfair.

He didn't even try. He just was.

And I was a sucker for it even though I knew that I shouldn't let the way he was grinning at me flip my stomach. I couldn't do anything to stop it.

"All yours." He lifted my hand and brought it to his mouth, and I was mesmerized as I watched his lips meet my skin. "And you're all mine."

"I don't think I agreed to that part."

He narrowed his eyes at me just as he pulled me in closer. "Don't worry. You did."

"Did I?" I cocked my head to the side and slowly ran my

tongue over the caramel apple that was becoming sticky in my hand.

"Be careful, Josie." Beck wrapped his hand around the back of my neck and pulled me toward him. He kissed me, the caramel on my lips mixing between us, but he didn't care. "I'll start getting territorial, and you might not like that."

I would definitely like that.

Just the words made me press my thighs together.

"And what exactly would you getting territorial look like?" I ran my tongue over my apple again, and he watched the movement as if he couldn't look away.

"Josie."

"Yeah?" I asked innocently just before he grabbed the apple out of my hand and chucked it in the trash. "Hey! I was eating that!"

He wasn't listening to me, though. He was too busy pulling me through the crowd and away from our friends who were still a few yards behind us.

He tugged me forward until we reached the end of the boardwalk that was scattered with ancient arcade games, and he didn't waste a second before he pushed me against the side of the wall where a loud pinball machine was going off.

"What are you doing?" I laughed as he kissed my jaw with his hands on my hips.

"Kissing you," he practically growled, and I did nothing to stop him.

"We're in public." I looked around, but no one could really see us where we stood. We were almost directly in the middle of the crowd, but we were far enough hidden away that no one was paying us one bit of attention.

"I don't care, princess." He snaked his hand up into my

hair, and I let my hair fall back against the machine. "I need you."

He was out of his mind. He hadn't stopped touching me since we had arrived. "Beck."

"Yes?" He was still kissing me, running his lips and tongue over my skin, and I felt like I was going insane. I knew that we shouldn't be doing this here, but God, I wanted him just as badly as he said he wanted me. I felt irrational in my want for him. In my need.

"We can't do this here." I chuckled as I clung to him harder. He pressed his thigh between mine, and I thought I was going to die from the friction. I needed more. More of this, more of him, more of anything he was willing to give me.

He leaned back to look at me, then tugged me forward. He didn't stop until we walked down the long pier of the boardwalk and onto the beach. And I didn't stop him.

I didn't stop him as the sand flew up around his stomping steps or as he found a spot on the beach that was mostly abandoned. I definitely didn't stop him as he sat down in the sand or when he pulled me down over him until my knees straddled his lap.

I ran my fingers through his hair as I stared down at him, and he was looking up at me with so much want that it was intoxicating.

"I'm so glad you're here." He tugged me impossibly closer to him, and I groaned as our bodies connected.

"I'm glad I'm here too." I nodded and let my fingers slip down his neck.

"And are you glad you're mine?" he teased me, and I couldn't deny him anymore. I couldn't pretend that I was anything other than his.

"Of course, I am."

He pushed forward, bringing his mouth to mine, and this kiss was much slower than the one before. This kiss was deliberate and seductive and made me feel like I was falling apart in his hands.

He ran his fingers down my back, and I couldn't stop myself as I rocked against him. My knees dug into the sand, but I didn't care. I just wanted to be closer to him. I wanted to forget where he began and I ended.

I wanted to forget that there was anything other than the two of us.

And he let me.

He held me as I fell into the kiss and he guided me as I rolled my hips against his. He felt as desperate as I did. The two of us not caring that there were plenty of people around us that we should have been aware of.

I couldn't bring myself to care.

Beck moved me off his lap and onto the sand beside him. I thought he was going to stop us, but he didn't. He rolled toward me, both of us on our sides, and he pushed my hair out of my face before he kissed me again.

He peppered kisses along my lips before sucking my bottom lip into his mouth, and I groaned as I moved impossibly closer to him.

"You are so much trouble." He ran his hand down my side as I lifted my thigh and draped it across his.

"I am not." I was still kissing him, and I didn't care that he thought I was trouble. I didn't care if he wanted to stop this. There was no way that I could.

"You are." He wrapped his arm around my back and forced my chest flush against his. "But I think I'm falling for you."

His words were a whisper, but they stopped my heart in its tracks. I was falling for him too. About that, I was one hundred percent certain, but he didn't give me a chance to respond.

He kissed me like he was dying to do so, and I let him. I let him kiss me and kiss me, and I kissed him back with just as much need. I kissed him back in a way that I hoped he knew how far gone I already was when it came to him.

I wasn't falling for Beck Clermont.

I had already fallen, and there was no way that I could take any of it back now.

Not even with my father's threats or the risk of my future on the line. Beck was more than any of that. He was more than anything I had ever known, and for the first time since I lost my mom, I felt like I might actually be okay.

As long as I had Beck and my friends, I would be okay.

I knew that deep in my gut.

Beck's finger toyed with the top of my jean shorts, and I pushed my hips forward. I wanted more from him. I didn't care that anyone could catch us on this beach. I didn't care that I could still hear the sounds of laughter on the boardwalk.

Nothing mattered but him.

He slid his hand just under the top of my jeans, and I gasped as his fingers skimmed the top of my bare pussy. It felt so forbidden, so risky, but God, it was thrilling. I peeked up around him before pressing my face back into his neck, but no one was watching us.

Everyone was lost in their own little worlds, and not a single one of them cared what was happening between us.

Beck rolled his fingertip over my clit, and I moaned into

his shoulder. I was already so close and he had barely even touched me. Beck knew it too.

He swirled his finger in my wetness as he forced his thigh between mine, and I clung to his shoulders as my legs began to shake. I could smell the saltwater and his addictive cologne, and I wanted to be lost in it. I wanted to be lost in him.

"Take me to the water," I whispered against his skin.

"Here?" His chuckle was deep and throaty, and I knew he was as far on the edge as I was.

I nodded my head, dying for him to move, and he quickly stood and lifted me in his arms. I wrapped my legs around his waist and kicked off my sandals as he pushed into the water.

He didn't care that he was fully clothed, or that I was, and he didn't stop until the water lapped at our shoulders. His mouth was on mine again. Teasing, tasting, devouring, and I was falling apart.

He didn't hesitate as he buried his hand back into my shorts, and I moved against him, chasing the friction of his hand. Chasing the feeling that only he could give me.

My clothes were soaked and sticking to my skin, but all I cared about was him and chasing the feeling he was giving me. The waves crashed against my back, and he crashed into me everywhere else. He wasn't gentle as he moved his hand over my clit in quick circles, and I tried to lift my body to give him better access as he moved a finger inside me.

I fumbled with his own clothes, trying desperately to get my hands on his skin, and he groaned loudly into my shoulder when I finally wrapped my hand around his cock. He was impossibly hard and slick under the water, and I wasted no time as I began stroking him in the same rhythm that he was moving against me.

Neither of us teased or took our time. We were both desperate for each other, desperate for a release, and if I was being honest, I was desperate to have him in my hand and know that he belonged to me. A part of me hoped that Carrie could see us now, I wished that she would know exactly what we were doing under the water, and I wanted her to report it back to Cami.

I wanted her to feel exactly how I felt every time I hear someone say that he belonged to her, that she was somehow his.

I wanted her to choke on that feeling like I had been choking on it for weeks.

Beck pushed his palm hard against my clit as he sucked my neck into this mouth, and I cried out as I could do nothing to stop the orgasm from rolling through me. I pumped my hand harder and faster as I tried to control the feeling that was rolling through me with his pleasure, but it was only a moment later when I felt his hot cum hit my hand and mix with the cool ocean water.

The two of us stood there, him holding us both up, while I sagged against him, and I didn't move for a long moment. I let the feeling he had just caused rock through me with the beat of the ocean and tried like hell to get myself back under control.

We still had to walk all the way back down the board-walk completely soaked, but I didn't care. I was with Beck and I was deliriously happy, and nothing and no one was going to ruin that.

Not now.

Not while we still had this moment in time where there was nothing but us.

I lifted my head from his shoulder and looked at him before smoothing some water from his face. "I think I might be falling for you too," I whispered words that didn't need to be said.

He knew. He had to know.

But his answering grin was enough to make my heart skyrocket again. It was enough to make me want him, even though he had just wrung every bit of pleasure from my body.

"That's good to hear, princess." Then he kissed me, and I knew that there was no turning back from this. Whatever Beck wanted from me was his. All he had to do was take it.

CHAPTER 21

BECK

Josie couldn't stop touching me, and I couldn't stop touching her.

I didn't want this weekend to end. I didn't want to give up this bubble we had created around us and our friends that blocked out the rest of the world, but we had to.

This wasn't real life. Unfortunately, both of us had to face our realities.

"One more kiss." I gripped her around her waist and pulled her back into me.

She giggled as her hands hit my chest. "You said that with the last kiss."

"I lied." I pressed my lips to her and ran my tongue over her soft bottom lip.

"I have to go." She pushed against my chest and grabbed her bag off the ground before jogging up to her front door.

I walked back around my car, my keys in my hand and a stupid fucking smile on my face, and I was still so lost in her that I almost missed Mr. Vos leaning against his garage door with his arms crossed against his chest.

My steps faltered, and even though I wasn't scared of the man, I would be lying if I said just the sight of him didn't put some fear in me.

I wasn't foolish enough to not realize how much power he held.

I didn't say a word to him. I simply walked to the driver's side door of my SUV and put my hand on the handle. Before I could open it, he pushed off the wall and walked in my direction.

"Beckham, I guess it's safe to assume that my daughter was with you all weekend instead of where she said she was going to be."

I hesitated but looked up at him. I didn't know what to say. He clearly saw me dropping her off, and if it wasn't for her, I would have told him to go straight to hell. But this was Josie's father. This man controlled everything for her.

"That's all right." He tucked his hands in his pockets and looked back toward his house. "I don't need you to answer me."

"What are you going to do?" I didn't know why I said it, but I knew that he was going to do something. I knew that he was going to hurt Josie for disobeying him.

"Beckham, I know you think you have life all figured out, but you're young. You are going to meet plenty of pretty girls in your lifetime, and you've had enough of your fun with mine."

His words enraged me, but I couldn't for the life of me form a complete thought to say back to him. "What?"

He just watched me, completely cool, fully at ease with what he was saying.

"My daughter is not going to be with you." He leaned

back against the hood of my car. "You're not good enough for her."

"From what Josie says, I'm surprised to hear that you care about her at all."

"Josie is my daughter. She is my blood. Of course, I care about her."

"I care about her too."

He pressed his lips together as he shook his head and looked away from me. "I don't think my daughter needs the kind of care you give her. I think far too many people learned about your kind of care a few weeks ago."

"I didn't..."

He interrupted me before I could finish my sentence. "Your ass is lucky that you're not in jail. The fact that you're still running around with her and that she seems to have forgotten that you showed her exactly who you are is nothing but luck on your part."

"Me?" I pointed to my chest, and my damn hand was shaking. "What about your stepson? I think both of us know that if anyone deserves anything, it would be him."

He nodded softly, and I knew that he was as aware of that fact as I was. Even if he was the one who got Lucas out of everything.

"We're not here to discuss Lucas, though, are we? We're here to talk about you staying the hell away from my daughter."

"And why should I listen to you?" I cocked my head to the side and studied this man that I hated so much. "What makes you think that I would ever do anything that you wanted?"

"It's called leverage, Beckham, and it's something that

you need to learn about if you're going to be half as successful as your father."

"You don't have any leverage over me anymore. You already used that card with your piece of shit son."

"Not on you. Her?" He nodded up to his house, and I knew that he saw the panic that must have flashed in my eyes. "She'll either leave you alone or she'll lose."

"She'll lose what?" I knew what Cami had told me, but I needed to hear it from his lips. I needed to hear the selfish bastard tell me exactly what he would do to his daughter if she didn't do things his way. If she didn't do exactly what he wanted her to.

"Everything." He pushed away from my car and began walking toward the house. "You leave my daughter alone or she'll lose everything she cares about. Her mother's house. The money her mother left her." He ran his hand over his hair and looked back at me. "Did she tell you that she plans on getting as far away from this place as she can once she graduates?"

She hadn't, but I didn't want him to know that. I didn't want to think that he had any sort of upper hand when it came to her.

"The only reason she's still here is because that's the only way she gets to keep those things. If she doesn't graduate, they're mine. If you don't leave her alone, they're mine."

"I don't want to leave her alone," I said to his back, and he paused.

"Then you don't care about her at all." He looked back over his shoulder at me. "You've already shamed her beyond repair. What do you think she'll do when she finds out that you were only pretending to want her again to ruin her further? When your plan all along was to make her lose everything?"

"That's not true."

"The truth doesn't matter, boy. Not after all the lies you've already told."

I knew what he said was true. She would have absolutely no reason to believe me over him. Not after everything I had already done.

I stared up at the house with my hands clenched into fists. Her father was cruel, but I knew he wasn't lying. Josie was going to leave this place and I would stay here. She was going to move on with her life, and she was going to fucking hate me if I had some part in taking away the things she wanted most.

I knew that.

Especially after this weekend and hearing her talk about how badly she missed her mom. After hearing her talk about her home.

My heart raced in my chest and every part of me wanted to run into her house and pull her away. I wanted to wrap her in my arms and protect her from any and everything that could ever harm her, but I knew that I couldn't.

I knew that I had harmed her almost as much as the others.

And that thought sobered something inside me.

And I knew what I had to do.

CHAPTER 22
JOSIE

I couldn't stop smiling.

I knew how stupid that sounded, but it was true.

Not even my dad or Lucas could knock the smile off my face. Even though my dad had been looking at me like he hated me since the moment I first ran into him on Sunday evening.

No one had been around when I got home. No one had even cared that I had been gone, and I knew that he had no idea where had been. He had no idea that I had just spent the entire weekend with the boy he told me I was not to see.

He had no idea that I had just fallen so far for the boy who I knew wasn't good for me that there was no way I could stop.

Not now.

It didn't matter what my father had threatened. It didn't matter that I could potentially lose everything because of Beck. I had fallen for him, and there was nothing else that mattered. There was nothing that could make me feel otherwise.

My stomach was in knots as I walked through the front doors of Clermont Prep. I was no longer the new girl or the girl who had been fucked over by the Gods of Clermont Bay. I was Beck Clermont's girlfriend, and somehow that made me forget that I ever gave a shit what any of these people thought about me.

The way they watched me and whispered and talked. I didn't care about any of it anymore.

I was Beck's and that was all that mattered. I was his, and I couldn't see anything past that.

"Oh my God." Frankie leaned back against the locker next to mine and rolled her eyes. "I'm so sad the weekend's over. It felt like it went by so fast."

"I know." She had no idea. It felt like it had flown by for me and Beck, and those few small moments that we managed to sneak away from everyone.

The small moments that seemed to change everything.

"I wish we could go back every weekend." I grabbed my books out of my locker and stuffed them into my bag.

"Me too." She sighed and looked over at me. "Have you seen Beck today? He left early this morning for baseball workouts."

"No." I shook my head and closed my locker. "And I passed out so early last night that we didn't even get a chance to talk."

"It's not like you all did much talking this weekend anyway." She waggled her eyebrows at me, and I smacked her arm as she giggled.

"We did plenty of talking, thank you."

"Oh my God. Yes." Frankie ran her hand over her neck dramatically. "That is not the kind of conversation I was talking about."

"You're an ass." I laughed and lifted my bag onto my shoulders. "For your information, we talked about a lot of things."

"Like whether or not you two are official?"

"Yes. Like that."

"And?" She leaned closer to me, and I knew that she was dying for the answer.

"We are."

"Oh my God!" she practically squealed. "Thank you!"

"Do not be so dramatic." I rolled my eyes and pushed off my locker to head to my first class.

"I am not being dramatic. You have no idea how terrible Beck was when you were mad at him. He's been moodier than he was when he hit puberty."

"Don't blame me. I think he's just generally moody."

"That's true, but you got him all in his feels and he was extra peachy."

I couldn't help but laugh. I couldn't imagine what it would be like to be his sister. To live in a house with him and have to deal with his intensity all the time.

"I'm just glad the two of you have finally worked your shit out so I don't have to deal with his attitude anymore."

I smiled, but it quickly fell from my face. As soon as Frankie and I rounded the corner, there stood her brother, in all his perfect fucking glory, with Cami leaned up against him. And it wasn't just her. She wasn't just leaning up against the guy who I thought had belonged to me. She was welcomed there. He was leaning back against the wall with one of his hands resting on her hip, and he was watching her like he had never seen something so riveting.

Like he hadn't just spent the weekend making me feel like I was the only girl he saw.

"Are you freaking kidding me?" I heard Frankie's words, but I didn't look at her. I didn't take my attention off Beck for one second.

I didn't want to miss a moment of what he was doing to me. I didn't want to allow myself to forget who he really was.

Because I knew I would.

I already had.

Beck had shown me who he was time and time again, and I never believed him. I never believed that he could be this guy he pretended to be in front of everyone else. Not when he was so different with me.

But I was an idiot.

And I knew I should have just walked away. I should have turned my back on both of them and never looked back, but I couldn't. I couldn't just stand there and let him make me look like a damn fool again.

I couldn't let him think he could get away with whatever he wanted without any consequences. I didn't care if that was how this town ran. I didn't.

I wasn't this girl.

I wasn't someone he could continue to play.

Frankie was talking to me, but I didn't hear a word of what she was saying. My head was spinning, and even though I hated it, he was still the only thing I could see.

"Oh hey, Josie." Cami's voice was full of honey and vinegar, and the sound of it snapped something inside of me. She was the only thing that seemed to pull my attention off of Beck and where his hand still rested on her body, and it only took a second before I knew that I was losing control.

Cami was the last person I wanted to see. She was the one person I never wanted to see Beck with again, and seeing her there like this when he was supposed to be mine. It broke something inside of me.

I felt Beck's gaze as I made my way toward them, but I didn't spare him another glance. Not as I reached forward and grabbed Cami's wrist. I pulled her toward me and as far away from him as I could, and I didn't stop until she was out of his reach and stumbling on her feet.

"What the fuck do you think you're doing?" she yelled at me as I pushed forward and backed her into the lockers behind her.

I was in her face, and I was so fucking angry. "What am I doing? What the fuck are you doing?"

She cocked her head to the side even though there was a flash of fear in her eyes. "Aww, honey. I told you that he couldn't be trusted." She lifted her hand and ran it over my trembling bottom lip. "Don't take it so personally."

My heart was thundering in my chest as I watched her. As I watched this girl who thought she was better than me, this girl who was taking away the one thing that felt right.

I didn't know what came over me as I grabbed her retreating wrist in my hand and used it to slam her body back into the lockers. The look of shock on her face fueled me. It made me feel like I was more than this pathetic, broken girl that they were making me out to be.

"Fuck you, Cami. You think you're better than me, but you're nothing but trash."

"But I'm the trash Beck actually cares enough about to be seen in public with, right? How was your little secret weekend away? Did he convince you that you meant every-thing to him? Did he tell you everything he needed to get right back between your legs?"

"At least he's the only one I'm fucking. What about you?

Does your other guy like to be seen with you in public or does his wife have a problem with that?"

I didn't know why I didn't see it coming, but I never thought she would slap me until I felt the sting across my face. It only took a second to register before I was on her. Before I knew what was happening, I had her hair in my hand and she had mine, and I slammed my fist down against her jaw.

I had never fought with someone before. Not like this, and even though I had no idea what I was doing, I couldn't stop. She was as angry as I was as our hands and fists slammed into each other, and I couldn't help wondering if maybe she cared about Beck far more than she let on.

I could feel someone tugging on me from behind, but I didn't stop. I couldn't.

Cami landed a blow to my jaw, and I winced as the pain lanced through me.

But I didn't let it stop me. I took everything out of her. Every bit of hurt and anger that I had been bottling up since I came to Clermont Bay was pouring out of me, and I wanted to tear her apart.

She seemed every bit as eager to destroy me too. Our hands and fists flew in the air, and I could barely tell what was happening beyond the contact of my hands hitting her and hers hitting me.

I was jerked away from her, and I pushed the hair out of my face just in time to see Carson pin her up against the locker to keep her from getting to me.

"Fuck you, Josie. You are so fucking dead."

"Go suck a dick, Cami. Isn't that your specialty? Surely someone around here has a life you can ruin." The arms around me tightened and pulled me further away from her. I fought against the grip, wanting to get my hands on her just one more time.

"Stop." Beck's voice was in my ear, and I went stock-still against him as he pulled me down the hallway.

I didn't want his hands anywhere near me, not now, not when he was standing there with her like this past weekend hadn't meant anything at all. Somehow I felt more betrayed now than I did when that stupid video was posted, and I knew why.

I knew the reason, but I hated it.

I was in love with Beck Clermont, and I was still nothing but a game to him.

I was nothing more than whatever he chose for me to be.

And I hated him for it.

That was the thing about him. Since the moment I met him, I had never felt neutral. Not one single part of me. My feelings for him were always extreme, and he was the one who controlled them. He was the one who determined whether I hated or loved him, and it had come from some sick game to him.

I could flip from one feeling to the next so easily, and he knew it. I had become just like the rest of the people in this town, so infatuated with this boy who didn't deserve it, and I couldn't bring myself to fight him as he pulled me into the girls' bathroom and away from the scene I had just caused.

He dropped me to my feet, and I tried to catch my breath as he started pacing up and down the length of the bathroom. I had no idea what the hell he had to pace about, but I was trying to calm my racing heart, and he was doing nothing but fueling my anger.

I closed my eyes, and all I could see was him and her.

I could just imagine the two of them talking about this

weekend. Talking about the way he made me fall for him like a damn fool.

Because I had.

I had fallen for him so damn hard that I knew I couldn't just walk away. I would never be able to walk away from him and not lose some part of myself.

Because he had stolen it.

He had stolen a part of me I would never get back, and I hated him for it.

"Get out."

I opened my eyes, and he was staring at me. He was running his fingers through his hair, and I knew that there was probably some slick line on the tip of his tongue that would make me question whether or not he was truly capable of breaking my heart, but I didn't want to hear it.

I couldn't hear it or I would let him win.

Again.

I would continue to let him take more and more from me even though I knew he wasn't worth it.

"Josie." His voice was broken and unsure, and it shouldn't have made my chest hurt, but it did.

It ached and my stupid heart begged me to look up at him and listen to what he had to say. Fighting it was almost impossible, but I had to do it.

I had to fight against every instinct that told me that he really loved me because he had made me believe that. He had made me believe it so well that even he couldn't seem to convince me otherwise.

Even when the proof was right in front of me.

I swallowed down a gulp of air and pushed my pride down with it. I didn't have the luxury of being a stupid girl. I needed to get my head on straight and forget that he ever existed.

"I said get out." I finally looked up at him, and I hoped he could see how angry I was. I hoped he knew that I was no longer going to be a part of his fucked-up world.

"Fuck." He reached out for me before thinking better of it and clasping his hand into a fist. "I just... I can't..."

"Then don't." I could feel every part of me shaking. "Just leave and go out there and check on Cami. God knows you're dying to find out if she's okay."

"If I wanted to be with Cami, I would be, but I'm here with you."

"So that's supposed to mean something?" I yelled at him, and I knew that I probably looked crazy. I could feel my hair sticking to the side of my face and my uniform was completely disheveled. "You don't get to choose when you want me or don't want me, Beck. That isn't how this works."

He was watching me, staring at me like he was dying to say something that would actually fucking mean something, but instead, he said, "You're right."

You're right.

Those two words echoed over and over in my head, and I tried my hardest to make them stick.

No matter what he said after this moment, I needed to remember that I was right, and I deserved more than whatever parts of himself he was willing to give me.

He started to walk toward the door, and I should have let him leave. I should have kept my mouth shut and let him walk away.

But I didn't.

"You're a fucking coward."

He stopped in his tracks, his body perfectly still besides

the rapid push and pull of his breath, and I waited for him to say something. To say anything.

I wanted him to yell at me, to tell me that I was nothing more than what he had made me; I wanted him to fuel this fire that was raging inside me, that would instill that I didn't forget how much I hated him, but he did none of those things.

He simply stood there for a moment with his back toward me, then he walked out the door as if I didn't matter at all.

CHAPTER 23
BECK

Josie wasn't going to make anything easy on me.

Not that I had expected her to.

Not after everything I had done.

And I couldn't tell her. I couldn't explain that I wanted her more than I had ever wanted anyone in my entire life, but I couldn't have her.

That I cared about her too much to have her.

Because I knew that she would choose me. If she was given the choice of me or everything her father threatened to take away, I knew that she would choose me.

She would choose me, and I would never forgive myself for it. Even if that meant I had to hurt her now. I knew that her mother's house was far more important to her, and I wouldn't be the one to take it away.

If Mr. Vos did that, it would be all on his own.

I would have nothing to do with it.

Even if every moment of every day had me dying to talk to her. It had me dying to call her and beg her to forgive me just one more time.

I couldn't do it.

Not when I knew that it would hurt her far worse.

I walked out of my dad's office, and I dragged my feet as I headed into the kitchen. My dad needed some paperwork from the kitchen manager, but I knew that Josie would be there. Even if she hated me, she hadn't given up her job, and I wasn't surprised when she had shown up on time this morning and looking like she hadn't been affected by what had happened between us at all.

Except for the fading bruises on her jaw that she tried to cover with makeup.

She hadn't looked at me when I saw her then and she still wasn't looking at me when I pushed through the kitchen doors. She was wiping down silverware, and as soon as she noticed me, she stared down at the fork in her hand as if the task took all of her attention.

I wanted to walk toward her and demand she look at me. I wanted to kiss that bottom lip that she constantly worked with her teeth when she was anxious, and I wanted to remind her exactly who we were.

Want, want, want. That was all I could see. My want for her. My need.

My want for her to have more than this life had afforded her.

It was the only thing I thought about as I distractedly grabbed the papers from the manager and walked back out of the kitchen. She glanced up at me just as I pushed through the door, and I swear that one look was enough to cut me. It was enough to make me bleed open and bare everything in front of her.

I closed the door behind me and leaned against it as I tried to catch my breath.

She was so damn beautiful, even when she was mad at me, and I knew that I wouldn't get a chance with a girl like her again. Josie was my lucky shot. She was my one real chance at something pure and good and beautiful, and I would never have her.

Not now. Not when neither of us had any real control over our lives.

And I couldn't help daydreaming about what it could be like after this chapter. When Josie moved away and I took over my dad's business. Would she ever come back? Would she ever give me another chance after she had already given me so many already?

I shook my head and pushed off the door. I couldn't afford daydreams like that. I couldn't afford to wish and wonder and hope.

Because even if I wasn't being forced to push Josie away, she would be leaving. I was staying here and she would leave, and I knew that would be the end of us.

Even if no one else had a hand in it, the two of us would end.

Sometimes people were only meant to be in your life for a short fleeting moment, and I had to believe that was what Josie was. But these small moments, these small things I loved about her, they weren't small in any way.

And I knew the effect of her would never be small. But I tried to convince myself that it somehow made what we had even more precious. These fleeting moments, rushed encounters, and broken hearts. Everything about us had been quick and unrealistic.

We were never meant to be more than we were, but God, I was so glad that we had been.

Even if it was over now. Even if she hated me.

I watched my feet as one footstep after the other led me away from her, and I focused on each and every one of those steps to force myself not to turn around. I was so focused that I barely noticed the door to one of the conference rooms near my father's office was cracked open just slightly, and it wasn't until I heard Cami's voice float through that crack that I stopped in my tracks.

"What do you expect me to do? I've done everything you wanted from me. I've been exactly what you wanted." Her voice was desperate and broken, and I knew that if I looked inside that door I would probably see her father being the asshole he was.

And I didn't know if I could handle him today. I didn't know if I could fake another smile to that man after everything I knew he had done.

He was a regular at the country club, a lucrative regular who was a huge contributor to the success of my father's business, and I knew that I shouldn't do anything here. Keep business and pleasure separate. It was something my father had always instilled in me, but I couldn't walk away from that door knowing Cami was in there with him.

I couldn't just hurt them both and walk away. Because despite what I tried to convince myself, I did love both Josie and Cami. Not in the same way, not even close. But Cami had been my friend for a long time. She had been one of my closest friends, and even though I knew that she had done shitty things to Josie, I couldn't just abandon her.

I took a couple steps back and looked through the crack in the door. But she was all I could see. She was standing there at one end of the large conference table that took up the room, and her fingers were digging into the wood as she argued.

"Please don't do this."

I could just barely see movement on the opposite side of the table, and it wasn't until he laced his fingers into her blonde hair that it hit me that her father wasn't the other person in the room.

He pulled her toward him with a roughness that told me he was as eager for her as she seemed to be for him, and I had never seen that look on her face before. She had never looked at me like I was the one who could change everything for her. I had been a temporary solution, but the way she was looking at him was like he could make every part of her life that she hated disappear.

This man what her knight in shining armor, and I could barely breathe as I watched Mr. Vos lean forward and capture Cami's mouth with his.

What the fuck?

I couldn't breathe. I couldn't think. I couldn't begin to understand what was happening right in front of me.

I took a step back to make sure he couldn't see me just as he spoke. "This is getting reckless, Camille. We can't keep doing this."

I fumbled for my phone in my pocket as his talking stopped, and as I peeked around the corner, they were kissing again. Cami was holding onto the lapels of his jacket like she never wanted to let go, and even though I hated her for what she was doing, I still felt guilty as I lifted my phone and hit Record.

My hand was steady as I recorded the two of them. It was perfectly clear on camera who they were. He was a man that no one in this town could ever mistake as anyone else, and she was a girl who had no business being anywhere near him.

She was a girl who had fucking lied to me and made me be a part of helping cover this sick little affair that the two of them were having. An affair that she knew I would hate. Because I hated him.

She knew that.

She fucking knew it better than most people.

But she was still here, clinging to him like he was the only thing in this world that could save her. She clung to him like she had no idea the monster he was.

Like she hadn't helped my sister cope with the destruction he and his son had caused.

She had looked her in the face, the both of us in the face, and acted like she had hated the man as much as we did. She acted like she actually gave a shit about what Lucas and Mr. Vos had done and all the while she was leaving my house and going back to him.

Acid filled my throat as I watched them through my phone.

Fuck Cami and fuck Mr. Vos.

Any loyalty or fucked-up relationship I had with Cami was so fucking over. I could barely stand to look at her or the way she pressed her body against his.

Cami was nothing but a whore, and she had used me so perfectly in her fucked-up lies. I had been the one to help her keep her affair with Mr. Vos a secret. I was the one who had allowed her to lie to everyone while thinking she was this perfect girl with the perfect life that everyone else wanted.

But she was none of those things.

Mr. Vos gripped her thigh in his hand and lifted it to bring it around his body. Neither one of them noticed as I quietly slid the door open and slipped inside, and I could tell that neither of them cared about anything other than each other as I pushed the door back just to the latch.

I watched them for a few more moments before I forced the door closed behind me with a loud thud.

Mr. Vos dropped his hands from Cami so quickly you would have thought she was burning him, and I was so damn happy that I was still recording when his gaze met mine and the look of shock and terror filled his hazel eyes that matched Josie's.

This was her pathetic excuse for a father. This was the man who had threatened to take everything from her because she wasn't exactly who he wanted her to be.

And look at him. He expected perfection from a girl who had just lost her mother, and here he stood with his body wrapped around someone who was the exact same age.

Someone who was underage. She was underage, and she most certainly wasn't his wife.

"What the fuck are you doing?" His voice held so much power even as he was being quiet and trying not to be overheard.

But that power in his voice was nothing but bravado.

I clicked Stop Recording and tucked my phone deep into my pocket before I answered him. "It looks like I'm getting a free show on the clock." I leaned back against the door and crossed my arms. He tracked the movement, and I loved the way he fidgeted as he watched me.

I had caught Mr. Vos with his pants down, and now he feared me. It was a heady and dangerous feeling, and I let myself bask in it for a few moments before looking over at Cami.

She had a pathetic look on her face as if she wanted to say something to me. As if she wanted to explain what I had just saw, but both of us knew that nothing she could say would ever make this better.

She had chosen her side. She had chosen it and made me look like a fool. A fool who had believed she was sleeping with a fucking teacher this entire time.

Cami was a good liar, and she had hidden her lies so well in almost truths that I had never questioned her. Because why would I?

Why would this gorgeous girl ever lie about sleeping with a married man?

But now I knew.

"Delete that video now, Beckham."

My gaze snapped back to Mr. Vos, and I couldn't believe he had the nerve to think he could actually tell me what to do. After everything this man had done, his audacity was astounding.

"Let me tell you how this is going to go." I drummed my fingers against my arm.

"This isn't his fault." Cami rushed out before I could continue. "Joseph had nothing to do with this. I made a move on him because I've been infatuated with him forever." She pushed her hair out of her face as her gaze bounced between me and him.

"Do you ever stop lying, Cami? Do you ever stop being anything other than a malicious bitch?"

"That's enough." Mr. Vos came to her rescue and watching him be so fucking weak tasted so sweet on my tongue.

"Let me tell you what's enough." I pushed off the door and stepped toward him. I didn't cower at the way this man still somehow made me feel smaller than him. I held the power now. I could destroy him so quickly, and we both knew it. "Stop fucking with Josie."

His back went ramrod straight as her name passed my lips.

"Beck, what are you talking about?"

I ignored Cami's question and stared right at him. He and I both knew exactly what I was talking about. We both knew how fucked up he was.

"You're going to sign over the deed to her mother's house now. Not when she turns eighteen, and you're going to give her all of her money."

He straightened his suit jacket and tucked his hand in the front pocket of his slacks. He seemed so nonchalant, so unworried by my demands, and I knew that this was the businessman that I had always heard of standing in front of me. His emotions disappeared, and what was left was nothing short of ruthless.

But I didn't care.

"Or what? You're going to blackmail me?" He shook his head before looking back at me. "And what exactly are you going to want after that? How long do you think you can keep this little charade up?"

"I want nothing else." I tapped my fingers against my pocket. "You give Josie what she wants, what is hers, and I'll hand over the video."

"Just like that?" He didn't believe a word I was saying, and I knew it was because if he was in my shoes, he would use the video for far worse. But I wanted to be nothing like him. I had already hurt Josie once by trying to stoop to their level, and I knew how insane that was. I wouldn't do it again.

I would make sure that he didn't hurt her like he had

planned, then I would step away. I would give him the video just like I promised, then I wouldn't think about the two of them ever again.

"I know this is a hard concept for you to understand, but I love Josie." I looked him in the eye and made sure he heard what I was saying to him. I wanted to make sure that he knew that I loved her when he didn't. "I will do whatever it takes to make sure that she's happy."

I could tell he wanted to argue with me, but I refused to let him.

"Even if that means destroying you. How do you think your wife will feel when she sees this video? Cami's dad? Your investors?"

"Beck, you wouldn't." Cami stepped toward me, but then thought better of it as I let my gaze snap to her.

"I will." I nodded and made sure she could see the truth in my eyes. "You've done nothing but lie to me and I'm done protecting you. It's time for me to protect Josie, even if she'll never forgive me after what he made me do. I'll protect her regardless."

"Fine." Mr. Vos ran his fingers through his hair. "I'll do what you demand, but I want that video, and I want proof that you're not keeping it anywhere else. I want a legal agreement."

"That's fine. You give Josie what's hers then I'll let you keep your dirty little secret."

"Don't talk about me like I'm not standing right here." Cami stepped toward Mr. Vos, and I almost winced at the look on her face as he stepped away from her.

"I need to get out of here." He didn't even spare Cami a glance as he headed toward the door, and I could see the heartbreak in her eyes.

And even though I knew she made the bed that she lied in, I still felt sorry for her.

She had lied to me and everyone else, and I somehow still felt sorry for her.

"Beck, please." She sounded so broken as I looked up at her, and I wondered what she truly thought was going to happen. Did she think she would somehow end up with Mr. Vos? Did she think he was her ticket to a happily ever after?

"How dare you?" I took a step back and put distance between us. "You've been lying to me for how damn long? How long has this been going on?"

She twisted the ring on her finger as she stared up at me. Mr. Vos's hand was on the door, and I knew that he was waiting for her response. "I didn't mean for it to happen."

"How long?" I demanded an answer from her.

"Since sophomore year."

Mr. Vos ran his hand down his face, but I didn't give a shit what he thought.

"This whole time you had me believe that you were with Mr. Weston but you were with him. After everything he has done, you were with him."

Cami searched Mr. Vos's face for something, but I had no idea what she was looking for. I had no idea what she thought he would give her. "You don't know him like I do. You think you do, but you don't." She shook her head, and I wasn't sure if she was trying to convince me or herself. "He's not the monster you think he is."

But he was. He was every bit of what I had painted him in my mind. Cami was the one who didn't know the man who was leaving her standing there like she meant nothing to him.

"You can't share the video, Beck." She reached forward

and grabbed my hand in hers. "You know what my dad will do."

Cami knew how to manipulate me as easily as she did everyone else, and even though I knew that was what she was doing, it was working. Because I knew that her father would die if he ever found out. He would lose his fucking mind.

But Cami had made that choice. Not me.

And I couldn't protect her from her own fucked-up decisions anymore.

"I won't share it as long as Mr. Vos holds up to his end of the bargain." I pulled my hand away from hers and looked between the two of them.

"You barely know her." Her desperate voice stopped me in my tracks. "I've been your friend for as long as I can remember, and you barely know her. How can you choose her over me?"

My heart was thundering in my chest, and I didn't know what to say to her. I didn't know how she could even ask such a question after the way she had betrayed me.

I didn't know how she could expect anything out of me.

"I love her, and I will do whatever I have to, to protect her."

The door opened, and Mr. Vos let out a deep curse.

"What the hell is going on?"

My gaze snapped to Josie's, and from the way she was looking around the room, I knew that she had just overheard far too much.

"Dad?" Josie looked to her father, and I swear I had never seen so much hurt cross her face. I had never seen her look at him the way she was looking at him now. Like she was desperate for him to me, more than he was.

"Nothing's happening." He reached out for her hand, and she quickly jerked it out of his touch. "I think it's time the two of us head home."

"You're sleeping with Cami?" She looked back and forth between them, and I couldn't imagine what was going through her head. After everything she had been through, that was the last thing she needed. This was the last thing she could take.

"Don't be absurd." Mr. Vos's face was filled with rage, and I knew that he hated this. He hated that he couldn't talk his way out of this situation that he had put himself in.

"I heard you." She glanced over at me before looking back at her father. "I heard what Beck said."

"This isn't the place to have this conversation." His gaze bounced to the door, and I knew that he was unraveling. Whatever plan he had with Cami was backfiring on him. For such a smart businessman, he was acting like a complete and total idiot.

"Where exactly do you think we should have this conversation?" Josie's voice was rising. "Should we talk about it with your wife, or maybe Cami's dad? Would those be better options?"

I moved closer to Josie and her gaze snapped to mine.

"We are not doing this." He shook his head, but I didn't care what he had to say.

"The video is yours." I nodded to Josie. "Make him sign over your mother's house and money."

"And what about you?" She looked so hurt, so full of questions. "You finally have the power to destroy him and you're just going to hand it over?"

"Yes."

There was an instant relief in her eyes at my answer as if

she hadn't believed it before that moment. As if she actually thought I would choose revenge over her, and I hated that I ever made her believe that. I had caused that doubt in her, and I would do whatever it took to take it back.

"Josephine, let's go. We can talk about this in the car."

But Josie wasn't looking at him. She was still looking at me. "I'm not going anywhere with you."

"Josie."

She jerked her head around in his direction, and I stepped closer to her still. I felt so overprotective of her, so eager to get her behind me where he couldn't touch her even if he tried, but I knew that she was capable of protecting herself.

And she needed this.

"I am not going anywhere with you," she repeated herself. "If I were you, I would leave."

"I am your father."

"You are nothing more than a man who thinks he's entitled to whatever he wants." She balled her fists up at her sides. "Now leave."

He stared at his daughter, but he didn't say another word. He ran his hand through his hair before looking back at Cami. He didn't say a word to her as he pushed through the door and left.

Josie let out a shaky breath, and I knew that Cami was about to say something. And I didn't know if Josie could handle anything else. Not today. Not after what she had just witnessed.

And I knew she probably didn't want to talk to me either, but I couldn't walk away from her. Even if that was what she wanted.

"I need to get out of here." She looked back at me, and I didn't give her a moment to second-guess what she was saying. I reached out and grabbed her hand in mine, and I pulled her away without a backward glance at Cami.

CHAPTER 24
JOSIE

I felt like I was numb.

I couldn't wrap my head around what just happened or what I should be doing or saying. All I could think about was Beck and the words I heard him say over and over in my head.

"I love her, and I will do whatever I have to, to protect her."

None of it made sense. Not anything that he said or did. His push and pull. It gave me whiplash, and I didn't think I could survive another round of it.

Because despite everything, I was in love with Beck Clermont.

But he was responsible for so much. Even though Lucas had told me that he was the one who had given Cami the video, Beck was the one who gave him access to it. If I had never met him, it never would have happened. I wouldn't be in this situation where my dad was fucking a girl from my school who I hated.

But it wasn't fair to blame Beck for that.

Because he didn't know.

He thought he knew Cami. She was his friend, and I had to believe that he didn't know. If he did, I would never be able to forgive him. But I saw the look on his face when I walked in that room, he was as shocked as I was.

Because who would believe a man like my father would do something like this? I knew the man wasn't the best father, and I had my own built-up hate for him, but this was beyond what I thought he was capable of.

But I knew he was guilty.

If I hadn't heard it with my own ears, that fact would be laminated by the fact that I received a large sum of money in my bank account this morning. A sum that was the exact same amount that my mother had left me.

But there were no calls or texts from him. No I'm sorrys or checking to see where I was.

My dad handled his business in money, and I guess I was no different.

And if the deed to my mother's house was waiting on me when I finally went back to his house, then I would be glad.

He could do whatever he wanted, and I would have nothing else to do with him.

Even if that meant that I had to leave Clermont Bay.

Even if I had to leave Allie and Frankie and Beck.

My chest tightened just at the thought.

Beck had held to his word when we arrived at his house last night. I walked behind him as he led me up to Frankie's bedroom, and once she opened the door, I didn't see him again.

I knew that was what I should have wanted, but I couldn't lie and say that I wasn't disappointed that he didn't come back for me. That he didn't demand I talk to him.

Because as much as I wanted to be nowhere near him, there was an even bigger part of me that wanted him to make me listen. I wanted him to make me understand.

Now, the whole house was asleep, and I was sitting by their pool wrapped in a blanket I stole from Frankie's room. And I was just replaying everything that happened yesterday over and over in my head.

I wondered if Lucas knew. If he was aware that his step-father, who he worshipped so much, was cheating on his mom with someone his age. I doubted it would matter to him.

And that thought made me sick.

It probably wouldn't matter to most people because they feared the power that my father held.

But I was just disgusted by him.

He was nothing that he should have been, and I couldn't understand how my mother could have ever loved a man like him. Because she did, even when they were no longer together she had loved him.

And he wasn't worthy of her love. Not one moment of it.

"Can I join you?"

I jumped at the sound of Mr. Clermont's voice. "Of course."

He took a seat next to me in one of the pool chairs and stared out toward the ocean. We were both quiet for a few moments before he finally spoke.

"You've had an eventful few months since you moved to Clermont Bay."

"You can say that again." I snuggled into my blanket and watched him. He looked so much like Beck, or I guess Beck looked like him. His usually clean-shaven face was covered in salt and pepper stubble, and he looked so peaceful. Like he hadn't had time to consider the rest of the world and their problems.

"I'm sorry about your father."

I winced. "Beck told you?"

"He did." He nodded and looked over in my direction. "He's scared that what he did is going to force you to leave."

I thought about what he said, and he was right. There was a good chance it would force me to leave because I had no other choice. There was no way in hell I was going to stay in that house with him. I hated it there before, but now? I didn't think I could come to terms with everything he was doing.

Especially with her.

And how was I supposed to look Amelia in the face and not tell her the truth? It wasn't something I was capable of, and once I got the deed to my mother's house, it wasn't something I was willing to live with.

"He's right." I nodded and stared down at the calm pool water. "I don't think I can go back to living with my father, but he's supposed to be giving me my mom's house back. I will figure everything out."

"What about school?" His question wasn't condemning. It was as if he had genuine curiosity about what my plans were.

"I don't know." I answered honestly as I shrugged my shoulders. "Hopefully, I can finish back home, or I'll have to get my GED. I'm not sure."

He nodded his head and sipped from his coffee, and for a moment I thought he was finished talking to me. The silence rode out before he finally said, "Both of my children will be really upset if you leave, and as their father, it is my job to ensure their happiness."

I knew he wasn't intending for them to, but his words were like a stab in the chest. He was right. That was what a father should do. "I'm not sure both of them will be upset. Frankie, yes, but surely you'll let her come visit me."

"I'd be much more likely to let her visit you if you stayed in the pool house." He tipped his coffee in the direction of the pool house that stood to the right of their pool. It was small in comparison to their massive home, but it was probably still bigger than the house my mom and I shared.

"What?"

"That is if you want your privacy. You're more than welcome to stay in the house with us. We can fix up the room next to Frankie's for you."

"Mr. Clermont, I can't stay here." I couldn't wrap my head around what he was saying.

"You most certainly can." He turned to face me more fully. "I know that my son has made some really poor decisions when it comes to you. Really stupid decisions, as a matter of fact, but he cares about you."

I shook my head, because Mr. Clermont was wrong. I thought that Beck had cared about me too, but he wasn't there at school when he treated me like I was disposable. After everything at the cabin, he had just pretended like I meant nothing.

"He does." He tried to reassure me.

"Your son likes to play games. That's all I am to him."

"Did he tell you that your father threatened him?" I sat up straight at his words and he nodded his head. "Right after you all got back from your cabin trip that I didn't know you were going on, by the way." He tapped my armrest with a smile. "Your father threatened to take things from you if Beck didn't keep his distance. He was using whatever leverage he had over you to keep Beck away."

"That's why he was pushing me away?" I asked out loud, but I was talking more to myself.

"Mmhmmm." Mr. Clermont took another drink of his coffee. "I didn't say he was making smart decisions. He should have just come to you and told you about your father, but he was doing what he thought was best for you." He studied me for a moment before speaking again. "He told me all of this last night, but he also told me something I'm not sure I should tell you."

"What's that?" My chest felt tight, and I wasn't sure if I could handle anything else.

"He told me that he's in love with you."

I opened my mouth to argue, but Mr. Clermont held up his hands. "My son may do a lot of things, but this isn't something he says lightly. If he says he's in love with you, I believe him. But I didn't need to hear him say it to know. His mom and I have known for a few weeks now."

I shook my head because I didn't know what I was supposed to say. Beck loved me? I knew that what I felt for him was beyond anything I had ever felt before, but it was so hard to understand.

"Now, my question is do you love him?" He asked the question like my answer was simple. But it wasn't. The answer to that question was earthshattering and confusing and beyond overwhelming.

"I don't know."

"Yes. You do." He looked at me with so much sympathy in his eyes. "It's just hard to say it out loud. I remember when I realized I was in love with Beck's mom." He chuckled as he rubbed his chest. "It hit me like a ton of bricks, but I was so damn scared to say it to her. It took me far longer than it ever should have, but every time I was with her or I thought about her, I had this feeling in my chest that I just couldn't brush off. I was so damn obsessed with her."

I thought about all the times I was with Beck and when I thought about him, which was always, and I knew the exact feeling he was talking about.

"Yes." I nodded my head. "I'm in love with your son."

Mr. Clermont's smile took over his warm face. "Then that's the only thing that matters. Everything else can be worked out."

"Mr. Clermont, I really appreciate you offering to let me stay here, but I don't know that it's the best idea. I don't think I can afford this place," I pointed to the pool house, "and I don't want to be a bother to you all."

"I didn't ask you to rent it, Josie. I told you that you can stay there, and you could never be a bother."

"But..." I didn't get to finish my argument because the sliding door opened behind us, and both of us turned around to find Beck coming outside. He was watching me with a guarded look on his face, and the urge to get up and kiss him was overwhelming.

The cabin felt like weeks ago, and I felt like I hadn't touched him in far too long. But Cami had, and I wanted to wash every bit of her off of him. It was irrational, but I hated that she had ever touched him at all.

"I think you two need to talk about some things." Mr. Clermont stood and patted me on my shoulder before he passed his son and walked back into the house.

I sat there in the quiet peace of the morning as the sun rose, and I stared at Beck. He looked so hesitant as he approached me. So unsure.

"Hi." He took the seat next to me and didn't move his gaze away from me for a moment.

"Hi."

"Did you sleep okay?" He ran his fingers through his unruly hair.

"I did. What about you?" I pulled my knees up against my chest and wrapped my arms around them.

"Not really." He chuckled. "I was a bit worried about you."

"You didn't have to worry. I'm okay."

"Are you?" He searched my face, and I knew he was looking for some sign that I was about to break.

I shrugged my shoulders because I didn't really know. In this moment, I felt okay. I felt like I could breathe and that the rest of the world wasn't crashing down around me, but I knew that I wouldn't feel that way for long. I was going to have to face the real world, and I was going to have to make decisions that would affect the rest of my life.

Decisions that would be so much simpler if my mother was still here.

"I'm sorry." He ran his hand over the back of his neck before taking a deep breath.

"For what?"

"For everything." He chuckled. "For hurting you, for not coming to you when your father threatened me, for what he's done to you."

For what my father had done. Beck was apologizing for the man he hated, and I knew how hard that had to be for him.

He leaned forward until he was close enough to touch me and his hand hovered over my jaw, and I knew he wanted to kiss me. But he was holding himself back.

"Beck." I shook my head because I didn't know what I

was trying to say. I didn't know what I wanted or needed or how to tell him that I just wanted him.

After everything, it was just him.

"I love you." He tilted my jaw until I was looking up at him. "I know that things are crazy right now, but I need you to know that."

He looked so nervous as I stared up at him without a word. "Please say something." He searched my face. "I'm kind of freaking the hell out here."

I couldn't help but laugh at that. This man who was so cocky and fearless was looking down at me with so much uncertainty, and this should have been the thing he knew about above all else.

Surely, he had to know.

"I love you too, Beck."

The small smile that took over his lips was so devastatingly handsome, and I knew that even though everything seemed stacked against us, I would never be able to walk away from him.

He leaned his forehead against mine, and his breathing mingled with my own. "Then nothing else matters. Not what your father did. Not Lucas, not Cami. None of it matters."

But he was wrong. It did matter.

And I knew that things would be different going forward. I didn't know where I stood or where things would lead, but I knew that they would be different.

Because my father had made far too many selfish decisions that would affect us all.

And a huge part of me felt so bad for Cami.

Because he had no right to be with her. Even if she made stupid decisions, she was a teenager and he was an adult.

My father was an adult.

And he had taken advantage of her.

And I couldn't just take what I wanted from my father and not have him pay the consequences for his actions. I would never be able to live with myself.

"It does matter." I nodded and buried my hands in his t-shirt. "But we'll get through it, right?"

"Right." He kissed me then, pressing his lips firmly against mine until I could think of nothing else but him.

Everything seemed to be falling apart around me, but here he was with his hands buried in my hair and his lips pressed to mine and everything was going to be okay.

But anger still stirred inside of me and I dug my nails into my palms. "My dad..."

"Is not your future." Beck pushed my hair out of my face and stared down at me. "He doesn't get to decide who you become. He threatened to take your future, and I believed him. I couldn't be the reason you lost everything you had left."

Tears fell as I clamped my eyes shut, and I knew that I was crying for far more than what my father had done. I missed my mother and the security she brought. I missed being so sure of my future with her.

Beck wiped away tears from my cheek as he cradled me closer to him.

"I don't know what will happen from here," I said my biggest fear out loud. I had no idea what was to come. I had no clue what my future held.

"You are my future, Josie." He leaned forward and kissed me. "Nothing and no one will be able to change that but you."

"I don't want to change it." I shook my head before burying my face in his neck.

"Good." He chuckled. "Because I've already fallen far too hard."

"Your dad asked me if I wanted to stay here." I had no idea why, but I was so scared to say that out loud. I was scared that I was actually considering his offer.

"I know." He nodded. "We talked about it last night."

"I don't think it's a good idea." I looked up at him and searched his eyes. "You'll probably get tired of me if I'm here all the time."

"That could never happen." He pushed some hair back out of my face before cradling it in his hands. "Who do you think came up with the idea? You can't go back to living with your father, Josie. You're miserable there, and there's no way in hell I'm letting you leave me."

"So, this is it then?" I looked around his parents' massive house. "Me and you?"

"Me and you." He leaned forward and pressed a kiss to my jaw. "And when school ends, you can decide where you want to go to school, and I'll be here."

"You'd wait for me to finish college then come back to you?" I scooted closer to him and ran my nose along his neck. He smelled so good.

"I'd wait for you forever, princess."

EPILOGUE
JOSIE

You don't really realize how hot guys look in baseball pants until you're in love with a baseball player. Don't get me wrong, they've always looked nice, but now that I sit here watching Beck run home and slide into the plate, I realize that I never knew their true power.

Because all I can think about is how to get them off. Well, not off exactly, but pulled down enough that Beck can easily lift me against the wall.

I hadn't even been able to keep up with whether our school was winning or losing. All I knew was that Beck looked so damn hot in those pants, and he was far better at baseball than I ever realized.

I thought that every single time I was at one of his games. I had no idea how someone could be that good at a sport. I could barely walk most days, and here he was diving toward balls and throwing them halfway across the field.

Of course, being at his baseball game meant that I also had to see Lucas, but I tried to pretend like he didn't exist and he did the same to me. It was pretty much the only way we functioned since the moment I moved out of my father's house.

Lucas had done nothing to defend me or shield me as my father lost his mind while I packed my bags, but I hadn't expected him to either. Beck had begged to come with me, but I knew that it was something I had to do on my own.

I had to face my father and tell him I was leaving. He reacted exactly like I expected him to, but I didn't care. There was nothing he could do to me now, not with the knowledge that I held over him. I made sure to remind him of that fact too.

I could see the edge of fear in his eyes when I told him that his relationship with Cami was to stop. I didn't care what he gave me or what power he held. I would use whatever I had against him if he continued anything with her.

He told me that he had already ended it as he handed me the deed to my mother's house. The deed that was still in my name from the beginning.

I knew then and there that there wasn't a single doubt in me that I hated my father.

And I would no longer be under his thumb.

Not as I packed my bags and carried them out to the driveway. I thought about him as I drove back to the Clermonts' house, but I refused to let him have any power over me anymore. For far too long, I had wanted that man to be the father he was never capable of being, and I was finally letting go of that hope.

He would never be anything more than exactly who he was.

"Oh my God." Frankie stood from her seat next to me and cheered. "Olly just got a double."

Allie was cheering too, so I quickly stood and yelled along with them.

Olly looked good in his baseball pants too, but not nearly as good as Beck. But I was sure that Frankie would argue otherwise because she hadn't been able to take her eyes off him for the whole game.

"Are you all ready for the Halloween party tomorrow?" Allie sat back down beside me as the excitement died down.

"No." I shook my head as I thought about the costume the two of them talked me into. "Are you all sure we have to wear costumes? Haven't we outgrown that?"

Frankie rolled and eyes and put her hands on my shoulders. "I told you, we've upgraded. We're into sexy Halloween costumes now."

"I feel like you made that up."

"I did not. Have you never seen *Mean Girls*? We don't want to be the girls who show up wearing something lame when everyone else is dressed slutty."

"It doesn't really matter to me, I'm already taken." I bat my eyelashes at them and grinned as Frankie groaned.

"Yes. We know. The two of you are practically attached at the hip. The only reason you're hanging out with us now is because they won't let you on the field."

I rolled my eyes because she was being ridiculous. "You're insane. I hang out with you all the time."

"Allie." Frankie leaned forward and looked at my other best friend. "Back me up here."

Allie shook her head and didn't bring her eyes away from the field. "I'm not taking either one of your sides. I'm just glad Josie is happy. But you two are missing the end of the game."

She was right. Olly had just run across the home plate, and the whole team stormed out of the dugout to celebrate.

"Ballgame." You could barely hear the umpire's voice over the sound of their cheering.

Beck made eye contact with me as soon as he started walking off the field, and I couldn't help but smile. Because Frankie was right. I could barely stand to be away from him most days.

Not that we were ever very far apart.

I had taken Mr. Clermont up on his offer and moved into the pool house. I thought it would give Beck and me a little more separation, but more nights than not, he snuck out to the house after his parents were sleeping. I was sure that they knew he did it and didn't say anything.

But I didn't care. I was far too wrapped up in him to care what anyone else thought.

Especially when he was looking at me like he was now.

He didn't look at anyone else as he made his way toward me and scooped me up in his arms. His warmth enveloped me instantly, and I wrapped my arms around his neck as he lifted me from the ground.

"Already with the PDA?" I heard Olly's teasing voice, but I didn't care what he had to say. I was too busy bringing my mouth against Beck's.

He kissed me softly before peppering a few kisses along my jaw and on the way to my ear. "He has no idea what kind of PDA we're capable of," he whispered for only me to hear, and I knew he was referring to the side of the school building where we had gone a little too far before the game.

"Don't be a hater just because you can't get laid, Olly." Beck and Carson chuckled, but I noticed Frankie tense up.

"I can get laid. I just don't put it in everyone else's faces."

"Your hand doesn't count." Carson slapped him on the shoulder before hiking his baseball bag up on his back. "Are we heading to get some food or what? I'm starving."

"You're always starving." Allie rolled her eyes. She was perpetually annoyed by him, and I knew that he was the same with her. If they weren't getting under each other's skin, they were ignoring each other altogether.

"I am." He waggled his eyebrows at her playfully but his eyes were full of steam, and I swear I would have been squirming if I were her. They may have acted like they hated each other, but they wanted each other more.

"You're a pig."

Carson didn't deny that fact. He just grinned harder because he knew he was getting to her.

"Let's go get pizza." Frankie linked her arm in Allie's and started pulling her toward the parking lot. "We'll meet you all there."

"Sounds good." Beck wrapped his arms tighter around my middle. "We'll see you all in a few."

He kissed my jaw again before letting go of me and grabbing my hand. He led us to his car and moved some hair off my shoulder before he opened my door.

"You're being very chivalrous today, Mr. Clermont." I climbed into the seat, and he leaned in against the door.

"I have to keep up good appearances because what I'm about to do to you in this car is not gentlemanly at all."

"We are supposed to be meeting everyone for pizza." I giggled because the look in his eyes promised so many things, and none of it was pizza.

"We'll get there eventually." He closed my door, then walked to the driver's side of the car while unbuttoning his jersey.

Watching him was like an aphrodisiac. I had no idea how he could make something so simple so damn hot.

He climbed into the car wearing his baseball pants and a white t-shirt, and he didn't say another word as he started the car and drove. He just reached for my hand and laced his fingers with mine before resting them on my thigh.

I had no idea where we were going until we passed the pizza place on the left and pulled down to a public beach access. He parked the car before leaning his head back against the headrest and looking over at me.

"This isn't pizza."

"Nope." He exaggerated the word with a devilish smile on his face. "It definitely isn't."

"We'll be alone at home tonight."

"I can't wait until then." He leaned across the middle console and gripped me by the back of my neck. He pulled me closer to him and I didn't put up any sort of fight. I let him pull me exactly where he wanted me, and I was instantly met with his sinful and insatiable mouth. He kissed me like he hadn't seen me in months, and I let the feeling of his want wash over me.

This was the way Beck always kissed me. Like he was scared he could lose me at any moment.

He buried his hands in my hair and tilted my head back to give him better access. His mouth moved over me, kissing my mouth, my jaw, my neck, and I was a squirming mess under his tongue.

"Beck," I whispered his name even though no one else could hear us.

It was all he needed, though. That one simple word, breathless, on my lips. He pulled me forward until I moved over the console and into his lap. He quickly scooted his seat back so I could fit comfortably between him and the steering wheel.

"You drive me crazy." He was talking to me, but he was staring at my body. He pulled my top down just enough so he could taste me, and I settled down against him.

I ground down against him as I looked out the window and noticed other people milling about on the beach. "Beck, we can't have sex here. There are people everywhere."

"We're not." His words were muffled against my chest. "I just have to touch you before I go insane."

I ran my fingers through his hair as I laughed. "You've been touching me all day."

He ran his tongue over my nipple as he gently pinched the other in his fingers, and I forgot my argument altogether. I moved my hips harder against him and held onto his head for leverage.

"It's not enough." He looked up at me and kissed me again as his hands worked their way down my body. He quickly unbuttoned my shorts before sliding his hand inside, and I held my breath as his fingers felt how wet I already was.

He moved his fingers against my clit, and I rode his hand like I didn't care who saw me. I was far too concentrated on the way he was making me feel to be concerned with anyone else.

I moved my hands down his body and fumbled as I undid his belt. Those baseball pants that made his ass look so good were easy to undo, and I pulled his cock out into my hand.

His growled as I worked him in my hand. There was no room between us. Our bodies and hands were cramped in the small space we had, but neither of us cared. We were a rush of movement and chase, and I felt like I would lose my mind if he stopped.

"I love you," he whispered against my neck as his breathing rushed in and out against my skin, and his words made my chest ache.

"I love you too." And God, I did. I love him more than I ever thought was possible, and it went far beyond this. Beck loved me without judgment or fear, and I was doing my best to love him back just as fiercely.

I had no idea what my future held, but I was sure about him.

"Beck." I could feel my body falling over the edge, and Beck knew it. I pumped my hand harder up and down the length of him as his fingers pumped inside me. He pushed the palm of his hand against my clit, and I was gone.

I kept working him as I rode out my orgasm and he followed right behind me. I leaned against his chest, not caring about the mess between us or that our hands were still resting against each other.

I nuzzled into his neck and wrapped my opposite hand around the back of his head to pull him closer.

"Are you ready for pizza now?"

He chuckled at my question and pulled my face up to look at his. "I'm ready for anything as long as I'm with you."

CHAPTER 1

CARSON

I fucking loved Halloween parties.

What wasn't to love? Almost every girl here was dressed sluttier than I had ever seen them. Everyone was drinking, and my chances of getting laid tonight were pretty damn high.

The slutty nurse sitting on my lap right now was proof of that. Everything was perfect. My ideal night.

Until Allie Taylor walked through the damn door dressed like a cowgirl who could never possibly ride a horse. Her rhinestone cowboy boots went up to her knees, and her shorts barely covered her ass. There was a black cowboy hat resting on the top of her head and a pink bandana around her neck that did nothing to hide her tits that were practically busting out of her top.

Frankie and Josie were both dressed similarly, but I could barely see them because Allie was so distracting.

How the hell did Beck let them walk out of the house like that?

"What the hell are you supposed to be?" I asked them all,

but I was looking directly at Allie. For the life of me, I couldn't fucking quit looking at her.

"We're rhinestone cowgirls." She grinned and adjusted her bandana.

I knew I should have just left her alone, but I couldn't. It was either be cruel to her or fuck her. Those were the only two thoughts I had when it came to Allie. It was all I had been able to think about for years, and there was no way we were going there, so cruel it was.

"You look like a slut with a cowboy hat."

Her face fell, and my chest ached for the smallest moment. But I forced that shit to go away. I hated Allie, hated her, and the sadness on her face wasn't going to change that.

I refused to let it.

"You are such an asshole, Carson." This came from Frankie, and she wasn't wrong. I was being an asshole. Allie looked beautiful, too beautiful, and it was driving me crazy.

There was no way in hell I was telling them that, so instead I simply shrugged my shoulders with a fake-ass grin on my face.

Allie's gaze slid away from me and moved to where my hand rested on the nurse's hip. I didn't even know her name. I knew how horrible that sounded, but I preferred it that way. Because I had no plans with this girl beyond tonight.

I never did.

"Do you have an issue?" the nurse asked Allie, but I wished for once she would just stand up and say that she did. I wished she would say exactly what was going on in that head of hers, but she never did when it came to me.

Not anymore.

Not since we were kids.

"I do." Frankie raised her hand and moved in front of me. She cut off my view of Allie, and I wanted to push her out of the way. I loved Frankie, but God, I just wanted to stare at Allie. I wanted to watch her be upset by the fact that there was another girl on my lap.

Frankie moved to my lap and sat down on the opposite knee from the nurse. She wasn't gentle, and almost squashed my balls as she forced herself closer to me and forced the nurse out. The girl looked back at me, but there was no way I would deny Frankie. Not after everything that girl had been through.

"Are you kidding me?" She was waiting for me to push Frankie away, but I didn't.

She stood, her fine ass swaying as she stomped away from me, and Frankie shooed her away with her hand like she was a dog.

I wrapped my arms around Frankie and nuzzled into the back of her neck. "You're such a cock-block, you know that?"

"I do." She patted my thigh. "But you're a slut. You didn't need that girl tonight."

"Wow, Frankie." I chuckled against her just as Olly and Beck walked up behind the girls. I hadn't seen any of them all night. "Tell me how you really feel."

Frankie was beautiful too, but she was innocent. She was one of my best friend's baby sister, and sometimes I felt like Olly and I were more protective of her than Beck was. But there were other times, like right now, when Olly was staring daggers at my head like he wanted to kill me, that I thought maybe Olly felt more for this girl.

But it was something that would never happen.

Not after what Lucas had done to her.

Beck would never forgive Olly for going there. Never.

Olly knew that too. It was why he caught himself and looked away before anyone noticed that tortured look on his face, but I noticed. I always did.

"Come on, girls. Let's go get a drink." Josie wrapped her arm in Allie's as she stared daggers at me, and I hugged Frankie tighter against me one last time before she climbed off my lap and walked away.

"I swear to God, you have to be the biggest idiot sometimes." Beck ran his fingers through his hair as he watched his girl walk away.

"I know." We had this conversation multiple times before. He and Olly both thought I was too harsh on Allie. They thought I just had a boner for the girl, but that wasn't it at all. They didn't know Allie like I did. They had no fucking clue what happened between us. "But I wasn't wrong."

"Every girl here is dressed like that, but you just had to say something to Allie, right?"

"I can't help it that she was the first one I saw." I shrugged.

"Or that she was the only one you couldn't quit eye-fucking." Olly shook his head. "I wish the two of you would just have it out and get it over with."

"Not going to happen, my man." I stood and patted him on the shoulder before I passed them to get a drink. I needed one, desperately.

A few of the players on our baseball team were gathered around a bottle of dark liquor laughing, and I quickly snatched it up before I took a long drag. "What the hell are you all up to?"

I liked most of my teammates, thought of most of them as brothers, except for Josie's stepbrother, Lucas, and his idiot friends. I fucking hated them.

"We've got a bet going." Seth, our center fielder, had the biggest damn grin on his face.

"A bet about what? I'm sure Vos is destined to lose." I patted Lucas on the chest and watched the anger rise in his eyes.

"You want to join?" He shook the baseball cap that was in his hands. There were dozens of folded-up pieces of paper inside.

"What are we betting on?" I matched his stare because there was no way in hell I was willing to back down from this asshole.

"Getting the girl." He cocked his head to the side, and there was so much challenge in his stare.

"You all need to make a bet to get a girl?" I looked around at my teammates. "I thought most of you had better game than that."

"Oh, we have plenty of game, but these girls are the ultimate challenge."

It was on the tip of my tongue to remind Lucas exactly what he had done in the past. I wanted to throw it in his face what a piece of shit he was, but he already knew. We both did, and bringing it up here would do nothing but hurt Frankie.

"So, what? We just have to get the girl? Make her like us?" This sounded pretty fucking lame to me.

"Make her like you. Fuck her. All before fall break."

"Damn." I chuckled. "You all need that long to get a girl in bed?"

Lucas stuck the hat out in my direction. "Draw a name, Hale."

I shook my head as I thought about their idiotic plan. "No, thank you. I don't need to play your little games to get pussy. I've got that handled." I winked at Lucas and a couple of the guys laughed.

"Suit yourself." He dropped it so easily, far too easily, before he moved around the group and let everyone draw a name.

He stopped directly in front of me and drew his own name out of the hat. There was only one sheet of paper left, and he pushed the hat back in my direction.

"Not happening."

He shrugged his shoulders before moving on to his buddy, Eli. Eli reached inside and opened the paper with a giant grin on his face.

"Frankie's name better not be in that fucking pile, Lucas."

He held up his hands innocently. "Never."

Then I watched in horror as the boys all started showing off who they got. Eli turned his paper around, the paper that Lucas had meant for me, and I stared down at Allie's name.

"That's not fucking happening." I tried to grab her name from Eli, but he quickly moved it out of my reach.

"Yes. It is." He tucked her name into his pocket as if that would somehow make a difference. "I've been dying for a chance to get a piece of her sweet ass for years. Did you see it practically hanging out of her shorts tonight?"

I lunged at him before I even had time to think about what I was doing, but far too many guys jumped in to stop me.

"Give me her fucking name, Eli."

"Hell no." This one came from Lucas. "You said you didn't want to play."

"I changed my mind. I'm in, and I want Allie's name." I would do anything to keep her from being a part of this. I could just picture her with Eli, falling for his stupid fucking charm.

"Too late." Lucas grinned and someone pushed against my chest to force me to back up. "I gave you multiple opportunities to participate, but you don't need help with pussy. Remember?"

I was going to kill Lucas. He used to be my friend, one of my best friends, and he was one of the only people who knew about what happened between me and Allie. He was one of the only ones who knew that I used to be head over heels in love with the girl.

"Lucas, I'm not fucking around."

He stepped up, his face just inches from my own, and I should have pummeled him right then and there. "I'm not either. It's Eli's job to get in Allie's pants now. I think you should probably give up after all these years."

"You're not going to touch her." I stared at Eli, and I could practically feel his fear. Good. That meant he knew I wasn't fucking around. He wasn't going to touch her. Not if I had any say in it. Not if I could stop him.

"There's nothing you can do to stop him." Lucas laughed and moved away from me. "Allie has hated you for years after how mean you've been to her. She won't listen to you if you try to warn her. She'll just think you're being the same cruel asshole you've always been."

He was right. Fuck. Both of us knew it. If I told Allie that Eli was only into her for a bet, she would absolutely think I was just being a dick. The girls would too. They had watched me be an ass to her time and time again. I wouldn't blame them. I would think the exact same thing.

But as much as I hated Allie, I couldn't sit back and watch her get hurt or humiliated by them. Lucas and his boys were nothing but douchebags, and Eli was one of the worst.

I may have been cruel to Allie, but I would never really hurt her. I would never do the things that I knew Lucas was capable of. I didn't know if Eli was capable of those things too, but I wasn't about to sit back and find out.

"Then I'll make her fall for me."

Lucas laughed along with half the guys standing around us, and my heart felt like it was trying to beat out of my chest.

"If that's what it takes to keep you all away from her, then that's what I'll do."

"Allie will never fall for you, dude." Lucas took a long swig of liquor. "It's a losing battle."

She wouldn't, but I still had to try. If I could convince Allie to fall for me, to spend time with me, then I could keep her as far away from these assholes as possible. Then that was what I would do.

"Then I guess you all have yourselves a bet."

CHAPTER 2
ALLIE

Carson Hale was the biggest asshole I had ever met.

He had been for a long time. For far too long. He had been this way ever since he decided that he no longer wanted to be my friend.

Because we were friends once upon a time, whether he wants to remember it that way or not, and he was the one who decided that what we were was over.

He made that decision, and I lost my best friend and the boy I had been secretly in love with all in one day.

Now he hated me.

And he made sure to take every possible opportunity to remind me of that fact.

I could usually deal with it. I had learned a long time ago to just let his comments roll off my back like they didn't even matter, but it was becoming so much harder these days. It wasn't just his comments either. It was watching him parade around with any girl he could get his hands on like he was constantly throwing them in my face.

I knew how ludicrous that was.

He didn't care about me. He sure as hell wasn't worried about making me jealous.

But it felt that way. I felt like every move he made was a deliberate act to get under my skin. It was something he had become very good at too.

Because I was jealous. I didn't even know who the hell Carson was anymore, but I was still jealous of every one of those girls who got to know him. Who got to have a piece of him that I would never have.

That I never got the chance to have.

I lifted the shot Josie just handed me and pressed it to my lips. The liquor burned, but it also eased the deep ache in my chest. At least a little. I couldn't believe that he said I looked like a slut.

Not only were Josie and Frankie dressed almost identical to me tonight, but we were also the most modestly dressed girls at the entire party. The girl that had been on his lap had on less fabric than my bra and panties, and he had the nerve to say I looked like a slut.

I grabbed the liquor bottle and filled the shot glass again.

I could see the concern in Josie's eyes and the way she kept looking at Frankie. They thought I was likely to snap, and they weren't wrong. I could feel my blood boiling, every bit of hate I had for Carson spilling over the edge.

I threw back the next shot as I avoided her gaze and looked around the party. Everyone was having a blast. The music was blaring through the speakers, people were dancing and grinning, and I hated that Carson had put me in a bad mood.

"Come on." Frankie grabbed my hand in hers and pulled me to the center of the living room. "Let's go dance."

There was no way I could refuse her. Instead, I followed behind her and tried to plant a smile on my face to match hers, and I let her twirl me around in a circle before a genuine smile took over.

"You're a terrible dancer," I yelled the lie over the music, but it made her smile bigger.

"That's what I hear." She shimmied her chest in my direction before finding the beat of the music. "But they say terrible dancers are really good in bed, right?"

"I have no idea." I shrugged. Frankie and I were probably the only two girls at this party who were still virgins. "Your guess is as good as mine."

Frankie started doing a super awkward hip-thrusting move that was drawing way too much attention, but I couldn't quit laughing. She didn't stop either. Not until I was clenching my belly and had almost completely forgotten about Carson.

Because that was the kind of friend she was.

"Hey there, cowgirls."

Frankie and I both stopped laughing and looked up at Eli Scott. I knew who he was because almost everyone did, but I had never spoken to him before.

"Hi," Frankie said dismissively and reached out for my hand.

But Eli's attention stayed on me. "It's Allie, right?"

"Yeah." I nodded as I answered.

"I thought so." He grinned, and I had to admit that it did something to his face that made him even more handsome than before. "If your girl wouldn't mind me cutting in, I'd love to dance with you."

As soon as the words passed his lips, a much slower song with a heavy beat rang through the speakers. Frankie squeezed my hand. I didn't know if she was telling me to say no or yes, but I knew what I wanted to say.

"I'd love to."

I pulled my hand away from Frankie's and placed it in Eli's outreached one. He tugged me toward him gently until my chest pressed against his, and I let my body move with his to the music. He was much better at this than I would have guessed.

"I love your costume, by the way." He tipped the front of my cowgirl hat with the tip of his finger before he let it trail down my back and rest there.

"Thank you." I smiled, but I couldn't keep the thoughts of what Carson had to say about it at bay. Here I was dancing with this guy who was far too attractive for his own good, and I was still thinking about what Carson had said. "And what exactly are you supposed to be?"

I leaned away from him slightly so I could get a good look at his costume. He was dressed in a dark dress suit with a vest included, and he wore a flat cap on his head that covered most of his sandy brown hair.

"Thomas Shelby." He looked down at me like I was supposed to somehow know who that was. "From *Peaky Blinders.*"

"I've never seen it." I shrugged, and he pressed one of his hands into his chest.

"It's only the best show ever." He sounded offended that I hadn't seen it. "I guess I know exactly what we're going to have to do on our first date."

My stomach flipped at his words, and I couldn't stop the stupid grin that I knew was taking over my face. Eli Scott was hot, and I didn't know how to react to him suddenly being interested in me. "I don't remember agreeing to a date."

"Are you sure?" He cocked his head to the side and pulled me in closer to him so our bodies were touching.

He was staring down at me like I had never been looked at before. I didn't have much experience when it came to guys, but I knew one thing for sure. The look he was giving me was one of want. Having someone look at me with such an open and easy desire was overwhelming and so attractive.

"I could have sworn you just asked me to introduce you to *Peaky Blinders*."

"What if I hate it?" I asked as he continued to sway us to the music.

"Then we'll have to end it right then and there. We could never go on after that." He was so playful and charming, and I felt light dancing in his arms.

"I feel the same way about *Gilmore Girls*, you know?"

He curled his top lip, and I laughed. "Does that mean we're going to have to binge-watch it after *Peaky Blinders*?"

"Only if you plan on getting serious," I joked because I knew that nothing was probably going to come of this after tonight, but it was nice to pretend.

Just for a few minutes, I could imagine myself curled up on a couch with him watching whatever he wanted to watch and begging my heart to slow down. I wanted that. I wanted it far more than I realized.

"It's a date then." He stepped back as the song ended and brought my hand to his mouth. He pressed a gentle kiss to the back of my hand and winked at me. "Next Tuesday, we'll meet up at six."

"Okay." I nodded as I stared at my hand that was still near his mouth.

He pulled his phone out of his pocket and handed it to me.

"Give me your number so I can text you."

I typed it in without hesitation, then watched as he typed in Gorgeous Cowgirl before saving it.

"I'll let you get back to your friends." He nodded over my shoulder, and when I turned around, I spotted the entire group along the edge of the room, including Carson. He was staring daggers at the two of us, but I attempted to avoid his gaze altogether. Eli pushed my hair over my right shoulder as he leaned forward and whispered, "I'll see you on Tuesday."

Goose bumps trailed down my arms. Then just like that, he was gone.

"Excuse me, but he's hot." Josie was watching me as I stepped up beside her.

Carson scoffed, but I ignored him.

"He is." I couldn't stop smiling. "He's charming too."

"You girls have really poor taste in men." Olly rolled his eyes at us.

"I'm dating your best friend, remember?" Josie asked.

"I do" —Olly nodded his head dramatically— "and he's about as charming as a wet noodle."

"I can hear you, asshole." Beck was far from offended. Instead, he wrapped his arms around Josie and nuzzled his face into her neck. From the details Josie had shared with me, Beck was more than charming.

"It seems that you have really poor taste in friends then, Olly, because you've somehow managed to pick two charmers." Olly laughed at my comment, but Carson didn't. Instead, he cocked his head to the side and studied me. I tried to avoid looking at him at all, but he was so unnerving.

"You picked me as your friend once upon a time too, remember?"

I was shocked by his comment. Carson had said plenty to me over the years, but he never brought up the past. I had almost convinced myself that we didn't have one.

"I do." I nodded and memories of us bombarded me. Memories of how much I used to care for him and how close we used to be. It was the memories of him that made me feel anything at all for him anymore. "And look how that ended for me."

I could feel everyone watching us, but suddenly, I didn't care. I was desperate for Carson to say something more, to be mean if that's all he was capable of. I just needed something more.

He had become a master of hiding his emotions, and I used to be able to read them so well. I would give anything to be able to see past that mask he wore these days.

"You ended up exactly where you wanted to be, Allie." His fingers skimmed over his jaw as he talked to me, and I couldn't stop myself from watching every inch of the movement. "Don't forget that you're the one who put yourself there."

He was so full of crap. I didn't put myself anywhere. I was his friend, I was in love with him, and he had dropped me like I was nothing.

"That's not how I remember things." I balled my hand into a fist. "But of course, that's how you do. You've never done anything wrong in your life, Carson. Have you?"

"Besides ever wasting my time on you?" He looked up at the ceiling like he was thinking and hadn't just wounded me to my core. "No. I don't think so."

"I hate you." I stared him straight in the eyes as I said it, and I meant it. This guy, this Carson that stood in front of me, he was nothing like the boy I used to know.

There was a flash in Carson's eyes, but I couldn't figure out what it was. It couldn't be regret and I knew that my words didn't hurt him, but there was something. It was there one moment and then it was gone. "Ditto, baby."

CHAPTER 3
CARSON

Allie had left hours ago, and I still couldn't stop thinking about how stupid I had been. Being cruel to her was going to do nothing but push her directly into Eli's arms, but I had been so angry when I saw him touching her. When I saw how pliable she had been under his hands.

Then she turned around and had that stupid fucking look on her face like he had just shown her the best time of her life. I wanted to pummel him, but more than that, I wanted to punish her. I wanted to ruin that moment she just had. I wanted her to hate it as much as I did.

So I pushed her like I always did, and I forced her to hate me. That was the only thing I was good at when it came to her.

But it wasn't what I needed.

Guys like Eli and Lucas. They would ruin Allie, and as much as I hated her, I couldn't let that happen. I couldn't be that cruel even if she already thought I was.

Even though Allie had hurt me once upon a time, I

couldn't let them hurt her. Not like this. Allie was mine to fuck with.

She was mine.

That irrational thought played over and over in my head.

She was the furthest thing from what I wanted but somehow, she was still all I could think about. Even now, with the fine-ass nurse from earlier pressed against my body and kissing up my neck. Allie was all I could think about.

It was infuriating.

I dug my fingers into her hip and tried to concentrate on what she was doing. It felt good. Fuck, she felt good, but it also felt wrong. It always did.

After all the girls I had been with, it was never enough.

None of them were ever enough.

But they were enough of a distraction that I normally didn't care. I need it. To distract my mind from everything that was going on around me.

From school. From my family. From her.

It never lasted long. There was only a small moment when I wasn't thinking of her. Then the girls' hair would remind me of Allie or remind me of how different she was. It was frustrating as hell.

I didn't want to think about her.

If I could completely erase her from my mind, I would.

And that was exactly what I was trying to do now.

"Do you like that?" the girl mumbled against my skin, and the sound of her voice grated on my nerves.

"Yeah." I gripped her arms in my hands and pulled her fully into my lap.

She moaned as her pussy pressed down against my erection. There was very little fabric separating the two of us, and I knew that she could feel exactly how hard I was.

I wanted her even though I didn't. I just needed her body, her escape, a fucking moment away from the constant bullshit in my head.

She ground down against me, and I leaned back in the chair. We were alone in someone's room, I had no fucking clue whose, and I could do anything I wanted to this girl.

Anything.

I knew that and so did she. She was eager and willing to let me do things to her body that I would probably remember for a very long time.

It was my idea of heaven.

Except I couldn't turn off my fucking mind.

At least that was what I told myself, but the reality was that I wouldn't think about her again after tonight. It felt like heaven and hell. She was nothing more than a quick distraction, a temporary high.

Her lips were full, but they weren't as full as Allie's. Her hair was brown and shiny, but Allie's was so blonde that it seemed to attract the sun. It always had been.

I reached up and ran my fingers through her hair, gripping the strands right at the base. She leaned her head back with a seductive smile on her face. She was right there, completely open for me, and still, I hesitated.

She moved against me harder, my cock was about to kill me if I didn't do something to her, but I just sat there. I let her ride against me through our clothes, and I held her hair firmly in my hands. She didn't seem to mind. Her eyes were glazed over with want, and I knew if I touched her, she'd be soaking wet against me.

She pressed her hands to my shoulders and held on as she brought her mouth down next to mine. "What do you want, baby?"

There should have been a thousand things on my mind in that moment. I should have given her all the ways I wanted to fuck her around this room, but I couldn't.

All I could think about was the way Allie had been smiling at Eli, and how I knew he was going to want to put her in this same position. He was going to want to fuck Allie like she was nameless and didn't matter.

And I fucking hated that.

I knew that was exactly what I was doing to this girl. But it felt different.

I knew how fucked up that was, but it was true.

Allie wasn't a virgin. I was almost one hundred percent positive of that fact. But I had rarely seen her show interest in any guy. She hadn't dated anyone that I was aware of.

And Eli fucking Scott wasn't going to be the guy who she thought would be her knight in shining armor.

I refused to allow it.

I wouldn't be either, but I could keep her as far away from him as possible.

But he was already a thousand steps ahead of me. He made her smile, and I saw her put her number into his phone. And she didn't fucking hate him.

That part was going to be tricky.

I shifted my hips and pulled my cell phone out of my pocket.

"What are you doing?"

I looked up from my phone at the girl who was still grinding against me. I held up a finger as I pushed myself out from under her. "Give me just a minute."

It was after two in the morning, and I was almost certain that Allie was probably already in bed. But I still clicked on her name. I hadn't called or text Allie in years. It felt odd.

But I refused to allow Eli to have the complete upper hand tonight.

I typed out a message to her, then erased it, then typed another. I did this over and over again as I thought about what to say to her.

I lied about you looking like a slut. You looked really hot tonight.

I hit Send before I could think better of it.

Her response came through my phone within a minute.

Who is this?

I grinned because she knew exactly who this was. Neither one of us had changed our phone numbers since we first convinced our parents to get us a phone when we were thirteen. Unless she had deleted my number. Shit. She might have done that.

Was there anyone else who was a complete ass to you tonight besides me?

Let me know and I'll kick their ass.

The three little dots danced across my screen before they disappeared. Then they started dancing again.

"Carson, can't that wait?"

I ignored the girl behind me and stared down at my phone.

Nope. Just you.

I don't know what you want but leave me alone.

I just wanted you to know how good you looked.

I should have apologized for saying she looked like a slut, but I rarely apologized for anything, and I never apologized to her.

Don't worry. Someone else already told me.

My anger was instant. I was telling her how slutty she looked while Eli was telling her the opposite. She didn't need me to tell her. She didn't need me to be anything for her.

Eli is a douchebag.

Her next response was instant.

Says the biggest douchebag I know. Do you need something, Carson?

No. I was just trying to be nice.

Well, don't. It's weird and giving me whiplash.

I grinned at her sass. It was one of the things that I had loved most about her once upon a time. It usually pissed me off now.

Noted. Back to being an asshole, I go.

She didn't respond after that, and I knew I should have put my phone down and left it at that. But I couldn't.

So I sent one last text message before I clicked off my phone and slid it back into my pocket.

Don't date Eli.

Then I turned around and faced the girl who was still waiting for me.

"I'm going to have to run." I ran my hand over the back of my neck.

"You have somewhere you need to be in the middle of the night?" She didn't believe a word I said.

"I do. A friend needs me."

"Is that why you were grinning down at your phone? I'm a big girl, Carson." She stood and grabbed her shoes from the floor. "You can just say that you're going to fuck someone else."

"All right." I shrugged my shoulders. "I'm going to fuck someone else." I was such a damn asshole.

She may have cared as little about me as I did her, but her face still fell when the words left my mouth.

"I can't believe you." She passed by me and headed straight for the door.

I didn't waste time as I followed her out. I needed to get out of this house. It smelled of beer and sex, and there were far too many bodies passed out on almost any available surface.

"Do you need a ride home?"

She turned around and stared at me like I had lost my damn mind. Maybe I had.

"I'm not letting my parents see me pull up to the house with Carson Hale," she snarled, her nose up, and I should have been offended but I knew she was pissed. I really didn't give a damn what her or her parents thought about me.

"Suit yourself." I pulled my keys out of my pocket and headed straight for the driveway.

I really didn't want to go home, though. My fucking parents were there, and even though they were probably asleep, I didn't want to deal with them. I never wanted to deal with them.

Not anymore.

Not after everything the two of them had done to each other.

I pulled my phone out of my pocket and text Beck.

Cool if I come over?

His text was instant and always the same.

Of course.

I tended to spend more time at his place or Olly's, and both of them knew why. If my parents weren't fighting, they were gone. Gone with other people.

It had been that way for a long time. Ever since that night that changed everything. The night that changed my family. That changed my relationship with Allie.

That was the night that I realized that even the people you love the most could let you down. It was the people you loved the most who would let you down beyond belief.

I learned that lesson the hard way, but it wasn't a lesson I would soon forget. The only people I trusted now, the only ones who I really let in, were Olly and Beck. They both knew about the problems in my family, but even they didn't know the full extent of it. The only ones who knew that truth were Allie and Lucas, and I wished more than anything that neither of them knew shit about me.

I wished that none of it had ever happened, but wishing wouldn't get me anywhere. I learned that a long time ago as well, because I had wished and wished and wished that my parents would change.

I wished that my father had never cheated on my mother, and I wished that I had never walked in on my mom after she found out.

That memory was nothing but a nightmare. I can still remember the way her face looked when her body was so limp, and I still hated her for it. I was far too young, and she was my fucking mother, but my father had been destroying her little by little over the years and it had finally become too much.

And nobody was there for me.

I didn't have my mom, I couldn't stand looking at my dad, and the girl I had been in love with let me down just like everyone else.

It had all felt like too much, and I hated even thinking about it.

I refused to think about it.

I climbed in my car and drove to the Clermonts' house without thought. I blasted music and rolled down my windows to stop my brain from thinking of things that were better left alone. But I knew that it was impossible.

If I was going to convince Allie to stay away from Eli, if I was going to convince her that she was better off spending time with me, I knew that I wasn't going to be able to bury everything I had felt for her anymore.

Allie was like an addiction. I didn't want her, I knew she was fucking poison for me, but every time I saw her, I could feel myself gravitating toward her more and more. It didn't matter that I hated her or had convinced myself I didn't want her. Just the sight of her or the smallest inhale of her scent made me feel crazy.

I wanted her even though she was bad for me.

I wanted her despite everything that had happened in our past.

And that only made me hate her more.

I climbed out of my car and didn't bother knocking as I walked inside. I knew Beck would leave the door open for me, and Mr. Clermont would die if I woke the whole house up in the middle of the night.

He was one of the nicest men I had ever met, but I still feared him enough not to test him.

As soon as I closed the door behind me, I could hear girly giggles coming from the living room. I smiled as I easily recognized Frankie's overzealous laugh.

"Shouldn't you all be in bed?" I rounded the corner, and the laughter died as soon as Allie's gaze met mine.

"Shouldn't you be off with some skank?"

I smiled because damn, these girls are protective.

Even though I'm still not quite sure how Josie feels about me, she makes it perfectly clear that when it comes to her friend, she will bury me before she lets me hurt her.

Fair enough.

But I don't have any real plans of hurting Allie. Not really. Not with anything more than the bullshit banter the two of us have every time we see each other. I never wanted Allie to be close enough to me again for me to hurt her or for her to hurt me.

But I was going to have to change that now.

I was going to have to convince her to get close to me. I was somehow going to convince her to fall for me.

And I knew that the simple solution would be for me to just tell Allie the truth. Fuck, actually, that was exactly what I needed to do.

Wasting my time and effort on convincing her to fall for me was futile. Because she would never fall for me. I may have had the slightest chance one upon a time, but not anymore.

Not after the way I've treated her.

I just needed to be honest with her.

"You know I don't bring the skanks home with me, Josie. They get too attached that way." I winked at Josie, and she rolled her eyes at my douchebag move. "But speaking of skanks..." I turned my attention to Allie. "I overheard a bunch of the guys talking tonight, and I should warn you. Eli is only interested in you because of some bet."

Her deep inhale was visible, and there was an instant look of defeat on her face. I told myself not to react. I didn't care that Allie was hurt by the news. She would have been far more hurt when he had done to her exactly what he had planned to do. I would much prefer that she find out now. That she find out from me.

"You are such an asshole." Her words were shaky, and

she forced herself to look away from me and down at her phone.

"I'm not sure how that makes me an asshole. I'm not the one who's using you." I shrugged my shoulders and made her believe I didn't care. I had become far too good at it.

"You seriously can't stand to see her be happy. Can you?" Frankie huffed and stood from the couch. There wasn't a trace of laughter or happiness left on her face that had been there when I walked in.

"This has nothing to do with me not wanting her happy. I figured she'd like to know now."

Frankie pushed her hand against my chest and forced me to take a few steps back and further and further away from Allie.

"Just like how that guy we saw at the pier last week wasn't really flirting with her."

"He wasn't." I chuckled even though thinking about that asshole made me feel ragey. "He was asking for directions."

"Right. And when Scott Noble asked for her number, but you convinced her that he just needed help with his homework."

"I don't really see your point."

She had pushed me so far back that we were now out of earshot of both Allie and Josie. It was just me and Frankie, and I hated that out of all of them she thought badly of me. She was pissed, and I knew Allie had become one of her best friends, but so had I.

"The point is that you are always telling Allie about how any guy who shows even the slightest bit of interest in her is after something else." She held up her hand and started counting on her fingers. "Schoolwork, sex, directions, her friend's number, and now, a bet. Come on, Carson. You're eventually going to have to get some balls and ask the girl out if you don't want her to be with someone else."

I shook my head and tried to ignore what she was saying. She had a point, but that wasn't what this was. I wasn't just bullshitting them. Eli was going to use her, and he was going to hurt her, and none of them believed me. "I don't care who she dates. I just think she should be prepared to be the laughingstock of both of our schools. If she still decides to trust the guy then that shit is on her."

She narrowed her eyes as she stared up at me. Frankie didn't believe a word I said. She had always been able to see right through me, and I hated that shit. "Are you sure that maybe you don't just want to be with Allie yourself, but you're too chicken to admit it?"

"Are you sure that you don't have feelings for Olly?" I stared down at her, and I hated that she flinched. I didn't want to hurt her, but I also wanted her to get off my back about Allie. "I see the way you look at him."

I could see her trying to come up with what to say. Frankie was always stuck in her head, and I had never called her out about Olly before. I didn't think anyone had. Olly would kill me if he knew. "How would you know what feelings look like, Carson? You never have feelings for anyone, right? And you definitely don't have any for Allie."

"You're right. I don't."

We stared at each other for a few moments without saying a word. I should have apologized for bringing up Olly. It was a low blow even for me. But Frankie spoke first.

"Stop being a dick to Allie."

I grinned down at her and gave her a grand salute with my hand.

"And don't bring up that other thing ever again. There's

no use talking about something that can never be." She looked so damn sad. So heartbroken by the thought that she could never be with Olly, and she was right. The two of them could never be together. Not if they wanted Olly to maintain his friendship with her brother.

Because as much as Beck loved us both like brothers, he would absolutely lose it.

"Don't worry, Frankie girl. Your secret is safe with me." I leaned forward and pressed a gentle kiss to her forehead, and I hoped it chased away some of the sadness that I had just caused.

She smiled at me, but it didn't come close to reaching her eyes.

"Good night, playboy."

"'Night." I didn't look back as I climbed the stairs to the Clermonts' spare bedroom. I didn't search the living room for another glance at Allie or tense as her laughter reached me once more.

And I sure as hell didn't dream about her that night or what I was going to have to do to convince the girl who hated me to fall for me.

Because she hadn't believed a single word I had said, which meant I was backed into a corner. I had no choice but to make Allie fall for me even though I had been convincing her to hate me for years.

CHAPTER 4
ALLIE

I kicked my feet through the pool water and tried to calm my racing thoughts. I had barely slept last night after Carson had come in and ruined my mood.

And what he said?

I couldn't stop thinking about it.

Was Eli just using me? Probably. But I didn't believe Carson about some dang bet or the fact that he thought he knew anything about the guy. He just didn't want to see me happy.

It was always the same. Any guy who was interested in me was always interested for some reason other than actually liking me, according to Carson. I knew that he was clearly still angry with me, that he had a deep-seated hate for me he couldn't let go of, but he was hurting me.

In the beginning, I tried to just let it roll off me, but his words refused to anymore. They struck me hard, and he always managed to hit me exactly where he was aiming. I guess that was part of the problem with making an enemy out of someone who used to know you so well. They knew exactly where to strike.

I could do the same to him if I wanted to. I knew where Carson hurt and where his weaknesses lied. Even if he tried to parade around like he was nothing but a careless playboy these days, I knew the truth. That wasn't who he was. Not really.

It was just some version of him that he had become.

Because Carson Hale was scared to get close enough to anyone who could possibly hurt him.

"There you are." I looked up just as Frankie and Josie walked out of the back sliding door. Frankie's house was massive, the pool to die for, and the view even better.

"Yeah." I ran my hand over my face and pushed back my soaking wet hair. "I couldn't sleep so I decided to go for a swim."

I smiled at them even though I knew they could see through it. The two of them were already in their bathing suits as well, and they each took a seat on either side of me.

"What's going on?" Josie nudged her shoulder into mine before laying her head on my shoulder. I pressed my head into hers and stared out over the view.

"Just stuck in my head."

"Do not let what Carson said last night get to you. You know he's always a dick to you for no reason. Eli wouldn't have asked you out if he didn't want to."

"No. I know." I nodded my head. "He actually already text me this morning."

"What?" Frankie leaned forward to get a good look at my face. "What did he say?"

"He said that he couldn't stop thinking about our dance last night and that he couldn't wait to see me again." I shrugged like it was no big deal, but the reality is that his text had made my heart race. Regardless of what Carson said, he had woken up this morning and thought of me.

"That's so cute." Frankie grinned. "What did you say back?"

"Nothing yet." I dragged my feet through the warm water, back and forth. "I didn't want to seem too eager."

"Good girl." Josie laughed before pressing a kiss to my cheek then sliding into the pool. "Make the boy work for it. No one deserves you if they aren't willing to put in some work."

"Do you..." I hesitated before taking a steadying breath. "Do you think he's really just using me like Carson said?"

"No." Josie's answer was firm. "Carson's just being an asshole. You know he always does this."

"I know." I looked back to the house because I knew Carson was still in there somewhere, and there was no way in hell I wanted him to hear me questioning everything because of a few simple words from him. "But Eli is on the baseball team, and we've never really interacted before. Maybe Carson is telling the truth."

"He's not." Frankie climbed into the water, too, before turning to face me. "Whatever Carson's problem is has nothing to do with these guys. It has to do with you. He's not like this with anyone else."

"I know." I groaned and ran my fingers down my face.

"What happened between you two? I know you don't really want to talk about it, but just give us something. It's hard for us to understand when we have no details."

I looked back to Frankie because I knew that she was close with Carson. She always defended me when he was being a jerk, but I knew she cared for him. It was hard not to when he didn't hate you.

"What has Carson told you?" I gripped the edge of the pool with my hands on either side of my thighs as I waited for her answer.

"He hasn't. He's as tight-lipped as you are about it."

"Come on, Allie." Josie moved in closer to us. "We're your best friends. We would never judge you or say anything about what happened. Did you two sleep together?"

"No." I laughed. I wished it had been as simple as that. "I don't know how much you all know about his parents." I looked back at the house again before continuing. "But they used to be so happy. When we were younger, Carson and I were close, and I would spend so much time at his house and him at mine."

"Okay?" Frankie encouraged me to go on.

"I used to be in love with him," I admitted out loud to them something that I didn't think I had ever said to anyone. "He was my best friend; he only cared about me as a friend, and I was in love with him."

"What happened?" Josie put her hand on my knee, and I didn't even realize that I was bouncing it until that moment.

"He was always interested in other girls. You know how he is. He can get any girl he wants. So, finally I decided that I was going to do the same. He didn't see me as anything other than his friend, and it literally killed me. This was years ago." I straightened and smiled and tried to play off how badly I had wanted him. "We were only fifteen at the time. He had just started hanging out with Lucas and the boys, and things were changing between us. I went out on a date, if you can even call it that, and he was so upset about it."

"Because he loved you too." Josie said it like it was so obvious, but she was wrong.

"No. He was just possessive. He didn't want me, but he didn't want anyone else to have me either. We got into a fight. The first one we had ever had because I went on the date. He blew my phone up while I was there, but I didn't answer. I didn't want him to ruin my chance with this guy who actually wanted me simply because Carson didn't want him to have me, you know?" I looked up to the sky and took a deep breath. "He wouldn't answer my calls or texts after. Wouldn't answer the door. I was so angry with him because I thought he was just punishing me. But I was so damn wrong. His mom had caught his dad cheating the night before."

Frankie's shocked inhale told me enough. They may have been friends, but Carson hadn't let them in. Not really.

"When Carson had gone home that night, he found his mother on her bathroom floor. She had overdosed on some pills she had in her cabinet and tried to kill herself, and he had been the one to find her. That was why he had been calling me. He was calling me because he needed me, and I wasn't there." I angrily wiped a tear from my face.

"You know that's not your fault, right?" Josie looked back and forth between me and Frankie. "There was nothing you could do."

"I know that." I nodded. "But I should have been there for him. I should have been happy with being his friend, not trying to make him jealous. Because that's all that date was. It was a ploy to try to get him to notice me as something other than his stupid friend, and I ruined everything."

"Allie."

I knew Josie was going to try to talk me off this ledge, that she was going to try to convince me that this was all on

Carson and his family, but she was wrong. If I had only answered my phone and been there for him, we wouldn't be where we are now.

He wouldn't still hate me.

"It doesn't matter." I shook my head and planted a fake smile on my face. "He never talked to me anymore after that. Not other than to insult me one way or another, and that's that." I shrugged my shoulders and both girls looked concerned.

"I didn't realize." Frankie looked up at the house then back at me. "I didn't know that about his parents. They are still together, and I didn't think what happened between the two of you would be this serious. I just thought he was pining after you."

"No." I laughed, just as the door opened behind me. "A girl could only wish."

I looked back over my shoulder to see Beck, Olly, and Carson walking outside. The three of them were talking, and I wasn't sure if they had even noticed us yet. I turned back to the water and quickly wiped at my face. There was no way I would allow him to catch me out here crying. It didn't matter if he didn't have a clue, it was over him.

I refused to give him any ammunition over me.

Frankie laughed and squeezed my leg just as I heard running behind me. Then Carson bolted past me, close enough that I could easily reach out and touch him, and jumped into the water. He managed to splash all three of us, but I was happy for the distraction.

I wiped the water from my face as he came back to the surface with a grin on his face. Don't look at him. Don't look at him.

"I didn't get you ladies wet, did I?" He grinned harder and Josie gagged audibly.

"I don't think you could get any douchier if you tried, Carson."

"Sure, I could." He swam toward her, and she held out her hands.

"I swear to God, Carson. Do not. Beck!" But Beck was too far away, and Carson had already gotten Josie's hand in his. He pulled her toward him, and she laughed as she tried to fight him off.

God, I hated him for who he had become, but when I watched him be like this with someone else, I also missed him. And I hated the deep ache in my stomach at the thought.

"Beck can't help you." He lifted Josie into the air, her body wiggling and trying to get out of his grip the entire time, before he tossed her in the air and to the deep end of the pool. "What are you two looking at?" He turned to me and Frankie. "Any comments you all would like to make this morning?"

"Nope." Frankie leaned against the back of the pool. "But it's not our fault you act like a prick before anyone has even had their coffee."

He dove for her before she even got the last few words out, and she squealed as he tried to grab ahold of her. "Say you're sorry, and I won't throw you."

"Not happening." Frankie laughed, and Carson caught ahold of her hand. His hand brushed my leg as they horse-played, and I tensed at the contact. I hadn't touched him in forever. His gaze met mine, as if he felt that brush as strongly as I had. It was only for a moment.

But it felt like a lifetime. I held my breath until he looked away from me. My stomach ached, my chest ached, and if I was being honest with myself, my thighs tightened from that one look alone.

"All right, Frankie girl. It was your choice." He lifted her in the air like he had Josie just moments before and threw her too.

I expected him to swim away, to not say another word to me since he didn't currently have anything to insult me about, but he didn't. He turned back in my direction, crossed his arms over his chest, and stared at me.

"What?" I asked consciously. I wished he would look anywhere but at me.

"You have anything that you'd like to say?"

"Absolutely not." I shook my head and gripped my fingers harder into the pool edge.

"You don't think I'll throw your ass into the pool too?" He cocked his head to the side, and I knew he was challenging me.

"I didn't think you even knew I existed when there wasn't another guy talking to me."

He jolted back as if my words shocked him, and I guess they probably did. I rarely ever said anything to him, let alone anything to defend myself in any way. Hell, before I became friends with Josie, I tried to avoid him at all costs.

"I think we both know that I'm well aware of the fact that you exist." He moved closer to me, and I straightened. What was he doing?

"Do we?" I looked behind him to where Olly was pulling Frankie to the shallow end of the pool. She was staring daggers at Carson's back, but he had no idea. His attention was all on me.

Nothing in this world scared me more.

The only time Carson paid me any attention was when he intended to hurt me, to berate me, to put me down. I couldn't handle any of those things right now. Not after the conversation I just had with the girls. The memories of who Carson and I used to be were still fresh in my mind, and I didn't want them tainted by this guy who stood in front of me now.

"Come on, Allie." He was less than a foot away from me. "Get in the water or I will drag your ass in."

"No." I shook my head and started to climb from the pool's edge, but he reached his hands out and grabbed ahold of my legs before I could. His hands held on to me just behind my knees, and I felt paralyzed by his touch.

"Carson, don't." My words were a whisper, only for me and him to hear, and I knew that he could hear the emotion in my voice that I had tried to hide.

"Why not?" His fingers tightened around my skin. "We're just having fun."

I looked down at him, and I couldn't help staring at his chest or the way it rose and fell with each of his breaths. His body was perfect, chiseled through athletics and years of surfing, and it felt so sinful to look at. There wasn't an innocent thought that ran through my mind as my gaze skimmed over his golden skin.

"You and I don't have fun anymore, remember?"

He chuckled and his stomach pressed into my shins. I couldn't remember the last time we had been this close, but it felt good. It felt so damn familiar. The warmth of his skin, the smell of his leftover cologne.

He was like the warmest of memories mixed with the harshest dose of reality.

Past and present. Then and now.

They were so different yet so familiar, and I couldn't keep my head on straight when the two of them became so clouded.

"I'm well aware, but honestly, I don't remember you being much fun back then either."

I knew he was trying to get a reaction out of me. That was what he wanted. "You're such a liar." I tried to pull out of his hold, but his grip was relentless.

"You're right." His truth shocked me. "Get in the water and remind me how fun you are."

"It's not happening. Let me go." His touch felt like a brand, burning me, consuming me, and I knew it wasn't meant to be. He was simply touching me, playing another one of his damn games, and I wasn't capable of having these stupid, insignificant moments with him. Every word, every look, every touch, it all meant too much.

"All right, Allie. Don't say I didn't warn you." He pushed between my thighs before he wrapped one of his arms around my back. He lifted me to him like I weighed nothing, and even though I didn't want to, I grabbed onto his shoulders to stop me from falling.

"Carson, put me down." My words were breathless in his ear. His hand tightened behind my back, his fingers relaxing before contracting again against my skin. My legs were wrapped around him, and I caught everyone watching us out of the corner of my eye.

"I'll make you a deal." Carson stopped in the center of the pool and looked straight into my eyes. "If you'll agree to go out on a date with me, I won't throw you."

"What?" I jolted backward, but his hands held me in place. "Have you lost your mind? Did you hit your head last night after we left the party?"

"No." He chuckled. "My head is perfectly clear."

"Is this a joke then? Are you trying to prove some point?" I squirmed in his arms and tried to put some space between us. "I'm not going to say yes, so you might as well go ahead and throw me."

"You wound me." He lifted me higher against him and readjusted his grip. I knew that I was about to be thrown into the water at any moment. "Can't a guy just be interested in his old friend?"

"Not you."

"I guess you would think that, huh?" He spun me in his arms until he was cradling me.

"Have you given me any reason to think differently? You hate me, Carson, and I don't think that fact has suddenly changed in the last few hours."

He stared down at my mouth before bringing his gaze back to meet mine. "I don't hate you."

Before I could take in his words or think of a response, he threw me. I flew through the air before hitting the water, and I let myself sink as the water surrounded me. I had no idea what the hell he was doing or why he was doing it, but I no longer trusted Carson Hale.

I knew that fact above all others.

But his words still shot through me like an assault. *I don't hate you.* They messed with my head and my heart, and I knew that was what he wanted.

I was nothing more than a game to him, and I refused to allow myself to get close enough for him to hurt me again.

THANK YOU

Thank you so much for reading Josie and Beck's story!

Don't worry! There is more from the crew in Carson and Allie's duet, The Taste of an Enemy and The Deceit of a Devil.

I would love for you to join my reader group, Hollywood, so we can connect and talk about all of your The Touch of Villain thoughts. This group is the first place to find out about cover reveals, book news, and new releases!

Join us for the fun: www.facebook.com/groups/hollyrenee

You can also sign up for my newsletter here:
www.authorhollyrenee.com/subscribe

ACKNOWLEDGMENTS

Thank you for taking a chance on reading this book!

I owe so many thanks to every blogger, bookstagrammer, and reader who shares, reads, reviews, and loves my books. I will never be able to express my gratitude.

I have so many people to thank for having my back and being a part of the best team ever.

I would like to think my wonderful family for always being so supportive and encouraging my dreams.

A big thanks to my beta team Sarah, Megan, Katie, Rita, Aundi, Heather, Elizabeth, and Christina.

Thank you to Christina Santos!

Thank you to Ellie and Rumi for helping make this book what it is!

To my author friends who keep me sane and pushing forward every day. I love you all.

And to the best street team ever, thank you for everything you all do! I am so thankful for you all!